ZOMBIE, ILLINOIS

ZOMBIE, ILLINOIS

A NOVEL

Scott Kenemore

SKYHORSE PUBLISHING

Skyhorse Publishing books may be purchased in bulk at special discounts for sales promotion, corporate gifts, fund-raising, or educational purposes. Special editions can also be created to specifications. For details, contact the Special Sales Department, Skyhorse Publishing, 307 West 36th Street, 11th Floor, New York, NY 10018 or info@skyhorsepublishing.com.

Skyhorse® and Skyhorse Publishing® are registered trademarks of Skyhorse Publishing, Inc.®, a Delaware corporation.

Visit our website at www.skyhorsepublishing.com.

10 9 8 7 6 5 4 3 2 1

Library of Congress Cataloging-in-Publication Data

Kenemore, Scott.
 Zombie, Illinois : a novel / Scott Kenemore.
   p. cm.
 ISBN 978-1-61608-885-9 (pbk. : alk. paper)
 1. Zombies--Fiction. 2. Chicago (Ill.)--Fiction. I. Title.
 PS3611.E545Z64 2012
 813'.6--dc23

                                        2012017903

Printed in the United States of America

For Delia, a fine Illinoisan

Avaunt! and quit my sight! let the earth hide thee!

Thy bones are marrowless, thy blood is cold;

Thou hast no speculation in those eyes

Which thou dost glare with!

—*Macbeth (III, iv)*

Chicago is a bare, bleak, hideous city.

—*H.P. Lovecraft to Frank Belknap Long*

Ben Bennington
Political Reporter
Brain's Chicago Business

The flag of Chicago has four stars on it: one for political corruption, one for high taxes, one for racial segregation, and one for...

Damn.

I think it's gang crime, but I'm not 100 percent sure.

Chicagoans always forget that last one.

My name is Ben Bennington, and I work for—don't laugh—*Brain's Chicago Business.*

Founded by publisher John Honeycutt Brain in 1973, *Brain's Chicago Business* is the leading source of business news for companies in the greater Chicago area. Now with weekly print and online editions, *Brain's* provides not only the cutting-edge industry news that our readers expect, but also award-winning themed issues like "30 Under 30," "Who's Who in Chicago Business," and, of course, "CEOs Making a Difference."

I'm a political reporter. (Politics and business are nowhere more intertwined than in Chicago—at least nowhere in the first world.) I'm a political reporter in a town that loves corrupt politicians. I mean *loves* them. *Really loves* them. Loves to hear them accepting a bribe on an FBI wiretap; loves to see photos of them associating with Italian mobsters or black gangbangers or the Chinatown mafia; loves to watch as they're led away handcuffed. And loves—above all—to believe them when they swear they'll never do it again. It occupies much of the local television news, yes, but Chicagoans also love to read about it—in the *Tribune, Sun-Times,* and, of course, in *Brain's.* That's where I come in.

You move to Chicago, and you think: How can a whole city behave this way? How can they *enjoy* this corruption, like it's a sport or game? It's not a sport or game, it's bribery and grift and graft. It's what everybody, everywhere knows is wrong.

And then you live here a little while and you slowly realize: Oh . . . it's not that Chicagoans enjoy it; it's not that *at all.*

Instead, it's a defense mechanism against having their hearts broken and torn from their chests every few months by yet another crooked politician. It's a hedge against their faith in humanity being reduced to a tiny nub by an endless series of betrayals. Because, when you believe in somebody enough to entrust them with your city—your home, the place you may have lived your whole life—and they sell you out at the first opportunity—and I mean the *very first* opportunity—you can do one of two things.

You can let your heart break and cry, "How *could* they?" (This option is painful, and most people can't stand to do it more than once or twice.)

Or you can choose the other option: You can distance yourself from it all. You can be bemused and act like it's all a big game. You can say, "That's Chicago for you." (This option makes you cynical, true, but it also allows life to go on. It allows the citizens—and the city itself—to continue to function, even in the face of mass corruption. Accordingly, it is the option Chicagoans overwhelmingly select.)

So when an Alderman takes a $10,000 bribe to re-zone her district for a developer, or the mayor gives his cousin an $80,000-a-year job as an elevator safety inspector (who somehow never gets around to inspecting any elevators), or the governor tries to sell a vacated senate seat when the senator becomes President of the United States—Chicagoans treat it like a game. The political news reads more like the sports page. Veteran reporters in fedoras and suspenders act unsurprised as they compare the current generation of scoundrels to the previous one, and then to the one before that.

And *I'm* supposed to be one of those reporters.

I have the fedora. (A nice, $500 Optimo, though I usually don't wear it.)

I have some suspenders. (Not so nice. From Kohl's. Also seldom worn.)

But *fuck me*, because I am *not* a Chicagoan, and I *do not* have that ability to treat it all as a joke.

I've lived in this city for twenty years, but I spent eighteen before that growing up in Iowa. And despite my many successful assimilations to Windy City life,[1] I have yet to make that one crucial crossover that will allow me to believe that politicians stealing from the people they're supposed to serve is funny.

Professionally and officially, I am as amused as the next reporter by the rampant corruption that pervades every ward. (I've got to keep my job, after all.) I adopt the "there they go

[1] I eat neon green relish on my hot dogs. I say "Shka-go" instead of "Chi-ca-go." I listen to Buddy Guy and Wilco on my iPod.

again" attitude. At press events, I shake hands and mingle with these politicians—these criminal aldermen (and women) who comprise our city council. We joke and laugh convivially. We never mention that some of them—even, perhaps, *most* of them—will one day fall from their perches in some form of scandal. Many of them will serve prison sentences. Some of those will be lengthy. (Since I've lived here, a Chicago alderman has been convicted of a felony every eighteen months or so, and those are just the ones that get caught! [It gets worse the higher up you go. Four of the last seven Illinois governors have felony convictions.])

But for the city to continue to function—to "work" as they say—we must, all of us, play this game. I must ask about their families, new projects in their wards, and their opinions of the Cubs' latest trade. Secretly though, I am disgusted with these people who use "clout" as a verb. (As in, "I clouted my way out of that one.") I feel like this is not a game. Like their corruptions and bribes and associations with gangsters are not funny. Like instead, they are a shame . . . a horrible, wince-inducing shame. Watching Chicago aldermen glad-hand and smile at city events is like watching fashion models who are ugly and weigh 400 pounds but expect to be complimented on their pleasing features and toned physiques.

If I know anything, it's that the men and women who run this town are not real leaders. If real leadership were needed, this city would fall. Our politicians would fail us utterly. Their sinecured appointees would prove useless. Their boring speeches would inspire no one.

I spend my days longing to see Chicago face some *real* test or trial that will expose these people for who and what they actually are.

I long for a crisis. For a disaster. For an invasion.

Pastor Leopold Mack
The Church of Heaven's God
in Christ Lord Jesus

It is the Book of Proverbs, I think, that most astutely describes the sin of adultery.

In the seventh chapter, we meet the harlot who has perfumed her bed with "myrrh, aloes, and cinnamon," and invites the stranger into her room to spend the night in lust. In verse eighteen, she entreats him: "Come, let us take our fill of love until the morning; let us solace ourselves with loves."

Solace.

That's an important word.

It's what the man in the Bible story is trying to find when he elects to sleep with a prostitute. It's also the thing my congregation on the south side of Chicago is looking for. And it is the one thing I cannot give them.

My congregants . . .

They are beset on all sides.

Firstly, they are poor. The good book says the poor will always be with us—and that's a point which, in a larger, philosophical sense, I wouldn't presume to dispute—but the *culture* of poverty that has persisted for generations in my parish (our neighborhood is called South Shore) is frustrating, because it feels so unnecessary and arbitrary—as if a few small changes could correct everything and set our residents back on the right track. Why can't my congregants make these few, small changes? Why can't I help them do it?

I ask myself these questions every day.

During this recession, unemployment in our neighborhoods officially hovers close to 30 percent. When I drive down the street and see so many idle young men chatting and selling cigarettes and DVDs to one another, I'm convinced it must be higher. Like 50 percent.

In my neighborhood, less than half of the high school students graduate. Of those, almost none are prepared for college. One year, a valedictorian from the neighborhood went on to a city college and flunked out her first semester. And you say, okay, she wasn't prepared. I can accept that. But she *was the valedictorian*. She was the best the school had. Something is definitely wrong here.

(This is where you say "Amen," by the way.)

With the girls, teen pregnancy is unacceptably common. Almost no babies are planned. With the boys, a culture of violence pervades. There are shootings nearly every day. In the summer months, the fatalities over a long weekend can stretch into the double digits. Statistically, it is safer to be a soldier in the U.S. Army stationed in Afghanistan than it is to be a young black man on the south side of Chicago.

The billboards in my neighborhood are for cognac and AIDS medicine.

Something is wrong here.

And now, the darkest detail…

My neighborhood is not the worst.

My neighborhood is *nowhere near* the worst.

White folks from the north side of Chicago—who never bother to visit us—view "the south side" as one uniformly harrowing and dangerous place where they must remember never to go. They close it off in their minds. It becomes almost mythological—a world they only hear about on the nightly news. But if they ever scratched the surface, they'd see that "the south side of Chicago" is a dynamic mix of about thirty neighborhoods, each with a distinct personality and character.

South Shore, Chatham, Back of the Yards, Kenwood, Auburn-Gresham, South Chicago, East Chicago, Pullman, Grand Crossing—all these neighborhoods are slightly different. "Better" and "worse" in some ways, yes, but also distinctive and uniquely colorful. This one has a vibrant community of immigrants from Senegal. That one is renowned for its block safety clubs and high school football tradition. This one has been the epicenter of black newspaper publishing for eighty years. That one has the finest soul food in Chicago, if not the world.

And yet, to the outsider...we are all "the south side."

Do we let that bother us? No, we don't. We cannot afford to. We—ladies and gentlemen—have more important things to do.

("Amen" also goes there. Thank you.)

I'm taking a trip now, and I want you to come with me.

I said my congregation is beset on all sides.... Let's see for ourselves. I'm going to pull my Chrysler 300 (yes, a big ostentatious "preacher car") out of the parking lot of The Church of Heaven's God in Christ Lord Jesus—a crumbling structure built in the 1920s that needs a new pipe organ and a new roof—and I'm going to head south, toward Indiana. We'll drive down roads called 12 and 41, parts of a lost highway named for General Grant.

As we drive, we will pass fish fry shacks, hot dog stands, dilapidated no-name hamburger joints, and Chinese restaurants that still advertise chop suey. What we *won't* pass are grocery stores. These neighborhoods are what sociologists call "food deserts." There are almost no businesses selling fresh produce. There's *one* grocery store chain in South Shore. One brand-name grocery store for a neighborhood of almost 50,000 people. Think about that. I don't even know if the store is profitable. Leakage—people stealing stuff—has to be through the roof. I think the franchise just keeps the doors open as a PR move, so in their TV commercials they can say that they're "committed to *all* of Chicago's communities."

So no, not many options for fruit and vegetables and whole grains. But fast-food that tastes motherfucking delicious (if you'll pardon my language)? Welcome to a fried grease wonderland!

Of course, this food isn't good for you (not to eat all the time, which is what most people do). It gives our communities the highest rates of diabetes and high blood pressure in the city. But it's affordable, and it tastes good. Most importantly, it provides—to quote the prostitute in the Book of Proverbs—solace.

For a lot of people around here, food is the most affordable kind of solace. It's what they've got when they want to feel better.

A close second—as the astute reader will have already guessed—is alcohol, the last great legal vice (until, that is, we cross the border into Indiana...but more about that in a moment).

Dave Chappelle has a comedy bit about driving in the ghetto and how the businesses go "liquor store, liquor store, gun store, liquor store..." But Chicago's strict handgun laws have arranged things such that the places where you can purchase a functioning firearm—and they are legion—can't exactly put up a sign.

Consequently, on our ride, the businesses simply go "liquor store, liquor store, liquor store."

At the end of nearly every block, a crumbling "packaged goods" establishment is making 90 percent of its money from liquor and beer sales. And liquor and beer—say it with me—are solace. They take away the pain. They are a short-term solution, but a solution nonetheless.

This is what I'm up against. This is what my congregation is up against.

("Amen" goes there, too. Hallelujah.)

Moving on, we pass into a neighborhood called South Chicago. Here we find illegal bars, derelict houses—tax delinquent and/or victims of mortgage fraud—and abandoned apartment blocks filled with squatters. We also find places to buy drugs.

And, I hate to say it, but drugs are one of the few vices that are *not* an overriding problem for my congregation, as least, not directly. Nobody sitting in my pews is smoking crack or shooting horse, but most people have somebody in their family who is lost to drugs. Parents with kids who won't behave worry that drugs are in that child's future, and unfortunately, they're probably right. Most certainly, drugs fuel the gang violence that pervades our neighborhoods.

But the people who actually make it into the pews on Sunday are, themselves, not usually on drugs. This is good. This is, as I remind myself, a start. I take encouragement from it because I must take encouragement anywhere I can.

("Amen" definitely goes there.)

As we draw nearer to the Indiana state line, we begin to pass large swaths of undeveloped land owned by the park district.

These swaths extend eastward and eventually border Lake Michigan. They are full of nothing—bleak and littered with garbage. They are lonely places, giving off the feeling of having been forgotten. Developers don't want to build here, and the city's park system has a shrinking budget and more pressing issues. The politicians would like to see these swaths built up—probably because wealthy people can see them from their boats out on Lake Michigan and are depressed by the sight. (These politicians—for what it's worth—have not voiced much concern for the urban neighborhoods *adjacent to* these nautically visible swaths.) The city's latest bright idea has been to use them to stage a three-day rock music festival every summer, featuring bands tending to the tastes of white fraternity members. Will this project, in any sense of the word, "work?" I do not choose to dignify that question with a response. For now, we drive on past these lonely brownfields where, 362 days of the year, local kids go looking for trouble, drunks pass out, and drug deals go down.

Closer to Indiana, we encounter shipping canals. Boats—most of them ugly, flat affairs laden with unpleasant cargo like animal offal or crushed cars—use them to pass into Lake Michigan. The area around these canals is something most Chicagoans never see. It is functional but unsightly, like an orifice or sphincter. (One knows it is there, but would, all things being equal, elect to never actually see it up close.) We pause in a line of stalled traffic—my preacher car standing out starkly against the rusted Neons, Corollas, and Fiestas—and wait for a bridge to be raised and lowered as a long, slow barge carrying refinery waste passes underneath.

Then we leave the shipping canals and cross into the Hoosier State by driving underneath the Illinois/Indiana Toll Road (known officially as the "Chicago Skyway"). It looms above us, a massive structure, thrusting upwards into the air. Since it was built in 1958, the neighborhoods below it have literally existed in its shadow. This is fitting. These are shadow places.

The character of the neighborhood begins to change a few blocks in, the racial demographic shifting from lower-class black to working-class white and Latino. Yet, this does nothing to diminish the temptations awaiting my parishioners here, in this short drive from South Shore. If anything, the temptations are compounded.

The back alleys and side roads are havens for prostitution. At night, the truckers driving the Chicago Skyway know to pull off here to find "lot lizards," prostitutes (usually grizzled and emaciated) who specialize in servicing truckers. They walk from rig to rig, climbing into each cab to do their lonely business. The interstate nature of a trucker's travel means my parishioners who seek solace from these same prostitutes can collect venereal disease from every corner of the lower forty-eight. For those seeking slightly tamer fare, the neighborhood is also riddled with topless joints. These are somewhat safer, yes, but still the last places the men in my flock should be spending their time and money.

Pressing deeper into Hoosier-land, we'll make a quick detour to a place called Whiting. At first glance, it's an All-American community sitting pristine and unnoticed on the lake just south of Chicago. The quaint downtown is practically picturesque, with cute restaurants and shops you could spend an entire Sunday exploring. There are well-kept residential streets and houses with white picket fences—but those picket fences have to be repainted annually because of the constant discharge from the massive BP oil refinery that sits right next door.

Since time immemorial—technically 1889—British Petroleum has owned this place: first literally, then only figuratively. Pollution lurks everywhere, always just below the surface. The U.S. Environmental Protection Agency has designated Whiting an "Area of Concern," whatever that means. The residents who choose to remain are the kind of people who can either accept a dark bargain, or who find the truth too unthinkable to credit. "Never mind the cancer-clusters and off-the-chart asthma rates," these folks will respond. "BP sponsors a nice fireworks display every Fourth of July and makes donations to our civic programs. Why, the basketball team wouldn't have those new uniforms if it weren't for the refinery!"

I exaggerate a bit, but only a bit. I have heard residents of Whiting, when questioned about how they stand the refinery-odor that pervades their town, answer with no trace of irony: "It smells like money." (I should add that the residents of Whiting, per capita, have only slightly higher incomes than my parishioners, which means that they are very poor. Certainly, they are in no substantial way privy to the wealth being generated next to their town.)

And despite BP's enormous resources, there is no magic dome keeping the pollution generated in Whiting from seeping over the border into the south side of Chicago. My parishioners' asthma rates aren't as high as those of the people of Whiting, but they're still too high.

And we sure as Hell don't get a fireworks display.

("Amen" sure does go there. Thank you kindly.)

But we have tarried long enough. Now let us grit our teeth and head for the belly of the beast. Into Calumet and outlying Gary, and the scourge that is the Indiana Riverboat Casino industry.

While there are no casinos in the City of Chicago proper—yet—"Chicagoland" has become the third largest gaming destination in the United States after Las Vegas and Atlantic City. If you count the casinos less than an hour's drive away in Michigan, Wisconsin, Western Illinois, and here in Indiana, then there are about fifteen casinos in Chicagoland. Their billboards are everywhere, as is their pull on those seeking solace.

And here's a secret: Casinos are racist.

And no, I don't mean "Do blacks get drink service as quickly as whites?" I'm talking about a quiet, sneaky, cultural racism that's virtually invisible but damnably damaging.

Here's the problem: The quicker a casino game is to learn, the worse the odds are for the player. I didn't grow up white—so this is next part is, granted, a guess—but whites (and also Asians and Middle Easterners, I think) grow up learning to play casino games. I don't know how this happens, but it does. Maybe the family trips involve gambling with cards in the back seat. Maybe the kids all play casino games at their expensive private summer camps. However it happens, they show up knowing how to play games like Texas Hold 'Em, Blackjack, Pai Gow—stuff like that. Stuff with the better odds.

When all these new casinos opened in the late 1990s, my flock didn't know casino gambling from hot air ballooning.

My flock hadn't been jetting off to Vegas for generations or spending summers on the boardwalk in Atlantic City. When my parishioners—curious and in search of a thrill—walked into the casinos for the first time, they were confronted by the new-ness and strangeness of the games. Naturally, they gravitated to the two you can learn the quickest: slots and roulette. Pull this lever, and you might win some money. Pick red or black, and you might win some money. Yet these are the two games with the *worst odds in the casino.* And they are no less addictive for it.

The players might care—might bother to learn the other games—if they were actually out to win money. But they're not. They only *think* they're out to win money.

Really, they're after the same thing they're always after.

Say it with me.

Solace.

("Amen" goes there, indubitably.)

To say that casino gambling addiction is rife on the south side of Chicago is like saying that water is wet. It's rampant within my congregation (and those, remember, are the churchgoing folk in the neighborhood—the folk who have, at least on some level, decided to make an ongoing investment in self-improvement). Many of the young couples in my pews have fights over money that one or the other has lost across the border in Indiana. Many of the grandmothers while away their pensions and Social Security checks on "the boats." *Most* of the grandmothers, if I'm being honest. Grandmothers are the biggest concern. (With all their sexy advertising and waitresses in low-cut dresses, you'd think the casinos were designed for men aged 18 to 35, but the average

Chicagoland casino patron is a woman over 60. The casinos aren't there to steal from the young brothers; they're there to steal from big mama.)

A gambling addiction is also easy to cover up. In my neighborhood, you don't need a reason to be broke this week.

("Amen" goes there, my brothers and sisters. "Amen" *definitely* goes there . . . .)

And so we pull away from the cluster of casinos and head just a little deeper into the Hoosier state. As we near the end of our tour—I'm now pulling my preacher car into one of the back-row spaces in a parking lot in Merrillville, Indiana—I have a confession to make. This drive was not for you. This drive was for me.

Like the members of my congregation, I am in the habit—now and then—of driving south in search of solace.

Like the members of my congregation, I have a vice. Something I must keep secret.

Come with me, then. But only a few steps farther.

I'll exit my car—along with the other, mostly middle-aged men—and walk with them into the Merrillville Hotel and Amphitheatre. The evening's festivities are about to begin.

They are my solace.

And they are my shame.

God help me.

Excuse me a moment . . . I'm trying not to cry.

Sometimes I just want something to come along and change my life, you know? Wipe it all away. This, me, my hypocrisy. The south side of Chicago. Everything.

But the pull is too strong. At least tonight. I know what I'm going to do. I am already seduced.

I walk inside.

"Hey Mack, nice to see you," says a man named David. (I sometimes see him at these things. He's a dentist in a suburb called Orland Park.) "Can I get you a beer?"

"Absolutely," I say, though I'm not much of a drinker.

And then the smell of the place washes over me. And memories it conjures flood back. And I am *there*; in that temporary place that is so wonderful and so awful at the same time. I am in that fire that will burn out and leave me covered in ashes, but the heat feels wonderful all through my body, and that's all that matters right now.

I am the old lady from the second pew, letting her Social Security check ride on black. I am the twitchy kid in the back of the church who can't wait for Pastor Mack's stupid, boring sermon to be over so he can go get high with his friends in the brownfields. I am the prostitute's customer 2,000 years ago in the Holy Land who only wants an evening of cinnamon-scented sex away from his troubles.

And in this instant, ladies and gentlemen, *I do not care.*

In this instant, I have solace.

(And I think—just maybe—"Amen" goes *there* too.)

Maria Ramirez
Drummer
Strawberry Brite Vagina Dentata

My name is Maria Gonzales Ramirez, and I want to fuck Stewart Copeland.

That's the one really defining, overriding thing to know about me.

There are other things, too, I guess . . . I mean, I'm 24. I'm from a neighborhood on the northwest side of Chicago called Logan Square. I live with my mother and younger sister. (I take care of them both, and they are the most outstanding ladies in my life.) And, oh yeah, I drum in an all-girl rock band called Strawberry Brite Vagina Dentata, which is *the best band in Chicago.*

But enough about me.

Stewart Copeland is a beautiful man. What? A man can be beautiful, and Stewart definitely is. He is beautiful in so many ways. He is my fixation, my fantasy, my obsession.

It's not just that he's the most important New Wave drummer of all time. His work with the Police should have been enough to solidify that. But there's also Oysterhead, Animal Logic, Curved Air, and then all of the films he's scored. I mean, the man's a musical genius. But he is also a gorgeous, *gorgeous* son of a bitch. And I don't mean "Stewart Copeland back in 1987" or some bullshit like that. (Though I *do* have that poster on my wall, and he *does* look damn fine.) I mean Stewart Copeland now. Sixty-something Stewart Copeland still looks *fucking hot.* Better than hot, actually, with his short gray hair and those glasses with the thick dark frames . . .

Oh Jesus God, do I ever want to fuck Stewart Copeland.

I want his skinny ass between my legs. I want his calloused drummer's hands interlaced with my calloused drummer's hands. I want to suck in his breath as I lie underneath him and fuck him.

Or he fucks me. I mean, Stewart can do anything he wants. *Anything.*

He can fuck my tits. (I'm told I have nice tits.) He can come in my mouth. He can fuck my ass, if that's what he's into. Could I be any more clear?

I. Would. Do. Anything. For. Stewart. Copeland.

See, drummers are a brotherhood. (It's a brotherhood that's 15 percent chicks, but a brotherhood nonetheless.) And I am— damn-straight—a brother. I can't explain how or why we drummers feel connected as we do . . . but we do. We look physically different. We play different styles of music. We even play different-looking drums and drum sets. What do we really have in common? Hitting things with sticks (or sometimes just our hands). Lugging heavy drums up and down stairs and in and out of cars, when the other musicians have long-since packed up and driven off. Being the butt of jokes from guitar players. ("What do you call someone who hangs around with musicians all day? A drummer.")

And yet, there's this bond. I don't know what it is—or why it is—but it's *real.* And sometimes it's magical.

I can bump into a drummer I've never met before—and with whom I have nothing else in common—and within five minutes we are talking shop like old friends. It's a bond that I don't think other musicians have. (Do clarinet players get together and bond over reeds? I seriously doubt that.)

But I don't want to fuck my brothers in this brotherhood—that would be incestuous, right?—I only want to fuck Stewart Copeland.

Anyhow, my drumming is important to the story.

It has to do with the zombies.

Strawberry Brite Vagina Dentata rocks harder than any other band in this city. Put us up against anybody—I mean *anybody*—and we'll take 'em down. (I love it when we're the opening act. There's no greater pleasure than knowing you are going to destroy the band that has to play after you. Nobody wants to play after SBVD, I'll tell you *that* for sure.)

Grizzled Chicago bluesmen? They look boring and about to die compared to Strawberry Brite Vagina Dentata. Twee, underfed indie rockers? They ride their fixies back to their trust funds when they have to follow us. Wilco? Okay ... someone has needed to say this for a long time: Fuck Wilco. (Guess what? Lots of Chicagoans don't like Wilco. There are waaaaay more of us than the local media would have you believe. This stupid town likes to assign musical standard-bearers for every era—probably because music reporters are lazy. It was Smashing Pumpkins in the 90s, and Wilco for the '00s. [And it's going to be SBRK for the teens. Just you fucking wait.] But being *told* that Wilco is the best band in Chicago by fat, old music critics doesn't *make* Wilco the best band in Chicago. It certainly doesn't make listening to them any less boring.)

Strawberry Brite Vagina Dentata plays all the best venues in the city, and our shows are fun as hell. You know ahead of time, if you're going to an SBVD show, that it's gonna be crazy. Stage antics, smashing guitars, sexy outfits—we do it all. All that shit.

But you gotta create scarcity. That's what Richelle—our bassist, who has a business degree—calls it. "Creating scarcity." Strawberry Brite Vagina Dentata can pack a venue like the Metro or the Double Door, but only once a month. The other three weekends we might play Milwaukee, Indianapolis, or some meathead sports bar out in the suburbs (where redneck guys just want to ogle at our asses, but whatever). But that's still only four shows a month. Is that enough rock for a girl in her prime? Hell fucking no.

Which is why, on weekdays, the members of Strawberry Brite Vagina Dentata become The Kitty Kats from Heaven, Chicago's premier all-girl cover band, available for weddings, private parties, and corporate events. (Corporate events might be the most fun because we wear these little pinstripe suit jackets and kitty ears. They fucking rule.)

Some musicians in the local scene call this prostitution. Maybe so, but it's at least high-end prostitution. A good cover band can make well into the four figures for a gig in Chicago. (And we *are* a good cover band, and we *are* in Chicago.) We'll play a rich girl's sweet sixteen up in Wilmette, a company picnic out at McDonald's' headquarters, and a neighborhood street festival, all in the same week.

The Kitty Kats from Heaven see a whole other version of the city . . . a boring one.

Jesus fucking Christ. I mean, is this what people really want—a thrashy version of "Brown Eyed Girl?" Watered-down Green Day? "Play that Funky Music White Boy" but with "Boy" changed to "girl?" Apparently so, because they're willing to pay us thousands of dollars for it.

Is that depressing? No. Because fuck these people. If idiots want to throw money at the Kitty Kats from Heaven, we can turn around and use it to fund a kickass punk band called Strawberry Brite Vagina Dentata.

What else? What else?

I should take care to mention the other girls. Sarah plays guitar and sings lead. Richelle plays bass and sings backup. Danna plays guitar and sometimes keyboards.

We met through an audition posting a couple of years ago, and now we're like sisters. These chicks can have a kidney, as far as I'm concerned. I would do anything for them. And we're all kickass Chicago girls. We're from different neighborhoods and backgrounds, but we all agree that Chicago is the greatest city in the world in which to rock.

East Coast? West Coast? Fuck that noise. How about no coast?! That's where you go to rock. Right fucking here. City by the lake, like Billy Corgan says.

When I'm playing with my band, I feel like I'm ready to conquer the world. I feel like I'm ready for anything. My girls and I are soldiers, and we're ready for a fight.

So now...

Let me try to step back and set the scene for you.

It's in downtown Chicago.

It's with my band.

It's on a dark and snowy night . . . .

Ben Bennington

On the evening when it starts, I'm downtown at the trendy new venue on the penthouse level of the Trump Tower. I don't want to be there.

It's the kind of place that, in Vegas or New York, they'd charge you a cover just to walk in. It has an incredible view, funky décor, and an expensive sound system playing the kind of lounge music that lets you know that drinks are going to be $14 a pop. But it's Chicago—not Vegas or New York—and it's a fundraiser for a bicyclists' lobbying group, so the vibe is laid back, and they let reporters in for free.

The venue has a little stage. A band composed exclusively of good-looking young women has just finished setting up their gear. There will be raffles for bicycle equipment, tedious speeches from local politicians (the reason I am here), a musical performance, and free hors d'oeuvres. (Though not—I note with some regret—complimentary cocktails.)

I wade into the crowd, shaking a few hands and nodding across the room to my counterparts from the *Tribune* and the *Sun-Times*. My stomach rumbles. I corner a waiter and steal a handful of chicken meatballs in cream sauce on frilly toothpicks, and then retire to a table at the back and plug in my laptop.

It's already been a long day. I just want to take notes on a few speeches, file, hop on the El train, and go home. It is snowing a little, and there's more in the forecast. I want to beat it if I can. Also, the more I think about how there is no alcohol at this event, the more I think getting some beers on the way home sounds good. And maybe a pizza.

Soon enough, the trendy lounge music is turned down, and we are underway.

Whoopee.

My fingers poise above my keyboard, but I have all the disinterest (and probably the empty stare) of a court reporter who has heard it all before and will hear it all again.

The first speaker is a thin, awkward man with a beard—he's the president of the bicyclists' lobbying group. He speaks about creating a climate of bicycle courtesy on the roads and the need for wider bike lanes. He drives home his point by telling a story about the time he broke his collarbone in a bike collision. He is not a good speaker, but at least his story is interesting.

The local politicians queuing up to go after him are what I'm really dreading—and what a couple of cocktails would considerably improve. None of them knows much about bicycling. They are here for political reasons and will hit all the predictable talking points. I can see it all happening in my mind before it actually does. Blah blah blah public transportation. Blah blah blah reducing carbon emissions. Blah blah blah the importance of promoting active lifestyles. Blah blah blah in conclusion, Chicago is a green city.

God. I. Need. A. Drink.

But no. The stars have not aligned…yet. (The liquor store in my neighborhood is called Vas Foremost. It has a high, pleasing smell when you walk inside, like Pine Sol and fruit juice. The kids in the neighborhood call the place "Vas Deferens," which I secretly think is clever. As the 23rd Ward Alderman takes the podium and begins to drone on about working with the police to reduce bike thefts in her ward, I begin to picture the cooler at the back of Vas Deferens—the one where they stock the giant Belgian beers. I mentally look them over and consider which one I might select for tonight. Hello ladies. How *do* you do?)

Maybe, if I write really fast, I can turn something in and leave before this shit has concluded. If I'm lucky, I can probably beat the worst of the snow. (My colleagues will likely be none the wiser, and it's a risk I'm willing to take tonight.) Then home. And pizza. And beer.

I look outside. The white stuff is still coming down, harder than before, which means crowded, snowy, wet trains that take longer to get you anywhere. Blech.

I wonder . . .

Is this the same laptop where I saved the story I wrote about the Green City Initiative fundraiser?

Scroll…scroll…scroll…

Yes.

Okay, okay. Focus, Ben. Focus. We can do this . . .

Find: "Green City Initiative." Replace with: "Bicycle Transportation Alliance."

Find: "Recycling programs." Replace with: "Bike lanes."

Find: "Renewable energy." Replace with: "Commuting to work on a fucking bike."

Find and remove: "fucking."

Aaaaaaaaand . . .

Not bad, not bad at all. Just a few more fixes. Switch out this alderman's name for that one's. Change the location from the Chicago Cultural Center to the Trump Tower. Plug in that last bullshit quote the CTA president just read from the speech his PR hack wrote for him . . .

Type type type.

Oh yeah. We'll be sneaking out the back before this is half an hour in. The article practically writes itself.

(Please understand that my alacrity to leave is not a slight on bicycles themselves. I like bikes. In the summer, I bike to work at *Brain's*. I like the bracing rush of negotiating city traffic. I like the other bicyclists too—the skinny kids on fixed gears, the hardcores in full regalia that think it's the Tour de France, the Mexican busboys on their fat-tire Huffys. I even like the aggressive African cabbies who like to roll down their windows and curse at bicyclists in Xhosa or Wolof. It's its own little ecosystem, with aspects that are way, way more interesting than city ordinances and helmet laws make it sound.)

Now . . .

If I file too early, it will look suspicious to my editor. I should probably pack up and hit send when I get home. The snow on the windows . . . gee. It's really coming down. But . . . oh Christ, is that Alderman Dunney waiting to speak? Fuck me, it is.

Alderman Dunney is supposed to be thinking of running for mayor. What if he announces tonight? He almost certainly won't—why would he *here*, at a stupid bicyclist's event?—but if he does and I miss it, I'm almost definitely sacked.

Okay, we wait until Dunney finishes. According to the program, he goes after the CTA guy. It won't be that long to wait.

I hope.

I decide to go take a piss so I won't have to later. I discreetly close my laptop and stand up. I unhitch a metal side-door as quietly as I can, and ease my way out into a hallway near the stage.

In this hallway, I am abruptly confronted by four young women in coordinated outfits. *Sexy* coordinated outfits.

That's right, I remember. The band.

The young women are huddled together around a tablet computer resting on a drummer's plastic bass drum case. The case is completely covered with stickers. Most of the stickers advertise women's roller derby in some form or another. Others bear clever variations on Rosie the Riveter. Others still declaim "Straight but not narrow," "Critical Mass," and "Twisted Scissors."

The young women—all of them—are absolutely beautiful. And they are sharing a case of beer.

Suddenly, I forget I have to take a leak.

"Oh my gee," says one of them. "It's *totally* a zombie!"

"It *can't* be," says another. "Can it?"

"Are you kidding?" says the first. "It totes is!"

"I heard they're all being made by a film student out at USC," says another still. "Like, a special effects guy who interned at ILM."

"Um, ladies . . . who's the old guy looking at our asses?"

Gulp.

The jig is up.

"Hi there," I say. I stand up straight and try to hold in my belly.

"Who are *you*?" one of them asks.

It's hard to tell which one spoke. All these women are beautiful. I am noticing that again and again, and becoming a little flustered as I look from face to face.

"A, uh . . . reporter," I answer.

"A 'uh reporter'?" one of them responds.

She turns back toward the computer. Another one—who is tall and black and showing *a lot* of cleavage—puts her hand on her hip and gives me a "May I help you?" look.

I sigh, turn around, and start to shuffle back down the corridor to the restrooms, my hopes of beer and hot-women-being-around thoroughly dashed.

But then the band member holding the tablet computer says: "Wait, why don't you see what *he* thinks?"

I slow my retreat and hazard a glance over my shoulder.

And she turns around too—the one using the tablet computer—and she is stunning. The other girls are beautiful, yes, but this one is stunning. She looks like a Latin Joan Jett in her prime. Dark eyes, dark hair, tremendous curves. Neck tattoos like snakes coming up from under her collar. A voice that makes you think of cigarettes, bourbon, and dark, musky perfume.

Wow.

"What're y'all looking at?" I ask in my most genial Iowan.

"The zombie clips," Latin Joan Jett says. "You know, the new ones on the internet?"

I nod. I do.

For the last three days, viral videos of what some people are saying are actual zombies have been circulating across social networking sites. Some are shaky, amateur video of corpses at funerals twitching spastically and then falling still again. Some are close-ups of bodies with fingers and toes that suddenly tense and flick like frog's legs dipped in salt. Other videos show full cadavers prepared for autopsy—or *during* autopsy—rising from metal examining tables and walking around as medical students or morticians stand by, flummoxed.

They've been all over the blogosphere, but hard news outlets have yet to report on them. Nobody is taking them seriously... yet.

"We were talking about those videos in the newsroom just this morning," I say. "We were cracking up."

"Cracking up?" she asks. "What if they're *real*, though?"

I make a face like this is a crazy idea. Latin Joan Jett frowns and turns back to her screen.

Then I remember that my fellow reporters are not looking over my shoulder.

"But um . . . there are some things about the videos that nobody can explain," I stammer. "Things that make me think they could be...real."

"Oh yeah?" she says, turning back to face me. "Like *what*?"

"Um, like . . . " I fumble. "Okay . . . like why the institutions where the footage supposedly comes from haven't disavowed it. They haven't said, 'No, that's not from our hospital.'"

"Why would they need to do that?" she asks.

"A lot of the videos are from *specific* hospitals and medical schools, right?" I say. "They're supposedly posted by med students who are like 'I shot this with my camera phone on such-and-such day doing rounds at such-and-such hospital.' Those places are full of doctors and scientists—the types of people who are straight shooters when it comes to what's real and what's not. I think if somebody had made fake movies of cadavers in their hospital getting up and twitching, then of course the hospitals would come out and say the videos are fake—CGI tricks or whatever. Of course they would. There'd be a humorously-worded press release about it. It would be cute and be picked up on all the news services. But the hospitals and doctors haven't done that. There are no cute press releases. No doctors have said that it didn't happen. They haven't done anything. *That's* what's scary...

"Yesterday, one of the writers at *The Exiled* called the PR office at L.A. County, where that video of the dancing zombie was shot—you know...*that* one?—and he posted the audio of the call, and it's terrifying. Because the PR guy won't say 'No, that didn't happen.' He just says things like, 'What do *you* think happened?' And 'I'm not making a statement like that right now.'"

"See, we're reporters, and we deal with PR guys all the time. And that's how they talk when they've got something to hide. The hospital where that footage was shot? It's got something to hide. At least its PR rep *thinks* it does."

There is a long pause. Have I totally lost Latin Joan Jett, talking about reporters and PR flacks? Have I been boring and old mannish? I almost certainly have.

Goddamn it.

And then she says, "My name's Maria Ramirez," and hands me a PBR.

I accept the beer—probably with comically wide eyes—crack it open and have a swallow. Suddenly, I find my urge to get home early has almost completely faded.

I may just stick around to see the show.

Leopold Mack

For all of its helpful pronouncements on subjects relevant to the human soul, the good book has little to say about regret. This is a shame because the topic is so rich. It runs deep. It affects us all.

There are many different kinds of regret. One can regret the done or the undone. (Or even the yet-to-be done.) There is the private regret that hits late at night as you struggle to fall asleep. There is the sloppy, flabby regret that comes with eating, drinking, or flirting too much. (Consequent vows of abstemiousness usually follow this one.) There is the inexorable regret that bombards you when confronted with the consequences of your misdeeds. There is the public regret expressed in front of others—dramatic, exhausting, and usually insincere.

The regret encountered as I climb back into my preacher car and begin the drive back north to Chicago is probably my least favorite of all.

I reactivate my cell phone almost absently. I'm lightheaded. Exhausted. I need a shower.

The tiny phone whirs to life, and soon informs me that I have one voicemail. I hit play and put the phone to my ear. I cringe as soon as I recognize the voice. I scramble to turn down the radio.

The voice belongs to Ms. Washington, one of my oldest and dearest parishioners. She comes from the part of my flock that I inherited when I first took over as pastor of The Church of

Heaven's God in Christ Lord Jesus many years ago. She is ancient and terrible. Smokes three packs a day, yet still breathes like a giant, healthy bellows. Now she breathes into my phone.

She is in need of her pastor, she says. She apologizes for calling at so late an hour, but she has something important to talk to me about. She would like to see me in person, tonight, if possible. Could I see my way to dropping by? Again, she would not call if it were not important. She sounds genuinely upset.

I look at the clock on the dash of my car. 9:30 p.m. And Ms. Washington's message is from 8:00 p.m. I should be there by now.

Regret.

I would have been there—would have been able to pop over from my house to hers in a few short minutes—had I not driven to Merrillville. I would have done what pastors are supposed to do. I would have been there to comfort one of the most venerable and vulnerable members of my flock. And instead, I indulged myself.

Bad pastor.

It is now snowing. A light snow, but growing steadily with each passing swipe of my windshield wipers. I don't remember hearing that a blizzard was in the forecast, but storms can sometimes blow in quickly off the lake. As I wind my way northward through dodgy neighborhoods dusted by snow, I dare to hope that Ms. Washington only needs some groceries before the storm hits. Something like that. I remember her as still getting around just fine, but she probably hesitates to use her car in weather like this. Maybe she needs her heart medicine from a pharmacy you have to drive to.

Please let it be something like that.

It has to be.

It almost has to be.

Regret ebbing.

Somewhat.

I turn down 71st Street and eventually merge into Lake Shore Drive, the highway that runs along the edge of Lake Michigan. I drive north at a good clip. There are very few cars on the road. To my left are parks and apartment buildings. The scene to my right varies, but usually shows thirty yards of trees and bike trails, then ten yards of beach, then the endless dark of Lake Michigan beyond.

The flakes are coming down, but not really sticking. Every time I drive this way in the snow, I can't help but think of the blizzard of 2011. It hit hard and fast, and hundreds of people were trapped inside their cars on this very road. The traffic slowed to a crawl and then to nothing. People couldn't drive forward or backward. The snow quickly piled up too high to try off-roading, even if you had an SUV. After a few hours, people started running out of gas. The city had to send the fire department out on foot to rescue folks from their cars. It was an all-night operation. The next day, chilling photographs ran in newspapers around the world showing this wintry wasteland—a snow-blasted highway with rows and rows of gridlocked, abandoned cars leading off forever into the distance.

Tonight, thankfully, traffic is light, and I'm doing forty-five miles an hour even in the snow.

I edge farther north and pass Hyde Park—home of such venerable entities as Louis Farrakhan, Barack Obama, and The

University of Chicago. Then I see something that makes me both
furious and utterly astonished.

There are people playing on the beach.

I can scarcely credit it. Am I seeing what I think I'm seeing?
I take one hand off my steering wheel and rub my eyes. When
I look again, the people are still there. It's almost unbelievable.

Every twenty yards or so, I see a person walking around,
knee-deep in the lake's icy water. They do not wear coats or winter gear, much less insulated wetsuits. Some appear to be coming ashore—walking from out of the water up onto the beach—
while others seem content to splash around in the waves. But they
are, all of them, *lingering*. Taking their time.

What the Hell?

Can this be some sort of polar bear club? Or a flash mob of
crazy young people that organized on the internet? A University
of Chicago hazing ritual?

I have no clue. The scene makes no sense.

I know, I know. This is where I'm supposed to say something
pithy, right? Something like, "White people crazy." But I can't.
For one, I can't tell for sure that these people *are* white, because
of the darkness and the falling snow—and, yes, because the eyes
of a man of advanced age are not what they once were—I am
unable to discern much more than silhouettes. The ages, sexes,
and races of these winter waders are obscured entirely by the
shadows. But one thing *is* sure: they are playing around in the surf
or walking out of the water and up onto the land, in the middle
of a snowstorm. Many appear dripping wet from head to toe.
Are there blankets and heaters secreted away amongst the rocks?

Are there warm, running cars hidden between the trees? There must be. There *have* to be. Otherwise, this activity is a recipe for frostbite and death.

But I can see no idling cars, and no caches of blankets and heating packs along the shoreline. I only see, every twenty yards or so, another wet person walking around in the surf, like an idiot.

Maybe some people don't have enough problems. Maybe they can't think of all the helpful and useful things they could be doing with their time. Maybe their lives are so boring and confused that they *need* hypothermia to make it interesting.

Okay, fine. I'm 'a say it.

White people crazy.

★ ★ ★

After twenty minutes, I exit Lake Shore Drive and take an off ramp heading past the Loop—downtown Chicago, where the tallest buildings are.

It's still kind of bugging me out—the polar bear club people— so I try to busy myself worrying about Ms. Washington.

The first thing to know about her is that she's one of the only members of my flock who left South Shore but still comes back for church. Ms. Washington moved up north a few years ago when she inherited a place from her sister who passed. The neighborhood is called Logan Square, after John A. Logan. (He ran for vice president 150 years ago and lost, is my understanding. Apparently, that's good enough to get a neighborhood named after you.) Forty years ago, Logan Square was as dangerous as South Shore; more dangerous maybe. Latin street gangs fighting for turf and shooting up the residents. Now it's better, and white people have moved in. That's how the neighborhoods generally evolve in this town—how the gentrification runs. White people pushing out Latinos. The Loop inexorably pushing its way west and south to where blacks live.

Too often, my Latin brothers and sisters are the buffer between the blacks and the whites. I do not envy them. They bear the brunt of the gentrification—having to make a choice every generation between staying in a neighborhood that no longer feels like home or uprooting to move a mile west if they still want the signs on the stores to be in Spanish.

God help them—for I, certainly, cannot. *Dios mío. Dios mío,* indeed.

But Ms. Washington . . . she is a firecracker. I like the fact that she's chosen to make her stand up in Logan Square. So what if she could sell the place and live out her final years high on the hog in South Shore? It's in the family, and she's gonna take it over. Amen.

Driving through neighborhoods and watching the demographics change like this has always made me wonder—what does "success" look like for Chicago? What are we all working toward?

I mean, The Church of Heaven's God in Christ Lord Jesus needs a new roof and a new pipe organ. That would feel like success to me. A roof that doesn't leak when it rains and organ music that people can hear back in the last pew would be a little bit of success. But think bigger, Pastor Mack . . . what about the whole neighborhood? What about the whole city?

These are the questions that nobody wants to answer.

Should there be no "ethnic neighborhoods" or Chicago-style segregation? Should the races all mix together like a true melting pot? Must we interbreed until the entire notion of "race" is lost?

Or should we instead proudly cling to ethnic heritages and neighborhoods—espousing how they enrich our cultural lives—but insist on economic equality? That is to say: Is success when there are still black and white and Latino neighborhoods, but they're all equally wealthy, and they all have schools and firehouses and hospitals that are just as good?

There is no consensus upon these questions—within my own brain or within the highest echelons of city government. The only thing that the clergy and the politicians and the community development people can agree on is that things are not okay as they are. Things need to change.

But change to exactly *what*? Ladies and gentlemen, nobody has any idea.

Nobody.

Anyhow, I pull off the expressway and head a few blocks into Logan Square.

That's when I start to hear the mysterious thumping noise coming from the back seat.

Maria Ramirez

So I decide he's kind of cute ... but also weird.

Those guys in their 30s who still dress like hipsters ... they don't look old, but they don't look young either. It's like plastic surgery. You're not old but you're not young. You're this weird, *third* thing.

He has a wrinkled dress shirt with the top unbuttoned and a tie hanging low on his neck. He's tall—which I like—but also a little thick around the middle. Not exactly Stewart Copeland. But then he does have the thick black Stewart Copeland-style glasses. I have to admit I like *that*.

And it turns out he actually does know a little about zombies. At least he's less cynical than what they were saying on Gawker and Drudge Report. That they may be a prank, or some new medical condition. That the stumbling, decayed people in the clips are mutated residents of a nuclear accident in some former Soviet republic. (A lot of the newer zombie videos *are* from Eastern Europe.)

He isn't calling them zombies though. He says he thinks that if they *are* real, that they're people. Maybe deformed. Maybe sick. He also thinks it could just be a giant internet joke though, or a hoax by a company to promote a product. (Stranger things have happened.) He says that something's up ... but not necessarily zombies.

So, yeah, he talks about the zombies with me for a while. Just when the conversation is winding down, he says, "Oh hey, SBVD. Right on."

He's looking at the Strawberry Brite Vagina Dentata sticker on the side of my drum case. He obviously has no idea that we're the same band. I tell him that we are.

"No shit?!? You guys just do this cover band bullshit for the extra scratch?"

"Ding ding ding," I say. "We have a winner."

"Really?"—not like he doesn't believe me, but like he thinks it's cool. "That's awesome. Wow!"

"I guess it's kinda awesome," I say. Now he's going overboard.

"You guys are amazing," he continues. "That one tune you do, 'Flip the Trick'? That's an *amazing* song. That part where the guitars drop out and it's just bass and drums? Amazing. And you're *that* drummer?"

I kind of step back and look him up and down again.

He doesn't look like a typical Strawberry Brite Vagina Dentata fan. At least ten years too old and thirty pounds too heavy. Also, he says "amazing" too much.

But he clearly knows our songs.

"Yeah," I say cautiously. "That's me. Did you hear us on the radio? We got played on 'Local Anesthetic' the other day."

"My wife . . ." he begins, and falters. For just a moment his eyes flicker around, and his lips curl like he's sad.

I wait.

"My *ex*-wife . . . " he tries again. "She made me a mix CD. 'Flip the Trick' was on there. The second song, actually . . . right after 'California Stars.'"

Fucking Wilco. Goddamn it.

"Can I just tell you—you're a really good drummer," he continues.

Without asking, I hand him another beer. He accepts it appreciatively, cracks it open, and continues to gush about my ability with the sticks. (Non-drummers are so cute when they try to describe what drummers do, but they don't know the right terminology or even understand how a drum kit works. He finishes by comparing me to John Bonham " . . . but, like, a sexy female John Bonham," and praising "that one part of the song where your hands go really fast.")

I open a second PBR for myself.

"What other songs are on this mix by your ex-wife?" I ask. "Other than... *Wilco*."

I'm always curious about other bands that SBVD fans like. We can try to poach their fan bases on social networking sites—get those people to come to our shows. Sometimes it actually works.

"Uh, lessee," he says. "She's kind of all over the place. There was some Beatles, of course. She loves the Beatles. Some John Mellencamp—she's a Hoosier. And then bands like Nickelback."

"Excuse me while I puke a little in my mouth."

"Oh," he says, realizing this selection is not to my taste.

"No offense," I tell him, "but if music were the human body, nu-metal would be the taint."

"Heh," he says. "That's a good line. I'm gonna steal that."

"It's fucking true."

He smiles. He's cute when he smiles.

"Not to bring up a sore subject," I say. "But . . . um . . . she can't have been your ex for long."

"Why do you say that?" he says, as if my question is confusing.

"If she made you a mix CD with 'Flip the Trick' on it," I clarify. "We didn't release that song until four months ago. So if she made you the CD and then you got divorced..."

"Oh, we were divorced before," he says. "It's been official for about two years now."

"But you still...?"

"We're still friends, if that's what you mean," he tells me. "I still care about her a lot. It just didn't work out."

"Did you *have kids* together or something?"

"No," he says.

"Good," I tell him. "Because eww."

He gives a big toothy grin.

"What, you're not into kids?"

"Umm, what do *you* think?"

He laughs again.

"No . . . my ex and I are just friends. Not every relationship that ends has to end badly, you know?"

I let him have that one.

I need to go warm up on my practice pad, and tell him as much. I have the feeling this guy's going to hang around for the show.

"Hey," he says as I began digging through my backpack for some sticks. "My name's Ben. Ben Bennington. I don't think I told you before."

Awww. He's trying to be bold.

"Hello Ben," I reply. "It's nice to meet you."

Ben Bennington

So I decide to stick around for the show. (It was fun to talk with Maria about the zombies. I wished I'd had more to say on the topic, but I still think I did okay.)

I leave the hallway, return to my chair at the back of the nightclub, and wait patiently for the remaining politicians to finish. All the speeches are so similar. So boring. I swear to God, if another person quotes Daniel Burnham I am going to start throwing things.

Can this get any worse?

Oh wait, it can. The serious looking alderman at the microphone just brought up Al Capone.

Ugh. That's the worst.

There's always somebody who wants to talk about how Chicago needs to be known for something other than Al Capone. They tell stories about how, when they travel—to other countries or just down to Indiana—the one thing that people know about Chicago is still Al Capone and gangsters. Non-English speakers will smile and say "Shee-cago?" then make a "*Rat-tat-tat*" sound as they mimic a gunner at the St. Valentine's Day massacre.

Yet, what do our gifted and wise politicians propose championing to replace these stereotypes? Bike lanes. Green buildings. Recycling programs.

Really? Can we not do any better than that, Chicago? Can we really not be any more interesting than low-flow toilets and solar panels?

Is something wrong with me that I would *prefer* fedora-ed gangsters as my civic heritage? That I find them kind of—dare I say—cool? At least compared with green roofs?

I've heard these speeches—in one form or another—all before. And I'll surely hear them again. Be like Burnham. Don't be like Capone. Blah. Blah. Blah.

I spend most of my time thinking about the cute drummer.

Maria. Her name was Maria.

It's still snowing outside. I watch it coming down through the polished glass windows of the Trump Tower. I more or less tune out the speeches, and stare off into the distant darkness of Lake Michigan.

Even though there's a band, this will wind up early. These things always do.

The final speaker finishes. No one says anything new. Nobody makes an announcement about being a candidate for mayor, which pisses me off. I boot up my laptop and file the story I could have filed from home with a beer in my hand. Then Strawberry Brite Vagina Dentata plays a forty-five minute set of covers under the name "The Kitty Kats from Heaven." They're really talented musicians—and that girl can drum!—but the song selection is tepid and predictable. Lots of classic rock. A couple of soul songs. A Wilco tune, during which Maria appears to wince. (How do you even draw up a set list for a room full of low level civic politicians and representatives from nonprofits? Maybe this is as good as it can get.)

I kind of want to talk to Maria again, but I also don't want to be a stalker. (Or creeper. That's right. The girls say "creeper" now.)

I'm sure I'll be able to find her later on a social networking site or the SBVD web page. Maybe in a few days I'll get up the courage to send her an email if I don't decide that I'm too old.

I give Maria a wave after the last song. She waves back from the stage, wiping sweat from her forehead with an embroidered Hello Kitty towel. Her mascara is running a little. It is super-hot.

I beat a quick retreat out of the Trump Tower and head for the nearest train.

Once outside, I realize the snow is not so bad. It's not even sticking.

So at least there's that.

The El ride back to my neighborhood is noisy and cold. I stare out the windows when the train goes above ground. The buildings are just visible through a blue-orange haze of streetlights and snowflakes. The wind is picking up, and sometimes it rocks the train a little. I find the sensation pleasant and calming.

I exit at the California Avenue stop and walk down the salted metal staircase connecting the platform to the street below. My neighborhood, normally bustling, is almost deserted. The few people I do see are scurrying here and there in heavy coats. (Maybe the forecast has changed and a blizzard is now predicted.) A weird tension pervades. Nobody is stopping to chat with anybody. I'm guessing they're hitting the grocery one last time before the snow starts piling. Or maybe the liquor store.

I ponder whether or not I am still in a beer and pizza mood. I decide, no. I'll just head home. Maybe pull up the SBVD web page and see if there is a "Photos" section.

Creeper, indeed.

I trek down a couple of side streets tracing the familiar path to my apartment. My block is relatively quiet. My footprints are alone in the virgin snow-slush underfoot.

I turn a corner by Palmer Square Park—almost home—and finally see another person. He's a frustrated-looking African-American guy, maybe in his late 60s, wearing a long brown trench coat. He's holding a tire iron and standing next to an immaculate Chrysler with a flat tire. It's right in front of my apartment building.

He notices me approaching, and his expression changes.

"Hello, my friend," he says with a smile.

"Hi," I respond tentatively.

"I wonder...could you give me a hand?"

And boom: I have that reaction where you're sure it's going to be some kind of grift.

I mean, this guy has an actual flat tire. He's not making *that* up. But I still feel like I'm a mark. That this is—somehow, someway—going to be a request for money. A new variation on the guy who roams the neighborhood with an empty gas can, saying he ran out and his wallet's at home and could he please just have $5.

I am going to get *taken*.

"Um, maybe I could give you a hand," I manage.

"This flat tire is stuck onto these bolts," he says, kicking it. "Maybe frozen on."

He seems genuinely frustrated.

"So you can't remove it to put on the spare?" I ask cautiously.

"Exactly. Would you be able to give me a hand? Maybe if two people pull together ..."

I kind of relax a little. Okay. This is feeling less like a grift.

"Yeah, man," I say. "I can do that."

"I keep slipping in the snow," he tells me. "Can't get my leverage right."

"Let's both try," I say, putting on my gloves.

I join him at the side of the car. He's got it jacked up, and the offending tire spins freely. We grip it together and prepare to pull. I just have time to imagine a nightmare scenario in which the jack slips in the slush and we are both crushed under the stylish automobile.

"Okay," he says, "one . . . two . . . three!"

We pull as hard as we can. The tire spins a little in our collective grip, but does not come loose. It is almost impossible to get a good footing in this snow. After just a few seconds of pulling, I can tell we aren't going to get it.

"Okay, stop," I say. "This thing is stuck."

We step back and examine the situation.

"Shoot," the man says. "I could call AAA, but I'm on my way to something important."

"And they take an hour to come when it snows like this," I observe.

"Shoot," the man says again, looking skyward in exasperation.

"Wait," I tell him. "I got it."

The man cautiously raises an eyebrow.

"What about hitting it with something? I bet you could smack it from behind—like from the inside—and knock the tire loose."

"That might work," the man agrees.

"I've got an old sledgehammer up in my apartment. Want me to go get it?"

He looks at his watch and shrugs.

"Yeah," he allows. "What the hey? Best to give it a shot."

I leave the man alone by his car and open the gate to my building. I trudge upstairs (third floor walkup) and find the ancient hammer; rusted, and with the handle covered in black duct tape. I wonder if the man is even expecting me to return? Maybe he has already called AAA. Maybe he thinks this was a pretense to get away from him.

He's still standing there, though, when I emerge from my building with the sledge.

"You want me to do it?" I ask him.

"Sure, it's your sledge."

"Yeah, but it's your car," I tell him.

"I trust you."

I creep to the edge of the wheel well and take a knee. Chopping from the side—long and slow, like a batter in an on-deck circle—I hit the side of the tire as hard as I can. It jostles loose and bounces up and down on its bolts. Success.

"Hot damn!" says the man.

"That should do it," I say, pleased with the result.

The man grips the tire and easily lifts it off the car. He sets it on the ground next to the nuts and bolts.

"I appreciate this, friend," he says. "Look, can I give you a couple of dollars?"

Here I had been afraid this was going to be a swindle, and now the guy is offering *me* money. Man, I am some kind of fuck.

"No," I tell him, privately embarrassed. "This was my good deed for the day."

"Well then," he says, extending his glove to me. "Thank you."

We shake hands, and he begins to replace the tire.

A few minutes later, I am upstairs at my desk with a cup of hot chocolate and a browser window containing Google Image results for "Strawberry Brite Vagina Dentata drummer." The results look pretty good.

I hear the car outside slowly pull away.

And that's when I realize I have forgotten to bring the sledge-hammer back up with me.

Fuck. Back into the cold once more.

Reluctantly, I leave the appealing search results behind and put my coat on. I trudge down the stairs and walk back outside into the winter chill.

The hammer has been thoughtfully propped against an oak next to the sidewalk, a final kindly gesture on the part of the man with the flat.

I walk over and pick up the hammer. Then I stop dead in my tracks.

Standing in front of my building is a young woman in a thin yellow dress. She has pleasing features and pale skin with a few freckles. She could be one of my neighbors from the building next door, but I can't place her face. Though underdressed for the weather, she doesn't shiver. Her skin is unmarked by goosebumps or windburn.

She also has what appears to be a baby's half-eaten arm dangling from her mouth. The front of her dress is covered in blood. (In the first instant, I had mistaken the crimson blotches for an artistic pattern woven in, but when she approaches I see that it's definitely blood.) She is looking at me. Her eyes are an unnatural milky-white, as if colored by layers of cataract. She takes one shambling step forward, continuing to masticate the arm like a carnival treat on a stick. Her expression is placid and curious.

"Is that a Halloween costume?" I whisper. (I'm afraid to say anything loud. Afraid to alert the universe. Afraid to make it real.

The young woman takes another shuddering step toward me...then another. She draws nearer, and nearer still. Then the baby arm drops from her mouth and her hands stretch forward as if to strangle me. Her mouth gapes and shows me hideous cruor teeth. Her lips curl into a smile.

My adrenaline surges. Fight or flight, I wonder?

Then I remember that I'm holding a sledgehammer.

Without thinking, I raise the hammer. (I've never been a strong guy, but I'm, you know, big. I can knock somebody down when I have to. In this instant of calculation, I feel confident I can take out this waifish woman, especially if I can just get my weight behind the hammer.) At the same time, she lunges forward and tries to scratch my face with her long fingernails.

I flinch back—reacting without thinking—and send the sixteen-pound hammer careening down into her.

If I had not flinched, the hammer might have obliterated her head. Instead, it enters her chest up to the handle. There is a moment of resistance when the head of the hammer meets her ribs, but only a moment. It smashes through them and sinks deep inside her chest cavity.

I am speechless. I release my grip on the cedar handle and take a step back.

The bloody woman does not fall.

She does not wince.

She does not scream.

Her legs buckle for a moment, adjusting to the weight of the hammer, but then she gains her footing once more, and takes another step toward me, the handle still protruding from her chest.

That's when I realize something is very, very wrong.

Leopold Mack

I arrive late.

My car is running on the donut, which has almost no traction in the snow.

Yes, I had a flat, but let's be honest, I'm late because I fucked off and went to Merrillville. I'm late because I chose to be selfish and put my own pleasure over being present and available for my flock, which is supposed to be part of a pastor's job. Maybe if I hadn't driven to Merrillville, the tire wouldn't have gone flat.

I get out of the car and stare up at Ms. Washington's house, feeling even more like a bad pastor. It echoes again and again, like a heartbeat in my chest. Bad pastor. Bad pastor. Bad pastor.

I take a deep breath and flap my arms, getting the blood flowing. You can do this, Mack. You can do this.

I walk up to Ms. Washington's front stoop and press the bell. (Just one bell. Ms. Washington inherited the whole place.)

"Oeah?" is the croak that comes back at me through the tiny, tinny speaker. The response is instant, as if she has been sitting next to the intercom, waiting for me, anxious and scared and in need of consultation with a man of God. (Bad pastor. Bad pastor. Bad pastor.)

"Ms. Washington, it's Pastor Mack," I call back, loudly and clearly. "I got your message on my phone."

"Oh Pastor," she responds. "One moment."

I hear a series of latches being unfastened, and the front door creaks ajar. A wave of smoke spills out, as if announcing the arrival of a denizen of the Pit. But the stout figure before me is no devil. It's just old Ms. Washington, puffing on a menthol and wearing her pink housecoat.

"Ms. Washington," I say again as she admits me. I receive a smoky, minty kiss on the cheek and am all but physically tugged inside.

"Oh Pastor Mack," she says. "I'm so glad you could come up north on a snowy night like this."

We take a seat in her kitchen.

"Yes," I say as she lights another cigarette. "I would have liked to have come sooner, but I had . . . obligations."

"Of course you did," Ms. Washington croaks. She offers me a glass of water, which I accept.

"Also, a flat tire," I say, taking the water.

"My lands!" exclaims Ms. Washington. "In *this* weather!? We should thank the Lord that you made it here in one piece. Don't tell me you tried changing it yourself! In the snow!?"

"I was . . . blessed with a helpful white boy," I tell her. "It wasn't so bad with two."

"Pastor, now I feel horrible putting you through all of this," Ms. Washington says.

She doesn't have to tell me about feeling horrible.

"It's no matter," I respond. "I'm here now. Please tell me how I can be of service."

Ms. Washington takes a seat and considers where to begin.

"This isn't about *me* exactly," Ms. Washington says, taking a pull on her smoke. "This concerns my neighbor, Miss Khan. But Pastor, she needs your help if anybody ever did!"

"Miss Khan?" I ask, as the name is entirely unfamiliar to me. "You haven't mentioned her before."

"Maybe I haven't," agrees Ms. Washington. "A young thing. Lives in the apartment next door. Always see her when I'm working in my garden and she's coming back from jogging in the park. She works as a flight attendant, I believe."

I stare hard into the ample forehead of Ms. Washington. This is a conversation I've had before. My friend—or neighbor—has a problem, Pastor. What should they do, Pastor? What should *we* do?

From what Ms. Washington has said thus far, I'm guessing the problem will be a boyfriend or husband who's physically abusive. That's one I get a lot. Most people can't understand why a woman stays with a man who beats her, but there is always a mitigating circumstance. Always a thing that makes it "not that easy." She has no finances. She has nowhere else to go. She has had children with him.

If it's not that, then it will almost certainly be a suspected drug habit or drinking problem—likely compounded by a correlating suspicion that children are being neglected. These suspicions—when they're accurate—are some of the most difficult for me to assist with. (If the troubled person cannot be convinced that they have a problem, then it comes down to a series of difficult binaries; choices where it's either this or that. We either call child protective services, or we don't. We either call the police, or we don't. We stage an intervention, or we wait until something happens again.)

A final possibility—a rare one, but something I still see consistently—will be a request that I use my connections in the community to lobby for some sort of minor municipal change that will benefit the neighbor. Pastor, that bus stop needs to be moved to the other side of the street—all those people right outside the window! Pastor, that traffic light just changes too fast— I can't haul my old bones across the crosswalk in time. Pastor, our new property assessment *can't* be right . . . can it?

So I have—or at least *think* I have—some idea of what Ms. Washington will ask about on behalf of her friend, Ms. Khan.

And I am totally wrong.

Ms. Washington takes another deep drag and says, "I ain't seen Ms. Khan for almost two weeks. And normally, I don't pay it no mind when she don't come around. We just been missin' each other. She's flying all over the world. She gets free tickets, you know, with that job? And the men she carries on with? The trips they take together? Mmm-hmm. And so I haven't seen Ms. Khan, precious little thing. Then, this evening, I go out to my box to get the mail and she's standing out in the cold—in the *cold,* Pastor— wearing nothing but her exercising top and those yoga pants. Can you imagine?"

I nod as if I can.

"And I ask her how she's been, but she won't say a word to me," Ms. Washington continues. "Not a word. She won't even communicate. She looks lost. And my mind says: Something is not right with this young woman! She is freezing outside in just her exercise clothes. I have got to get her someplace warm."

I nod again.

"But she won't go back into her building," Ms. Washington continues, sounding genuinely exasperated. "So I think, maybe she just needs to come inside and have a cup of tea with me. Warm up, you know? And if that doesn't work, I say to myself, I'm going to call the hospital. So I take her by the hand and bring her into my house. I try to make her to sit in a chair—the same one where you're sitting now, Pastor—but she won't. She just *wanders* through my house. She is bumping around, knocking things over, like she doesn't even see them! I cannot, for the life of me, understand. Then something happens you won't believe!"

As if to punctuate this declamation, a loud scratching sound—like a dog trying to open a door—rises from the back of the house. It falls away after just a few seconds.

Ms. Washington looks over her shoulder uneasily.

"What happened?" I press, following her gaze toward the mysterious noise.

"She got . . . *bitey*," Ms. Washington whispers seriously—as if this is something more sinful than sex or drugs or rock and roll.

"She got . . . ?" I try, hoping for more explanation.

"She tried to *bite* me!" Ms. Washington answers, vibrating nervously like a round mound of pudding. "She snapped at me. With her *teeth*! I asked her what she was doing. I said I was trying to *help* her. I told her to stop. But she wouldn't listen. No sir! She got this mean look in her eyes. Her eyes had started to get sort of milky and dark at the same time. They had this look like she could see me, but she *didn't* see me. You follow? She didn't know me anymore. And I tried telling her, 'Ms. Khan, we've known one another since I moved into this house! Tell me why you are trying to bite me!' But she didn't say a thing; only *kept* biting. That's when I locked her in the guest bedroom."

Again, on cue, the scratching noise rises and falls. That dog really, *really* wants out.

"Is that *her*?" I ask, as I point in the direction of the scratching.

"When I saw that look in her eyes—my lands, it was horrible! Just so horrible!—I knew I had to call you, Pastor." Ms. Washington replies, ignoring my question.

"Show me where she is right now!" I say, rising to my feet. "We need to call an ambulance."

"No!" entreats Ms. Washington. "This is no sickness! This isn't medical! Pastor . . . can't you tell? This is *possession*!"

I lower my head and look hard at Ms. Washington. She stares back at me, unwavering.

"Take one look in her eyes, and you'll see it. Just be careful of the biting."

Ms. Washington rises to her feet and slowly conducts me to the back of her house. As I trail her, I take the phone from my pocket and prepare to dial 911.

This is a surprise. A venerable and usually likeable congregant who has suddenly gone batshit crazy, confining another human in the back of her house? It's a surprise. A big damn surprise. And totally new. I've never seen *this* one before.

As we walk toward the back of her pleasantly appointed home—past a collection of dream-catchers, matching rugs and table runners, and a framed photograph of herself at last summer's "Witness to Fitness" event at the church (stretching out her XXL t-shirt and smoking a KOOL), I wonder for how long I have been missing the signs of dementia. I see her face in the pews every week without fail, but it's been a long time since Ms. Washington and I really talked. Too long, apparently.

We near the end of a hallway at the back of the house. It terminates in front of a thick white door. I can sense the presence of another human behind it, though the scratching sounds have temporarily stopped.

"Now . . . I'm going to open this just enough for you to see," says Ms. Washington. "But Pastor, don't you go sticking your fingers anywhere near her!"

I look at Ms. Washington doubtfully and prepare to dial for emergency services.

She then opens the door, and I forget all about my phone call.

Inside the quilt-festooned guest room stands an athletic, Asian woman in a sports bra and yoga pants. She looks insane…utterly insane. She's rocking back and forth—very slowly—on the balls of her feet. A thin rivulet of red drool falls continuously from the corner of her mouth. It has pooled on the floor beneath her. Her face is a mask of living death.

It's like everything I've seen before—and nothing I've ever seen before. What can I compare it to? What *can't* I compare it to?

I think of the wasted addicts I've seen dying in back alleys on hot Chicago summer nights. The empty stares. The snot and spit and plasma. The numbed, destroyed facial muscles. I mean the ones who are really, really far gone.

I think of the people inside the group homes run by the Illinois Alliance on Mental Illness—the ones that I thought maybe were past being in a group home. The ones who give you the feeling that maybe there is not an entire person in there anymore. The ones that make you think things about euthanasia and assisted suicide that a pastor probably shouldn't.

Something about her is already cadaverous, and so I also think of the many—too many—dead bodies I've had to identify at the Cook County Morgue over the years. That dead stare coming up at you from the metal examining table. The organs that no longer function, in a chest splayed like an anatomy lesson. The outstretched tongue taking in one final taste of the air.

Jesus Christ.

I take a step past Ms. Washington to see Ms. Khan more clearly, and the confined woman suddenly starts. Violently. There is something else here. Yet another aspect is revealed.

In the face of this woman, I now also detect a murderousness. It is something I have seen only a handful of times in my life. And I thank God for that fact.

I got my first look when I was just nineteen years old, in a jungle in Southeast Asia. I've seen it on the faces of gangbangers when I'm called in—usually as a last ditch effort—to talk them down from a revenge killing. To convince them not to head out with a gun to kill the killer of their fallen friend.

Now I see that same angry madness in this woman's face.

Before I can speak, she lunges forward and emits a low moan. Ms. Washington expertly stops the door with her foot, preventing the insane woman from breaking through. (The woman is considerably athletic, but Ms. Washington has mass going for her in a big way.)

"You *see!*" Ms. Washington exhorts as Ms. Khan begins claw-ing at the door with her fingernails. "Possession! Demonic spirits! I'm sure of it, Pastor Mack. This is a young lady who is being cor-rupted from *the other side.*"

I don't believe Ms. Washington for a moment. But also, I find—in this strange, horrifying moment—that I can't think of what else it could be.

Before I can formulate any answer, Ms. Washington makes a fatal mistake.

"Don't you *believe* me?" Ms. Washington says, noticing the bewilderment and hesitation on my face. "If you need to take a second look, Pastor, you be my guest and go ahead."

Ms. Washington takes her foot away from the door, which opens it another crack. Then her foot slips, and the crack becomes a two-foot opening. The thing that was Ms. Khan reaches its sinewy arms through and grabs Ms. Washington by the throat.

"Oh my Lo-" manages Ms. Washington as the thing's arms close around her neck.

I try to jump between the two, but my boots are slick with snow. We all three lose our footing and tumble to the hardwood floor of the hallway.

My trench coat gets tangled and goes up in my face. Then I hear a horrible noise like a basketball being punctured with a knife.

By the time I push the coat out of my eyes and get propped up on an elbow, the Khan-thing has already bitten away the throat of Ms. Washington. There is blood everywhere. Ms. Washington looks toward the ceiling, dead-eyed, as the Khan-thing chews at what used to be her ample neck.

(Ms. Washington was heavy and she went down hard. She hit her head and died in the fall. She was at least unconscious when the thing bit through her windpipe. This is what I tell myself to stay sane.)

Oh Jesus, there is a lot of blood.

I spring to my feet and leap backwards, away from the women. The Khan-thing no longer acknowledges my presence. It merely feeds on the flesh of Ms. Washington.

"Hey!" I manage to yell out, treating this creature as if it's a dog.

The thing gives no sign that it has heard me.

What the fuck is going on?

I am paralyzed with fear. Do I call the police? Do I run? Do I attempt to subdue this monster inside the body of an athletic Asian woman? (Should I try to *kill* her? My mind and heart are both racing at the possibilities.)

Then, something astonishing happens.

I hear a "*fwack*" from the entryway of Ms. Washington's house. The wind has blown her front door open. And the sound is followed by the steady shuffling of feet.

"Hello?" I cry out, afraid to take my eyes off the gorging Khan-thing. "Is someone there?"

The feet shuffle closer. From the corner of my eye, I see a body round the corner at the far end of the hallway. I risk a glance. Then a do I a double take.

The figure rounding the corner is a Latin man in his late 50s with an ample belly, wearing blue jeans and the remains of a well-stretched wife beater. I say "remains" because the lower half of the wife beater has been blown away—as has much of his chest—by what was almost certainly a close-range shotgun blast. There is a gaping hole, and I can see his heart, which is *not beating*.

The man's eyes are rolling but aware. His arms extend in front of him, like a sleepwalker. He begins to advance. I should be scared, but all I can think about is how that heart isn't beating. He is a corpse…and yet…he walks.

The walking dead man lumbers down the hall. He moves nearer, then nearer still. I am terrified. My brain races for some frame of reference, for something—anything—that explains this.

I've seen some shit, okay. In my many years on this earth, I have seen some *shit*. I've seen things I don't need to tell you specifically, at least not here. I've seen things that I would not have hesitated to call "unthinkable."

People like to throw around that word. I am among them, I admit it! It's unthinkable that two-fifths of my platoon were killed in a single mortar attack. It's unthinkable that there are 400 young black men killed in the City of Chicago each year. It's unthinkable that the people we love the most pass away and then aren't there anymore.

Unthinkable, right?

But this is something else entirely. This leaves me with a feeling of alarm, like I've stumbled onto a plane of existence where I shouldn't be. This is the fourth dimension. This is Hades. I'm an existential trespasser. I have walked in, and now I want to walk out again.

The thing that used to be a Latin man walks right up to me. I let it. I'm not convinced I have the power to stop it. Besides, I'm at the end of the hallway, and there is nowhere to run.

Then the thing notices Ms. Khan feasting on the body of Ms. Washington, and it abruptly changes course. It brushes past me, and gradually kneels down—clumsily—next to Ms. Washington's corpse. It reaches for her bloated, diabetic, arthritic leg, and tucks in. It chews away slowly and methodically. There is clearly nowhere on Earth it would rather be.

"Move Mack!"

The voice is inside my head, but it feels real, like someone shouting it. It's a combination of my father, my high school football coach, and my drill sergeant. All three of those men are dead now. Whether it is their spirits coming through the void to save me or only my memories, it does the job. They command me to move. To fight my paralyzed legs and to get out of that house. To save figuring out what the Hell is happening for later.

And I do.

I take one last glance at the horrible things feasting on Ms. Washington, and then I run without looking back.

Maria Ramirez

"Ever wish you played the piccolo instead?"

That's a smartass comment you hear all the time when you're a drummer and it's time to load-out. The guitarists have an amp, a guitar, and maybe one gear bag. You've got a small mountain of heavy drum cases and hardware to carry.

And, I mean, okay. The joke has a point. Drummers have the most shit to lug. But also, what the joke neglects to account for is that when you're the drummer, *you're the drummer.* You get to be the one to play the drums.

That's a pretty fair trade-off, if you ask me.

After the show at the Trump Tower, I load my drums into their black plastic cases, load those cases into the freight elevator, and take it down to the basement parking level underneath the giant building. The other girls have finished loading by the time I arrive in the parking bay. They're already warming up their cars to drive home. We wave goodbye and shout "Good gig" to one another.

We have a show the very next day—a corporate event for a diagnostics company up in the northern suburbs. This schedule is typical for us. Most nights, my drums never leave my car.

"Watch out for zombies," Sarah shouts with a laugh as she pulls away in her Nissan Cube.

"Totes!" I call back from the loading dock.

The other girls follow Sarah's Cube out of the parking garage, and I am all alone. The ugly, utilitarian surroundings remind me that this is not a place for hotel guests or residents of the expensive condos upstairs. This is a place for serfs and servants, where comfort is not a priority. I'm surrounded by ugly concrete floors below and cheap lights above (the kind that will make anybody look haggard).

I get into my SUV and carefully back it up to the ledge by the freight elevator where my drums rest. I get out, open the back, and put on my weight-belt. I begin lifting the heavy cases one by one into my car. (This shit is good for your upper body. I've got some sexy-ass arm muscles, and they're not just from the drumming.)

Behind me, someone calls the freight elevator. Its wooden doors close automatically, and it hums softly as it's carried away to the upper levels of the hotel. I set my kick drum case on the concrete beside me, and it makes a loud "crack." I listen to it echo through the vast subterranean levels of the garage. It starts out loud and then fades away into nothingness. After that is only silence.

I feel very alone, and it's not an awesome feeling. I'm a social person who doesn't like to be by herself. This is a little eerie.

I try to think about something other than being alone down here.

Something else.

Not zombies.

Stewart Copeland.

Yes.

★ ★ ★

So I'm there loading out, straining and sweating under the weight of my hardware cases and remembering watching Stewart play Wrigley Field with the Police back in 2007. (Sting's son was in the opening band, and that made me think about wanting to make a bunch of little Stewart Copelands. At the end of the show, Stewart threw his sticks into the audience. I was sitting too far away to have a shot at catching them. The next day one of them was on eBay, but some jagoff beat me to it. Fucking goddamn "Buy It Now.")

I finally begin to hear other people-noises coming from distant parts of the garage. Someone moving something heavy. Footsteps. Workers. It relaxes me a bit. (I'm sure there are plenty of security cameras in the upper parking garage—the one for *guests* of the hotel. [They probably even have security guards watching them.] But I don't see *any* security cameras down here.)

I get the last of my cases into the back of my Jeep, and shut one of the doors. Then I turn around and almost scream.

Standing by the front of my vehicle is a large man who looks . . . well, he looks a lot like a Strawberry Brite Vagina Dentata fan. He's imposing—at least six feet tall—with a red beard, a face full of piercings, and tattoos that creep out from beneath a ripped Slayer t-shirt. He's on the younger side, but his skin is mottled in a way that makes his age hard to determine. His skin is also an alarming shade of light-blue. His face looks immobile, like he's wearing a mask. I'd say it *was* a mask, except *all* of his exposed flesh looks that way. He is wet. Dripping. His hair and beard are ribboned with green algae.

I realize that he looks like just what he is—a corpse that has been underwater in the Chicago River for a few weeks.

Did this guy drive his car into Lake Michigan? Get drunk at a Slayer show at the House of Blues and fall off the State Street Bridge? Whatever the case, he's been sleeping with the fishes for a while now. He's got that strange city-fishy smell you get after it rains: 25 percent blacktop, 25 percent dead fish, 25 percent sewer, and 25 percent unknown.

And then he takes an awkward, sopping step toward me, and I know instantly.

Zombie.

Those internet videos are real, and this is definitely a zombie.

All I can think is: How do you do, Mr. Zombie? Get ready, because you're going to be my first.

★ ★ ★

First question: Fast or slow? (I have lots of other questions too, but you've got to start somewhere.)

Never taking my eyes from the shambling dead man, I back to the rear of my vehicle. The squishy corpse clearly wants to follow me. His water-logged eyes roll in their sockets, watching my retreat. He struggles to raise one leg, and then carefully takes a sopping step forward. It doesn't bring him far, but it's still progress. He raises his other leg and tries to take another.

Slow zombie it is.

This is exhilarating. My heart is racing. I wonder how the hell it snuck up on me. How it got so close without me hearing it! Then I look down at its feet. The shoes have partially rotted away and the remaining leather has congealed into the foot—which has, itself, congealed into a blue mass. What's left is a sort of fleshy, leathery *matter* acting as a natural dampener against the concrete floor. The zombie might as well be wearing slippers.

I look around for more of them. (That's the first thing you learn from watching zombie movies.. There's always more than one...)

I look left. I look right. Nothing. Nobody behind me on the loading dock, either. Nobody in the dark corners of the giant garage, at least as far as I can see.

Well then . . . an early riser.

I stand still and try to breathe quietly. The zombie takes another squishy step in my direction. In the distance, I begin to make out human voices. Are they from people in another part of the parking complex—perhaps on another level—or are they voices from another section of the building entirely, piped down to me through ductwork and vents?

"Hello!!!" I scream. "Can anyone hear me???"

The zombie doesn't even start.

"I could use some help over here!!!" I try again. "Young woman needs help!!! Hello???"

My voice echoes and fades away. After a moment, I can still hear people in the distance. They do not respond or return my cries. The zombie takes another step forward.

I'm going to have to do this my damn self. (I could run, sure, but I realized a long time ago that if you run once, you'll be running forever. Whatever I'm up against, I prefer to stand and fight.) But what to use?? I've got to get to the brain. Everybody knows that's how you kill zombies. I immediately start looking around for weapons.

The back of my car is full of drum gear that looks like crazy metal spider arms on stands. They'd appear intimidating in a fight against a human, but they might just annoy a zombie. They certainly aren't going to get to his brain. I also have heavy drum cases full of drums. I could throw one of those and knock the zombie over, yes, but that would only stop him for a moment.

Nope. We're going with sticks.

I reach inside the backseat of the Jeep and find my backpack. I grab a stick in each hand and strike a stance like I'm a martial artist fighting with Sai. The zombie regards me intensely, water softly dripping from its soaked clothing. Though it may be wet and slow, it is still filled with dangerous intent. It gnashes its teeth. It looks at me longingly. It *wants.*

Timing my movements to the zombie's plods, I lunge forward and jam the right stick into its eye as hard as I possibly can. There is a moment of resistance, and then something gives within the socket and I'm able to drive the stick further in. Unfortunately, the zombie jerks back before I can go quite as deep as I'd like. It cranes its neck, momentarily disoriented, with three-quarters of a drumstick extending from its face. In the same breath (mine, not his [obviously]), the zombie rights itself, and lunges forward once more.

Fuck, I think. Only one socket left.

Transferring the other stick to my right hand, I bob and sway in front of the zombie like a boxer waiting for the right moment to strike. It lowers its arms and leans in, like it's smelling me.

Gross.

I jump forward and jam the drumstick hard into its remaining eye. The zombie staggers back again, blinded.

Once the stick is secure I step back and Karate-kick the butt end as hard as I can, driving it even deeper. This seems to do the trick. The tattooed giant falls to its knees and then plops un-ceremoniously onto its side. It moans once, and then ceases to function.

I lean against the side of my Jeep and try to catch my breath. I feel like I've just run a series of wind sprints.

Before I can even start thinking about how I just killed a zombie—how I just *killed a zombie!!!*—I hear a loud shuddering noise and flinch. The doors of the freight elevator behind me are opening up. Two smiling porters with Trump Tower embroi-dered on their uniforms exit the elevator. They are pushing a small dumpster on wheels.

One of them is talking: "And so she's putting her pants on outside my door, and then my mother comes around the corner and before I can say anything she . . . *holy hell!*"

The porters freeze. They are confronted by an exhausted young woman and a dead body with drumsticks driven into in its eye sockets.

"Shit . . ." one of them says, and runs back into the elevator. The other pulls out a cell phone and starts dialing.

"Are you okay, miss?" he asks as he hastily dials.

"Okay?" I answer distantly.

Then I kind of think about it.

"Yeah, I'm okay. I'm pretty fucking awesome, actually. I just killed a zombie."

"You did *that*?" the porter asks, gesturing to the crumpled body.

I nod.

He frowns and goes back to his phone. He cancels one call, and then places another. Three numbers long.

That's when I decide maybe the next thing I should do is get out of there.

Ben Bennington

The next part is like a dream. (I think because it involves a lot of running but never escaping what you're running from.)

I leave my rusty sledgehammer buried in the zombie's breast and run.

Zombie.

Yes, "zombie." For so I know it to be.

When people see a zombie, there seem to be three typical reactions. There are those who, instinctively, feel themselves qualified to attack—to start fighting the zombie with whatever's handy—and this is what they do. There are those who instantly retreat to a safe place and start battening down the hatches. And then there are those who simply go mad and start running, anywhere and for no reason.

I'd like to think I would be in the camp retaining enough sense to at least run *for cover*, or with a purpose in mind…but no. I just run. I run down the dark Chicago streets as fast as I can.

Something primal kicks in and I want to find someone who'll take care of me. A policeman. Mom or Dad. Any type of authority figure.

But I'm not seeing anybody. The streets are dark and empty. Holy fuck.

I notice that I'm saying "Jesus Christ" over and over under my breath as I run. Is it a prayer or a curse? I have no idea. I just keep saying it.

A few moments later I find myself in Palmer Square Park. I'm hardly registering locations or navigation points as I flee in cowardly terror, but some part of me remembers that this large green space has a name. Palmer Square is a friendly area where you can normally count on finding joggers and kids playing soccer. At worst, you get a couple of gruff, smelly homeless guys minding their own business.

In the orange glow of the streetlights ringing the park, I make out a furtive group of figures huddled together. I stop and look more closely. Two are naked. One is half-naked and has what appears to be the broken arm of an embalming apparatus dangling from the side of his chest. Two are dressed nicely, wearing a tuxedo and Sunday dress, respectively. I stifle a scream and run in the opposite direction.

My brain starts trying to work. I try to think of where to go or whom to call. I toy with the notion of heading back to my apartment, but I'm afraid the zombie in the yellow dress will still be there waiting for me.

I head away from the park, running north. In a few moments, I find myself at the traffic circle containing the Illinois Centennial Monument. A fixture of the neighborhood, the 70-foot Doric column emerges from a stout base atop a shallow hill. The base itself is about 10 feet high.

I draw near and see a cluster of figures huddled around the base. Even from a distance, I can tell from their stiff, lumbering movement that they are zombies. They are trying to reach two young women who have climbed up the 10-foot base. The women are trapped.

I approach the monument. The two women—perhaps in their early twenties and wearing different styles of ironic fuzzy coats—appear terrified. They look how I feel.

And before I can help myself—my terrified, running, chicken-shit self shouts "Hey!"

The zombies don't look at me, at least not at first. But the young women do. They have a horrible, dire pleading in their eyes. I'm just one lumpy reporter, slow and unarmed. They aren't hoping I've got a shotgun underneath my coat that I'll use to save the day. No. They are hoping that the zombies will decide to come after me instead.

Which is exactly what happens.

After a few tense moments, the zombies notice me. They look back and forth between the reporter and the girls, and choose the reporter. Whatever their mental handicaps, they seem able to deduce that someone on the ground is easier to reach than someone atop a stone base.

The zombies move away from the monument and come after me. They lumber off the traffic circle and into the street. I pray for a giant truck to appear and squash them. But no. Nothing. Somehow, the streets on this nightmare evening are entirely empty.

I turn around and head back in the direction of the park. The zombies keep following.

As Palmer Square comes back into view, I remember that—oh yeah—there are also zombies in it. Then I see them. They have left the park and started heading up toward the Centennial Monument. I am pinned between two groups.

I stop running, terrified. Only the side streets are left. Dark, cold alleyways with parked cars and dumpsters. I'm not sure if these streets contain zombies, but they suddenly look better than the alternative.

Then, out of nowhere, a pair of headlights appears. They are attached to a familiar-looking Chrysler with a flat face and a faux-Bentley grill. The Chrysler speeds past Palmer Square Park and crosses to the wrong side of the road to give the group of stumbling zombies a wide berth. Then the headlights fall on me, and it slows down.

I wave frantically. The car pulls up close and stops. The driver reaches across and pushes open the passenger side door.

"For God's sake, young man," a baritone voice calls. "Get in!"

Leopold Mack

Christians can disagree—sometimes respectfully, sometimes not so respectfully—about whether certain stories in the Bible are literally true.

Some of us believe that particular passages in the good book are only parables, intended to illustrate how we ought to live our lives and understand the world. And that they may not—*some* of us contend—have actually happened.

There is Jonah and the whale. Does the Bible contend that a man actually survived inside the stomach of a giant water-dwelling mammal for seventy-two hours? Or could it instead be that the Bible intends Jonah's tale as a fable illustrating how God protects the blessed man when he is doing the work of the Lord?

Does the Tower of Babel grace the pages of the scriptures as a parable, reminding us the price of succumbing to pride…or is it an account of a real place destroyed by God for sinfulness?

And so on and so forth. I assume you understand the point I'm making here.

So what of Biblical tales in which the dead arise? There are, after all, quite a few of them.

We are told in the Book of Kings that God answers the prayers of the prophets Elijah and Elisha by raising a person from the dead. In another Old Testament account, a dead man whose body merely touches the body of a prophet is miraculously restored to life, almost as a matter of incidental contact. In the New Testament, Jesus thrice raises the dead. Also, he speaks at length on the larger resurrection awaiting us all when we come into the kingdom of heaven. When the Judgment comes—on that blessed hour, on that blessed day—we are told the faithful will live again. The resurrection is consistently emphasized throughout the four Gospels. Luke speaks of a "resurrection of the righteous" as though it is quite literal, in a physically-getting-up-and-walking-around sort of way.

So, Pastor Mack, that means our souls will all get up and go to Heaven to be with Jesus, right? Right?

It's certainly nice to think so.

I have told worried parishioners hundreds or thousands of times that this is the case. That that's what these passages mean. The souls of the faithful shall rise and be joined together with God in heaven.

But here's a secret about the Bible. It's full of different versions of the same story, and different phrasings of the same idea. It's also full of strange tales that defy explanation. It's full of stories that are disturbing and make no sense. Only a precious few of the Bible's accounts are actually comforting to the dying or useful to those seeking information about the next life. The pastors, reverends, priests, and preachers of the world mediate almost *exclusively* upon these few comforting and coherent passages. Thus, because they have only heard *these* stories from their priests, most people as-sume the *entire* Bible is comforting and coherent (or, at the very least, not frequently insane and troubling).

This is not the case.

Parts of the Bible advocate killing, slavery, incest, and rape. Parts of the Bible repeatedly advocate breaking the Ten

Commandments. Most disturbingly, parts of the Bible portray a world of chaos ruled over by a vengeful, insecure God who demands horrible, violent deeds from his followers at regular intervals.

And, gentle Jesus, have you read the Song of Solomon? Have you *actually read it*? Because that thing is straight-up Two Girls, One Cup. (I have the internet just like you do.)

We preacher-types read our parishioners the *other* passages . . . the ones about how murder and rape and stealing are bad. And we trust (almost always correctly) that our congregation is indolent enough never to actually read the Bible on their own time, so that they will never discover the passages and stories where God seems to advocate things like incest, rape, murder, revenge, and slavery.

So when it comes to ideas about resurrection, you can bet your bottom dollar that there are comforting versions . . . and not so comforting versions. There are the ones you've heard at every single funeral you've ever attended…and then there are ones you've probably never heard of unless you read the Bible on your own. Versions of the resurrection story that priests and preachers are careful *not* to use during services. But they are there, these "minority reports." They are real, and they chill my bones.

Consider the Apostle Paul's version in First Corinthians. This is important, so let me just give you the whole passage:

> *Behold, I shew you a mystery; We shall not all sleep, but we shall all be changed, In a moment, in the twinkling of an eye, at the last trump: for the trumpet shall sound, and the dead shall be raised incorruptible, and we shall be changed.*

That's pretty wide open if you ask me. What *exactly* is going to happen to us, Paul? We're going to be "changed." We're going to be "incorruptible." Is this the clearest you can put it? What if I don't like being "changed?"

Elsewhere, Paul says, "The body that is sown is perishable, it is raised imperishable."

It. The body. Not the soul. The body. Imperishable.

Like, if a shotgun blasts through it, but it still keeps going? *That* kind of imperishable, Paul? *Could that be what the fuck you meant???*

(And here I have just cursed out the Apostle Paul. Merciful God, forgive me. Bad pastor. Bad pastor. Bad pastor.)

All this time, I've looked at the Bible and told myself that really, it is the coherent passages showing a loving, forgiving God that are true. No matter what new example of human depravity confronts me, nothing has ever been able to shake my faith that it is these parts of the good book that limn the true nature of the world. Like every other pastor I know, I never for a moment worry that it could be those *other* parts of the Bible—the ones we *don't* talk about on Sundays—that best describe the universe.

The ones that portray a blind, idiot God who lashes out like a spoiled child. The ones where the Israelite tribes murder, rape, and pillage as God looks on approvingly. The ones where God says that a woman must marry her rapist, or else be killed. That anyone who is gay, a "fortune teller," or a nonbeliever must be executed.

You see, there is a possibility darker and more unthinkable than atheism. More troubling than our lives being Shakespeare's "tale told by an idiot," signifying nothing.

There is the possibility that it is these *other* passages in the Bible—the ones showing a world of horror and terror and bigoted, useless nonsense—which correctly reflect the nature of God.

And so . . . what if they are? What do we do in that case?

It is a possibility, I must admit, to which I have never devoted much thought. But when the ravenous dead walk the earth, it begins to feel like something you should probably start considering.

★ ★ ★

I race my car away from Ms. Washington's house as fast as I can. Zombies are already appearing plain as day on the city streets. Next to me, the young man who helped me change my tire is breathing more normally. He has also stopped screaming.

"What the fuck is happening?!" the young man manages when he has his breath back.

"We're getting out of here," I say, "That's what's happening."

I see no need to trouble him with the theological misgivings digging at my brain, but he presses the issue.

"No . . . what is *happening* happening? What are these things?"

Before I can give an answer, he adds, "Are they the zombies from the internet? I hit one with my sledgehammer, but it didn't die. It just kept right on walking."

"Zombies from the internet?" I repeat slowly. Somehow, this calms me, making me feel like there's an explanation. The internet knows everything. Wisdom is always waiting on that one webpage that you didn't think to check. That blog you're not hip enough to know about yet.

"Yeah," says the young man, still breathing hard. He tells me that gossip and rumor websites have been posting grainy cell phone videos of moving corpses for the past few days.

"Nobody thought they were real."

"Did they show people walking around with no hearts?" I ask. "People that couldn't possibly be alive? Did it show them eating the living?"

"No," he gasps. "But I think that might be the next step. I think that maybe this is what they do next."

"Can they be killed?" I ask. "Put back down? Does the internet say anything about that?"

The young man shakes his head.

"People seem to think you can kill a zombie by destroying its brain," he tells me. "The one I saw…I didn't stick around to find out."

"God bless and protect us," I say instinctively.

The young man looks me over.

"Are you, like, religious?" he asks. We drive in silence.

"Sorry," he says. "I wasn't being critical."

"My name is Leopold Mack," I tell him. "*Pastor* Leopold Mack. Of The Church of Heaven's God in Christ Lord Jesus."

"Oh," he says. "My name's Ben Bennington. I'm a reporter for *Brain's Chicago Business*."

"Nice to meet you," I say.

"Your church has a long name," Ben says.

I exhale deeply and keep my eyes on the road. Another moment of silence.

"I'm sorry," he says again. "I shouldn't have said that. I'm just nervous and talking without thinking."

"Apology accepted," I tell him, and pull the car over to the side of the road.

"Whoa!!!" Ben says in alarm. "Are you kicking me out because I said that about your church name? Look, I'm really sorry. I wouldn't normally speak that way. It's just these zombies have got me feeling crazy."

"I'm not kicking you out of the car," I tell him, putting a hand on his shoulder. "I need a moment to think."

"Think?" he asks, still alarmed.

We have paused at the entrance to Humboldt Park, a large city park with ponds, ornate boathouses, and statues of long-dead Germans. Ben looks around anxiously through the windshield, I assume for zombies. None seem to be around. There are also no people. A few cars are on the roads, but they're all speeding by. Behind it all, there is now the wail of distant sirens. Everything is still here, but the world feels . . . *different*.

"What are you thinking about?" Ben asks, still alarmed. "We need to figure out where to go."

He pulls out his phone and begins to go online.

"That's exactly what I'm thinking about," I tell him.

And, mostly, it is.

★ ★ ★

The story of how Leopold Mack became Pastor Mack?

Well, you're in luck. It's a tale I have practiced telling. It is also a tale strengthened by a few notable omissions.

I know by heart the version that makes my life sound ordered and even laudable. How I grew up on the rough south side, got excellent grades in school, served my country without hesitation when it called, and then returned because I wanted to change things for the better. I went to seminary, became a pastor, took over one of the community's most historied congregations, got married, had a beautiful daughter who is now full grown, and held myself together when the Lord called my dear wife away only two short years ago.

It may not be especially notable as pastor's biographies go, but it gets the job done. When people want my story, they get that. And they like it. Why did I become a pastor? I wanted to help my community by fighting the drugs and crime that beset our neighborhood.

What I don't tell them is that before I was part of the solution, I was part of the problem.

In no small way.

The root cause was a simple one. You have likely heard it from others who were in my place. Who were called to be knee-deep in Southeast Asian jungles at the ripe old age of nineteen.

It started when I was exposed to drugs in Vietnam. And by "exposed," I mean "addicted."

Good old Leo Mack—the nice young man who went to Sunday school and had respectable friends, who never got in trouble with the police, and who didn't hesitate to serve his country when called—had never tried drugs. It was more than just that I hadn't; I was never *going* to try drugs. It was completely off my radar. You kind of block drugs off in your mind as a real possibility, you know, when you make that decision. You think, as long as I never go down to such-and-such street corner where the prostitutes and dealers hang out, then I'll be okay. Drugs are something I'll *never* have to worry about. *Never* have to deal with. I'll have problems, sure, but drugs won't *ever* be one of them.

But things have a way of getting in through the back door. They find a chink in your armor and slither through in the dark when you're not even looking. That's life.

See, there are things you won't ever try...and then there are things you won't try when you're pretty sure you're going to die in the next few days. And let me tell you, the first list is longer than the second.

Awake for seventy-two hours, half-starved, and ankle-deep in the freezing tributaries along the Mekong Delta; unthinkable things have a way of becoming thinkable. When the second lieutenant in charge has been making bad decisions all month—and, to boot, is a white guy from Mississippi who sends the black guys in the platoon to do all the most dangerous shit—it begins to feel more and more likely that you won't be seeing home again. And you start to cross a few items off on that list of things you'll never do.

Then that fateful night happens when the guy awake with you on guard duty says he has some pills that can help you stay awake. Stronger than coffee. Better. So much better, they're technically illegal. And apparently, in addition to waking you up, they have the side effect of making you feel *amazing*. And you just sort of say okay, whatever man, gimme one.

And that's it. Boom. You like them. They work. You feel better. You feel up and optimistic. Getting through the night isn't so jackshit horrible.

You then ask about getting some more. Pretty soon you want your own personal supply. Then you learn that there are other pills, and others still. Things that make you go up, down, and sideways. Sure, there are some side effects—most of which you don't notice right away because you're young and strong—but overwhelmingly, they just contain different ways of making you feel amazing. And you sure aren't thinking about the side effects that'll hit years later, or how this could turn into an expensive habit that you sure-as-shit don't have the money to pay for. You're only thinking about how there are a million North Vietnamese coming down the river to kill you, and you don't expect to live out the month.

So . . . yes.

By the time I got back to Chicago, I was hooked on uppers and downers and smoking reefer to boot. Some guys had it worse, but that was bad enough for me.

The first thing I realized was that if I wanted to keep taking these drugs—which I did—I needed entirely new friends.

People back home said, "The war has changed him." They didn't seem too surprised by how I was different, because hey, it's war. It'll do that. Everybody had an uncle from WWII or a grandpappy from the first one who'd come back a different dude.

So when I started running with a new crowd, became unable to hold a job, and got shifty when asked about my future, people just assumed it was the war.

And it wasn't.

It was the drugs.

A year after Vietnam, I was an amphetamine and opiate addict.

Two years after Vietnam, I had added cocaine.

Four years after that, I was a stone cold criminal, doing jobs right and left to support my habit.

In the 1970s, Chicago's south side was changing. Or…wait… maybe the most accurate thing to say was that it had *stopped* changing…and that *that* was the change.

Once upon a time, Chicago's south side had been *the* destination for blacks leaving the Deep South hoping for a better life. Beginning in 1910, people started calling the Illinois Central Train Depot "Black Ellis Island," because so many African Americans made it their entryway to the North. The Pullman Porters circulated Chicago's black newspapers like the *Defender* and the *Crusader* all throughout the South. A whole lot of people read those papers and thought they were reporting on a place that was better than where they were. Eventually, Cook County had more black people in it than any other county in the United States, which it still does. Most of those black people lived on Chicago's south side. It became its own city within a city. You never had to leave the south side if you didn't want to. Your job, church, doctor, dentist, insurance agent, grocery—they were all black and all on the south side.

And no one will say it was a perfect time—or even a good time—from, oh, about 1910 to 1970. There was racism, housing discrimination, and race riots. And when Martin Luther King came to town, they hit him in the face with a damn brick. But it had this feeling of impetus. Of momentum. Ours was a community that was growing, you know? New people were arriving every day to come be part of it. It was a thing.

But then, around 1970, it started to change. The immigration stopped. All of the blacks who had wanted to move north had pretty much done so. Maybe there was less racism and more opportunity in the South, or maybe the dew was just off the lily for Chicago. Whatever it was, people started to leave the south side. Couple that with a massive national recession and huge spikes in crime, and you began to see a new south side. The one—you *could* argue—that we still have today.

There started to be these things called "shopping centers," and then "malls" that were fun to shop at and cheap, and you could get to them on the El trains. So boom, suddenly there's no reason for all of these local businesses on every block. Most of the trusted family-owned stores die out. The businesses that replace them are usually terrible. Lousy restaurants. Second-hand wig shops. Fly-by-night places that do your taxes.

It was hard times. The first Daley was still mayor, and he took the south side for granted. Instead of the social programs and real investment that were needed, he trucked in free swimming pools in the summer and created scholarships to bad city colleges where a degree didn't help you much. It was putting a Band-Aid on a cancer, and everybody knew it.

This was the south side in which I found myself after the war. I was hooked on drugs, and I came back to a neighborhood that no longer was growing. Instead, it had a feeling of stasis. There would be no new people or stuff. Now it was just trying to hang on, and criminals were starting to fight over whatever was left.

When the world around you is changing for the worse—and everybody is filled with the same feeling of sickness and unease—turning to crime is not so hard for a young man to do. There were gangs—not quite like what we have today, but still technically gangs. (What we had in the 1970s was like the Cro-Magnon man of gangs. Evolving, but not there yet.)

I was never a major player. I carried a gat but never shot anybody. Mostly, I just did B and E's. A little stick-up work now and then. A whole lot of intimidation. And I'm basically high the whole time.

And then God saved me. There is no other way to say it.

God "accelerated" my life, is how I like to put it. I was "fast-forwarded" to rock bottom ahead of everybody else. He let me reach my lowest moment after just five years, when I was still salvageable. Still young. Most young men who choose drugs and crime can keep it up a lot longer—ten, fifteen, even twenty years before they want to get out—and by that time they're just dead husks that don't have long to live.

The walking dead indeed.

The Bible tells us that the wages of sin are death. Nothing in the entire book is more demonstrably true.

And I can remember the moment when I changed like it was yesterday. My best friend—or the man I *thought* was my best friend—had been shot to death the night before in a robbery. We'd been upping our intake of pills and blow to superhuman levels. We knew we couldn't maintain that lifestyle, but we were crazy. We did it anyway, because . . . well, I don't fully know why we did it. I still don't. We should've stopped. We should've known it could only be the road to ruin. Maybe we were blinded by the pleasure of it all, in love with the dark magic of our existence. Maybe we were just young, high, and stupid.

I remember looking at myself in the long, cracked mirror that we'd propped against the wall of the basement of the dingy two-flat in South Shore where we were living . . . and it was like God touched me. Like, he physically touched me. He said, "I'm going to take these bad things from you and make it right. It's going to happen right now."

I flushed my pills and cocaine down the toilet—trying not to think about how much money they had cost—and left my apartment. I started walking with no destination in mind. I walked down to the decrepit shopping strip on Jeffery Boulevard, not knowing what was happening or what to do next. I was just walking.

Then God tested me.

I suddenly started thinking about how I would never take another pill in my life—never feel that warm rush that made everything okay, that let you relax about things, that made sex feel like the greatest thing ever (even if it was with some hoochie you didn't really care for). I started thinking about how I'd driven away my family and all my childhood friends. I had no real job or prospects. What would come next? What could?

A horrible panic seized me. My chest felt like it was going to explode. I had this strange tension running down of the backs of my legs, like a cramp that wouldn't go away. My heart was beating fast. (I had this new *awareness* of my heart, too. I was afraid it would wear out, and I had no idea how to make it slow down.)

Then I thought to myself: So . . . this is *probably* death. I've never died before, so I can't say for sure, but this feels about right.

I stopped right there on Jeffery Boulevard, clutching at my chest with everyone looking at me like I was crazy. I started looking around, turning in circles. I could have gone to a hospital. I could have called for a policeman or an ambulance. But then— looming above the other buildings—I saw the steeple of The Church of Heaven's God in Christ Lord Jesus.

Go there, my brain said to me.

So I stopped spinning, and I walked over to that church. It wasn't the biggest or best church in South Shore. It had a small congregation for its size. The pastor was nobody I had heard of, certainly nobody powerful in the community. The building was an old synagogue that had been converted to a Christian church in the 1940s when the last of the Jews in the neighborhood gave up and moved away. The addition of a cross and steeple left it looking not quite right, like a lizard that has scurried underneath a cast-off shell and insists it's now a turtle.

These shortcomings didn't matter at that moment. To me, it looked absolutely perfect.

When I reached the church, I was too scared to go inside. I didn't know a soul there. Also, I thought that if I stopped moving— like in a pew to pray—my heart would explode and kill me. Instead of going in, I walked circles around that church, peering up at the dark lead glass windows and the steeple that didn't match the roof. After a few minutes, I began to feel calmer. I still felt like I might die, but I felt like *if* I died, that it would be all right. It was up to God now, and not up to me.

And you know what? God let me live.

After about half an hour or so, a man came out of the church (I later learned he was a deacon named Reynolds) and looked at me. I must have been quite a sight—troublemaker in a thug's coat with the rolling eyes of a maniac. He probably thought I was casing the joint to rob it. He didn't say anything. He didn't tell me to skedaddle. He just looked at me—up, down, and all around—to make plain they knew I was there. Then he went back inside.

The next Sunday I attended services. Sixth months later, I was sitting in my first class at divinity school.

I'll always regret that part of my life. I'll never be fine with the fact that I was a drug-fueled stickup man for most of my young adulthood. That I robbed women, children, and the elderly. It will always be with me.

You don't "get better."

You don't "get over it."

You maintain.

You maintain, and—when you can—you try to help people. That's the only way it ever gets a little less awful.

★ ★ ★

Sitting in my car in Humboldt Park—looking at the man next to me who is also scared shitless—I realize where it is that we need to go.

"If this is happening all over the city, then people are gonna head to church."

"The church?" the man asks, as if I have invoked the notion of religion.

"*My* church . . . where I'm *Pastor*. If their relatives are coming back from the dead and it might be the end of the world, then people are going to be heading for the church. It's where *I* would go. Where anybody would. They're going to go talk to Jesus."

The young man nods thoughtfully.

"You're welcome to come with me," I tell him. "It's down in South Shore. We can be there in thirty minutes, maybe less."

"Yeah, okay. I sure as shit don't wanna go back to my house."

"Do you have family you need to check on right now?"

"No, they're back in Iowa," he says, not looking at me. "I have an ex-wife, but she went to Florida for the week."

"I see. . . . Then you should come with me."

I put the Chrysler back into drive.

"You seem really certain," he says.

For the first time, he smiles.

"The Bible shows us that in times of portent and mystery, almost nothing is a coincidence," I tell him.

"Oh," says the young man. "Well okay then. Let's go."

We speed south through Humboldt Park, its verdant lawns and ball fields covered with a thin dusting of snow. I notice one person—or zombie—milling about, waist-deep in the center of a nearly frozen pond. Probably a zombie. It is far too cold for a swim tonight. Sirens continue to rise and fall on the streets around us. (I think any kind of siren anybody owns is going off tonight.)

Occasionally, I see groups of people who clearly aren't the risen dead standing around in front of their houses. They're trying to figure out what's going on. They talk to one another, like neighbors might do during a power outage or when there's a fire on their street.

We drive beneath an overpass with a stalled (or possibly abandoned) train on top of it and enter an African-American neighborhood called Garfield Park. It's a rough place, like South Shore. More criminals released from prison return to Garfield Park than to any other neighborhood in Chicago. I wonder how the residents are faring? The streets are deserted. The snow on the sidewalks is undisturbed.

Next to me, the young man—Ben—starts talking into his cell phone.

"Caroline? Hey, how are you guys? How's Florida? Hey listen, this is going to sound crazy, but I'm *not* joking, okay? This is *not* a joke . . . have you seen the internet videos about zombies and stuff this week? Yeah, well it's real. The zombies are *real*. I just got fucking attacked by one. Is it happening there in Florida? Is . . . hello? Caroline? *Caroline*?!"

Ben looks down at his phone and shakes it like an Etch A Sketch.

"Here, try mine." I pull my phone out of my coat pocket and hand it to him. Ben accepts it and tries to make a call.

"Nothing," he says. "No service. What the fuck is this!?"

"Can you bring up the internet?" I ask. "See what the news websites say."

"Fucking nothing," Ben says after a few tries. "It just gives a 'No Service' message."

"I guess the whole grid is down," I tell him. "Everybody is trying to make phone calls at the same time . . . *and* trying to use the internet. The system can't handle it. It's what happened in New York on 9/11. I was there that day for a fellowship conference in Queens. Our cell phones failed for most of the morning. They'll probably have it fixed in the next few hours."

"The next *few hours* . . ." Ben says, as if this is devastating news. "Something tells me the next few hours are going to be really fucking important, Pastor."

I watch the road and nod. I do not disagree.

Maria Ramirez

As I gun the engine on my Jeep and pull out of the parking garage underneath the Trump Tower, all I can think about is how if I saw one zombie that means that there are more zombies. It's like seeing a cockroach. Those things don't roll solo. You've got an infestation, and the only way to deal with it is extreme violence.

Kicking the ass of thousands of zombies is going to be a big job. There's only one thing that matters more to me right now…my family. I merge onto Highway 94—in traffic that is surprisingly light—and dig my phone out of my purse.

I try the house first. It rings and rings with no answer, which is not surprising; my mother is usually in bed by nine and has a habit of silencing the ringer. I try her cell next, which goes straight to voicemail. Crap.

That leaves my sister, Yuliana, who is an even dodgier prospect. She's seventeen and has been in the habit of sneaking out at night to see this twitchy kid I don't like named Santiago. (He's not in a gang, but some of his friends are. My sister wonders how I can tell this, and it's like, I've been around the block, little sis. I grew up in Logan Square, too!) Also, my sister hardly uses her phone for calls, insisting on doing virtually all of her communication by text. This being the case, I hastily pound one out as I careen through the snow-dusted roads.

Yulie. Where R U? Where is mom? Need to talk ASAP. Will be home in 10 mins. Stay indoors. No joke.

I hit send, and wait for a response. Sometimes Yuliana can be lightning-fast with a reply, like she has been waiting for it. This time, there is no response. Nothing at all. Not even a damn emoticon.

I try again.

"R U there? Bad things r happening."

If that doesn't intrigue her, nothing will.

Aaaaaand...nothing will.

I wait and wait, but she does not reply. I double-check the volume on my ringer. I look at my 'Sent Messages' folder and make sure both of my texts went through. They did.

Still...no response.

I take the exit at Fullerton and race toward the little blue house where I live with my mother and sister. Something is wrong in my neighborhood. At first, it's hard to say exactly what. Despite the cold, there are a lot of people standing around—like how the queues get crazy at bus stops when the El has a breakdown. But these people are just chatting with each other . . . and other funny things. A few of them are drinking beers outside, which you can't do. In front of Quencher's Bar, people have carried their glasses out onto the street. Some are even holding homemade weapons—clubs and bats and things.

So then...I'm not the only one who knows.

I keep on driving and the not-rightness doesn't go away. It is everywhere. Even the houses that are dark and quiet manage to be dark and quiet in a bad, ominous way. Something is definitely wrong.

After a few blocks, the house comes into view. The lights are out. There's no sign of my mother's car.

Fuck.

I pull into the drive and just sit there for a moment. I look at the front door through the window of my Jeep. I'll be honest, I'm scared to go inside. It's my home—where I live with the two people in the world I love the most—but now it feels like a haunted house or something. I scan the shadows in the nearby alleys. Who knows how many zombies they hold?

Come on girl. Time to go.

I exit the Jeep and advance toward the front door. Then I pause and return to the Jeep and fish a couple of drumsticks out of my bag. (If it worked before . . .)

Still edgy, I stalk up to the front door and dig out my keys. I open it slowly, expecting…I don't know. The inside is dark and quiet.

"Mom?"

"Yuliana?"

Nothing.

Then I notice that a light *has* been left on—at the back of the house, in the kitchen.

I make my way over. On the dinner table is a notepad with writing on it. The notepad is my sister's, but the hand is clearly my mother's.

Maria, your father called and we need to meet him at his house. It's serious. Tried to call you but the phone and internet stopped working. Be safe. Meet us at your father's.

Double fuck.

If there's one thing that could make this worse, it's my father.

I sit in the kitchen for a moment and consider my options. I soon realize that there aren't any. I feel my body beginning to relax. Which is bad. The adrenaline that started with the zombie in the garage and got another injection when I couldn't raise my family on the phone is now beginning to ebb. A part of me suddenly says, "Relax into this chair and do nothing, Maria." Then adds, "Or maybe crawl upstairs and lie down in your bed under that giant picture of Stewart Copeland. Drift off, and when you next awaken, all your problems are likely to be solved."

Fuck fucking you.

I force myself to my feet, take a slug of orange juice from the carton in the fridge, and head out the door. Back inside my Jeep, I lock the doors, fasten my seatbelt, and get back on the city streets.

My fucking dad. Goddamn it.

When I reach Kedzie Boulevard, I start heading south.

Ben Bennington

We get there, and the pastor is right.

The Church of Heaven's God in Christ Lord Jesus—which, yes, appears to be the actual name—is crowded like it's Christmas or Easter. It's a venerable structure with a tall steeple that somehow doesn't quite match the rest of it. A group of official-looking men has gathered at the entrance. They gesture and point as the pastor's car comes into view. They have been waiting for him.

Mack pulls up to the front of the building, and the crowd parts. We exit the Chrysler. Everyone is looking at Mack like he's a celebrity—a rock star or something—but they seem hesitant to be the first to speak. Younger people are helping groups of the elderly into the church. A member of this elderly contingent finally cries, "Oh bless my soul, Pastor. I knew you'd come."

Several of the men standing near the church door have half-concealed guns. In the shadows by the side of the building, I see a corpse on the ground. The picket from a fence has been shoved through its forehead. The body looks like it died a long, long time before this latest injury. A group of kids is looking at it, and one is poking it thoughtfully with a stick. Moments later, a disapproving mother appears and shoos the children into the church.

"Pastor, what kept you?" one of the armed men asks.

"Attending to Ms. Washington," says the pastor, and his eyes betray a strange sadness or guilt. "She is . . . no longer with us."

"Pastor, do you know what's happening?" asks another man. "Have you seen what's on TV?"

"I know that the dead are walking among us," Mack replies. "I know that some of them are eating people. I saw that myself. What does the news say?"

"It's happening all over the city, maybe all over the state," says a nervous looking man with glasses and a black fedora.

"It's national news," says a man in a suit who lets his Desert Eagle dangle conspicuously from one hand.

"*International news*," says another. "Everybody talking about what's happening in Illinois."

"Pastor Mack, the congregation needs to hear from you," says fedora-guy. "They've been waiting."

Mack sighs deeply. "I'm sure they have. I'm sorry that I was delayed."

"Let's get you inside, Pastor," someone says.

The group parts to allow the pastor to pass. I wonder if I should follow. Nobody has acknowledged my presence.

Then one of the armed men standing guard by the door says "Pastor, who's your friend?"

Everybody turns and looks at me.

Mack smiles.

"That is a Good Samaritan who helped a traveler in need," says Mack. "We must repay him, as in the parable."

The men nod thoughtfully.

Mack clasps me around the back of the neck and we walk together into his church.

Everyone inside is looking at us…I mean everyone. Maybe this is what it feels like to be in a celebrity's retinue; to be in a rapper's posse or a rocker's entourage. The Church of Heaven's

God in Christ Lord Jesus feels enormous once you're inside, and every pew is filled with people looking my way. People line the aisles, but they make way as Pastor Mack passes.

The stares don't stop as we get further in, though people do start to fall silent. I am probably the only person present who is not a part of this congregation. I am definitely the only white person.

Some onlookers give me the same hopeful looks they give Mack, hoping perhaps that I am part of an ecclesiastical team here to explain what is happening and to save the day. Others appear merely confused or annoyed by the uninvited interloper.

The church does not have a high ceiling—or even a peaked ceiling for that matter—but it does feel holy. Maybe a better word is regal, like where a king lives. That kind of ancient, lofty place. Special.

Yeah, this is *definitely* the kind of place you run to in a zombie outbreak. No question.

Ahead of us is the altar. To one side is a choir loft and a nest for musicians. An unattended drum set and piano sit silently. The carpet beneath our feet is red and well worn. It, too, exudes a feeling of old royalty.

His hand still on my shoulder, Mack leans in and says, "I have an important question for you, Ben."

"Sure," I say, advancing with him toward the old oak pulpit that now looms above us.

"The newspaper where you work—*Brain's,* right? Does it cover crime?"

I look him up and down, trying to make sense of this query.

"Um, sometimes," I answer honestly. "Like white collar crime, or when a business gets robbed. We might report that. It's a business magazine, but you knew that."

"Uh huh," says Mack, never averting his gaze from the pulpit. "And when you report a crime, does *Brain's* disable the online comments when it's a story about a crime committed by a minority? Say, when a black person robs a white person?"

Mack's tone is mischievous. It's the last thing I expected to be asked about, here, in the midst of his congregants.

"I've never heard that we do," I answer and believe it to be the truth. "I mean, not as far as I know we don't. What do you... Why ..."

"Good," he says. "That's all I need."

I swallow hard.

"I should go get vested," Mack says. "Why don't you come along?"

"Oh, okay," I say, still not entirely sure what that means.

We near the pulpit and break off to the side. There is a small door which admits us to a hallway crowded with costumes and props. It feels like the backstage of a play. Choir robes and sheaves of printed music are folded in piles or placed atop the large boxes that line the walls. Musical instruments are strewn higgledy-piggledy. A few steps down this dim hallway, and we pass through another door and into Mack's office.

It has the same regal red carpeting but looks fresher, not as worn. There is a desk full of papers, knickknacks, and an aging computer with an old-timey cathode monitor. Photographs of smiling people locking arms at church events cover the walls.

There are several bookcases crammed to bursting with religious texts. Portraits of Abraham Lincoln, MLK, and Obama complete the decorations. Six or seven dog-eared copies of the Bible sit in different places around the room, each containing at least a hundred day-glo Post-it notes.

Mack gestures to an old TV in the corner and says, "Why don't you see if you can find us some news?"

With that, he passes through a doorway set into the wood paneling behind his desk. It closes silently. Just like that, Mack has vanished, leaving me alone in this cluttered room. It smells like pipe tobacco and old library books.

I take a deep breath and approach the pastor's small, dingy television. What are we going to get? Cable feels out of the question. Does it even have a digital converter box?

I find a power button and turn it on. The old TV—standard definition (do I even have to say it?)—winks to life. And what it shows me changes everything.

★ ★ ★

Every virus has an epicenter. Every outbreak starts somewhere—in a lab or a jungle or wherever. Things have beginnings. There is always a point of origin.

We know that AIDS started in Sub-Saharan Africa, but then spread all over the world. We know that, for most of history, English and Spanish were spoken by only two tiny European kingdoms . . . now half the world speaks at least one of those languages. And that hilarious cat video your mom likes so much—the one that now has 25 million YouTube views and counting? It started out on a site that was previously lucky to get twenty-five hits a week.

And so with the undead.

Though it would eventually consume the entire world, we know that the great zombie outbreak—for whatever reason (accident, dumb luck, destiny)—had its epicenter in the State of Illinois. Corpses around the world had been inexplicably shuffling their feet or blinking their eyes for weeks. But when they finally decided to stop mucking about and start eating people, the corpses in Illinois got a head start on the rest of the world by just a few hours.

When Mack's tiny office television finally boots up, it shows me a local network newscast. They have broken in over the standard late night comedians and talk shows to bring news of . . . *something*, but they're not sure what. At least, they want to *act* like they're not sure. Nobody wants to be the first to make the call. Nobody wants to use the "z" word prematurely. (Can you imagine a news bureau calling "Zombie Outbreak" and then being wrong? It'd make "Dewey Defeats Truman" look like a fucking typo.) A graphic at the bottom of the screen merely announces "Violence Crisis."

Well yes, I think to myself. Zombies *do* involve violence. They got that much right.

The veteran newsman in the anchor chair looks pleased to actually have some real news to report for once. Years of gently informing viewers about predicable aldermanic scandals, foreseeable gang violence, and annual neighborhood festivals have not addled him. His sonorous voice does not shake or stammer. This is his hour and he knows it. You can see it in his steely eyes. In his radiant silver hair. This is the big one. After all these years. Finally.

Footage begins to come in from all over the state. The anchor does his best to narrate. Many of the shots show locations I've visited for work; places where my friends live; towns I've heard of in television commercials for carpet warehouses or car dealerships, but haven't gotten around to visiting.

The rushed-looking reporters doing remotes from the field are visibly struggling to maintain their composure as they tell tales of people attacked, gangs of vigilantes, and unexplained concentrations of violence around cemeteries. None of them mention the z-word. They have few concrete answers, either for the anchor or for the viewers at home.

After a few minutes, we're informed that new footage has just arrived. The anchor attempts to narrate. He is coming to this cold, as are we all.

The first shots are from the streets of downtown Chicago. They show people gathered on corners with guns, police and emergency vehicles rushing to and fro, and city officials looking into the camera and shrugging. Basically, it is what Mack and I saw on our drive down to the church, but even more so.

The next selection of footage takes us north to Zion, Illinois—a small, traditionally religious town. The fervent residents have barricaded themselves into a large church (as, I note, have we). Unfortunately—the anchor reminds us, drawing on his Illinois history—the zealous city founders designed Zion so that all roads would lead to its central church. (The roadmaps of Zion look like a British flag with a church in the middle.) A camera crew sent down from Milwaukee captures the residents' final moments as the barricaded church doors give way and a horde of filthy zombies forces its way inside. We have only a moment to see it; the camera—apparently shooting from the window of a moving news van—is soon driven away at top speed.

Then, abruptly, another shot. Handheld. Shaky. The anchor tells us we are looking at an area downstate along the Kankakee River. Zombies are attempting to cross a bridge that spans the river, and a team of stalwart construction workers are preventing them. Having converted their construction equipment into weapons, the workers dump sacks of nails into a long-range mulcher. The resulting blasts cut down huge swaths of zombies (and send others skittering out over the rails and into the water below). When they're out of nails, the workers break out pickaxes and chainsaws. They close on the zombies to finish them off.

The camera cuts away. Another shot. Amateur footage that the anchor believes is from Joliet or Romeoville, taken while there was still a little daylight left. It shows what appears to be a hot dog stand with life size statues of Jake and Elwood Blues on top of it. A zombie has also climbed onto the roof with the statues. The camera zooms in. It is a desiccated, moldering cadaver with only one eye and only one arm. It lopes pitifully around Elwood and Jake, examining them. After a few moments, its lone eye appears to fix on the camera operator, some 30 or 40 feet away. The zombie then straggles toward the edge of the roof and steps off, falling 15 feet to the concrete below in full faceplant. It remains prone for a moment, then slowly rights itself and rises. It begins a slow lope toward the camera. The footage then becomes a messy blur as the camera operator sprints away.

Then another shot. This time from a marina up near the Wisconsin border. It shows the walking dead crawling up out of man-made shoals and onto land. A lone frozen zombie shuffles across an empty winterized dock. An overalled local in a CAT baseball cap saunters into shot and prods the zombie with a long dowel. The zombie begins to moan and flail its arms. The man looks back at the camera and smiles. Keeps poking. A moment later he misses the zombie and begins to lose his balance on the icy wood underfoot. The zombie lunges in and bites for his throat. The feed goes black.

Back to Chicago again. More random clips from the Loop. These are the places I walk every day. Places I have lunch or meet friends after work. The guardhouses along the Chicago River are being attacked by crowds of zombies. People trapped inside are trying to push them away with long poles. The zombies are smashing windows and forcing their way in. Along Michigan Avenue, shop windows are broken and retail displays upended and destroyed. One shot shows a multi-level store selling cookware. Shoppers and staff have retreated to an upper level and are raining down pots and pans on the undead figures slowly working to climb the escalators.

Then the station cuts back to the newsreader, who asks a reasonable question. Where, then, is the mayor during all of this? Why has he not given a speech to calm the souls of his city's populace? This is his Rudy Giuliani moment, yet he has not appeared. There has been no press conference with him standing alongside the governor—both men covered in dust and zombie parts, perhaps carrying chainsaws—urging the citizenry to keep calm and carry on.

Then a producer talks into the newsreader's earpiece. The newsman's face falls as the implications of whatever he's been told become clear. The mayor's office, says the anchor, has just confirmed that the Mayor of Chicago's itinerary for this evening included a trip to Mt. Carmel Cemetery with his family to pay respects to his wife's departed relatives.

Good God, I think. Mt. Carmel! Those massive, endless fields of graves!

And then the broadcast cuts away to, yes, the sequence you have doubtless seen so many times already—that shaky helicopter footage that was broadcast all around the world, the thing that everyone, everywhere thinks of when they picture the outbreak in Chicago.

I'm sure you're already familiar, but I'll try to describe how it struck me that first time.

The news helicopter hovers over the great, suburban cemetery with its well-manicured lawns and stoic mausoleums. The snow-dappled paths between the monuments spread out below like a skein. The mayor's motorcade is there—two jet black SUVs. But while the helicopter's searchlight finds the cars, there is no sign of the people who should be inside them. The doors of the SUVs hang open, despite the chill.

Then, in the darkness that surrounds the spotlight, there appears a furtive movement. Something in the shadows is shifting. Is it only the play of the beam against the headstones? Or is it… something else? The operator zooms out and begins to explore the periphery around the mayor's motorcade. This exploration reveals . . . zombies. Lots and lots of zombies.

The ancient creaking corpses stumble like drunk men around the network of tombs. They are wearing grave clothes and covered in dirt and snow. Occasionally, they pause and become hard to notice. They camouflage themselves against the headstones. Then they move again—just a little—and stand out. It is like looking at a Thanksgiving turkey and realizing, very slowly, that it is entirely riddled with squirming translucent maggots.

Moments later, there is a flash from a firearm in the periphery of the shot. The camera follows. Red and white fire spits out into the darkness—tiny pops of handgun discharge. The shaky spotlight swivels wildly toward the source.

Then…the scene. The one we all know. (So often, in playback, it is censored. Well, I can tell you it wasn't censored the night it went live.)

The mayor and his wife—and three men in trench coats with guns—are retreating from the inner graveyard back toward their cars. They are surrounded on every side by the walking dead. Two of their police escorts are firing back at the zombies with handguns. Now and then they strike home—one of the zombies is shot in the head and goes down—but there is no way they can win; no way they can hold off a horde that looks as if it might be endless.

One of the police escorts—the one who is not shooting—turns and runs into the darkness. He has gone mad or abandoned his post. He will almost certainly be eaten by zombies.

The remaining policemen have run out of bullets. They decide to make a break for the cars. They aren't going to make it. That's completely clear to anybody watching.

The mayor and his wife have been abandoned. Left to fend for themselves. The mayor puts his arm around his better half and swivels his head. He is looking for something. What can it be? His smarmy charm and empty political promises cannot save him now.

Meanwhile, one of the sprinting policemen dives for an SUV but doesn't make it. He thrashes heroically as he is ripped apart. The remaining policeman fights back against an oncoming wave with the butt of his gun. He is slowly overwhelmed. The mayor and his wife retreat from the cars until they are backed up against the flat wall of an enormous marble mausoleum.

Then it happens.

From the shadows beyond the spotlight, a nightmare figure lopes into view. It wears a traditional Italian funeral suit and has a porcine, jowly demeanor. Few alive today have seen the face in life, but there is no not-recognizing it.

Good God. It is Capone.

Even as I watch in horror, some part of my brain begins working. I start to remember that the people buried out in Mt. Carmel are some of Chicago's most famous—yes—but also its most infamous.

Frank "The Enforcer" Nitti, Vincent "The Schemer" Drucci, Sam "The Cigar" Giancana, "Machine Gun" Jack McGurn . . . and, of course, Capone himself. All of them are out there in Mount Carmel. It's full of gangsters. Men the city would prefer to keep buried (in more than one sense). Men the Mayor of Chicago had hoped to make the world forget.

As Capone stumbles forward and sinks his flabby, rotting maw into the mayor's forehead, you just have time to see an expression of complete surrender cross the mayor's face. This is rare. The mayor isn't the kind of guy who likes to lose. This surrender is profound and deep. He's not just surrendering his life. It is an "Okay, I give up" that goes far beyond the stare of a condemned man. Yes, in that remarkable, horrible, haunting instant, you just have time to see the Mayor of Chicago realize that he—like the city itself—will *never* escape from Capone.

"So the mayor . . ." the anchor begins soberly. "The mayor is now having his brains eaten by what I'm going to go ahead and call a zombie. A zombie that, in this reporter's opinion, looks a whole lot like Al Capone."

He doesn't say more. He doesn't have to.

Leopold Mack

What kind of tie do you wear to the apocalypse?

I stand in my dressing room and eventually select a bright pink one with shiny, iridescent stitching. I consider for a moment, and decide that, yes, it will complement the gray-black pinstripe suit I have already donned.

It could be worse, I think as I attempt my Windsor knot and consider the task before me. I could be a downstate Pentecostal preacher trying to explain to a roomful of corn-fed farmers why they are not being lifted physically to the heavens right now. Indeed, I have said little about the end times during the course of my Sunday sermons. I have always been focused—perhaps too focused—on the times at hand. (Why eschatology connects with rural white preachers, and not inner-city black ones, remains a mystery.)

I don't know what's going on. I don't know if this is truly the end times or the Rapture. I just know that a lot of people who are scared most of the time anyway are now really, really scared. And they're in *my* church, and they're looking to me for answers. Not to the police. Not to an alderman. To me. People in my neighborhood can't trust the cops. They can't trust their politicians. The only honest person left—if they're lucky—is their preacher.

In other parts of Chicago—the north side, say—the residents have a good relationship with the police. The cops are there to protect them, not to harass them. It's rare in north side neighborhoods to have a family member who was shot to death by Chicago police. Five families in my congregation can claim that distinction.

In other parts of Chicago, you can trust the politicians to be effective…at least sometimes. They occasionally have enough power to bend the mayor's ear and get something done. But in our neighborhoods, it's different. Our politicians can get a boondoggle like the Harold Washington Cultural Center built… and then mismanage it into bankruptcy by putting their no-sense relatives in charge of it. They can bring the south side a convention of church groups (who don't eat out, drink, or ever spend a dime more than they have to), but they can't bring the kind of conventioneers who throw around enough money to actually improve a local economy. They can give speeches in schools about how drugs are bad, but then you see them on the street chatting with guys that everyone knows are running drugs. These people cannot provide real assistance in times of need. They cannot even be trusted to put the needs of the community above their own craven scrabblings to get ahead.

For that, you need a man in a shiny pink tie who knows a lot about Jesus.

★ ★ ★

I emerge from my dressing room to find my new friend looking into the TV set. He appears bewildered, as if by the technology itself.

"Pastor Mack, you won't believe this. Zombies are coming up all over town. The mayor just got eaten. This is fucking crazy!"

"Mmm hmm," I pronounce evenly.

"Pastor you . . . *damn*," he says, turning in my direction. "You clean up nice."

"Thank you," I say. "My congregants expect it."

This is true, and something many folks in the white community don't fully grasp. When they see the pastor of a poor congregation driving a nice car and dressed to the nines, they shake their heads suspiciously and look at you like, "Is *this* how you should be spending your congregation's money, when *they* struggle to pay their heating bills? When *they* use usurious payday loan stores to get to the end of the month? When *they* have children who can't concentrate in school 'cause they're so hungry? Can't you just be modest? You know . . . like the pastor in our white neighborhood?"

What the people behind these accusatory glances fail to understand is that a pastor in the ghetto of Chicago has to do a lot more. In addition to his duties in the pulpit, the south side pastor often has to be a policeman, a financial advisor, a marriage counselor, a lobbyist, and a community organizer. The pastor is the advocate of the people. He's the one who'll go to bat for you. And when you need a new hospital in your community, or better teachers in your schools, or youth programs not to be shut down just because of a recession, you want your advocate to be as impressive as he possibly can. He has to look like a man who can make things happen. Like a man who you can't dismiss with a department secretary or fluster with paperwork or city permits. For whatever reason, a nice suit and automobile seem to really help make that happen.

Ben turns his head to the side, as if something important has occurred to him.

"What on earth are you going to tell the people out in your church?" he asks. "What is there to say at a time like this?"

"You know those verses in Matthew and Mark about how, one day, the first will be last, and the last will be first?"

Ben nods.

"I think I'll start there."

I walk over to my desk and unlock the drawer containing my father's Bible, the one he held on his deathbed. I pick it up and place it tenderly in the crook of my arm. (*Tonight,* I think to myself, *we're using the good china.*) It doesn't get any bigger than this . . . or at least I hope to God it doesn't . . .

I grip the book tightly for a moment—thinking of my father—and take a deep breath. The book feels good in my hands.

"All right," I say to Ben. "I think it's time."

Maria Ramirez

Fathers...

They're not my favorite subject, but let me tell you a bit about mine. It will pass the time while we make this long-ass drive down to the south side (which is not a place I like to drive normally and *really* not where I want to be going on the night of a zombie outbreak).

I probably don't have to tell you about growing up in a fucked up family. Lucky for me (I guess), the only thing that was fucked up in our house was my dad. He grew up in Logan Square back when it was really tough. Back before the gangs all had three names that went "adjective-Latin-plural noun" (like Insane Latin Kings, Hardcore Latin Tigers, or Crazy Latin Playboys). In my dad's day, they just had one name—like the Broncos or the Devils—and they were much, much meaner. My dad was a perfect fit for them. He was a thug and an abuser of women. He hit my mother about once a week, but the emotional abuse was always worse. He was like an alcoholic, but he didn't need the booze to change personalities. He did that on his own, for what seemed like no reason at all.

His main vice was women who were not my mom.

I was still a little girl when I figured out what my parents were fighting about night after night: my father's girlfriends. I think my poor mother lived in denial for the first twenty years of her marriage. She'd see things or hear rumors but sort of forced herself to look the other way. Then—when I was fifteen or so—it all came crashing down.

Some of my mother's friends in the neighborhood just couldn't keep silent any longer and told her about a new string of women he had. Women my mother knew. Women half her age. That was when the fights got crazy, and the hitting started happening every night. I used to hold Yuliana's ears and hum so she wouldn't have to hear it, but we'd wake up the next day and mom would have black eyes or bruises. (Sometimes, when we couldn't see the bruises, it was worse—'cause you heard the hitting and you knew the bruises were there under her clothes.)

I wish I could say I was the one who stood up to him, but it wasn't me. Really, none of us did. He eventually got tired of dealing with my mother and left on his own. He started living with a girlfriend, some high-up administrator who worked for the city. After a year or so, he moved to a different neighborhood to live with her and divorced my mother. Then he left that woman and took up with a new one. And then one after that.

Now, of course, he is all contrition.

I'm proud of my mother for never taking him back. He has tried in his horrible, cloying way to weasel back into our household a couple of times. We have not allowed that to happen. We've shown him that we can support ourselves. I mean, it's me who does the financial supporting of our household, but I would be nothing without my mother and sister. We're a team.

Which is why it's disappointing and confusing and worrying that two thirds of the team just decided to high-tail it for my fucking father's house. He lives on the edge of the south side in a sketchy neighborhood called Farrell Park. What the fuck possessed my mother and sister to go there with him? It's sure not going to be safer than Logan Square.

Then I have a thought that makes me really, really sad.

What if all the progress that we've made since my father left doesn't matter? What if all that strength I thought we had—as three women banding together to stand against the world—wasn't as strong as I thought it was? Sure, we've had some times when the three of us were tested. There have been money troubles and cancer scares and even an actual stalker (who is now doing fourteen months in Statesville, thank you very much). Those sure felt like real tests at the time. But maybe they meant nothing . . . maybe, when zombies come out of the ground, we are really just a group of weak women who want a big fatherly man to protect us, even if he hits and cheats and makes you feel like shit. Maybe we only thought we were strong.

It's like no matter how much we work out and lift weights, we'll still never be stronger than most men. Maybe we have been lifting our little five-pound aerobic dumbbells all this time—convincing ourselves that we were getting "totally strong"—and then when a situation happened where we needed a real, actual tough person we were like, "It's not us! We just made little girl muscles. All this work has been for no real progress! We still need a man!"

I don't feel that way . . . but now I've got a horrible suspicion that my mother and my sister do.

Christ.

I hit the gas pedal and speed south toward my father's house.

This is *not* how I wanted to spend the zombie apocalypse.

Ben Bennington

I file back into the crowded church. All eyes are on me. I have emerged from the pastor's private office. The *sanctum sanctorum*. People are wondering who I am and what I have to do with whatever is going to happen. The congregation is now silent, like music fans waiting breathlessly for a performance. Am I the man who walks onstage to introduce the performer?

No.

The men from Pastor Mack's praetorian guard motion me over to a pew in the front row. I quickly join them, planting myself on a well-worn wooden seat. I look up to the pulpit, waiting for Pastor Mack like all the rest.

Moments later, he emerges. Resplendent in his thousand-dollar suit and shining tie, Mack has the majesty of a dragon. It is otherworldly.

It suddenly feels impossible that this can be the same frustrated commuter I helped with a flat tire hours before. This man is powerful. This man is collected. This man would certainly have no problem getting a tire with frozen bolts off his car.

Can it be the same person? Somehow it is.

I look around. The people next to me are similarly transfixed by the pastor. Unlike him, they are wearing whatever they had on when the outbreak started. With the exception of one older woman who has topped off her Minnie Mouse sweat suit with an elaborate church hat, few have thought to dress for the occasion. Some people have on uniforms from their jobs or even pajamas. Initially, this gives the church a casual feel, as if it is being used as a community center or a giant AA meeting. But such is the power of Mack's suit that suddenly it is Sunday, and we are—all of us—sporting our finest. We are all made formal by his majesty.

For a moment there is silence—I mean complete, pin drop silence.

Then a woman in the back says, "Pastor!" in a voice that's happy, but also a little hurt. It's a tone that says, "How could you have left us for so long?" and "Please, don't ever leave again."

Her voice is joined by others, and then others still. A groundswell of cries and applause echoes off of the walls of the church. People shout, "Pastor, what's happening?" or "Pastor, save us."

Others simply stand and applaud. I find myself clapping along.

Mack holds a small leather-bound Bible and a pair of reading glasses. He frowns like a stoic gargoyle intended to illustrate resolve. He carefully puts on his glasses. They nearly dangle off the end of his nose.

Mack opens the Bible and places it on the lectern before him. He grips a microphone on an umbilical holder and bends it up to his mouth. Then he raises his eyes and looks out over the congregation. This is, apparently, the cue to fall silent, because that's what everybody does. There is electricity in the air. Every few moments, someone cannot contain herself and lets loose with another "Praise you, Pastor Mack!" and is hushed accordingly.

He begins to speak.

"Let us pray," Mack begins, opening the good book.

*"In green pastures you let me graze; to safe waters you lead
me; you restore my strength. You guide me along the right
path for the sake of your name. Yea, though I walk through
the valley of the shadow of death, I will fear no evil, for you
are with me; your rod and your staff, they comfort me."*

"Amen."

The church echoes with a resounding "Amen."

For the first time tonight, I see hope in the eyes of people.
Not alarm. Not confusion. Not fear. Hope. This opening invoca-
tion has not offered any specifics for how to survive a zombie
outbreak, but the parishioners are relieved just to hear Mack's
voice. Someone is in charge. Someone is explaining things. Daddy
is here.

The voice with which Mack reads from the Bible is unlike
his speaking voice. It's superior to his speaking voice. Not just
different. Better. Sonorous and musical. It feels like it doesn't lie.

Mack closes his Bible, looks down at the congregation, and
says, "Thank *God*."

There is kind of an awkward silence. (One person manages
a "Hallelujah," but it's quiet and half-assed. Nobody knows what
Mack means yet.)

"Thank God for this," Mack says.

"Is it the end?" shouts a congregant.

"Is it the Judgment Day, Pastor?" asks another.

Mack closes his eyes and raises a hand above his head.

"Brothers and sisters, I can't tell you what is happening. I can't
tell you why—near as I can reckon—the dead are coming back to

life. I can't tell you what has roused the sleeping from their slumbers and made them walk on earth once more. And yet surely it is so. You have seen evidence yourselves, haven't you brothers and sisters?"

There is a murmur of assent from the audience.

A very tall woman in thick glasses and a floral dress announces that earlier this evening, she saw her dead brother attacking people in the park. Then a man in blue work overalls shouts that he saw a dead baby crawling out of a dumpster in an alley. He knew it was dead because it was in two pieces. A grim silence descends.

"Now, I have seen things like this myself," Mack intones. "And while no one could be pleased about it, I thank God—*I thank God*—that we are a congregation in a neighborhood like South Shore. *I thank God* that we have not been allowed to become dependent on easy things. *I thank God* that we have been tested...because it has made us strong."

Several "Amens" echo through the church, though tentative and uneasy.

"I do not need to tell you that this city has failed you. I do not need to tell you the ways in which this . . . *place* . . . Chicago, Illinois...has aligned against us. And I have tried—oh how I've tried—to do the best I could for you."

"You have, Pastor!" someone shouts. "You're a good man, Pastor!" says another. Others still murmur in nonspecific adulation.

Mack waves them off.

Then Mack looks at me. Right. At. Me.

"Even the forces in this city that claim to have an interest in truth and justice have failed you. Just the other day I was thinking about how the newspapers in this city disable the feedback on the internet every time they report on a crime committed by a person from our neighborhood. Now why is that? Why do they do that?"

The audience is silent. He has lost them. Why is he bringing up the internet when there are actual zombies knocking on our doors?

"Now...if you ask them, they say they don't want to provide a platform for racism. They say that it gives redneck chuckleheads from the suburbs a chance to write that they aren't at all surprised that blacks are killing one another, because blacks are ignorant, violent, and spoiled by a welfare state. Then that same Chicago newspaper will run front-page editorials about how we are a post-racial society and show us a picture of Obama out riding his bike with his little safety helmet. They will say because we elected a black man from Chicago's south side to the White House, things must have changed in Chicago. They say you don't see *real* racism anymore, not like you used to.

"Sure. You don't see it anymore . . . when you refuse to show it. But that radio silence—or internet silence—doesn't mean that in every collar county suburb there aren't legions of racists who still refuse to hire blacks. That doesn't mean that—even here in the twenty-first century—there aren't bigots teaching their children to hate people based on the color of their skin. That doesn't mean that it doesn't force us to rely on ourselves. To become strong. To become blessed."

"Amens" echo off the church walls, but again, they are tentative.

Mack adjusts the microphone, pauses dramatically for an instant, and then continues.

"Nothing could be more helpful to an understanding of race relations in this city than for them to enable comments on stories about black on black crime, or black on white crime, or, for that matter, white on black crime, and Latino on black crime, and so on and so forth. Certainly, it would reveal more than any undercover expose.

"Will it 'give racists a voice,' as they fear? Absolutely. And then people will be reminded just *how racist everybody still is.* They'll remember that racism is why young men in our communities aren't getting jobs. Why nobody wants to invest in our neighborhoods.

"Just because you don't read it doesn't mean it's not there. Doesn't mean it's not prevalent everywhere. Doesn't mean it's not determining how people vote, where they choose to live, and where they choose to open businesses.

"Can you imagine if it was the 1850s and the papers in the North thought the best way to fight slavery was to not report it? Can you imagine?"

This gets several "Amens" and one "Tell it, preacher!"

Mack continues.

"And yet, you have become resourceful. You have become like the heartiest plants that can thrive in the most inhospitable soil. You have learned to create community—a vibrant, beautiful, blessed community—in this hostile soil. You are surrounded on all sides like Elisha in the Book of Kings—and though you have been tested, your faith has not wavered. And tonight, I think, brothers and sisters . . . the good Lord is going to show you how blessed you truly are."

Mack pauses, and there is a cautious swell of approval from the congregation.

"You've learned to survive in one of the hardest neighborhoods in Chicago. You know how to keep cool in the summer and warm in the winter, *without* any help from the city. You know how to keep safe from crime without help from police. We don't have security systems on our apartments . . . we have bars on the doors and ten different locks!"

Some Amens.

"We don't depend on the police to come when we call . . . so we call for Pookie across the alley to come over with his baseball bat!"

Some more Amens.

"We do what we have to do. We do what *no* north side neighborhood in this city does—not Lincoln Park, not Wrigleyville, not Wicker Park, not Old Town. We *handle our business*. We depend on ourselves, on our friends, and on our neighbors to do what the city can't or won't. We know one another. We know what protects us, and we know it sure isn't the CPD!"

Cheers and Amens follow.

"Something profound is happening tonight. The dead are walking among us, and not as the people they once were. They are hungry for murder. They are cannibals or worse. Right now, alarm is spreading across the city. Along every alleyway and avenue, the call is going out. 'Oh no,' the northside people cry. Hang on . . . if I cup my ear I think I can hear them in the distance . . ."

Gentle laughter as Mack cups his ear.

"Yes, they're crying out. They're saying 'Help us Mister Mayor. Help us Mister Po-Lice Man; there are monsters on my street. Whatever shall I do?' But we aren't saying that, are we? Because we have monsters on our streets every damn night! We *know* what to do when killers are on the loose. And now we have the skills that everybody else in the city wishes they had. We are a loving, caring, righteous congregation that already knows how to handle its business when assailed on all sides. I don't know about them, but *we* will survive!"

Applause. Amens. Cheers.

"If we can survive the drug users roaming our alleys . . . if we can survive the gangstas and dealers on the corners . . . if we can survive the decades of neglect and underinvestment by the establishment . . . then I think a few punk-ass zombies are gonna be *no damn problem.*"

The congregation begins to applaud and cheer. I find myself cheering as well.

"Now, it's not all good news," Mack says. He smiles but holds up a hand to stay his audience.

The applause dies slowly.

"It's not enough for us to simply *endure* this newest test. "Nonono. Anybody can *endure*, like a bump on a log. We must do more. We must reach out to those who cannot help themselves in this time of reckoning. No, I don't mean we have to drive north and help a rich lady whose security system isn't keeping the zombies from trampling on her thousand-dollar rug. Not at first, anyway. But I want us to take care of one another. Crenshaw Cemetery is closer than any of us care to think about right now."

Serious nods and "Mmm-hmms" ripple throughout the congregation.

"We need to start by taking care of each other. That means what it has always meant. We don't hide inside our houses—or inside a church. Instead, we go out into the community. Those of us who are able, we check on the old, the sickly, and the infirm. We help them if they need help. We do what Jesus would do…in a zombie outbreak."

Applause. Amens. A few folks raise their palms skyward.

"We've had to take back our streets from gangs and drugs, and tonight we're going to take them back from the walking dead. Those of you who need to seek sanctuary are welcome to stay in The Church of Heaven's God in Christ Lord Jesus. Those of you who are able bodied and willing to follow me, then come along. We're going to go take back our neighborhood—one more time."

And it's here that I begin to feel a little faint, because I realize the full extent of what the man in the pulpit is proposing. As Mack briefly elaborates on the incumbency of going out to kill zombies—I try to consider the direct and subsequent upshot of his words. Those of us who are not sickly or infirm are being encouraged to follow him into the streets of South Shore and… try to protect it from zombies? Wait…really?

It is definitely a lightheaded-making prospect.

Mack begins reading once more from his father's Bible. An eerie stillness settles over the church. The parishioners are probably used to hearing his words accompanied by organs, choirs, and drums. Tonight, however, there is only his voice; sonorous and slightly fuzzy in the aging microphone. It's sort of like when a band turns off all the distortion and special effects and does an acoustic number. It really makes you listen.

After a final reading from the Book of Psalms, Mack closes the Bible and directs the parishioners to remain in their seats. A din of polite conversation breaks out, like the intermission at an orchestra performance. Mack stalks to the side of the altar and motions for me—and, I realize, the other men at the front of the church—to join him. We're a big group, maybe thirty or so as I look around. I don't know who got selected for it or why. Some are seniors—Mack's age or older —while others are still in their teens.

We follow Mack to the door at the back of the altar, past his office in the corridor, and then down a side staircase into the basement. The red regal carpet crunches loudly under our feet. Not so much as a word passes between us. Idly, I wonder if Mack will be wearing his expensive suit for the rest of the night. Right now, it looks like yes.

Mack flicks on the lights. The basement before us has been converted into a daycare. It contains toys, posters, and walls of corkboard with children's drawings tacked to it. Mack stalks into the room, and we follow him.

When we're halfway across, the lights flicker for a moment, then turn off completely, then come back on. We look at one another silently, everyone contemplating just how shitty a power failure would be in this situation.

Mack fishes a jangly wad of keys from his pocket and uses one to open a large janitor's closet. We all step inside, joining a floor-waxer and a wall of shelves stocked with paper towels and toilet paper. There is another, much smaller door, at the back of the closet. Mack opens this with a different key, and we step into an even smaller space. It contains a wooden table and an enormous safe. The latter is—I realize after a moment—a gun safe.

Mack flips a switch and a bare light bulb above our heads buzzes to life. The room is so small that most of our group cannot fit inside. I am one of the lucky ones at the front of the pack. Mack takes a knee in front of the safe and carefully punches numbers into a keypad. He then turns a circular flywheel, and the safe creaks open. Inside are more assault rifles and ammunition than I have ever seen in one room. (And that includes the time I did an article about the gun dealerships out in McHenry County.) I'm surprised, as are the other men around me.

"Hey now," an older man intones with a smile.

"Sheeee, Pastor," a younger one whispers. "You been holdin' out on us."

Mack carefully withdraws the weapons and places them on the table. There are easily as many guns as men in our group.

"Why do you have all these?" I can't stop myself from asking.

Mack begins to pass out the weapons.

"A couple of you know that I do my own gun buyback program," Mack says. "It's a standing offer to anyone in the community. Private. No questions asked."

"Mmm hmm," says one of the men next to me, indicating either that he knew of the program or just thinks that gun buy-back programs are good.

"Well…what'd you *think* I did with all the guns?" Mack says with a grin.

We all laugh . . . nervously.

"You out to give the cops some competition?" I ask, as Mack gives me a semi-automatic AK-47. "In the gun buyback depart-ment, I mean."

He shakes his head.

"The cops offer folks fifty or a hundred bucks for a gun," Mack says. "That'll convince somebody to get rid of their grand-pappy's rusted rifle from World War II, but not much else. I offer more—a lot more—and I make sure that the gang members around here know it. When one of them decides he's ready to get out of the game—*really* get out and change his ways—he knows bringing me his weapons will result in some serious money. Usually a G or two. Sometimes more. That's enough to help a young man start a new life. Rent himself a place in a new neighborhood away from his gang friends. Buy himself some work clothes. Clean up and get it together."

"Thassright," agrees a newly-armed parishioner next to me.

"Of course, my offer is one of the reasons why this church still has a leaky roof and a pipe organ that sounds like a constipated cat," observes Mack.

We laugh a little more at this, but just a little.

★ ★ ★

By the time everyone is equipped with a ponderous and heavy firearm, we depart from the cramped closet and walk back into the basement. My weapon is new and strange, and I feel terrified. I haven't shot a gun since I was a Boy Scout back in Iowa. Am I really expected to use an AK to fight these 'things?'

Apparently so.

"Now," says Mack, "the plan is simple. Defend South Shore. Help those who can't help themselves. As I see it, the zombies are gonna come at us from two sides—east and west."

Next to me, one of the younger men wrinkles his nose and says, "East? East is the lake, Pastor."

"Have you been to the lake tonight?" Mack asks the young man. "Did you drive up Lake Shore two hours ago, like I did? Did you see what I saw? All of the bodies that gangsters and gangstas ever dumped into Lake Michigan are getting back on their feet and walking ashore tonight. They're hungry for my brain and yours. They're coming for us."

"Understood, Pastor," says the questioner, cowed.

"And on the other side," continues Mack, "you got that massive cemetery, Crenshaw. I'm no expert, but I think we can expect some action from there as well."

The men murmur agreement.

"If you can hit them in the brain, it's an instant kill," says a man in a faded green beret. "You know . . . kills them *again*."

"Yes," says Mack. It's unclear if he is hearing this information for the first time or if he already knows it.

"I already kilt one up at my place," says Green Beret. "Torso didn't do nothing. One through the head, it went down, *splat*. I just wish it hadn't been my old friend Keith, you know?"

"Yeah," says Mack. "I know."

We look at one another, then over at the stairs leading back up to the church. Back up to South Shore. Back up—I realize on some level—to what may very possibly be our deaths.

"All right," says Mack, deadly serious. "Now it's time for a real prayer."

The men all take a knee around Mack, like we're at football practice and he's the coach. I follow suit, wondering what a "real" prayer might be. We fall silent. There is only the distant noise of the parishioners upstairs, chattering away nervously.

Mack closes his eyes and raises one hand like he's swearing on the Bible in court.

"O Lord. You know what's going on. You know what kind of test this is you're giving us and why. You know what this is. And we don't."

I expect a round of "Amens" or murmurs of agreement to follow. There is nothing. The men stay silent. This is different from upstairs.

"Lord, please give us the wisdom to accept that *you* know what's going on," Mack continues. "Please allow us to trust that *you* have a plan—and a reason—for what is now occurring in our community, in our City of Chicago, and in our State of Illinois. Please grant these men around me the strength to protect our loved ones from the walking dead. Help them to understand that you have always called upon the righteous to stand with you in times of turbulence and to protect those who could not protect themselves. Lord, please make these men protectors. Arm them. Make them mighty. Though some are young, grant them judgment beyond their years. Though some are old, grant them the strength of youth. Help all of us to serve you in everything that we do. Amen."

And here we do speak, and we say, "Amen."

The AK-47 starts to feel lighter in my arms.

We stand up and face the stairs.

It is time to go kill zombies.

★ ★ ★

We follow Mack back upstairs. The parishioners look at our guns and fall silent. Again, every eye is trained on us. Children are hushed. Every person we pass takes a few steps back. An old woman halfway up the central aisle whispers, "Bless you boys."

We walk to the front of the church, and Mack opens the doors. Not gently or slowly. He throws them wide open.

We are not greeted by a slavering mob of zombies…but what lies beyond is hardly encouraging.

We step outside into it. We can breathe it in our lungs and see it all over the horizon. We can smell it and hear it. It is everywhere. The *wrong*.

Nothing is what it should be. The city noises are all incorrect. Where we ought to be hearing cars and commerce, there are only distant shouts and occasional pops that are probably gunfire. Half of the businesses and buildings near the church appear to have lost power. The streetlights are still on, but many flicker continually. Some give off a sickly yellow hue that feels unnatural, a consequence of either too much or not enough power. Turning north, where the Loop and Chicago's tallest building rise in the distance, we can see what look like giant fires. The cold somehow makes the smell sharper and more distinct. Things are burning. Things that shouldn't be burning are burning. It's not a nice smell, like logs on a fire. It's metallic and industrial.

Burning, burning, burning.

Then another smell hits me. Seaweed, docks, and dead fish come to mind.

A man next to me screams, "Look out!"

I turn and see a zombie stumbling around the corner of the church. He has on a bright white jacket and a do-rag. He has two gunshot wounds in his chest. He is sniffing the air and rolling his eyes like a malfunctioning automaton. The zombie shambles slowly, more or less in our direction.

"Damn," says a member of our armed contingent.

"I've seen that boy around," says another. "His name was Lester. Never was no good."

Mack steps forward, marching seriously until he stands right in front of the zombie. It is as though he's greeting an old friend. The undead man flails his arms like he's covered in an invisible sackcloth that he's trying to slough off.

"You need some help there, Pastor?" I ask, genuinely worried.

Mack waves me off and draws closer to the zombie. Then closer still. The men around me smile genially at one another, as if to say they've seen this before.

"What's he doing?" I whisper to no one in particular. "He's going to get bitten."

"Pfft," says an older man in a black leather jacket. "How long you known Pastor Mack, son?"

"I met him tonight," I answer honestly.

"I see," he responds, like a detective making deductions. "Then maybe you haven't seen him standing up to the dealers when they forget what he said about selling on certain corners, or the times he's gone to stare-down a whole family who are bent on making a revenge killing. You should step back and watch the man work. You'll learn a lot."

I do.

Mack leans in and gets even closer to the stinking zombie—like reach out and touch it close—and the thing still does not strike. Mostly, it lumbers like a constricted, half-blind drunk. Like its skin doesn't fit. Like it's trying to sober up.

Suddenly, the zombie seems to find a new flexibility in its arms. It begins to move its previously stiff fingers and bend its arms back and forth at the elbow. In a flash, it flexes its knees and lunges forward at Mack. Before I can speak or think, we hear a deafening report. The zombie's forehead explodes. Its legs go limp. It collapses in a heap at the pastor's feet.

Mack turns, and we just have time to see the glint of a burnished nickel disappear back inside his leather jacket.

"They're frozen," announces Mack. "The ones from the lake are frozen and stiff with ice. This is good news for us. If we can approach them—and hit them right away—we can put them down before they have a chance to get flexible again."

We all nod. Mack peeks around the corner of the church to see if there are any additional zombies. There does not appear to be, but Mack still stands there, staring toward the lake, for a long, long time.

"See, that's Pastor Mack," the old man in the leather jacket whispers. "Always learning himself something new."

"Yeah," I say. "I see what you mean."

Leopold Mack

Sometimes the first *are* last. And, accordingly, the last are first.

For all that's been written and said about the outbreak in Chicago—about those first twenty-four hours especially—I've never seen a write-up of what the murder rate was like in different neighborhoods. And I mean murder by zombie *or otherwise*.

I know that in north side neighborhoods, it was high. Too high. I'm not happy about that. I hope that's clear to you. I didn't want to know that rich people would prove twice as violent as poor people. I didn't want live-in domestics to rise up against their masters and abscond with the silver and credit cards into the zombie-filled night. I didn't want the expensive electronic security systems—all suddenly rendered useless—to create an environment where the most defended homes were suddenly the most defenseless. I didn't want the cops who patrolled the rich neighborhoods to abandon their beats and go protect their own families.

But it happened, didn't it? It happened all over the north side. Folks who were not self-sufficient and who had not formed a community now sorely regretted it.

On the south side, those of us who were working for good—working to improve the community, working to fight the drug dealers, working to create businesses and jobs—all knew one another. House by house, block by block, street by street, we were able to recognize one another. We were still aligned and now playing for stakes that were, unimaginably, even higher.

On the south side, we had already picked teams.

★ ★ ★

My men and I broke up into squads of three.

People in the church were all anxious to tell us where we needed to go. A queue formed almost immediately when I explained the process. There were shut-in relatives who needed to be checked on. There were homes that residents hadn't secured (and feared might now contain the undead). There were relatives who didn't know where other relatives were—people wandering lost in the darkness. We went and checked on them.

There still weren't phones, so "calls" came in through word of mouth. People kept arriving at the church like waves of refugees, each more wide-eyed and scared than the next. The moment they heard we had organized groups who were armed and ready to act, it seemed like they all had somebody they needed us to go help.

There was also a sizable group of parishioners who didn't want me to join the street teams. They wanted me to stay at the church instead.

"Oh, Pastor," they'd say. "We need you here with us. You're our spiritual center."

I'd just point to the cross and say, "You see that man up there? He's your spiritual center. Him."

★ ★ ★

When we finally run in to Maria Ramirez, it has to be coming up on midnight.

I've driven to a side street off Cottage Grove Avenue because a member of my flock hasn't heard from her sister. The sister is morbidly obese and might have some difficulty leaving her home to seek shelter. It is now our mission to bring her to safety.

With me are Ben Bennington—my Good Samaritan—and a retired bank security guard named Mr. James, who is one of my deacons. In the hours since my sermon, our team has already found a missing five-year-old, shot three zombies from out our car window, and verified that a parishioner's small business is adequately boarded up against looters.

"Miss Martha!" I call, leaping from the Chrysler and cocking my shotgun. Ben and Mr. James follow me into the cold, windy night. There is still a burning, chemical smell in the air. It is distant but distinct, and it mixes in my nostrils with the odor of Lake Michigan.

The address I've been given is a dark two-flat with lead stained windows and no lights on. The little alleyways to either side of the place are pitch black and could contain looters . . . or worse. Something tells me right away that nobody's home—that despite her enormous girth, the woman inside made a break for it after all. (Can the morbidly obese outrun zombies . . . and would it be any fun to watch? Bad pastor. Bad pastor. Bad pastor.)

I've got this sneaking suspicion we're wasting our time, but I approach the first-floor windows anyway and knock hard through the bars with the butt of my gun.

"Miss Martha! Miss Martha, it's Pastor Mack! Anybody home?"

I fall silent and listen. There is nothing to hear.

Then, behind me, Ben says, "Hey, I think I see someone coming."

I turn and follow his outstretched finger as it indicates a flicker of movement down a side street.

"Someone running," I pronounce. "Too fast to be one of those things."

"Looks like a woman," Mr. James says. "And she don't look in a good way."

"No she does not," I say. "She looks hurt."

The young woman is sort of loping along like an injured dog that still has a lot of energy. She doesn't appear armed, but nothing about her mien comes off as friendly.

The young woman lopes a little closer.

"What the hell?" Ben says. "I . . . I think I know her."

"Funny," I say. "I think I do, too."

Ben opens his mouth, but before he can reply, I wave to the young woman and call out: "Over here!"

She notices us—standing right there by the alley, practically next to her—and starts like we've spooked her good. Then her neck cranes back and forth like she can not quite believe what she's seeing. After a few seconds, she smiles, shakes her head like she's shaking off a bad dream, and jogs on over.

"Well...I'll be *fucked*," she says brightly, breathing hard.

She's got some recent-looking scrapes on her face and some puffiness that may be the beginnings of a full-on black eye, but no serious injuries. The front of her clothes bear traces of spattered blood.

"Maria, wasn't it?" I ask.

She nods, panting.

"And you're Pastor Leo Mack," Maria responds with some contempt in her voice. "How could I forget?"

Then she notices Ben and says, "And *you're* . . . the reporter from the show tonight!"

"Yeah...hi," he says, shouldering his AK awkwardly. I can tell he likes her. Even in a zombie apocalypse, kids will make eyes.

"What do you think about those internet videos *now*?" Maria asks him, still catching her breath.

She smiles at him. Her knees buckle, and I fear she may swoon.

"Are you okay?" Ben asks, rushing in to steady her.

She brushes him away and appears to recover just as quickly.

"Am I *okay*?" she asks angrily, without opening her eyes.

"It's all relative, young lady," I tell her. "None of us are okay in the way we were a few hours ago."

She opens her eyes and shoots me a look like she wants to punch me in the face. Then she turns back to Ben.

"I got jumped...I think," she says, rubbing her eyes and then stopping when it obviously hurts. "I was looking for my mother and sister. I live with them, but they went to my father's place in Farrell Park, just north of here. I got to the house no problem, but they weren't inside. The door was open and the place was dark and empty. Also, it was all messed up—ransacked and looted, I think. Then somebody came at me out of the darkness, and I got knocked out. I can't remember anything else. They took my keys and money, and they drove off in my car. I came-to about twenty minutes ago and just started running. You guys are the first people I've seen."

"You didn't want to stay in your father's house . . . for safety?" Ben asks. "Lock all the doors?"

Maria shakes her head. "No. It didn't feel like a safe place. There could have been more looters inside . . . or zombies, for that matter. Plus, I still need to find my mother and my sister. Hey, can I have a gun? You guys all have guns."

Ben looks to me.

"She should probably have a gun," Ben says. "For safety."

"I've got a handgun and this shotgun," I tell her. "Which do you want?"

Maria wrinkles her nose, as if these are both unsatisfactory choices.

"*Ben* has an *AK*," she says flatly.

"Yeah, do we have any more AKs?" Ben asks.

"Mr. James, what are you packing, all-in-all?" I ask, calling back to the retired security guard behind us.

There is no response.

I look back at Miss Martha's shuttered house. Mr. James was standing in front of it a moment ago. Now he is nowhere to be seen.

"He was just there," Ben whispers.

"Dammit," I whisper back, lowering my shotgun.

"Mr. James?" Ben calls tentatively. "Mr. James, where are you?"

There is no response.

I take out my handgun and give it to Maria, grip-first. She accepts it silently, and checks to make sure there is one in the chamber. Then she holds it like a pro.

"Mr. James!" I call, no longer trying to be subtle about it. "Mr. James, are you there?"

My voice feels deadened—by the snow, yes, but also by the strange burning smell in the air.

After a few moments, we detect a low shuffling sound coming from an alley by the side of the house. It is followed by what can only be the sound of gas escaping; an enormous, prolonged fart—unnaturally huge.

"That can't be good," Ben whispers.

To my surprise, he takes the lead and stalks into the darkened alleyway.

"Careful now," I tell him, following after.

"I got this," he says.

I realize that he's trying to impress Maria. It's almost cute. (It *will* be cute…if he doesn't get himself killed.)

I trail Ben into the darkness. The streetlights don't cast their glow down this shaft of brick and concrete, and there are no lights in the windows. The shadows could conceal almost anything.

"Mister James?" I try again.

The only answer is another shuffling sound. We stare cautiously into the darkness ahead.

"Hang on," I say, pulling out my Maglite and turning on the beam. I hold it up and train it down the alley.

We are greeted by a surreal and grisly pastiche, like something out of Bruegel. On the pavement before us—quite close, really—two zombies are having their way with Mr. James. It's like some exotic three-way sex position, but with cannibalism substituted for the sexual act.

The first zombie is a slim white woman in a t-shirt and shorts. She has short black hair—maybe lightly salted with gray, maybe just with snow—and her right arm is a full sleeve of tattoos. From the waist down, she is almost completely skeletonized. Her legs are twists of tendons and visible bone that look like they cannot possibly support her slender frame…yet they do. This zombie is cradling the head of Mr. James—who is obviously dead—and eating into his face through his eye-sockets. Both of Mr. James's eyeballs are completely gone.

At the other end of him is another female zombie. I shudder to realize that it might be Miss Martha. She is a hulking, obese woman, entirely nude except for an adult diaper. She looks like she hasn't been dead for long, and could even pass as a living human—albeit an insane, naked one—were she not tearing the skin from Mr. James's backside and stuffing it into her mouth. She chews chunks of raw, yellow fat from his ass. Her mouth is covered with blood.

"Oh what the fuck?" cries Ben. He tries to shrink back from the sight, and ends up slipping in the snow. He falls ass-backwards to the ground. His AK bounces out of his hands and fires off into the wall.

The obese zombie notices this pratfall. It looks Ben over, and slowly rises to its feet. It belches—seemingly involuntarily—and then extends two chubby arms toward him like an overweight Frankenstein's monster.

"Oh shit," says Ben, scrambling to either rise to his feet or pick up his gun, but accomplishing neither. His slips and falls twice more on the ice.

"Blearrrrg!" roars the obese zombie. Her heavy calf manages a shambling, wobbly step in Ben's direction. A dollop of Mr. James meat falls from the corner of her slavering mouth and lands on Ben's boot.

"Good Christ," says Ben.

In the next moment, there is a bright flash and report from behind us as Maria discharges her weapon.

BLAM!!!

The obese zombie's head rocks back as Maria's bullet puts a perfect circle through its forehead. The zombie's eyes cross, and its flabby legs buckle. Unfortunately for Ben, the zombie's massive body then pitches forward. In a moment, he is covered by the limp corpse of a housebound and incontinent 600 pound woman.

"Bah!" Ben chuffs, struggling to push away the body. "Omigod . . . this is awful."

Then, before I can help him up…

BLAM!!!

Maria fires again. It's another headshot, and it takes out the tattooed zombie on bone-legs. This one goes to its rest more gracefully, simply curling into a motionless wisp like a spent firework.

All that remains is the eyeless—and now largely assless—corpse of Mr. James.

And . . . did I just see its fingers twitch?

★ ★ ★

"We need to get out of here, and fast," I announce. The smell of gunpowder from Maria's weapon is still in the air.

Maria and I work together to extricate Ben. The corpse is too big for either of us to move alone.

"One . . . two . . . *three!*"

We push at the same time. The giant, motionless zombie rolls away.

Ben is wide-eyed, stunned, and covered in blood. He walks a bit like a zombie himself, struggling to regain his balance. His hat has fallen off and his hair is a wild, sweaty mess. However, he does not appear to be injured.

"Damn," says Maria. "You look like you just got laid."

Ben sheepishly picks up his AK and does not make eye contact. He takes a few deep breaths and steadies himself against the wall of the alley.

"You probably smell like it too," Maria adds. "In fact, you totally do. You smell like ass, boy. Was it good for you? Ha ha!"

Something in me flinches.

"Maria, a man has just *died*!" I pronounce in my most stentorian tone.

Maria visibly bristles. She stuffs her handgun down the front of her pants and stalks over to me as if she wants to fight. She's a full head shorter than I am, but she stands really, really close and stares up at me like an angry animal. She exhales, and I can smell the brackish smell of a sweaty, worn-out woman on the wind.

"Ooh, I'm *soo sorry*," Maria spits sarcastically. "Did I hurt your feelings? Well *excuse me,* 'reverend.' I love how you get to call yourself that, by the way. 'Reverend.' Like how you just decide you're something people should 'revere.'

"It's pastor, actually," I remind her. "Not reverend."

"Who . . . fucking . . . cares!!!" Maria shoots back. "Even in a zombie apocalypse, you've got to act like you know everything, huh? Would you like to tell me why the dead are coming back to life and eating people? No, because you don't know. "

I cross my arms and look down at her sternly, refusing—for the moment—to be tempted to wrath.

"I mean…" Maria continues—wheeling around on her heel and then coming right back into my face. "What do you even *get* from it? Is it the fancy suits? The expensive preacher cars? Seriously, tell me, because I can't figure it out. Maybe you just need to get your ego stroked every Sunday—to hear a bunch of people go 'Amen' after you speak…right after *you fucking tell them to*. 'Revere me! Say Amen after I talk!' Could you *be* any more insecure?"

I move quickly, without thinking. It's an animal reaction.

Bringing the shotgun up with both hands in a single motion, I brace it hard against my shoulder and pull the trigger.

Twenty feet beyond Maria, the head of the thing that was Mr. James explodes into a shower of a thousand fleshy pieces . . . about five seconds before it could take a bite out of Ben's neck.

The headless body takes two steps forward and falls to the ground, coming to a rest next to the thing that was Miss Martha. His dead arm cradles her torso, like an exhausted, headless lover. They are, the pair of them, spent.

Ben looks at the dead zombie and says, "Damn."

I lower my weapon.

"Tonight, I'm just a guy trying to kill some zombies," I say, turning back to Maria. "And when everybody else is losing their damn minds and running around like a bunch of chickens with their heads cut off, I'm out in the streets trying to save my community. I'll let *you* decide if that's worth revering."

★ ★ ★

We pile back into my Chrysler and prepare to rendezvous back at the church.

Mr. James, to my knowledge, had no kin in the pews at The Church of Heaven's God in Christ Lord Jesus. He was a loner. An orphan. There is no family to notify.

Still, this is no consolation. Mr. James was a good man, and I liked him. Moreover, I'm his pastor, and he was a member of my congregation. And I let him get ambushed by zombies. And then he became a zombie. And then I blew his damn head off.

There is nothing good about this. It is still horrible.

Just . . . less horrible than it could have been.

I resolve to remain thankful for small things.

Maria Ramirez

Mack drives us back to The Church of Heaven's God in Christ Lord Jesus. Unlike everything around it, the church is crowded and well lit. In fact, it's the only crowded place I've seen since I got down to the south side. It's like everybody in the neighborhood came here. The church is filled to bursting, and there are people spilling out on the landscaping around it. When we pull into the parking lot, there is a visible reaction from some people when they see Mack's car. Their faces brighten. This is what they've been waiting for.

"Stay here," says Mack, pulling to an abrupt halt near the entrance. He springs out of the car with the step of a much younger man. Five paces toward the church, and he is mobbed by crowds of parishioners, each one eager for his attention.

I take a deep breath. Ben has mostly been sitting quietly in the back seat—I'm assuming humiliated and cowed by the ordeal of being pinned under the fat zombie. I wouldn't be surprised if he's fallen asleep, actually. He looked beat.

Then, out of nowhere, he speaks.

"So . . . why don't you two just fuck and get it over with?"

Silence.

Then I explode laughing. Ben laughs too.

And it's like, okay. Right on. I like this guy.

"I don't mean to be nosy or anything," Ben continues as my giggles die away. "It's clear that you two already know each other, and that something's...*up*. I just met Mack—by the way—right after I met you, so I'm not picking sides, here. I'm just curious. What's this about?"

I turn around in the seat to face him.

"He has a daughter named Richelle," I explain. "You might say that I seduced her away from Mack, and he's pissed about it."

"Oh," Ben says evenly.

He's still smiling, but suddenly there are wrinkles his brow. I can tell that he's disappointed. (It's so cute how much this guy is into me.)

"It's not like *that*," I clarify. "I might have kissed a few girls, but I'm not into Richelle that way. She's not my girlfriend. She's in my band. You saw her earlier tonight. The black girl with amazing tits who was playing bass?"

"Oh, okay," Ben says. "I remember."

"First, Richelle joined my band. Then she moved north out of this neighborhood. And then she started thinking for herself. Which, I think, she had always done. But she kind of started not pretending anymore. Not letting her father think she was someone she wasn't."

"Aha," Ben answers cautiously.

"Don't let Mack fool you into believing he's a perfect person. He's come to our shows before to confront Richelle publicly— to shame her, in my opinion. And I've let him know he's not welcome. I've gotten in his face and told him exactly what he needed to be told. Told him Richelle was a fucking adult who could do whatever she wanted. I sort of think Mack respects me for that, but he's also still pissed about it. And I still think he's a total jagoff. He spends all his time down here on the south side—with people kowtowing to him and telling him he's a big, wise man in the community—that he forgets he doesn't know everything. And, let me tell you, Leopold Mack most certainly *does not* know everything."

Ben takes another look over at the church. I follow his gaze. We see Mack entirely surrounded by a needy throng. They look at him like he's the only one with an answer to the world's problems.

"What's the issue for Mack?" Ben asks. "It's not the 1950s. Nobody's calling rock and roll the devil's music anymore. There are Christian rock bands, for fuck's sake."

"Mack would say there are *issues*, plural. But it really comes down to one thing. Richelle wants to be her own person, and it's not who Mack wants her to be."

"And what's that?"

I sigh. "Richelle is a smart successful black woman who has zero interest in living on the south side. Her father is a preacher, but she's a freethinker. She doesn't go to church on Sunday because she doesn't believe that the stories it's founded on are true. And she doesn't—what's that phrase she uses?—'owe fealty' to the south side. She has friends of all different colors. She certainly dates guys who are all different colors.

"From what I can tell, Mack had this vision that—after college—Richelle would move back to the south side, marry a religious black guy like him, and work for some community organizing group or something. But Richelle doesn't want to play on that team. She's just like, 'I'm not playing.' Richelle wants to live her life how she chooses. Which means being the bassist in the best fucking rock band in the City of Chicago! You'd think that would be something a father would be *proud of*, you know? But not Mack."

"It's still a problem for him?"

"Let me put it this way. Have you heard Mack mention his daughter once—*once*—this whole time? It's a zombie outbreak, and he's down here helping his church people instead of going to check on his own flesh and blood. His own daughter. If that doesn't make it clear, then nothing will."

"Yikes," Ben says.

I nod and say, "Yeah…yikes."

★ ★ ★

A few minutes later, Mack returns to the car and throws open the door. He moves brusquely, no nonsense. He hands each of us a bottle of water and a granola bar, which I actually appreciate.

"Thanks," Ben says.

"Yeah, thanks," I tell him. "What's the plan…'*Pastor*?'"

"We're going out again, of course," Mack says, all business.

Another member of Mack's congregation climbs into the back seat. He's a balding, older man who carries an ancient hunting rifle.

"This gentleman is Mr. Perry," Mack says.

The older man nods hello.

"What's up?" I say to him. "You the next ensign in the red uniform, ready to beam down to the Class-M planet with us?"

Ben chuffs, trying not to full-on laugh.

"I get that, you know," the man says quietly. "Unlike you, I can remember back when that show was on television."

Mack climbs into the front seat and starts the car.

Stragglers are still creeping into the parking lot from the surrounding neighborhoods, and the streetlights are beginning to flicker more frequently. I've been wondering if a complete power failure is in our future. I feel like that would be catastrophic.

"We have to go to Crenshaw Cemetery," Mack says cryptically.

"What?" says Ben. "But the zombies! Won't we be overwhelmed?"

"We'll be fine," Mack says, as if he knows something we don't.

"Wait...why are you taking *me*?" I ask.

"It's true; I don't like you," Mack says flatly, never taking his eyes from the windshield. "But I must admit, you've got energy... and you know how to shoot."

This makes me smile, and I cross my arms in satisfaction.

"Wait," Ben says, still unconvinced. "We're going to a graveyard...in a zombie outbreak...on purpose?"

Mack nods silently.

"But why?" Ben presses.

"Because something is wrong," Mack says.

"What?" I ask. "Bodies *aren't* coming up out of the ground?"

Mack drives silently for a moment, as if he has elected not to answer the question. We pull away from the church and back into the snowy city streets. I look at the clock on the dashboard. It is just past midnight.

Mack says, "No. The problem is that bodies *are* coming up... just not where they should."

★ ★ ★

We head northwest. It's a short drive to Crenshaw. The streets are mostly empty. A couple of times, we pass shambling, huddled figures in the shadows—maybe they are zombies and maybe they are cold, confused humans. Whatever the case, Mack never slows the car to investigate. All along the avenues and boulevards, the lights intermittently flicker and dim. (At least Mack has a flashlight. Suddenly, I want one too.)

We draw close to the cemetery, which is surrounded by a massive wall of pink and red bricks. The cemetery has a mixed history. Its inhumed residents tell the story of immigration and emigration on the city's south side. The earliest, oldest graves—the ones from the 1800s—are all white Protestants. Then from the 1920s to the 1950s, the internments are solidly Jewish. Finally, from 1950s on, they are almost exclusively African American.

"Crenshaw was creepy enough before," Ben says. "I really don't wanna see it in a zombie outbreak."

Mack slowly pilots the car along the exterior of the cemetery wall, apparently looking for the entrance.

"How do you figure, son?" says Ensign Perry.

(He called him 'son.' LOL. Ben is *totally* old.)

"Crenshaw is located at the epicenter of a lot of bad shit, if you'll pardon my French," Ben tells him. "I'm a political news reporter, so I have to follow this stuff. You've got some real messed up local politics because this location is where three wards touch. Crenshaw is technically in Royko Square, the Fifty-Third Ward. Marja Mogk is the alderman, and it's, you know…a black neighborhood. But then just a couple of blocks west is the Fifty-First Ward, Farrell Park, which is Latino. And to the north and east is the Fifty-Second Ward, where Igor Szuter is the alderman, which is mostly white. It's like a racial and political nexus, and it all meets right at this cemetery."

Ben takes a breath. "Then, of course, there's Burge Wheeler. But I don't need to tell you all about that."

He's right. He doesn't.

I don't keep up with city politics—which just seem like a bunch of ugly, old people arguing about boring things—but even *I* know about Burge Wheeler. He didn't make the national news, but in Illinois, he was unmissable.

Burge Wheeler was a police commander who ran the precinct around Royko Square until about three years ago. He was a decorated Vietnam veteran. In the 1980s he'd gained a reputation as a kind of hero-cop. He saved kids from burning buildings, got in shootouts with drug dealers, and once stuck his finger in the firing-pin of a suicide's gun—saving the woman's life and almost severing his finger in the process. He also had one of the best arrest and conviction records of any precinct in the city. The papers said Wheeler's clearance rate for murders was close to sixty percent, which is unheard of in *any* Chicago neighborhood, much less a low-income, high-crime one. He was held up as a model for the rest of the department to follow. He was proof that one brave, determined cop *can* make a difference.

Then, in the 2000s, some law students at Northwestern started examining some of Wheeler's old arrests as part of a class project. Suspects brought in by Wheeler had an unusually high confession-rate, and it was these confession cases the students examined. They started filing motions for retroactive DNA testing in cases where no DNA tests had been done, and in almost every instance, the DNA between convicted perpetrator and that found at the crime scene did not match.

The students and their professors organized appeals. Scores of criminals arrested by Burge Wheeler began to have their convictions overturned. When asked about their confessions years before, they told tales of secret torture rooms in police station basements where Wheeler presided personally, using techniques he remembered from Vietnam. There were beatings, whippings, electrocutions, and more. Burge had waterboarded for years (in a time before most people knew what waterboarding was). He had burned suspects' testicles with his cigarette lighter. He had threatened to kill suspects' family members and friends (or just suspects themselves). And it had worked. The men he arrested, almost uniformly, confessed. The suspects Wheeler and his men grabbed off the streets—when they needed to "solve" a crime— were always young black men and always known gang members or thugs. They had no idea of their legal rights and believed Wheeler when he said they could be killed on his whim. They were people everybody in the community would believe were guilty. They were seldom missed.

The floodgates opened around 2010, just as Wheeler was preparing to retire and move to Florida. With all the falsely convicted offenders pointing together to a single man, the public outcry became too much. Internal Affairs launched an investigation, and Wheeler's old cronies quickly flipped on him in exchange for immunity. One by one, current and retired police officers stepped forward to confirm tales of Burge Wheeler requesting to be left alone with suspects in holding cells, Burge Wheeler bragging of coerced confessions, and suspects who routinely displayed mysterious injuries after private interrogations.

The Feds swooped in, and there was a quick trial. Many said the mayor had put in a word to keep it brief, to make Burge Wheeler the sole scapegoat. And he was. The Feds had been reminded that they didn't need to try and convict every dirty cop on the south side of Chicago. Keep it to one guy. Get in and get out. Make a quick, surgical incursion. Don't linger too long in a neighborhood like Royko Square. Don't let too many of its residents take the stand and start talking about the things they've seen over the years. (They say that sunlight's the best disinfectant, but both the mayor and the prosecutors knew they didn't have enough to scrub clean the south side of Chicago. *Nobody* has that much.)

So anyhow, it was a quick trial. Burge Wheeler was overwhelmingly guilty, and so he was found. But the prosecutors went for what they knew they could get, which turned out to be things like perjury and lying about having followed proper interrogation procedures. (The actual incidents of torture were hard to prove. Wheeler was a master at beating and strangling and burning in such a way that no marks were left. And any scars that *did* crop up had had twenty years to fade.) The sentence he received was far less than anyone thought the man deserved. Though in his late sixties and now an amorphous blob of cholesterol and broken blood vessels, Burge Wheeler would probably *not* die in jail.

Has justice been done? Can it *ever* be done?

Nobody knows.

But when Ben reminds us that we're driving into Burge Wheeler's old neighborhood—in addition to driving into a graveyard in the middle of a zombie outbreak—it adds another layer and makes it even more unnerving. This is a place with a horrible history. This is a place where secret things have been done. And maybe, just maybe, the things we know are only the tip of the iceberg.

From the front seat, Mack says, "Hush now."

We do.

A moment later, I hear gunshots coming from within the graveyard.

"Holy cow, people are in there," I say. "They might need help."

Mack responds by turning off the headlights on his car.

"I'm not sure they want our help," Mack says cautiously. "Or that they'd take kindly to being interrupted. Best to be cautious for now."

We continue to follow the road around the outer wall of the graveyard. Then, abruptly—with no entrance yet in sight—Mack pulls to a halt and kills the engine.

"Mr. Perry," Mack says, "tell me again what Aisha and Alexia said they saw."

The gunfire inside the cemetery crackles again. Mr. Perry shifts uneasily in his seat.

"It was very odd," begins Perry. "This was when they were leaving their house and heading for the church. They said they passed a group of cars that looked like police, but unmarked. Or maybe government. Some had those special license plates that city workers use. And everybody had guns. Alexia and Aisha said they looked into the cemetery and saw there were already walking corpses, but they weren't by where the headstones are. Of course, you can't trust Alexia half the time. And Aisha, she does like a drink."

"Well, somebody's in the graveyard," Ben points out. "And from the sound of it, they're packing heat."

"Is the city sending teams into graveyards . . . to put down the zombies?" I ask. "That's *good*, right?"

Ben laughs—a deep, thunderous belly laugh.

"Has the city ever done *anything* to make you think it could be that organized? Has it *ever* dealt with a disaster bigger than needing to move snow? Kiddo, I just saw the mayor get his brain eaten on live TV. I don't know if anybody is even in charge right now . . . but it's Chicago, so there are at least fifty-some people who think they ought to be. Can you imagine them coordinating and cooperating this fast to put down zombies?"

"I agree," says Mack. "The city doesn't work like this. That's why I want to take a look."

Mack gets out of the car like we've arrived at our destination. I wonder how this can be, because all that faces us is the pinkish red brick of the cemetery wall. Puzzled, the rest of us follow him out into the chilly night air. A wind whips up, and I hear a gentle creaking somewhere nearby. I crane my neck and detect its source.

On the other side of the graveyard wall—which is perhaps eight feet high—is an ancient oak tree. Its thick, heavy branches sway almost imperceptibly in the wind. I look up above us and see that one of the thickest branches extends out over the graveyard wall and hovers just above the sidewalk.

"I used to climb up this way when I was a little boy," says Mack, handing his shotgun to Ben. "We liked to run around inside Crenshaw at night, just because we could. Simpler times."

Mack looks old—I mean, I said Ben was old before, but Mack is properly ancient—but he manages a running jump, presses up off the wall with his foot, and grips the oak branch with both hands. He runs up the side of the wall with his feet and eventually pulls himself up until he's sitting on the wall. He's definitely done this before.

"Okay," he says, extending an open hand. Ben tosses him the shotgun.

"What do you see, Pastor Mack?" Mr. Perry calls hoarsely.

Mack stares intently into the graveyard like a man looking out to sea for a distant ship.

"Anything?" Perry asks after a moment.

There is another ripple of gunfire in the distance.

"It may have been too long since I last went to the eye doctor," Mack finally allows, squinting into the darkness and shielding his brow from the sputtering streetlights' glare.

"Don't look at *me*," says Mr. Perry. "I can hardly pass the seeing test at the license branch."

For a moment, the group appears to consider me. At barely five feet tall, it is doubtful that I could make the leap up onto the branch.

So that leaves…

Ben Bennington

There's a bit of emasculation involved when a man who is about seventy has an easier time climbing up onto a wall than you do. And a cute girl is watching.

But hey, you do what you have to.

Once my fat ass is finally up there—with more than a little help from an aging pastor—I follow Mack's gaze and look deep into the graveyard. My glasses are new, so I'm sure I can see things 20/20. The scene before me is crystal clear. And it makes *no* fucking sense.

"I can't tell . . . I mean, I don't . . . I don't understand what I'm seeing."

"Just tell us what's over there," Mack says, putting a steadying hand on my shoulder. "Describe it plainly. You don't have to understand it."

It feels good to have Mack's hand on my shoulder. Reassuring. He has that kind of effect on people.

I swallow deeply and look back into the graveyard.

"Okay, to start with, there are five or six cars parked near the entrance. The cars have their hazards on. There are a group of people—like ten or fifteen—on the far side of the graveyard. It's hard to see them through the trees and graves. Most of them have guns. Long guns, as well as handguns. They are standing around a heap of dead bodies. Dead zombies, got to be. It's giant. A hundred of them, at least. Now the people with guns are waiting. A couple of them are smoking cigarettes."

"Do you recognize anyone?" Mack asks.

"No, it's hard to see their faces."

"They're probably just some concerned citizens who came to put down the zombies," Maria insists from the sidewalk below.

"Yes…" Mack says hesitantly. "I'm still not sure."

"What do the cemetery grounds look like?" Maria asks. "Have the zombies dug out of their coffins?"

"Only a handful of the graves look opened. In a few places I can see where something pushed away the dirt and crawled out, yeah. But there aren't many. Way fewer than I was expecting."

"It's just as I thought!" Mack says. "The cemeteries are a canard. A paper tiger. Most of the zombies can't escape. They're trapped inside their coffins, and by six feet of dirt. They're too rotted to get out, or the coffins are just too strong."

"But *some* are," I say, gesturing to the pile of zombies on the far side of the graveyard. "Plus, I saw Al Capone eat the mayor's brain on TV. That was real. The TV anchor nearly shit himself."

"I'm not saying 5 or 10 percent don't get out," Mack says. "Just that most don't. Also, the cemetery at Mt. Carmel— where the mayor was—is different than here at Crenshaw. It has mausoleums where all a zombie has to do is sit up and open the door."

Then I see something.

"Wait a minute," I say, touching Mack on the shoulder. "There's movement and activity. The people over by the cars are doing something."

"What?" Mack whispers. "All I see is blurry movement."

"Two guys just got big green gas cans out of the back of an SUV, dumping it on the pile. Yep. They're going to burn the zombies."

Moments later, there is a *fwoosh* sound as the giant pile of zombies ignites.

"They're burning them now," I inform the group.

"This is very odd," Mack says.

"Okay, but listen; I haven't even told you the crazy thing!" I say, shaking my head like I'm trying to get out of a stupor.

"You haven't?" quips Maria. "Then tell us, dumbass."

"There are holes all around the cemetery in the places *where there are not graves.*"

"What's that?" Mack says, inclining his head.

"The landscaping along the interior drive, at the very entrance to the graveyard? It's full of holes. *Man-sized* holes. They're maybe two or three feet apart. Real consistent."

Mack furrows his brow.

"And the flowerbeds along the west wall?" I say, pointing for Mack's benefit. "For you, they're probably just a dark brown blur…but I can see where the soil has been recently upturned. It's the same thing. A bunch of man-sized holes. There are other places too. That area there, about twenty yards from the east wall? It's totally empty except for new holes in the soil. And then all along the northeast wall there's more of them, a bunch more— like, I dunno, forty or fifty."

"How many total?" Mack whispers. His face has gone serious, his body completely still. He looks like a man who has just realized he might be sitting atop a leviathan, and wants to be very sure he doesn't wake it up.

"I'd say . . . you mean in total? The *whole* cemetery?"

"The whole cemetery, yes," Mack repeats with some urgency.

I try to take in the entirety of the strange scene before me, surveying the oversized gopher-holes where the cold earth has been pushed aside.

"More than two hundred."

"My God Jesus Christ who lives Heaven," Mack says ominously. Somehow, this appeal to a deity carries more rhetorical consequence than any four-letter curse I can think of.

"What?" Maria calls from below. "What's the problem? What's happening?"

"Someone has been burying people in this graveyard secretly," Mack pronounces quietly. "I imagine for years. Two hundred people don't just disappear. Someone has been using this as a private body dumping ground. And now they're trying to cover it up."

"What about the people who run the cemetery?" I ask in confusion. "Surely they'd notice if—"

"In on it," Mack says, his voice managing to be sonorous even in a whisper. "Whatever this is, they cemetery people are involved."

"Who would hide bodies in a cemetery?" I ask.

"You're the one who can see them," Mack reminds me. "But my first guess is the police. As you reminded us, this is Burge Wheeler territory. Lots of things happened in this neighborhood that people want to forget. That phony baloney trial just scratched the surface. Then there are street gangs, organized crime families, drug dealers...even professional hitmen! This is Chicago, after all. Crenshaw Cemetery might have had a relationship with all of the above. Maybe they hung out a shingle. You want to get rid of a body someplace where nobody will ever find it? For a fee, we'll put it in the last place anyone will ever look . . . a cemetery."

"They kinda *look* like cops," I allow, gazing again into the distant group of men (and, I now note, a few women) illuminated by the blazing zombie-fire.

"Kinda look like cops?" Mack echoes.

"They look serious, the way cops do when people are watching, except..."

"Except what?" Mack urges me on.

"Except none of them has a police uniform on. Their guns don't look like cop guns; they just have a mishmash of different guns, like we do. And the cars are official-looking, but not cop cars. Alexia or whomever was right. They're the kind of cars that get issued to city officials."

"Like the mayor?" Maria quips.

"Yeah, but I don't think he gave the word for this—whatever *this* is—because the moment the mayor realized there were zombies, it was too late for him."

"Curse these old-man eyes!" Mack says as he squints into the darkness. "Ben, can you tell me *anything* else about these people?"

"No," I say, shaking my head. "They're all different colors, I guess. Is that useful? They're white, black, Hispanic . . . a regular Benetton commercial."

"Naw," says Mr. Perry from down below. "You need some Asians and Indians for that."

Mr. Perry's tone immediately changes to a genial greeting, and he says:

"Howdy, young man…"

He is not addressing any of us.

Mack and I look at one another with a "What the?" expression and swivel around to see who Mr. Perry is talking to.

A fresh-faced black man in his mid-thirties has just rounded the corner. He wears a tan baseball cap with no insignia and a dark blue jacket. In his right hand is an automatic handgun. His left hand holds the right one down, forcing the gun toward the ground as if it is a bucking animal that must be kept at bay.

At first, he looks only at Maria and Mr. Perry, sizing them up. He does not return Mr. Perry's broad smile.

Then he sees the two of us sitting on the wall, and his eyes narrow.

His left hand suddenly loses the battle, and the gun comes up firing.

BANG! BANG! BANG! BANG! BANG!

The first shot is directed at Mr. Perry. He is hit in the solar plexus and goes down, stone dead.

With the next shot, the shooter changes his trajectory and comes after Mack and me up on the wall.

We both fight to get out of the way. I end up going backwards and falling to the ground outside the wall. Mack falls forward and disappears into the graveyard.

The next thing I know, I'm on the ground and looking over at Maria. She has dropped to one knee and taken her handgun out of her coat.

She aims and fires. Twice.

BANG! BANG!

The gun's recoil rocks Maria's tiny frame, but she stays balanced. The strange shooter is hit twice in the chest, and falls to the ground, motionless.

There is a moment of stillness and silence as the report of Maria's weapon fades into the distance.

"Ben, are you okay?" Maria calls.

I get up and pat myself all over. My elbows and knees hurt from the fall, but I can't find any bullet holes.

"I'm fine. I think Mr. Perry is a goner though."

"Christ," says Maria, seeming genuinely sad. "I shouldn't have made that *Star Trek* joke."

"It's not like *you* killed him," I blurt, not knowing what else to say.

We look around, surveying the two dead men.

"Where the fuck did Mack go?" Maria says after noticing he is no longer atop the wall.

"Mack?" I shout. "Pastor Mack, are you over there?"

Mack does not answer, but a chorus of raised voices suddenly swells from the distant side of the graveyard.

"Pastor Mack!" I call again.

He does not respond.

A tinny electronic voice blurts out of nowhere and makes us jump: "*Petey, what's happening? Petey, come back.*"

The dead shooter has a walkie talkie somewhere on his person. Something tells me I need to find it—though I can't say if I intend to talk into it or shut it off. I walk over and begin rifling through the shooter's bloody jacket.

"This is bad," Maria says. "Ben, we need to get out of here."

I find the walkie talkie. I depress the biggest, most brightly lit button, and the device falls silent. Then I see something else that has fallen out of the shooter's pocket. I do a double take.

"Maria?" I say.

The voices across the graveyard grow louder, like they are not all the way across the graveyard anymore.

"Ben, we need to go," Maria insists.

"Look at this envelope," I say, pointing to the dead man's splayed jacket.

Maria rolls her eyes and wearily stalks over to the shooter's corpse.

On the ground is a plain envelope. The word "Maria" has been hastily written across it in ballpoint pen.

"What?" she snaps.

"That envelope from his jacket says 'Maria,'" I say.

"So?" she responds. "Lots of people are named…"

Maria trails off as her eyes light on the envelope.

"I thought maybe he was coming to give it to you," I say. "Did you know this guy?"

"No," Maria says, kneeling down to pick up the envelope. "But that's my father's handwriting."

"Oh," I say, confused.

Maria opens the envelope. Inside is a single sheet of paper from the same stationery set. There are perhaps five lines written on it, obviously penned in great haste. I try—without compunction or shame—to read over her shoulder. Alas, the note is in Spanish, which I do not speak.

After a moment, Maria rises to her feet and puts the note into her pocket.

"Come on," she says soberly. "We need to go."

Leopold Mack

I am perhaps 10 feet off the ground, fully halfway up the giant chestnut. I am as silent as a church mouse. I am also terrified. People with guns are searching the cemetery grounds beneath me. With their trench coats and rifles, they look like old-timey federal agents—the kind who busted bootleggers in this town almost 100 years ago. A Kevin Costner in *The Untouchables* kind of look.

If you'd told me yesterday that I'd be climbing trees in a cemetery at midnight…well, let's just say I'd have had a hard time believing you. Now it's happening. The supple, slick bark under my gloved hands is as real as real gets—as is the terror that courses through my veins.

The strange people below are now close enough for me to see their faces, even with my aging eyes. Nothing about their appearance helps me solve the mystery of who they are or what they're doing. Ben's descriptions were about right. They look like cops or civil servants out of uniform, but the guns don't match. There are no badges or CPD-emblazoned turtle-necks. They lack the conviviality and good humor of cops who think they're unobserved. (Even at the direst of murder scenes, I've seen how Chicago cops crack wise and smile when the reporters are gone. There's not a shred of that here. These men and women have still, mannequin faces. These folks are still on the job.)

Miraculously, they shine their flashlights everywhere but up. My clothes are dark enough that I remain concealed against the tree. My only concern is my bright pink tie, which I have not removed. Perhaps an inch of it is exposed to the winter night, right at my neck. If a flashlight beam were to find it, it would dazzle back, and there is no question that I would be found. Very slowly, I slip my chin down, attempting to cover the bright swath of iridescent color with the wrinkles in my neck. I cannot be sure that this tactic is effective, but the flashlights never find my shoes, much less my neckwear.

All they do find is my shotgun. It sits on the ground where I landed. One of the flashlight people immediately takes it away.

From my perch, I cannot quite see over the graveyard wall. Ben and Maria are gone. They yelled for me and then ran off. I didn't hear Mr. Perry's voice anywhere. Something tells me that he's no longer with us.

Who are these people, so murderous and organized? What in the world is happening?

I cling to the cold, slippery tree and pray. It's not for deliverance. It's not for my own life. It's just for understanding.

Lord, when you take me—because someday you're *going* to take me—just please . . . please Lord . . . please let me know what the fuck is going on in the city of Chicago.

★ ★ ★

After ten minutes or so, the flashlight people get tired of looking for me and leave. There is the sound of car doors closing and engines starting.

After fifteen minutes, I get brave enough to turn around and risk a look toward the entrance of the cemetery. The people and their cars appear to be gone.

After twenty minutes I get brave enough to climb down from the tree, my slick dress shoes slippery against the bark. I almost lose my balance a couple of times and count myself lucky to get to the ground without breaking anything. How long has it been since I climbed a tree? Probably decades.

For a while, I creep around the back of the cemetery, wondering what to do next. I have a vague notion that I must—somehow, someway—return to my flock at the church. It all feels distant and theoretical. I don't even know if I can get out of this cemetery. The flashlight people may have locked the gates.

Confident now that I am at least unobserved, I creep to the nearest hole in the ground—one of the ones Ben was talking about (with no headstone or marker to signify that it's a proper grave). I see that many such holes ring the cemetery wall. I bend down and take a good gander. There can be little doubt that a zombie has pushed up from under the dirt. I notice that the grave looks shallow. They all do. Very shallow. Maybe a foot deep. Maybe less.

Following the trail of empty graves—in places where there should not *be* graves—I eventually make my way up to the giant pile of zombies. They are still smoldering. It is horrible to see so many charred corpses, zombies or no. Some have moldered to little more than flesh and bone, while others appear fairly recent. The burning, however, has been thorough. Now and then—in the horrible, tangled pile of flesh and limbs—I'm able to make out a face that has escaped the fire. In most cases, I can't. The flames have rendered them anonymous. Whoever burned these bodies really wanted to make some evidence disappear, and they nearly did. I wonder if we interrupted them before they could finish. Whatever the case, they did a pretty thorough job. I try to garner what I can.

The bodies look mostly African American, but there are a few whites and Hispanics thrown in. They are wearing street clothes. In most cases, they appear to have been shot through the head at close range. (This does not tell me how they died in life; it's a sign of their recent re-execution for the crime of being zombies.)

Otherwise, there is no unifying feature among the perhaps 200 charred bodies at my feet. Certainly, I recognize no one I know among the half-burned faces. For that, at least, I am thankful.

Then, just a few moments into my investigation of the smoldering pile, I hear a cough in the trees a few feet away. I jump as though it were a gunshot.

My hand goes for my shotgun, which is not there. All it finds is my Maglite, still in my coat pocket. If somebody's got the drop on me, I'm already dead. That much said, if this *is* my last moment, I'd sure like to see who pulls the trigger.

I turn on the flashlight and train it in the direction of the cough.

Nothing.

Nothing at first. Nothing but trees.

Then…yes, there is movement in the shadows against a giant oak. I bring the light closer.

I see a sleeveless jacket with pockets down the front, like something a movie director or archaeologist wears. Then a person comes into focus inside the jacket. It's a black woman—maybe a good looking sixty, maybe a terrible looking thirty-five—whose lined face tells the story of a difficult life. Whatever her age, she looks low-class; mean and hard. She's maybe five-foot-one, and a good fifty pounds overweight. A thick roll wobbles around her middle. With one hand, she supports herself against the tree, and with the other, she adjusts her wig, which has fallen askew.

Before I can notice anything else about her, she falls forward into the dirt.

I wait to see if this is some kind of ruse. If she's going to suddenly rise up with a gun and plug me three times in the chest. No such thing occurs. After a few moments, she moans—long and low. That's when I notice the rivulets of blood running out from underneath her coat.

This woman is no threat. She is a victim.

I hurry to her side and take her by the shoulder. She rolls over to face me, responding to my touch. As she does so, I detect the pair of bullet holes in the center of her lower belly. I kneel at her side, remembering that there is no cell phone service (and, probably, no emergency services to be summoned if there were). There is no hope for her. This will not be the first time I've sat with the dying, but it will definitely be the first time I've done so in a cemetery.

"I'm here," I say, hugging her close. "The pastor's here. I gotcha."

"Who are you?" she wheezes.

"This is Pastor Leopold Mack from The Church of Heaven's God in Christ Lord Jesus. I'm the one holding your hand. Can you feel that, child? Do you feel my hand? I'm with you."

"Oh Pastor," the strange woman says familiarly, as if we knew one another well. "I've got some sins, Pastor."

"Do I know you, child?" I ask, still thinking she could be a lapsed parishioner who has slipped my mind.

"No," she says soberly. "But I got sins on my chest. I got to tell somebody."

"Who did this to you, child?" I ask, struggling to redirect the conversation. "Who were those people?"

The woman looks away from me, unable to make eye contact. She stares up at the sky, then over at the pile of smoldering zombies.

Sins indeed.

"I knowed it was God sent them to punish me. Them walking dead. When they started up—out the ground—I ran and locked myself in the mower shed. I was screamin' and screamin'. I stayed there with them horrible things bangin' on the door. They just kept on. Then—after forever, it felt like—I heard people out there shootin' 'em. I was so happy. I busted on out that shed. Then I seen Shawn Michael…and he shot me in the belly. He shot me like I was a dog. A damn dog! I laid down and pretended I was dead."

This gives me pause. I know a Shawn Michael from around the neighborhood. He works for an alderman.

"Shawn Michael Recinto?" I ask the dying woman. "Him?"

She nods, still unable to look at me. Tears are running down her cheeks. Her expression says that the confession is still coming. I've sat with people who have skeletons in their closets. They know they need to let them out before they go to be with God. But this woman's face says that she has a whole graveyard.

Literally, it turns out.

"Is this where you work, child?"

She looks at me for a moment—and only a moment—and then looks away.

"I'm the cemetery manager. Been for well-on twenty years."

"And what happened here?" I ask, cradling her closer to me. She responds to the touch almost like a lover, gripping my arm and holding me tight, thankful for the contact.

"I did bad. I helped them bury they dead here. I took they money for it. Been takin' it for years. I buried the bodies all around the graveyard. I never asked no questions."

"Who?" I ask, now gripping her back. "Whose money did you take, child?"

For the first time, the dying lady smiles. Then her eyes roll and her tongue begins to hang from her mouth. Death is close. I won't have her for much longer.

"I never knew myself, pastor…until tonight."

She pauses, drifting off again.

"Who was it, child?" I entreat, shaking her as if to jostle a sleeper awake. "You need to tell me."

"All of them," she says quietly. "Pastor…it was *all* of them."

Then she is gone.

I say a prayer for the cemetery manager—a quick one, lest she decide to reanimate and come after me—and hurriedly make for the front gates. They appear to be ajar. At least I'm not trapped inside with these bodies. A small blessing, but I'll take all I can get tonight.

I pass the pile of burned zombies on my way out. It's like something out of a Holocaust documentary. The stuff of nightmares.

Despite the gruesomeness surrounding me, I feel strangely invigorated. I am, so far, still alive. And I think I have my first clue about what the Hell is going on. The cemetery manager wasn't able to tell me much, but it's enough to get me started. Someone brought her bodies to bury—illegally and secretly—no questions asked. Who was it? "All of them." Whatever that means. She also told me who shot her. She named a name. And it chills my bones.

Shawn Michael Recinto.

He works for Alderman Marja Mogk, whose ward technically contains this graveyard. He's her assistant, her #1 guy. I've met him at community functions all around the south side. He's a memorable person, to say the least. A tall, smiling man. Physically huge. Played one season as a backup wide receiver for the Dallas Cowboys after college. Didn't manage his money well. Ended up back in Chicago looking for a job. Found one with Marja.

Lots of aldermen like to surround themselves with guys like Shawn Michael, especially aldermen who are physically small or female. Drivers. Assistants. Chiefs of staff. Call them whatever you want. They're tough guys on the payroll who do whatever the alderman says. A guy like Recinto is not *technically* hired muscle, but if anybody ever wanted to start some shit, there's no question he'd be able to handle it. (In my darker moments, I have also wondered if Marja sleeps with Shawn Michael. I doubt I am the only one who ponders this.)

Anyhow, what in the name of the Lord is Shawn Michael doing executing a graveyard caretaker? What is he doing with a bunch of people with guns? Why is he piling up zombies and setting them on fire?

I pass through the cemetery's iron gates.

The streets outside are dead. The houses quiet and dark. (I'm guessing anybody who looked out a window and saw what was happening in the cemetery has drawn the shades, hidden under the bed, and prayed not to be discovered.) The streetlights above me blink intermittently. Sirens wail in the distance—not police sirens. Other sirens. Air raid.

I have no food, no car, and no gun. But I am damn straight about to get some answers.

You've been bad, Chicago. I don't know *exactly* what you did...yet. But I know it was bad...really, really bad. Forget the bribes and backscratching and giving your relatives jobs. This is a whole new level of bad. Pastor Mack is coming to hold you accountable. Somebody, somewhere, is about to get the whoopin' of their lives.

And it looks like I might have to be the one to deliver it.

Maria Ramirez

After we have run and then walked for what seems like forever, we stop to rest in front of a looted convenience store. The back door has been pried open with a crowbar, and there is a pallet of neon green energy drinks sitting outside in the snow. We look at one another and wordlessly head for the pallet. Ben and I each drink two of them, relaxing against the store wall to catch our breath.

Between gasps of air and gulps of colored sugar-water, Ben starts to pick my brain.

"Did you know that shooter?" he gasps. "How did he have that letter from your dad?"

"No, and I don't know. Do you think Mack's okay? Did he get shot when he fell over the wall?"

"I couldn't tell. He might have been hit in the back or he might have jumped into the graveyard on his own. It all happened so fast."

"Who the fuck *were* those people? What were they doing in there?"

"I described everything as well as I could. You know as much as I do."

"Well…they were inside my dad's house earlier tonight. We know *that* for sure."

"Huh?" says Ben, a look of consternation settling over his face.

"This note from my dad…he left it for me inside his house. I was supposed to find it. It says he's taking my mother and sister to our aunt's place in Hyde Park. Except…for some reason…he doesn't say that exactly. He's vague and uses code."

If I were being more forthcoming with Ben, I would tell him that it is unlike my brash, commanding father to communicate in subtle, high-context language. And the fact that he's done so scares me deeply.

I don't want to look at it again, yet I force myself to bring the note out of my pocket and read it to Ben in English.

"*Dear Maria,*

Your mother and sister are with me and safe. We are heading to the place where your mother and I had our first date. Meet us as soon as you can. My cell phone is broken. Don't talk to anybody from the city, or any other aldermen. Come right away."

I put the note back in my pocket.

"My mother and father had their first date in my aunt's kitchen," I explain. "It's a famous family story. He was supposed to take her to the movies, but they got snowed in by a big blizzard, so instead my aunt cooked them dinner, and they watched TV. My father's referring to it so that anyone outside of the family who reads this note won't know where he means. But why? Why would he do that? It's like he *expected* his house to get broken into, right?"

Ben opens his mouth to speak, but nothing comes out. His eyebrows and eyes dance back and forth. He's asking himself if he's heard me right.

He has.

"Yes," I tell him, rolling my eyes. "The note says *other* alder-men."

"Your dad is?"

"Frankie Munoz. Alderman for the Fifty-First Ward. Farrell Park."

Ben looks at me with an expression that neatly comports the entirety of "And when *the fuck* were you going to tell me *that*?"

"You have different last names. When I met you, you said your last name was Ramirez."

"I go by my mother's name."

"Oh," Ben says cautiously. "Any reason for that?"

"Yeah. I—what's it called again? Oh yeah—*hate* him. I *hate* my dad. That's the reason."

Ben furrows his brow.

"You hate your dad. You hate Pastor Mack. Who do you *like*?"

"Other than my mother? Not too many people over thirty."

I watch Ben swallow hard.

"Does your dad have a lot of enemies? I mean, more than a typical alderman? Is there anybody who'd use a zombie outbreak as an excuse to break into his house?"

I shake my head. Not to indicate no, but because I don't like to think about this. My father's always been such a shit. Some-times I fear that—as bad as he was when he lived with us—my mother and I only saw a small swath of his crimes.

"I don't know," I answer honestly. "But probably yes, he does."

"What interests me," Ben says, clearly trying to be tactful, "is that the guy who had the note on him was part of the cemetery extermination group. They were the same group."

"That seems pretty clear, but I don't know how they're connected. Maybe zombies breaking out are a chance to kill everybody you don't like all at once—human and zombie both."

"You know, come to think of it, I've met your dad a couple of times at city events where I was reporting."

"And what did you think?"

Ben shrugs.

"I never really formed an opinion. The paper I work for covers business, and there's not a lot in his ward. Maybe a new dry cleaner opens up or a bank opens a new branch; that's about it. But I know he's the last Latino alderman on the south side. You've got this little pocket of Latino residents here in Farrell Park. They barely have a majority. Maybe Latinos were fifty-five percent as of the last census. And they're about to release a new one and redraw the ward maps like they do every ten years. He's a transplant, right? Most aldermen grow up in the neighborhood they represent. But your dad didn't?"

"No, he didn't. We grew up in Logan Square. My dad ran the Boys and Girls Club there. When he left my mom about ten years ago, he and his new lady moved down here. He got a similar job at a community center. Pretty soon he was running it. Then he ran for alderman. I couldn't believe it when he got elected. I wanted to fucking die. How can the universe reward someone for being a pushy, bullying asshole?"

"I ask myself that every time I meet an alderman," Ben says quietly.

That makes me smile.

Then there is a crackle of gunfire, maybe a block away from us. Someone—a woman—screams for five full seconds at the top of her lungs. Then she stops with a horrible gurgle.

"We need to keep moving," I say, looking warily in the direction of the scream.

"Back to the church, you think?" Ben asks. "Do we even know the way? I always have to use a GPS whenever I drive below 35th Street."

"No. What we should do is go find my father. I mean...that's what *I'm* going to do. You can come along if you like."

Ben seems to consider it.

"Where is your aunt's house exactly?"

I describe a route to the house a few blocks to the northeast where my aunt has lived for nearly sixty years. It will take us through one of the south side's nicer residential areas, across a city park, and then back into a less-nice residential area.

"How many bullets do we have left?" Ben asks.

I inventory the clip of my automatic and see that I have three.

"I don't know how to check on an AK," Ben says, "but I already squeezed a few off. It could be empty."

"Yeah, well don't throw it away just yet. We're not just worried about zombies out there. Looks count for a lot. An AK pointed in your face will make you think twice, whoever you are."

Ben nods and grips his weapon resolutely.

"Do you think your dad will tell us what's going on?"

"Honestly, probably not, but I'm damn sure going to ask him."

★ ★ ★

We head out into the neighborhoods due northeast. It gets fancy real fast. These are nice homes, ones with fences and yards. A lot of African Americans who make it big but still want the street cred of being able to say they live "on the south side of Chicago" buy homes here. There are also a lot of University of Chicago professors and real estate speculators. It's a weird little pocket.

We mostly stick to the backyards and avoid the main streets. We trail along wooden fences and scurry through flowerbeds. On any other night we'd look like burglars casing a joint. These massive houses are quiet and dead. Some give me the feeling of actually being abandoned, but others exude the sense of people hiding inside with the lights off. It's weird how you can tell, but you can. Empty or not, we treat nowhere as safe. Every window, every bush, every abandoned automobile holds the potential for an ambush. The snow continues to fall, silently, all around us as we move.

We pause beside a backyard swing set creaking in the wind. I narrow my eyes and contemplate the rest of the route ahead. We're almost to the park. Once through, we'll almost be home-free. Right at my aunt's house. I blow on my fingers to warm them up, and then wrap them back around my handgun.

"Where'd you learn to shoot?" Ben asks as we begin creeping forward again.

I shrug and say, "I grew up in Logan Square back when it was *Logan Square*, you know?"

This seems to satisfy him.

Suddenly—as if the universe has heard our conversation topic—we hear gunshots. Something ricochets off the swing set with a loud *piiiing* that seems to go on forever. We both hit the ground.

The gunshots continue. They're maybe half a block away. It sounds like a back and forth—two groups out to kill each other. Two groups that don't particularly care how much ammunition is being expended. They only seem to be using handguns . . . so far.

"I think that was a stray," I whisper.

"Huh," Ben manages from his cowering position.

"I don't think they see us. They just hit the swing accidentally."

Moments later, the guns stop. The silence is deafening. The snow muffles all. All at once, it feels like it didn't really happen.

"Is that the way we need to go?" Ben asks with some trepidation, nodding ahead in the direction of the shooters.

I nod back.

"You want me to go take a look?"

And it's small. It's almost nonchalant, as if he's asking if he can take my coat or get me a drink of water. Except he's asking if he can scout ahead to see if we'll be shot at and killed.

In the midst of a survival scenario, he wants to make me feel comfortable. For an old guy, he's a gentleman.

But I say no. I can handle myself. And if anybody goes first, I want it to be me.

"Let's go together, then," says Ben.

We rise to our feet and carefully survey the homes ahead of us. I scan for movement or light, detecting neither. The wind picks up and makes me squint.

The nearest house is a giant, prairie style structure. Must be worth millions. As we get closer and closer, the area starts to look more familiar. It turns out Ben is thinking the same thing.

"Wait, where do I know this neighborhood from?" he whispers from above his AK.

"A lot of famous people live here. Obama's house is down the block. Then you got the Nation of Islam leaders over yonder. A few of the old synagogues are still operational too."

"Fuck," Ben whispers. "I forgot about Obama."

"His home's right over there, though I'm sure he's not in it."

"Do you think there are any Secret Service?"

The wind whips up again. For a moment, it's so fierce we can't even talk.

"Gotta be," I say when it dies. "Of course, they're there to do Secret Service shit, not to help us."

"I wonder…" Ben begins to say, then stops dead in his tracks. We can now see around the side of the prairie style house, and the street is full of bodies. At least four corpses are splayed across the road.

We stand stock still, like cockroaches hoping not to be noticed when the lights go on.

"Speak of the fucking devil," Ben whispers.

I take a closer look, and see what he means.

The dead men in the street before us are wearing overcoats with suits underneath. Two of them still have guns in their cold, dead hands. One has a visible earpiece.

"What the fuck?" Ben asks no one.

We edge around the side of the house and get closer. Four more bodies come in to view. That's eight total. Jesus. Nearby, a driverless car is running. A cheap-looking stencil on the door identifies it as belonging to a Black Islamic organization. Three quarters of the cadavers on the street are black men.

We don't have to ask what happened. Somehow it's obvious. They killed each other.

Ben and I look at each other. We both know it.

"Do Secret Service people and Islamic security not like each other? Is that a thing?"

"Government secret service versus religious secret service," Ben pronounces, not answering my question. "I could write a whole *series* of articles about this. Government versus religion, settled in a Chicago street fight. This is some Pulitzer shit right here."

"Pulitzer . . . is that the thing Roger Ebert always brags about having?"

"Yeah," Ben replies. "Not that the Pulitzers are necessarily going to exist anymore. But if this is *localized*—if this is just happening in Chicago—then yeah, I think I got a shot."

"What would you write about this? To get a Pulitzer, I mean?"

I don't know if I mean "this" as in the shootout that just happened or "this" the entire zombie outbreak. I don't think Ben does either. He thinks and rubs his chin a moment.

"The interesting thing about cities isn't what they do when people *are* looking," Ben says. "It's what they do when they think *nobody's* looking. Like, the shit the city is proud of? The shining skyscrapers downtown, the sports stadiums, the public art? You can't judge a city by that. That only tells you what the rich people are doing on a good day. It's what people do on a bad day—a bad day when there are no security cameras watching— that tells you what you really want to know. It's how people act during a blackout, a hurricane, or a siege that tells you the truth about a city."

"I think these guys wanted to kill each other," I tell him.

We look down at the corpses some more. Some could be peacefully sleeping, but others have twisted faces as if they died in anguish. I get curious.

"If you die with a grimace on your face, does it stay that way?" I whisper. "It seems like your face would just . . . *relax*, you know? But apparently not."

"Apparently not," echoes Ben.

We stand there a moment longer, shivering and looking at the dead men. Before long, one of them begins to twitch his legs.

"We should move along."

Ben agrees. Each of us pockets a dead man's handgun and we continue down the snowy street.

★ ★ ★

The rest of the journey to the park is uneventful. We draw our guns on a shuddering figure in an alley, only to find out it's merely a homeless man. He seems intoxicated and insane. He's not coherent, so we just pass him by.

"You know what this is like?" I say to Ben as we enter the park and begin to creep through the trees. "This is like the first day when the snow melts in the spring. You know what I mean? That day when all the trash and dog poop and plastic bags are suddenly there on the street?"

"Yeah," Ben says. "I totally do."

When it snows in Chicago—like the big snow, the one in January that's gonna stick around for a while—Chicagoans start to notice that they can stop looking for a trash can when they have to throw something away. If they drop a cigarette butt or candy wrapper, the snow will cover it. If they fail to clean up after Fido does his business, no one is the wiser. It's kind of a test to see if we'll keep putting rubbish in its place, even if nobody can tell if we did. And it's a test Chicagoans always fail. Each year when the temperature shoots up to fifty, we step outside—breathing in that invigorating spring air—and we're confronted with our own bad citizenship. The sidewalks and yards are strewn with our trash and animal shit. All the things we tried to conceal are staring us—and everybody else—in the face.

"The criminals of this city thought they could hide dead bodies under the ground and under the water," I say to Ben. "They're just like litterbugs in mid-January. They convince themselves nature will conceal what they did...but it never does."

"At least not this time," Ben replies dourly.

We trudge deeper into the park. On the far side—where we're headed—looms an old National Guard armory. It's a giant stone building from the 1920s with twenty-foot statues of medieval knights and WWI soldiers built into its columns. It has a crenulated rooftop like a castle and flat grates on one side—possibly meant to mimic a portcullis—where heat escapes. On cold evenings, the homeless crowd around and bivouac there by the grates. As we get close, I can see the clothing, blankets, and sleeping bags that comprise their impromptu tent city.

As we get even closer I can see it's all been ripped to shreds.

The tattered blankets of the homeless are covered with blood and body parts, and there are empty husks of eaten-out corpses. The zombies have found this place and they have fed. The residents were likely sleeping restfully, lulled by the warm grates. With no cell phones or televisions, they would have been perfectly unaware of the outbreak. It is horrible to imagine their collective surprise.

Next to a plastic bottle of vodka lies a severed human jaw. I hope the homeless here were drunk. I hope they were all passed out and beyond consciousness when the zombies attacked. Still, there are signs of resistance and panic—not least of which is a scrabble of bloody handprints extending seven feet up the side of an armory wall. This was a massacre. People make fun of how easy it's supposed to be to get away from a zombie, but when you're freezing, drunk, and clinically insane…well, it's more easily said than done.

We pass the armory and head out into the street again. These streets aren't so nice. Obama never lived here. Not even *before* he was president.

A block in, we spot a mob of the undead up ahead. They have fresh gore on their faces and it glistens in the flickering streetlights. It's also clear at a glance that these are Lake Michigan zombies. Their skin shows signs of having been eaten away by water and sea creatures. Some are wrapped in a sticky blackness that could be rotted skin or could just be gunk from the bottom of the lake. Others lack skin entirely and look like horrible walking anatomy charts. It is only a moment before they start moving in our direction.

"Oh no," Ben whispers.

"Relax, they're way down the block."

"But they see us. I don't think we have enough bullets to kill them all, even if you *are* a good shot."

I ponder the situation. The zombies slink a few feet closer. A couple of them moan. Others manage horrible, aquatic gurgles. Their rotted out throats give them the voices of half-evolved monstrosities—like things you'd see floating in glass jars in a freak show trying to speak. And what they're trying to say is that they're coming to eat us.

"We go around," I tell Ben. "We'll cut through side streets. Or, wait! Better idea. We'll just go back into the park and head north a few blocks to 43rd Street."

"Uh, no we won't," Ben says, tapping my shoulder hard.

I swivel around and see another group of zombies about the same size. They have just crested the hill at the entrance to the park. They are even closer to us than the other group. If they haven't noticed us yet, they will in a few moments.

"Side streets it is."

Ben Bennington

In my job as a reporter, I'll often ask a colleague how a particular alderman or state senator—who seems so dense that he'd be hard-pressed to remember where his penis is located each time he has to urinate—has managed to rise to a position of power in city or state government. It's not uncommon for the response to involve a knowing wink and a jocular "Him? Let's just say he knows where the bodies are buried."

Zombies, though, *are* the bodies that are buried. When a zombie outbreak happens and the dead reanimate, where bodies are buried ceases to be classified knowledge. It ceases to be a source of power. Everybody can see where the bodies are buried—or, perhaps more accurately, *were* buried—because they're climbing out of the ground and coming to eat you.

Following Maria down these twisting side streets and alleys of the south side, I am terrified, exhausted, and—if I'm being honest—a little turned on. But I'm also aware of a world around me that has changed forever. The bodies are no longer buried. The laws—at the least the old ones—are no longer in effect. Even the back alleys know that things are different. Even the dumpsters riddled with bullet holes and gang graffiti seem to have got the idea. This is a different world. A new one. Though thousands of people have passed through these darkened side streets, we're the first to be traversing them in a zombie apocalypse. Things have started over again. This is the year 1 A. Z. *Anno Zombi.*

Maria and I are explorers in a new world. Who knows what we will find in it?

★ ★ ★

We run and run through these streets that were never well known to me but are now completely foreign and strange. My gut shakes, and sometimes I'm afraid my pants will fall down, but they don't. I can feel my waist rubbing raw against my belt, though. It's not pleasant.

Maria seems to be having no belt-oriented difficulties. She jumps over rotting garbage and hurdles fences like an African deer of some kind. She still has scratches on her face and some swelling around one of her eyes, but none of it is slowing her down. I struggle to keep up and hike up my pants whenever she's not looking.

"Here," she says as we turn down a new street. "I think I know where we are. We just need to go around this corner and through the alley. My aunt's place is like a block past."

"Okay," I say, trying to conceal just how hard I want to pant. "Sounds good. No problem."

We round the corner and trot down an alley bordered on one side by garages and on the other by the flat face of an apartment building. Halfway through, the alley is narrowed by rows of green dumpsters placed side by side. Past that, it becomes an obstacle course of dumpsters—some overturned—where no garbage truck could ever pass. I can't decide if someone has done this recently and intentionally as an impromptu fortification or if this is just an especially horrible part of town where ordered garbage collection is not in the cards.

Ahead of me, Maria slows to a creep and holds her automatic at the ready. She carefully picks her way through the maze of dumpsters. Some are five feet tall. Trash and filth cover the street. Most of it is not covered with snow. I realize this maze must be a recent development.

Maria suddenly freezes. Does she see something? Is something wrong? Without looking back, Maria very slowly turns and shakes her foot at the ground next to her. I look and see a dead man in the trash. A hunting rifle is still in his grip. His throat and the back of his head have been mashed in or eaten out. Probably a little bit of both.

If this was the guy who built this dumpster-maze, then where's the zombie that got him?

Seconds later, my question is answered in a horrible way.

Maria passes through a shadowy pair of overturned dumpsters. Before I can do the same, a single white limb extends from the shadows between us.

A figure emerges. It's a woman, maybe five foot six, with dark blonde hair. She moves slowly. Lithe. Confident. Like a living human being, which—I realize moments later—she is not.

Gore is matted into her hair, and her fingers are red with blood. Moreover, it's freezing and snowing, but she's wearing a green sun dress. She does not appear to shiver.

"Maria!" I call. She wheels on her feet and ducks just in time as the zombie claws for the back of her head.

"Move, dumbass! I'll hit you!" Maria cries back.

I fall to my stomach and take a face full of snow.

Ka-POW! Ka-POW!

Maria puts two bullets into the zombie's skull. It falls motionless to the snow. Wary of repeating the ordeal with the overweight, diapered woman, I quickly roll away to avoid contact. It's the right move. The dead woman's head comes to rest in the place where my body had been moments ago. Her green eyes stare up into the darkness. I watch a single snowflake land on her pupil. It does not melt; her eyes are very cold.

"Any others?" Maria asks, peering all around us, brandishing her weapon.

I look around the lonely dumpsters and strewn trash. I see nothing.

"Nope," I say, rising to my feet and dusting myself off.

"C'mon, let's get out of here," Maria says. "Camouflage works both ways. I don't think the zombies use it on purpose, but they still use it."

We hurry through the remaining dumpsters and head toward the buildings beyond.

★ ★ ★

Maria's aunt lives in a Chicago-style bungalow. Between Frank Lloyd Wright, the legions of skyscrapers in the Loop, and the Prairie School, the bar for architecture in Chicago is pretty high. Which makes bad, uninspired, boring architecture—like every Chicago-style bungalow ever built—stand out all the more starkly. As is typical of houses on the city's south side, all of the windows are barred. Even from a distance, I can see that the front door has three or four locks on it.

As we draw closer to the yellowish-brown house, what stands out are not the bars and locks. Rather, it's the very large man waiting outside the front door. His arms are crossed, and he looks up and down the block every few moments. He is not trying to conceal his presence. He looks like he is here for a reason. There is nobody else on the street.

"Do you know him?" I whisper to Maria. We huddle in the shadows of a garage across the street.

"Never seen him before."

"He doesn't look armed."

"He's armed."

"But I don't see—"

"He's armed."

I rub my chin and wonder what to do.

"What's he doing in front of your aunt's house?"

"That's the question, doye," she shoots back. "And I think the best way to answer it is from a position where he can't shoot me. I don't think he's a friend of my dad's. I don't think my dad would post somebody outside like that."

"No?"

"No," insists Maria. "It's supposed to be secret that we both know to meet at this place. A dude out front just attracts attention."

"We could get the drop on him."

"Um . . . I think *I* could," Maria says, looking me up and down. "Do you mind being the diversion?"

"Huh?"

Maria proposes a scenario in which I get the large man's attention while she sneaks up from behind. I'm the bait. I'm the one he's going to see.

And, I mean, *maybe* I'm right about the gun thing. *Maybe* this guy is unarmed. There's no way to tell from here.

The real question is if I'm man enough to do this.

I decide that I am.

Maria slinks into the shadows and takes a circuitous route to the back of the house. She is unobserved by the man. A few moments later, I step out of the darkened garage and begin to stride across the street. The man notices me after just two steps.

He is perhaps thirty, black, and wears a stocking cap on his head. He also wears a slightly puffy North Face coat. He's also huge. As I get closer, I can tell it's not just the cut of the coat—this guy is built. He has a v-shaped torso and very large arms. For an instant, I feel protected by my AK. Then his hand flies to his hip, where a gun is sequestered.

"Hey there," I say with a smile. I try to give off the vibe of neighbor coming outside to commiserate about a power outage. (But instead of flashlights we carry guns, and instead of waiting for the electric company are waiting for…who the fuck knows.) I keep a smile on my face and approach slowly. If he's used to guns at all—which I am not—he's almost definitely going to be able to draw and fire before I can even correctly shoulder my AK…and I'm not even sure it has any bullets left.

The man does not smile. He frowns and cocks his head to the side. His fingers dance above his pocket like a typist working an invisible keyboard.

Oh fuck, I think. Where the hell is Maria?

Moments later I have my answer.

With the dusting of snow masking her lithe footfalls, Maria steals out from the shadows and creeps up behind the man. She takes exaggerated steps, like a cartoon character sneaking. I try not to look directly at her so the man won't notice. At the same time, anything that will keep him from deciding to shoot me sounds pretty good. Still, I manage to keep my line of sight mostly just straight ahead.

Maria reaches a spot directly behind the man. For an instant he seems to sense her presence and begins to turn his head. In that same instant, Maria presses the barrel of her gun into his ear. She looks supremely confident. Has she done this before, or is it just the primal need to find her family that lends such courage? Either way, it's pretty cool.

"Do not take even so much as a step," Maria says. "If you don't want to die, you're going to raise your hands right now."

The man obeys, blinking frantically and shrinking from Maria's gun like it's electrified. He has a look on his face like a losing coach whose team has just been defeated by a trick play.

"Who are you and what the fuck are you doing here?" Maria asks plainly when the man's hands are raised.

"Now hang on, hang on," he says.

He's cowering but still articulate. This is—I realize—probably much more than I would be in the same situation. I raise my own gun and hurry over.

"Where the *hell* is my father?"

"Lady, who's your—?" the man begins.

"Frankie Munoz," she clarifies. "Alderman Munoz."

The man's eyes shoot back and forth.

"I don't know where he is…but he's safe," the man insists. "Please. I work for the city council. I'm *supposed* to be here. Please."

"Why are you standing in front of my great-aunt's house?"

"The mayor died a few hours ago, out in Mt. Carmel Cemetery," the man says.

"Yeah," I say, piping up. "I saw it on TV."

"What does that have to do with my father?" Maria asks. She shoots me a daggered look, annoyed that I have interrupted her interrogation. She presses her gun deeper into the wincing man's ear.

"When the mayor dies in office, power shifts to the vice mayor," the cowering man explains. "He or she is in charge until the city council can elect a replacement."

"Vice mayor?" Maria asks skeptically. "Is that a real thing?"

"Actually, it is," I tell her. "They made the rule back in '76 after the first Mayor Daley died in office. There was this chaotic period of nobody in charge. It was bad. The city wanted to keep it from ever happening again, so they created a vice mayor's job. But Jesus, it's such an obscure post. I'd forgotten all about it myself. The vice mayor has no real powers or duties. The mayor appoints him or her. It's usually a member of the city council— some alderman—right?"

Even as the words are leaving my mouth, I guess what has happened.

Then Maria confirms it.

"It's my dad, isn't it?"

She lowers her gun.

"Yes," the man says soberly. "Your father is the new mayor of Chicago."

★ ★ ★

"Well, doesn't this beat all," Maria says to herself. "We finally got a Hispanic mayor in Chicago. And all it took was a zombie apocalypse."

We ride in the back of the man's SUV. Perhaps because he is the bearer of good news—that her dad is alive and the mayor—or perhaps because he is an enormous, hulking presence she can hide behind, Maria seems completely taken with this friendly giant, which, even in these strange and dire circumstances, depresses me.

The large man says he's taking us somewhere safe, but I notice that now he's driving back in the direction of Crenshaw Cemetery. This makes me nervous.

"What else do you know?" I ask him. "I mean, about what's going on. The last few hours have been crazy, and I only saw the TV broadcasts for a few minutes."

I'm genuinely curious about the state of the city, but I'm also hoping that when this guy speaks more he'll turn out to be dumb. And that Maria will notice this and be disenchanted with the galoot. (And man, I'm still thinking that if—and it's a big "if"—there's some way this zombie outbreak is confined to Chicago, I'm going to write the best story ever. I've got a front seat to city history...or at least a backseat. They're going to add a fifth star to the city flag to commemorate this. I'm gonna be the one who was there to witness the transition of power. You want to know what happened after the mayor got eaten? How his daughter found out? Here, let me write you that story.)

"The city council is convening informally at the Harold Washington Cultural Center," he says. "The Loop's too dangerous."

Damn. He said "convening informally" which doesn't seem like a dumb-guy phrase.

"Some alderman just put the word out informally," he adds. "We've sent runners to just about every district to let people know."

He used "informally" again. Maybe it's his go-to word. His one smart-person phrase (like that local financier who begins every other sentence with "Quite candidly...").

"What about my dad?" Maria says.

"We've..." the man begins awkwardly, then starts over. "Last I heard, somebody had a line on him. He may already be at the Cultural Center when we get there. Every effort is being made to loop him in and keep him safe."

"Okay," says Maria. "I've got another question. Do you know anything about city employees shooting up and burning the zombies in Crenshaw Cemetery?"

The man visibly flinches and then stops the car.

"What are you—" I start to say. Then I see.

On the dark street in front of us—by a row of cheap-looking shops selling hair-care products—ten or so zombies are lumbering toward a very old woman with a cane. The woman is wrapped in several layers against the chill and swinging her cane over her head like a battle axe. She is waiting for the zombies.

Our driver springs from his seat and takes an automatic handgun from his pocket. He strides toward the zombies with no hesitation. "No ma'am," he shouts. "It doesn't have to end like this!" Maria and I look at each other, wondering if we should follow.

The zombies notice him when he's about fifteen feet away. They are a motley and mottled crew that has obviously fed once already. Their mouths are red with blood. Some look like iced-over cadavers from the lake. Others bear the marks of rot in the ground—a horrible black *matter* that clings to their bones where healthy flesh should be.

"Hey zombies, what's up?" he says brightly. And opens fire.

He's a good shot. Like Maria (and unlike me), he can hit the zombies right in the forehead most of the time. When about half the zombies are returned to the ground, his gun goes "click, click." He immediately stops and changes clips. The old woman—who has not yet lowered her cane—looks on in wonder. She has been snatched from the jaws of certain death and doesn't know how to feel about it.

The second clip is in his gun. He continues to fire. The remaining zombies are confused. Some of them charge the shooter, but he backpedals easily and they never much close on him. A couple of his shots miss their mark—at one point, I see an ear fly off and go twirling through the air like a seed pod on its way to the ground—but most of the time he hits home. In less than two minutes, all of the zombies are dead…again.

"You okay, Mrs. Watson?" he asks when the last zombie is still. The woman nods.

"Where you headed?" he presses. "It's not safe to be out."

"My place is right here," she says, indicating a nearby apartment building with her cane.

"We'll wait," he says.

The three of us watch as she shuffles to her doorway, takes out a jangly ring of keys from her purse, and lets herself inside.

"All right then," she shouts back, and disappears inside the building. Only then does our driver return to the SUV. Maria looks up at him, and I can see from her expression that all that pick-up artist bullshit about women wanting dominant protectors is not actually bullshit at all, and that I have lost her to him for good. As he starts up the SUV and we continue the drive, I console myself with the fact that I still have the story. Still have my Pulitzer, right? And I'm still not dead from zombies.

As we drive, I try to remember who I am. I start to think like a reporter. I need the who, what, when, where, and why.

Start with the who.

"Nice work out there," I tell our driver. "Say, I didn't even get your name yet."

"Oh," he says. "Sorry. It's Shawn Michael. Shawn Michael Recinto."

Leopold Mack

It's well past midnight when I run into Kurdy Jakes.

I'm making my way back to The Church of Heaven's God in Christ Lord Jesus as carefully as I can. I try to stick to the side streets and stay in the shadows. Now and then cars whiz past, but it's impossible to tell if they're friend or foe. Certainly, I see no police, fire, or emergency vehicles. I glimpse a couple of possible zombies but leave them in the dust.

At one point, I pass Jackson Park Hospital. They've got three armed men stationed outside—two of whom are still wearing their stethoscopes. They look like exhausted medical interns and carry expressions of "I never expected being a doctor to be easy, but Jesus Christ..." If any place has generators, it's a hospital. Keep out the zombies and criminals, and they should be okay. Even if the power grid fails, they'll be all right for a while. (The local pharmacies—in stark contrast—appear to have been the first hit by drug-seeking looters. I pass no less than four smashed-in Walgreens and CVS stores. The $9-an-hour security guards have long since abandoned their posts, which is the right decision, if you ask me.)

Anyhow, I run into Jakes at the entrance to Valenwood Cemetery. It's a smaller burying-ground located between two old brownstones. Real estate speculators who don't know the neighborhood drive by and stop their cars, thinking there might be a swath of undeveloped land to buy. Then they see the few headstones and monuments—displayed in awkward rows like teeth that need dentistry—and get back into their cars and drive away.

Valenwood is old and not taking many new applicants from what I hear. (These days, to have someone interred there, you pretty much have to have a family plot . . . which is what Kurdy Jakes has.)

Even if you know about it, you tend to forget about Valenwood.

Kurdy is sitting out front. He has brought a folding chair out onto the sidewalk and is seated—a rifle at the ready—facing into the cemetery. He has also brought a thermos of steaming coffee, which rests next to him on the ground.

I did the service when Teddy Jakes, his son, was shot in a drive-by. It happened about a year ago. Teddy was out with his friends one summer night and didn't know one of the friends had insulted a gang member. Teddy was standing in the wrong place at the wrong time. Somebody drove by and popped off twelve shots. Wouldn't you know, they missed their intended target and got Teddy.

"Kurdy," I shout. "It's Pastor Mack."

He looks in my direction. I expect the expression on Kurdy's face to be somewhere between grim determination and outright horror—he is, after all, watching over the same burying ground where his own son's interred. Instead, he looks bemused, even slaphappy. (Maybe it's Irish coffee inside that Thermos.)

"Yo pastor!" he calls back warmly. His smile is broad and gentle.

I saunter over.

Kurdy relaxes in his chair, but doesn't rise. He looks at ease and convivial, as if I have spotted him fishing in Lake Michigan and not gunning for the undead in a zombie outbreak. He doesn't feel dangerous . . . but I still wish I had my shotgun.

"So…" I begin awkwardly.

What do you say to a man who is waiting to kill the zombie of his own dead son?

"Beat all, don't it Pastor?"

"You got that right," I tell him. "I never expected the dead to rise. And they're not just 'the dead,' are they? They're our own family members over whom we still grieve."

Kurdy looks left and right, as if I am missing the point.

"Yeah Pastor…" he begins cautiously. "These zombies certainly *do* pose a curiosity. But I was thinkin' more along the lines of ol' Mystian Morph over there."

"Mystian Morph?" I say. "What's he got to do with…"

Kurdy indicates the cemetery with a poke of his rifle.

I look into the field of headstones. There are three or four dead zombies splayed here and there, but what catches my attention is a man wielding a meat cleaver and leaning against a very large monument. He is wearing a suit, and his arms are folded.

"Jesus help us," I say when I realize what I'm seeing.

Mystian Morph is a local businessman and politician, proud of himself for holding a variety of positions in banking and state government. Most people hadn't heard of him until he got appointed by the old governor to fill a U.S. Senate seat. Among other things, Morph was famous for spending a small fortune on a fancy mausoleum for himself. (A mausoleum—I now remember—located here in Valenwood.) On the wall of the mausoleum is inscribed a list of Morph's accomplishments, and above them the legend "TRAIL BLAZER." Which, of course, should be one word, not two.

Most importantly, unlike the zombies stalking through the cemetery grounds, Mystian Morph is very much alive.

"I came here first to watch for my son," says Kurdy quietly. "He come up—just as I thought he might—and I put him back down. I wanted to be the one to do it, y'see? When he come out the ground, I looked him hard in the eyes. That wasn't him anymore. That was some other thing."

"Amen," I say with a nod, putting my hand on Kurdy's shoulder. "You did what had to be done."

"But no sooner do I finish," Kurdy continues with a laugh, "than ol' Mystian Morph shows up with his little cleaver and sets down next to his gravestone."

"What's he getting at?" I wonder softly. Morph is well within earshot.

"Hey Mr. Morph!" Kurdy calls out, cupping a hand to his mouth. "What you getting at over there?"

Morph appears not to have heard. I look at Kurdy, who gives me an expression that says "Just wait."

Then we hear him.

"I'm protecting what's mine!" Morph nearly screams. "This is my legacy! My legacy! I'm not going to let any *damn zombie* upset what I've worked for."

Really?—I think to myself. He's out here like this so that zombies don't overturn his misspelled headstone and its list of middling accomplishments?

"Ain't like he Martin Luther King," Kurdy quietly offers from the side of his mouth, evidently thinking along the same lines that I am.

"Yeah," I reply with a chuckle. "Seems like Martin Luther King was Martin Luther King. Mystian Morph feels more like a yes-man and corrupt Illinois politician who accidentally lucked his way up the ladder ... and then spent all his money to buy a giant gravestone."

Kurdy laughs in agreement.

"Pastor, I think you hit the nail on the head."

Yet, there he stands. Insane. Implacable. Determined to protect his "trail blazing" for future generations to see. Illinois's own Ozymandias.

"I can't just let him die," Jakes declares. "You see a person this crazy...*this* pitiful and insane...you got to help them. It's the Christian thing to do."

Again Jakes reads my thoughts. My shameful thoughts. Namely, that a zombie apocalypse would be a good time to let a man like Mystian Morph get what he deserved. That letting him die might be the *first* step to setting things right again. (Bad pastor. Bad pastor. Bad pastor.)

"Doesn't Mystian have a wife?" I ask, remembering this important fact.

"Heh," says Kurdy. "He sure do. Who you think brought me this coffee? It's good, too. You want a sip?"

I politely decline.

"He ain't doin' shit with that meat-cutter," Kurdy continues. "I shot three zombies so far rose up and come after him. *So far.* I sure wish he'd leave. But just you watch . . . he'll stay, and soon there'll be another."

Kurdy cups his hands to his mouth again.

"You need to get yourself on out of there, Mr. Morph! You need to go home to your wife."

Morph mumbles back something under his breath. The only word I catch is "legacy."

"You're a good man," I tell Kurdy. "Here I was worried about you having to see your son again… and you're trying to save the life of somebody that . . . well . . . most folks wouldn't put first on their list at a time like this."

Kurdy shakes his head and looks at the ground.

"Losing a son is hard," he says softly. "After that, a bunch of damn zombies ain't nothing."

Maria Ramirez

Okay, so do I need to tell you that sometimes a girl likes the wrong kind of man? Because sometimes a girl likes the wrong kind of man.

And people try to make it like we don't know. Like the guy has been all…deceptive. Like we're all innocent, and we've been tricked into following a man who is no damn good for us. But please, we *know* he is no damn good for us. We just want him anyway.

That was the kind of vibe I got from Shawn Michael.

I could tell a mile away that something was up with this dude. My creeper-senses were tingling, sure. But other parts of me were tingling too. That was the problem. And the way he jumped out of the car and shot up those zombies like out of an action movie? Hot damn.

Let's just say a girl wants what a girl wants…

★ ★ ★

By the time the SUV pulls up to the front of the Harold Washington Cultural Center, I am already undressing Shawn Michael with my eyes. (His body is unreal. Like a sculpture from olden-times or something.) But I'm still getting, you know, the creep-factor. The way he shot those zombies tells me he done things with a gun before. Probably, the best-case scenario is former military. As for the worst-case…well…I'm not excited to think about it.

The Cultural Center—like Mack's church—has apparently become a rallying place. It's a large, modern building with an indoor theatre that has twice as many seats as The Church of

Heaven's God in Christ Lord Jesus. Also, there just isn't much else in the surrounding neighborhood. If you were looking for a gathering place, you'd probably go here.

This part of Bronzeville is desolate and bare—and just plain boring, if you don't find the possibility of being mugged "interesting," which I don't. A few years ago, the city tried to clean up and fix this neighborhood. They started with an official decree designating it a "Blues District" because it had had blues bars in it fifty years before. It was in all the papers. They put up fancy streetlights with silhouettes of blues musicians on them and built this giant cultural center. It was supposed to convince people from other parts of the city to come down and spend money and turn a swath of payday loan stores and fried fish shacks into respectable businesses. Maybe actual blues clubs. It didn't work.

The neighborhood stayed lousy and barren. No tourists came. One blues club opened, but it burned down under suspicious circumstances. An ex-alderman was brought in to run the Cultural Center. She gave her kids jobs there and mismanaged it to near-death before they finally wrested it away from her. These days, it's only open a few days a week. Mostly, it hosts community events, traveling shows, and second-rate standup comedians.

Tonight though, Chris Rock might as well be headlining.

Cars are parked up and down the block, and the Cultural Center is lit up in all its glory. People stand all around the building—some armed, some not. There are even a couple of uniformed police, praise Jesus. In a few places, dead zombies have been piled together—not giant stacks or anything, but groups of two or three. Around the periphery of this outpost of civilization, men with drawn weapons patrol at the edges of the darkness.

For the first time since seeing that Slayer-shirt zombie in the parking garage, I start to calm down. I start to feel like somehow things are going to work out. I'm with a big strong man who has taken me to a place that almost looks like civilization, a place with people who know where my father and mother and sister are. It's not perfect, but I'm well aware that it's more than I should hope for in a zombie outbreak. More than a lot of people will get tonight.

This feeling washes over me. Thankful. That's it. I'm feeling really, really thankful.

Shawn Michael tries to find a parking spot that doesn't block somebody in. (He's so considerate.) Ben sits quietly, looking around. Actually, he looks unhappy. He has this expression on his face like he's just smelled something bad. I think he can sense that he's just been outmanned. That a real, take-charge dude is now present.

Shawn Michael pulls to a halt in the parking lot of a restaurant across the street from the Cultural Center.

"I'm gonna go let them know I've found you," Shawn Michael says. Then, like an afterthought, he adds, "I'll check to see if they've gotten in touch with your father yet. I mean, maybe he's there already. If he's not, I'll see that they drive you to his location."

SLAM goes the door. Shawn Michael runs toward the brightly lit Cultural Center, waving at the men with guns. They recognize him and wave back, mostly in a way that seems deferent.

A protector. A leader. The guy they look to to handle shit in a crisis.

Yes you are, Mr. Shawn Michael. Yes indeed you are.

Oh my God, can you please just fuck me right now?

Then out of nowhere, Ben says, "We have to get out of here. We have to leave before he gets back!"

Fucking spoilsport.

"What are you *talking about*?"

Ben's face is a mask of terror. For some reason, it makes me think of a little kid being taken in to get his first shot. Like everything, everywhere in the doctor's office could hurt him. It's that pure, paranoid terror you don't often see in adults. Especially not in grown-ass men.

"We need to go," he insists, opening his door. "C'mon."

"No! What's wrong with you? They know where my dad is. He might even be inside."

"These are the same men from the cemetery where they were burning the bodies," Ben says, whispering now that the car door is open.

"What...*all these people*?" I ask.

"No, but some of the ones standing outside with the guns definitely are," Ben replies. "*You* weren't looking into the graveyard, okay? *You* didn't see them. *I* did—and I'm telling you, these are some of the same guys who were trying to kill us."

"Ben, they know where my dad is," I insist. "My mother and sister are with my dad. They're all I care about right now. See how it works?"

"Maria, this feels *really* bad to me," Ben says, making one final pitch. (He's appealing to my feelings. Trying to get me to make a "heart" decision and not a "head" one. [What he doesn't know is that there's another part of my body making a pretty strong case that I should stay around and try to get some time alone with Shawn Michael.])

"Well it feels the opposite to me," I tell him. "All these people are here. There's cops, even. It feels totally safe. The men with guns are just keeping the zombies away, which frankly I'm sick of doing myself."

Ben pauses and looks at me for a moment. Looks me up and down. But it's not creepy. It's kind of sad. I realize he is saying goodbye.

He exits the SUV, closes the door without a word, and races madly into the night.

Ben Bennington

Gah!

Out of the frying pan and into to the fire. Is that the expression? That certainly feels right. My God! My fucking God!

I race down the snow-slick streets away from the Cultural Center as fast as my legs will carry me. I have no idea where I'm going. All I know is that the people Shawn Michel took us to are the same ones who tried to kill us. Murderers. And Maria is letting them have her. Serving herself up.

How could this happen?

They say you're supposed to be careful what you wish for, because you might get it. As I jog—badly, slowly—along the sidewalk leading away from the Cultural Center, it strikes me like a crossbow bolt to the chest that I may have gotten exactly what I wished for.

I knew Illinois was a state filled with fakers and losers. With self-interested politicians who had long ago sold their souls to the first bidder. With men and women who had marinated in the filth and corruption for so long that it no longer felt like corruption (and only a little like filth). It was just Illinois, just Chicago, the way things were done. So you did it; you got your money, and you moved on.

I knew they would suck and be terrible in a disaster...and I was right.

And it is, as I'm beginning to realize, little consolation.

I stop jogging for a moment and let out a deep sigh.

To win the Pulitzer for my exposé of this shit, I first have to live through it. As of this moment, that's the only project left.

★ ★ ★

I can't jog all the way north to the Loop…or south to Indiana. (Are Hoosiers better prepared than Illinoisans for a zombie outbreak? Maybe they have their own set of problems…)

Even though I'm fueled by terror, I'm well aware that I'll start to flag before long. Compounding this, it's fucking winter. I need to find shelter and heat eventually, or I will die. The zombies will have a frozen Bensickle on which to feast.

A few blocks away from the Harold Washington Cultural Center I encounter a caved-in cop car—smoldering, and with the charred skeleton of a policeman inside. I stop to rest and put my hand on the hood. Still warm. I wonder if the charred CPD officer is going to reanimate and come after me. For the moment, he remains still.

Without warning, a mangy white van comes screeching down the street. It's got one headlight out, and its bald tires are for shit on the snowy streets. It weaves precariously back and forth.

I move around the side of the police car-husk, instinctively wanting to put something between myself and the oncoming van. As it turns out, my efforts at self-preservation are premature.

Before it's halfway down the block, the van veers fatally into a mail drop box, which explodes in a shower of white letters. The snowy street is covered with mail. The van's driver explodes out of the driver's side door. He is naked to the waist and not wearing shoes. He takes off running down the street. He goes right past me.

"Aaaaaaaaahhhhhhhhhhhhh!" he screams as he passes.

I watch him race off into the darkness.

Then there is a noise. I turn around—back to the van—and see movement. I squint to get a better look.

A zombie emerges from the van. It is the most awkward zombie I have ever seen. Its arms are bound with rope and its mouth is taped shut with electrical tape. It shuffles awkwardly, like a worm trying to walk upright.

A moment later there is a KRA-KACK! And the zombie's forehead explodes. Two men in puffy winter jackets emerge from the shadows behind an abandoned bank. They both carry shotguns. I watch as they enter the van and begin to look through it.

They have to see me. I'm exposed by a cop car. How can they not see me?

Then I realize that they do see me. They probably saw me before the van drove up. They just don't care.

The illusion, I realize, is that these dark streets mean that I am alone.

The neighborhood may look empty, but eyes are everywhere.

★ ★ ★

I head vaguely northwest—away from the Lake and the people who tried to kill me but toward what…I'm not sure. I pass a small city graveyard called Valenwood. A smiling man carrying a folding chair and a Thermos is walking the other way. He has a rifle slung over his shoulder and gives me a friendly salute when we pass. I salute back.

When I get even with the graveyard, there is a horrible sight. A man in a suit is being pulled apart by several zombies.

One zombie has worked a giant strip of skin off his forehead with its teeth. Two others are chewing on one hand each. At first I think the victim is completely dead, but then I see his leg twitching spastically like a scratching dog. Something's still alive in there, if only nerve fibers. Dear God, it looks awful.

A couple of the zombies look up from their carnival to size me up. I cross the street and quicken my pace. For the moment, they leave me alone and stick with the sure thing.

I merge back onto Martin Luther King Drive and soon reach 35th Street where an ancient monument to African-American soldiers hunkers in the center of the intersection. A black soldier in a doughboy helmet stands resolutely atop a pillar. He holds a rifle and faces south, on the lookout. But the Kaiser is long dead. Tonight, he's looking out for zombies.

At the base of the monument stand three men in winter jackets…all armed with rifles. Two are drinking coffees from Styrofoam Dunkin' Donuts cups. They look approachable and friendly but keep their eyes on my gun.

I point my AK at the ground and give them a wave. They cautiously return it, searching my face to see if they recognize me. (This neighborhood, called Bronzeville, is about ninety-nine percent African American. There are a few white folks who live down here, but if you live here you probably recognize most of them on sight.)

As I get closer, I see two bodies—possibly human, possibly zombie—piled at the foot of the monument. The bodies are not dressed for the chill. Zombies.

"You keepin' it safe out here?" one of the men asks when I draw within earshot.

"Trying to," I say wearily.

"Where you comin' from?" another asks.

"The Cultural Center," I say, hooking my thumb to point back down MLK.

"How did it look?"

"No zombies," I answer. "A lot of people."

"A lot of assholes," says one of the men from atop his coffee.

"Yeah," I answer, and laugh. "That's right! How did you know?"

The other men laugh too.

"Let's just say we backed the wrong candidate in the last aldermanic election," says one of them. "The one who didn't meet with gang leaders and didn't have a criminal record. Don't know if we'd be welcome down there right now."

There is an awkward pause as the men consider this grim reality.

"Where you headed, son?" another asks me.

"North…I think."

The men smile.

"Keep it safe," says one of them.

"Believe me," I tell them, "I'm trying."

A few blocks to the north, there's an on-ramp that leads up to the network of roads leading away from the city. The giant raised highway lurches across the top of MLK. The roads go north to Milwaukee, south to Indiana, and west out to the suburbs. These are the central arteries that pump the commuters into and out of Chicago every day. Food, materials, tourists—all of the things a city needs to live come through here.

But not today.

To say that these asphalt arteries are now "clogged" would be a ridiculous understatement. Neither can I accurately describe the scene before me as "a parking lot," for parking lots—even during the height of a midnight madness Christmas sale— generally maintain some semblance of order and organization. What I see here is closer to a pile-on. The result of a lawless scramble to be the first to get out of Dodge. The highways are utterly blocked.

The almost archeological layering of the rows of trapped cars makes it possible for me to envision exactly how it happened. First, the two or three lanes of traffic crawled to a halt and then stopped completely. Then other folks said 'heck with it,' and drove on the shoulder, creating another lane of traffic...which then also became completely clogged to a halt. Then, the small space that was still left between the cars on the shoulder and the concrete divider got filled by brave or terrified souls whose small cars or motorcycles were just narrow enough to squeeze in. Then people started driving on the landscaping. Commuters in the central lane found themselves pinned in on both sides by two or three cars. That's when, from the look of things, they went crazy and began ramming the cars around them in a frantic attempt to get out. Going forward and backward was not possible. They were trapped. The only question became how long to wait before abandoning your vehicle . . . or attacking your neighbor.

What remains is a madness of immobile metal, smashed windows, and utter hopelessness. Though almost all of the cars are now empty, many of them have been left running (or at least left the lights on). What's scary is not the cars. What's scary is imagining the people who did this to the cars.

Just as I prepare to turn around and head the other way, something catches my eye. There is movement atop the expressway amongst the cars. Moments later, a zombie staggers into view. A zombie or a very injured person. (Please be a zombie. Please be a zombie.) Either way, the most merciful act may be to shoot it. Then it—she—stumbles into the beam of a headlight from a pinned-in pickup truck, and the horror becomes real.

It is not a zombie—just a woman in a brown coat with mussed hair and some kind of head injury. Her lipstick is smeared like a Hollywood portrayal of an insane woman. She's clearly not insane though, or wasn't until a few hours ago. She's cold. She's scared. She doesn't know what to do.

I lower my gun. I certainly can't kill her. Not even a mercy killing. Not even if she asked. Not even in a zombie apocalypse. Somehow I know this instantly.

She, however, apparently has no such compunction.

Just as I'm wondering if I should wave to her—or maybe shout hello—she stumbles to the edge of the overpass, legs it over the concrete railing, and jumps. The fall is an undignified one. Though the lady isn't fat, she falls like an overweight diver who has slipped at the last moment. She is all flopping coat and flailing arms. And finally…splat.

The fall is at least forty feet. Will it be enough to do her in?

Oh please. Oh please.

I stand and look at the mound of woman and coat for a while.

And it moves.

It twitches its fingers. A leg flexes and retracts.

I walk over to the lump. It's a zombie, I tell myself. She's already reanimated, and I need to put her down before she rises to her feet and comes to eat my brain.

I lower the AK and…click.

It *is* empty.

The leg twitches again.

Handgun. I have a handgun also. I took it off of the dead Secret Service officer and Islamic security guys.

I drop the AK and fumble into my pocket until I find the automatic. I'm not sure how to use it, but I'm guessing point and shoot. Those guys had been killing each other, so probably the safety is off.

Aaaaaaaaaaaaaaaaaaand…

BLAM!

It is.

The thing at my feet—zombie, woman, whatever—ceases to twitch. Did I hit the head or just the torso? The woman is such a mass of rags and hair that I can't even tell. I take a few deep breaths and replace the gun into my coat pocket.

Have I just put a fellow human out of her misery, or have I only killed another zombie?

I will never know.

Unless…

I dissolve into the shadows next to a pylon underneath the highway and watch the corpse from a distance. If it reanimates, that woman was still alive. If it doesn't, it was a zombie, and I killed it for a second time.

I give it a full five minutes before deciding I can walk away. Then, when I do, I hear a noise behind me like someone slopping a wet mop onto a floor.

I don't look back.

Leopold Mack

My God. What a sight.

When it comes into view, I'm rendered almost breathless.

The Harold Washington Cultural Center is lit up like a beacon. A beautiful, glowing beacon. Here are people! Here is humanity! Heaven be praised!

I've never seen the Cultural Center so crowded. It didn't even look like this at the grand opening—the sight of which is the only thing I can compare it to. But the grand opening wasn't quite this crowded. Neither did it have a perimeter of armed guards, huddled masses of cold people waiting to get inside, nor frowning men with crossed arms preventing this influx from happening.

And…unless my eyes deceive me…

Neither did it have Shawn Michael Recinto walking inside, arm-in-arm with Maria Ramirez.

★ ★ ★

"How's is it with you, my son?" I say to the giant man at the door.

He doesn't look like a regular church attendee, but neither does he look like a murderer. Somewhere in between. Let's say… bouncer at a strip club.

I look up into the man's face. (I'm pretty tall, but this guy is taller. Also fat. Very fat. That kind of fat where you start to look Asian because your cheeks are pushing up and your brows are pushing down.) He's like a Buddha statue that somehow has real, human eyes. They roll in their sockets of fat and eventually train on me. The heavy brow furrows as he sizes me up.

Who is this man—well dressed, in a pink tie and expensive suit—who acts like he's somebody?

"The councilmen are meeting inside," he says—a statement that wonders if I can legitimately claim to have anything to do with the proceedings. This is practiced rhetoric. I am dealing with a pro.

I play my first card.

"I'm Pastor Leopold Mack of The Church of Heaven's God in Christ Lord Jesus." I extend my hand so that he will shake it. He looks down at my beckoning glove. No other response.

I play my second card.

"I'm the personal spiritual advisor to Alderman Marja Mogk." This is a half-truth . . . maybe a quarter-truth. She has been to my church a couple of times, and I've seen her at events in the community. It's a safe bet that she's inside. (Where Shawn Michael Recinto is, Alderman Mogk is likely to also be.)

Nothing.

The man at the door may as well have turned to stone. A Buddha statue indeed.

"And I have a message for Alderman Mogk," I whisper confidentially. "*About Crenshaw Cemetery.*"

This is also a half-truth.

True or not, it is—apparently—the magic word. The large man remains expressionless but steps backward and pushes open the door for me. A frustrated and confused crowd looks on enviously as I am admitted to the inner sanctum.

What I see inside the lobby of the Harold Washington Cultural Center is . . . not what I am expecting. The mix of armed men and women is equal parts police officers, clergy, city officials, and gang members. And their families. It kind of looks like that footage you see on the news when commuters get trapped at O'Hare Airport overnight in a snowstorm. People are sleeping on improvised cots. Benches have been turned into beds. Clothing and luggage are everywhere.

Everybody looks at me when I walk inside. I try to appear as if I know where I am going. I unzip my coat and flash my suit and tie. The gaudy pink neckwear—that I had fumbled to conceal in the graveyard—is now the thing that will allow me to glide past unfettered.

And glide I do.

At the top of the grand staircase, I see Shawn Michael and Maria going through a doorway. Maria appears to be struggling. Shawn Michael shuts the door behind them.

I begin to climb the winding stairs when a voice as deep as my own booms.

"Pastor Mack!"

I turn and see the guard from the front door.

"Alderman Mogk is on the lower level," he says, regarding me with suspicion.

"Oh, thank you, my son."

The guard's face remains immovable. I slink back down the staircase and open the side door that leads to the reception and meeting rooms underneath the lobby. As I do, I take one last look at the door to the room that now holds Maria Ramirez.

After a quick, one-story elevator ride, I find myself in the network of passages and meeting rooms underneath the Cultural

Center. The hallways are clean and tidy, but also drab and functional. Not like the shining wood and glass above.

In the hallway before me is a cranky-looking man with a chrome revolver sticking out of his waistband. I smile at him broadly. He grudgingly steps aside, allowing me to pass.

I've been down here a couple of times for different events. (If my memory serves, there's a very large conference room at the end of this hallway.) The side rooms are filled with people, most of whom look like they work for the city. I smile at everyone and try to fit in.

The giant oak doors to the conference room come into view. Standing on either side are two large men wearing handguns. They look like thugs who work for aldermen—somebody else's Shawn Michael Recinto. They are chatting and smiling, but they face away from the door. (Whatever is happening inside, it's clear that somebody thinks it needs to be protected.) When they see me, they fall silent and begin to frown.

I make eye contact with the men—and wonder what the fuck I'm going to say to them—when suddenly the oak doors open slightly, and a young woman edges herself out as silently as she can. In her hands are a pen and a legal pad full of scribbles. She turns around, and I realize I know her.

Jessy Knowlton. She is a reporter for the *Chicago Defender*, Chicago's oldest and most venerable black newspaper. Jessy can't be older than twenty-five. She mostly does human interest stories—a high school football team's woe as a coach is lost to gang violence, a famous actor returns to his south side neighborhood to share the wealth, R. Kelly does . . . something—but I've also seen her at church-sponsored events around the community. She seems smart, and I like her. I also wonder what on earth she is doing here.

"Pastor Mack!" she says brightly, juggling her legal pad around so she can shake my hand.

"Jessy Knowlton. How are you...you know, considering?"

"I'm wonderful," she says, conducting me down the hall, away from the glowering guards. She walks me to a very small commissary with vending machines. It's empty except for us.

"This is incredible," Jessy says, galvanized. "Almost half of the city council is in that conference room. *All* of the south side aldermen and a few from other neighborhoods made it too. Apparently Aldermen Mogk and Szuter put the word out with street teams. Said that everyone should try to meet here because the roads are clogged up and it's impossible to get to the Loop. We had aldermen arriving by *bike*, but they still made it!"

"Crazy."

"Hang on," she says, holding up a notepad full of jottings. "The plot thickens! So the mayor got eaten by zombies. You knew that, right?"

I nod.

"Okay, so the power goes to the vice mayor, who is Frankie Munoz. You know Frankie, right? The south side alderman for that little Hispanic pocket? Anyhow, Munoz has gone insane. Fled the city and, apparently—Alderman Mogk thinks so, at least—taken a lot of city resources and cash with him. Mogk says she had a conversation with Munoz where he said 'Fuck you,

I'm leaving'—right before the phones went dead—but I can't verify that…yet. What I do know is that the city council and its lawyers are working to pass an emergency measure to give power to Alderman Mogk—make her the interim mayor."

"Can they do that without everybody present?"

"This zombie situation is pretty unprecedented, but yes, I think they can. Like I said, they've got almost half the city council in there, and more aldermen are showing up by the minute. This is historic. And it's a hell of a scoop!"

"You're…reporting on this?"

"Are you kidding? Of course I am!"

"They're *letting you*?"

"They *wanted* me to. Marja's people came and found me. It turns out she wants a record of all of it. And you know the best part?"

I shake my head, not seeing a "best part" anywhere.

"I'm the only reporter here!" Jessy beams. "There's nobody from the *Tribune*, the *Sun-Times, Brain's,* the *Crusader,* the *Hyde Park Herald*…nobody! This is the scoop of a generation, and it's all mine! At first I was like, 'This is a Pulitzer, easy!' But then I was like, 'No, aim higher, Knowlton. This is a book…or two.' Either way, I'm gonna pay off those J-school loans before I turn thirty. Hot damn!"

"I am, guardedly, happy for you," I respond as Jessy fumbles to activate a vending machine.

"So, look, I just left to get a cup of coffee. This is gonna be an all-nighter, and I want to be there for all of it. Every moment of what's going on in there is historic!"

A thought occurs to me.

"Jessy, did Alderman Mogk give you access to *everywhere* in the Cultural Center?" I ask, beginning to see an opportunity.

"I guess, yeah. She told all the big guys with guns I was with her. But see, I only *want* to be in that meeting room. That's where the action is."

"What if I told you there's another side to the story?" I say cautiously. "What if I know something that makes it an even bigger scoop?"

Coffee in hand, Jessy takes a glance down the hallway—back toward the oaken doors and the conference room.

But then she looks into my eyes and says, "I'm listening…"

Maria Ramirez

Believe it or not, the worst part is *not* the being tied to a chair like a damsel in distress from some goddamn B-movie. Neither is the betrayal. (I think of how excited I felt when Shawn Michael returned to the car. How I began to tell him that Ben had fucked off, and then having a gun stuck into my ribs, being disarmed, and being dragged inside. I thought, *A second ago I would have said yes to a quickie in a broom closet, and now you're dragging me around like a prisoner. This is definitely your loss, bub.*)

No. Instead, the worst part is the utter lack of explanation.

I'm sitting in this little storage room, tied to a chair with rope and with electrical tape over my mouth, and I have no clue what is going on. None! There is only one entrance, and Shawn Michael is standing in front of it, looking back at me. And that's it. That's all the information I have.

I regret not resisting more when he brought me inside the Cultural Center. All those people just accepted it when he pulled me upstairs. Maybe they're on his side—whatever's happening— but maybe they're not. Maybe I could have screamed for help.

I should have at least tried. I should have said *something*.

Now there is electrical tape over my mouth, and I can't say anything.

Fuck…

★ ★ ★

After what seems like forever, there's a knock at the door, and a thuggish-looking man in a blue blazer walks inside. He and Shawn

Michael stay by the door—maybe 15 feet away from me—and start to whisper. They think I can't hear them, but I can.

"What did she say?"

"He's got one other relative, out in Oak Park. He got to be there…if he ain't dead already."

"Fucking Oak Park. What do we do?"

"She says send a street team. Cars as far as you can. Then on foot. Or bicycles. Whatever it takes."

"I heard the highway's too clogged even for bicycles."

"Mmm hmm. She says go anyway. Make it look like a robbery. People might get curious when the CPD comes back. No shell casings they can trace. Use bats and knives if you can."

"Oh, I'm goin'?"

"Yes."

"And kill everybody?"

"Yes."

"So what's *she*, then?"

Both men look over at my taped mouth. I pretend not to pay attention.

"Insurance. Munoz won't come out and fight? You let him know we got his daughter."

"A'ight."

"She said you did real good with this, Shawn Michael. She said when this all over, maybe it's time for you to get a ward of your own. Be an alderman yourself. Maybe when they redraw the ward maps comin' up, there's one in there for you."

"A'ight den."

"A'ight."

The man in the blue blazer leaves.

Shawn Michael seems to relax a little. He takes out his phone. There is still no service—on cell or land lines—but he starts to play a video game. It is disgusting. In the car, he seemed like an articulate gentleman. I realize, now, that that was all an act. This is the real Shawn Michael.

I try hard not to cry. If he sees my makeup running, he will know that I have heard them. That I now understand why I am tied to a chair and what they plan to do with me.

Not knowing is no longer the hardest part. Now it's trying not to cry.

And trying to figure out how I'm going to kill Shawn Michael Recinto.

★ ★ ★

I'm doing a pretty good job of winning the war on crying—and imagining having Shawn Michael pinned down on some kind of medieval torture rack (where I can get at him easily, and make it really slow and painful)—when there is another knock at the door.

Shawn Michael looks like he's playing a game he can't pause. He frowns and sighs, annoyed. He opens the door with one hand, still clicking and dragging with the other.

Standing in the doorway is a woman I've never seen before. About my age, black, short hair, and conservative clothes with a yellow legal pad in her hand.

Is this another drone of Marja Mogk's? Will I hear more stories about plans to kill my family? I brace myself for whatever comes next. (I would give my life if it would save my mother and my sister. If I know anything for sure, I know that.)

"Hi there," the woman says.

"Mmm," says Shawn Michael, his eyes flitting up and back down to his screen.

"Alderman Mogk said I should talk to you." She looks past Shawn Michael and sees me tied to the chair.

"Mmm," Shawn Michael says again.

"Yeah, uh, here's the thing..." she stammers. At that moment the door cracks a fraction wider. And there, standing behind the visitor, is the unmistakable visage of Leopold Mack. I see him, and in the same moment, he sees me. His eyes go wide.

Before the mystery woman can say anything more, Mack kicks the door. It flies open—knocking the hulking Shawn Michel to his knees and making him drop his phone. Mack pounces on Shawn Michael, and the woman shuts the door behind them.

Wham! Wham! Wham!

Pastor Mack delivers three giant punches to Shawn Michael's face before the aldermanic henchman can right himself. The blows have unexpected ferocity. I hear the horrible muffled crunch as Shawn Michael's nose breaks.

The gal rushes over and begins to untie me. Mack hovers over Shawn Michael with a raised fist. He's like Ali in that famous photo, wondering if the prone man deserves a final shot. Shawn Michael is not unconscious but curls in on himself like a broken insect. His hands are trying to shield his nose, which is now a centimeter or two out of place. In the end, Mack decides on a kick to the ribs instead. A hard one. Shawn Michael bucks ferociously and then lies still.

The young woman frees my hands from the ropes. I rip the duct tape from my mouth myself.

"Yeeeaugh," I scream. "What the fuck is this!?!?"

"Quiet," says Mack, pointing at me. "There's a damn army on the other side of that door."

Mack turns to the woman unbinding my legs.

"Jessy, this is the one I told you about. His daughter."

I look at Mack and wrinkle my nose.

"You...know about my dad?"

Mack nods.

"You never said anything before."

"It never came up. Let's just say I might have wanted to know about you after you convinced my daughter to leave her family and friends. I might have done a little asking around about *you* . . . "

"Hooooooo," moans Shawn Michael from his curled ball in the corner.

Mack pivots and gives him another quick kick to the belly.

"Quiet, you," he barks. Then, to me, "This one killed the caretaker at Crenshaw."

"Why?" I say, freeing myself from the remaining ropes. "What the fuck are these people up to?"

"I'm not sure, but I think they aim to steal the city."

"They want to kill my father," I hiss, rising to my feet. My legs hurt and my mouth feels dry.

"This is Jessy Knowlton," Mack says, indicating the woman with him. "She's a reporter for the *Defender*. She might know how they plan to do it."

"Your father is Frankie Munoz, the legitimate mayor?" Jessy asks. I nod.

"My God," she says. "What a scoop!"

"We need to get out of here, guys," Mack says. He reaches down into the curled ball that is Shawn Michael and comes away with a Glock.

The idea sinks in.

"How do we get past all those people in the lobby…and then all the ones outside?" I ask.

Mack checks the safety on the pistol, and then points it at me.

"You're going out the same way you came in," Mack says. "With a gun in your back."

We exit the storage room and stand at the top of the staircase like royalty waiting to be announced. We look down into the mass of humanity below us. It has not changed. If anything, it has swelled. Police, city officials, and armed citizens mill about or talk confidentially. Through the Cultural Center's windowed walls we can see that there is a massive crowd outside the building— hoping perhaps to be admitted inside, or only to be told that somebody is in control.

"Struggle," Mack whispers to me. "Look at me like I just kicked your dog."

With that, the pastor sticks the Glock into my side. Hard.

Fucker.

The scowl that crosses my face is not manufactured.

We head down the staircase toward the crowded first floor. Mack and I take the lead, with Jessy following. All eyes are on us. Mack wears the expression of a teacher who has just caught the most notorious delinquent tagging the walls of the gym for a third time. He keeps the gun in my ribs. Once, when I stumble on the stairs, he pulls me up by my hair.

Most folks seem bemused. They look at Mack's scowl—and his manhandling of me—and smile to one another. A couple of young men look like they want to intercede on my behalf, argue for gentler treatment of the prisoner. Mack stares them down.

We reach the first floor of the Harold Washington Cultural Center and head toward the front door, where a giant man is standing guard. I'm acutely aware of each *tick-tack, tick-tack* of our shoes on the floor. Each step is one closer to freedom, yet it still feels like—at any moment—these curious faces might train their weapons on us and fire. Or just rip us apart with their hands. It is like something out of a dream.

We reach the giant man and the exit he guards. For a moment, I wonder if he's on our side. He says, "Pastor Mack" and opens the door for us. But then there is a commotion from behind us. People are muttering, and I hear one: "Oh my God!" I turn and risk a glance (before Mack rights me forcefully) and see Shawn Michael standing at the top of the staircase with blood running down his shirt. With one hand, he holds his nose. With the other, he is gesturing in our direction.

"Whoa," says the giant guard, stoically extending a huge, meaty leg to block our exit.

Without missing a beat, Mack takes the gun from out of my back and shoots him in the kneecap.

The weapon's report is deafening as it bounces around the frosted glass windows of the Cultural Center. It is followed by screams of alarm. The giant man goes down, gripping his leg like an NFL lineman with a hammie. His moan, however, is otherwordly, like a wounded ox.

"Run, you idiots!" Mack shouts.

Dropping all pretense of captor and hostage, we sprint through the door and head into the crowd beyond. The reporter follows us. Mack is surprisingly fast. He's also tall, so the people crowded around see him coming and move aside. Mostly. A couple end up tasting his shoulder. They fall reeling to the landscaping below.

Other people are running too—away from us, or just away from the sound of the gunshot. After a few tense moments, we get through the crowd and into the street.

"This way," Mack calls, taking us north up MLK along the sidewalk.

We still face a perimeter of watchmen. They patrol the intersection around the Cultural Center. At least one of them is dead ahead of us, carrying a rifle and wearing an orange cap. He's heard the shot but is looking past us, sniffing the air, trying to figure out what is going on.

Suddenly, there is a *KA-POW, KA-POW, KA-POW* from behind us.

A man emerges from the crowd, chasing us and firing a handgun.

"There!" he shouts, gesturing to us. "Stop those people!"

Mack veers off into the shadows by a row of parked cars. We follow. The man with the rifle raises his weapon and shoots it twice. There is a terrifying *P-PING* as one of the bullets ricochets near us.

We duck down behind the cars. Mack motions for us to keep moving. We creep north, using the shadowed row of cars as cover. More shouts of alarm arise from the Cultural Center.

Mack reaches the end of the row and stops. I join him, and we survey the grim landscape before us. We've edged past the confused guards, but just barely. And they're looking for us. We're by no means safe.

To our right is a row of shuttered three flats, without yards or alleyways between them. They might as well be a castle's impenetrable façade. To our left is an open boulevard, streetlights, and a few thin trees. No cover at all. That would be the worst place to run. That leaves north, where there are—yes—clusters of trees and a few more cars, but it's going to be very spotty in some sections in terms of things to hide behind. We'll have to sprint from shadow to shadow.

Mack, who has also reached this conclusion, whispers, "We'll head for the cars up ahead. Get behind that Toyota. If they still don't see us, try to make it behind that heap of recycling dumpsters. You see where I mean?"

Then, behind us, Jessy says, "Ben Bennington?"

Mack and I look at her.

"There!" Jessy says, gesturing. "On past the recycling cans. Look! I know that guy. He's with *Brain's*."

We look again. Jessy is right.

There, coming south along the sidewalk, is Ben Bennington. He is not in a hurry and does not look alarmed. Has he even heard the shots?

"Oh my God," I say. "They'll shoot him on sight."

Before I can say anything else, Mack starts sprinting toward Ben.

★ ★ ★

We run north. Ben is still ambling south. He sees us almost immediately . . . so do two armed guards from the Cultural Center, and they open fire.

The guns bark and bullets begin to ricochet.

Ben pulls a handgun from his pocket and begins pointing it in all directions.

"Ben!" I call. "It's us!"

Ben trains his gun in our direction, and for a moment I'm certain he's going to shoot me in the face. Then he recognizes us. He registers bewilderment and lowers the weapon. Then he sees the men with rifles farther down the street who are shooting at us. He shoots back.

We round a pile of blue recycling cans and hurdle the hood of a Toyota with a cheap spoiler that doesn't match the paint. (The words "Trust No Bitch" have been carefully painted across the rear window in Germanic script.) Mack hurdles it like an athlete, sliding over the hood and taking cover on the far side of the car. Jessy and I follow as best we can.

Ben squeezes off a couple more nervous shots and then lowers his gun. Nobody shoots back. It's unclear whether the guards from the Cultural Center are dead, in flight, or just not shooting anymore. Ben jogs over and joins us behind the Toyota.

"Mack!" Ben says, rubbing his eyes with his gloves. "What's going on? I thought you were dead."

"I am the resurrection and the life," Mack says with a little chortle. Then, after a thought, he adds, "Not really."

"Maria, you're okay!" Ben says.

"Relatively speaking," I tell him.

Then Jessy Knowlton says, "Little help…"

We look back and see that Jessy is not taking cover. Jessy is not even on her feet. She's lying curled on her side, head down against the sidewalk. There is a hole in her chest the size of a golf ball. Blood is pooling beneath her.

"Omigod!" I say, unsure what to do.

"Bennington…" Jessy says, her voice suddenly a croak.

Ben is clearly aghast but creeps closer to Jessy.

"Here," Jessy says, thrusting a blood-spattered legal pad at Ben. "It's *your* Pulitzer now."

Ben smiles at this idea. Then frowns at the tragedy before him.

Three bloody, croaking breaths later, Jessy Knowlton is dead.

"Oh no!" Ben says. "Who shot Jessy? Who were those people? What is going on here?"

We give him the quick and dirty version. The city government trying to get a quorum at the Harold Washington Cultural Center; Marja Mogk trying to install herself as mayor; sending some guys out to kill my dad so there are no other people in line for the throne; Shawn Michael taking me inside the Cultural Center and tying me up.

"See!" Ben says, a little too loud. "I *told* you that guy was up to no good."

I look at Ben and sigh, as if to say that this post-game analysis is not useful.

"We need to keep moving," Mack says. "How's north?"

"It's fine, I guess," Ben answers. "A few people. Nobody shooting at least."

"Let's move before they realize which way we went," Mack says.

We leave Jessy Knowlton's body in the gutter and scuttle north like crabs, staying low behind cars and fences. I hazard a few looks back as we move up the block. There are figures in the distance that look like they might be with the group from the Cultural Center, but they're not following. It looks like we just might escape.

We reach a corner and turn down a side street. I risk one final look back. I see Jessy standing erect and resting an arm on the Toyota next to her. I stop and point this out to Ben and Mack. Mack just shakes his head no. We continue down the darkened street.

Ben Bennington

Maybe, if you're reading this, you might not think Chicago is worth fighting over. Not worth the constant political jockeying, the gerrymandering, the literal and figurative backstabbing.

Well, it is.

The City of Chicago has an annual gross metropolitan product of over half a trillion dollars. That's trillion with a T. That's more than the entire GDP of countries like Sweden and Poland and Saudi Arabia. And Chicago is only 228 square miles, which makes it significantly smaller than Sweden and Poland and Saudi Arabia. It's a tight little funnel through which all of that wealth has to pass. And the people behind that half a trillion dollars all want favors, want to be taxed less, and want to be connected to whoever's in charge so those things can happen. If you can get your hands on that funnel—or even just a teensy little part of it—then everybody wants to be your friend and make you rich. (I haven't experienced it personally, but I have to guess this feels really, really good.)

Most people who aspire to be leeches on the money-funnel get in line at an early age. They help a local politician get elected or re-elected. In return, they expect to receive an appointment or a job with the city. Something small at first, but larger as time goes on. Something where they can manage people, get supervisory experience. Then, when the party bosses bless it, they can run for office themselves. Above all, aspirants to the money funnel must prove themselves good soldiers who will do anything asked of them. This includes mercilessly attacking anyone who dares to stand against the party.

You've heard of the way Scientologists go after anybody who criticizes them like it's suddenly a fucking war—labels them "suppressive persons" and attacks their children and families and so on? I think L. Ron Hubbard got that idea from Chicago politics. You take a run at a sitting politician in this town, and they come at you with all the resources of the city. Suddenly, the city inspectors find your house out of code, and you're hit with hundreds in fines and thousands of dollars worth of fixes to make. At the same time, the tax assessor may determine that he grossly undervalued your property last time around. Expect a new bill for the difference. Is the city sticker on your car in the wrong place? Have you parked more than six inches from the curb, or *touching* the curb? Are your windows tinted just a little too dark? Expect to find new traffic citations waiting underneath your windshield wiper every damn day.

When you go to war against someone entrenched in this system, they will use every resource and connection they have to harass you. And it's all nice and legal. Indeed, it is *through* laws that they will assail you. Everybody who got their phony-baloney city job because of the incumbent will come after you in any way they can. Why? What elicits such loyalty? The promise of a slightly larger space on the money funnel.

It's *that* good.

★ ★ ★

A couple of blocks shy of 35th Street, Maria mentions that her feet hurt. We stop for a moment, and she sits on a building's front steps and removes her shoes. I take the opportunity to review Jessy Knowlton's bloody notes in the glow of a lonely streetlight. Like most reporters, her handwriting is atrocious. Even so, I am able to make out the gist of what she has recorded.

Marja Mogk and a team of her fellow aldermen are attempting to convene the city council and appoint a new mayor. When they have a quorum—over 50 percent of Chicago's aldermen present—they will be able to operate legally and appoint the new mayor. Which, from what I can tell, will almost certainly be her. (I imagine every alderman who comes through the door is privately taken aside and informed of what is happening. Mayor dead. Vice mayor presumed to be. We've decided Mogk will be the one to take over. You can either support her and be rewarded—"How would your sister like to be the new head of Streets and Sanitation in post-zombie Chicago?"—or you can fight it, and lose, and gain nothing.)

The preliminary proceedings which Jessy Knowlton has recorded may lack official power, but they are clearly intended to have the force of the law behind them. In noting the absence of the vice mayor—Maria's dad—Mogk and Szuter use phrases that have almost certainly been prepared by a lawyer. Jessy has recorded some of them in whole or part. "Best efforts have been made to locate the vice mayor" and "It is reasonable for the council to presume him dead or missing" are my favorites.

That's why she was there, of course. Marja Mogk could give a fuck about the freedom of the press. Jessy was there to make it all look nice and legal. To write down the bullshit kangaroo court proceedings, while the real deals were being cut privately in the next room each time a new alderman arrived.

"Do her notes say anything about Crenshaw Cemetery?" Mack asks, sauntering up to my streetlight.

I quickly flip through the remaining pages.

"No. What they're doing inside the Cultural Center is creepy enough, though. Unless Maria's dad pops up, Mogk's going to be in charge by morning. This shit is like medieval times. House against house."

"Chicago wasn't ever *not* like medieval times," Maria says, rubbing her foot.

Mack stares thoughtfully at the ground.

"It's all connected," Mack says. "It *has* to be."

"What do you mean?" I say, looking up from the notes.

"Before I left Crenshaw, I spoke with the caretaker," Mack tells me. "Shawn Michael Recinto had shot her."

"That's no surprise," Maria interjects.

"The caretaker said that people had been paying her to hide bodies there," Mack continues. "When I asked who, she said it was 'All of them.' I'm still trying to figure out what that means."

"Maybe all the cops?" I say. "That was Burge Wheeler's beat."

"What if it means all the aldermen?" Maria says, replacing her shoes and joining us under the streetlight. "Or everybody who works for the city?"

"Would that include your dad?" I ask.

Maria is apparently unfazed by this possibility and answers, "It damn well could."

"We need to find him," Mack says.

"My father?" Maria says.

Mack nods.

"From what you told me, it sounds like Mogk and her people believe he could be out west," Mack says.

"I have a cousin in Oak Park," Maria tells us, invoking the suburb contiguous with the west side of the city. It's probably best known as the home of Frank Lloyd Wright and young Ernest Hemingway.

"But the note we found…" I object. "It said your father was headed to your aunt's house."

"Yeah, that's right," Maria allows.

We explain to Mack about the note we found on the shooter at Crenshaw. Mack rubs his chin and thinks some more.

"What if it happened like this…" Mack begins carefully. "Your sister and mother arrive at your dad's. He writes you the note, and then all three head over to your aunt's house. But when they arrive, they can tell something's wrong. They see Shawn Michael Recinto guarding the door. Your dad realizes he's been second-guessed. So what does he do next? Where would he take his family?"

Maria looks down and shakes her head.

"Would they go to your cousin's?" Mack presses.

"I guess they might," Maria says. "I can't think of anyplace else. We have no other family here."

"At the very least, there are bad people headed there who will kill your cousin," Mack says.

"Franco," Maria interjects. "His name is Franco."

"At the very least, they will kill Franco if he's home," Mack says. "If the rest of your family is there too, they will also be killed."

Maria walks away from us and flaps her arms in frustration. Then she walks back.

"What do we do?" she asks.

"It's simple," says Mack. "We get there first."

★ ★ ★

We stand atop the highway—where there is barely room to stand at all—and look west, out of the city in the direction of Oak Park. From our elevated vantage point, we can see for miles. The sight is enough to take your breath away.

The highways leading west out of the city are blocked. Either clogged completely with traffic or barricaded intentionally. And it's not just the highways and byways. The city streets also appear terminally blocked. Red taillights extend endlessly, like the blood seeping out of a corpse. The city's living have left it—or tried to—and this is the final sign of their mass egress.

"Now do you believe me?" I say to them.

They both nod absently. Mack's jaw has dropped.

"Why would people barricade the roads like that?" Maria asks. She gestures to a swath of street right below us where several tanker trucks have been parked side to side, blocking off a three-way intersection.

"To protect themselves, I'd say if I'm being charitable," I tell her. "To create a funnel in which they could trap and rob people, if I'm not. Maybe they just did it because they could. Think about how many people who live along the main thoroughfares spend their time wishing they didn't have to put up with rush hour traffic. With no cops around to stop them, they just went out and put up barriers."

"I say it was fear," Mack opines. "When there's a crisis, a whole lot of folks want to keep strangers out at all costs."

I nod silently in agreement and look out again over the glowing stopped arteries of the city.

Most people have abandoned their cars, but a few, against all reason, still have occupants. These people must have iron resolves and iron bladders. Are they hoping that somehow, someway the traffic will eventually start to move? Are they unable to bring themselves to leave their cars behind? Do they simply have no other idea about what to do—no place to go?

"I think this gives us a chance to reach your cousin first," I say to Maria. "Even if Mogk's people begin the trip in cars, once they get near *this* they're going to be on foot just like us."

"What if they have motorcycles or bicycles," Maria objects.

"I don't think it will help much," I say.

"I agree," says Mack. "This is an obstacle course to end all obstacle courses. Even the sidewalks look impassible in most places. If I had a motorbike, I wouldn't feel comfortable going at much more than a crawl. This is such a sight! I still can't believe it happened so *fast*."

"I dunno," I say. "Traffic reporters can tell you how one accident—or one dog running around in the road—can create a rush hour jam that goes for miles. Add to that a bunch of shit that people throw on the roads intentionally? I'm not surprised that by—what is it now? 2:00 AM?—We've got complete blockage. Chicago already had some of the worst traffic in the nation. And that was before zombies."

We take another moment to gaze thoughtfully down at the tangled glowing highways leading off into the cloak-black night.

"That's where we're headed," Mack says, pointing northwest across the glowing lines.

"So let's go already," Maria says.

We do.

Leopold Mack

A dark idea starts to broil and burble in the back of my mind. It's so dark that I don't want to acknowledge it at first. I certainly don't want to say it out loud.

Why don't I want to say it? That one is easy.

Fear.

I'm afraid. *Very* afraid.

In a city filled with zombies and looters, I know a place that's even scarier. I know a place that might have even worse things lurking in its depths. And I'm about to propose that we go there... if I can only summon the courage.

Which, right now, I feel like I can't.

Bad pastor. Bad pastor. Bad pastor.

Jesus . . . please help me. Good Lord, please give me the strength.

★ ★ ★

We're a couple of blocks west of the elevated expressway ramp by the time I get the guts. It's like going to the doctor when you know you're due for an unpleasant test. You just have to turn your brain off, everything except the part that can remember to tell the receptionist, "Leopold Mack. I'm here for my procedure."

And apparently, I am.

"Hold on guys," I say, raising my hand. "I want to bring something up before we go any further this way."

Ben is leading us directly west into neighborhoods where the last vestiges of the south side abruptly intersect with the beginnings of Chinatown. We're a long way—hours yet—from Oak Park. Twice already, we've had to adjust our trajectory because we encountered streets sealed off by local residents. (One group had upended a school bus and used it to completely block the road.) We're also near a police station that I know well, as I've had to identify bodies there. It has a huge parking lot that's usually full of squad cars and cops' personal cars. Tonight though, it's empty— although the lights are still on inside the station building.

Ben and Maria look at me.

"What is it, Mack?" Maria asks. "Why do you look so scared?"

"Uh…" I begin, my voice almost failing me. (This is unusual for a man who more or less speaks for a living.) "Do you guys know about the coal tunnels?"

There is a moment of silence.

Maria wrinkles her nose and shrugs. I'm guessing that's a no.

Ben has gone perfectly still. Frozen, in fact. I can see it in his eyes. The fear. The *understanding*. He *does* know. And he's guessed what I'm about to propose.

"Whoa…I don't think we—"

I cut him off.

"The coal tunnels are a system of underground passages built in the late 1800s that stretch from the downtown Loop all the way out to the suburbs. They predate the El train. They were dug back when buildings were heated with coal. Every morning, train cars would bring in coal to heat the buildings in the Loop, and every evening they would come back to carry away the coal ash."

"Uh huh…" Maria says, not seeing the point.

"Not many people know about them," I continue. "They stopped being used around 1950. I'm thinking Marja Mogk's people wouldn't remember them either. Most aldermen don't know anything about the city's history."

Ben stands by with his finger raised, waiting to get a word in.

"Why are you bringing this up now?" Maria asks. "Old tunnels where they used to ship coal? Why does that matter?"

"Some of the tunnels go straight to Oak Park. *Straight* there. Along a route that's not encumbered by barricades and crazy people. There's an old warehouse just north of that police station where my uncle used to work. That warehouse had an access point into the tunnels. It might be worth trying to see if we can get in. If we *can*, it'd be a straight shot. I don't see how we wouldn't get there ahead of Alderman Mogk's people."

Maria smiles. She likes that idea.

Then Ben speaks, and he says *everything* I am not allowing myself to think.

"Um, *no*. The coal tunnels? Are you *serious*, Mack? No! I can't think of a worse idea! They were dangerous *before* a zombie outbreak. They're condemned and unsafe. Shit might collapse on top of us. You know that as well as I do. The city can't even seal the damn things up safely."

I assume that Ben is referencing an incident that happened back in 2009, when the city tried to fill one of the tunnels by pumping thousands of gallons of wet concrete into it. (After 9/11, Homeland Security told Chicago it didn't like the idea of a major American city having a bunch of easily-accessed, empty tunnels running directly underneath all its tallest buildings.)

But the city's engineers misgauged the strength of the tunnel walls. The injection of concrete made the tunnel collapse and the ground above the tunnels buckled. It shut down traffic on the highway at rush hour, and everybody was pissed. (There have been no concrete injections since. Filling in the tunnels remains an expensive, lose-lose issue that the city doesn't want to deal with.)

"But that's not even the worst part," Ben continues. "There's bad stuff down there, and everyone knows it. I mean... when you talk to a guy who works for the CTA—the regular subway system—and ask him what's the most fucked-up thing he's ever seen down in the subway tunnels, he'll be like 'A really big rat.' But have you ever talked to a city worker who had to go into the *coal tunnels*? They've seen shit they don't even want to talk about. Sacks of aborted fetuses; discarded murder weapons covered in blood; altars where people snuck in and did Satanic rituals in the 1970s; shafts where gangsters have been dumping corpses since thirty years *before* Capone. One worker told me that he saw a severed head stuck on a pike. It was old and rotted, but he could still tell it was a head . . . on a goddamn pike!"

"You can't be serious, Ben," Maria says, giggling and placing a hand on her belly. "That's too much. Someone was being funny with you. I hate to tell you, but you're the kind of guy people would play jokes on."

She then looks over to me and sees my frown. She sees that I can credit everything Ben is saying. Maybe more. (Definitely more. I've heard worse stories. Things my uncle told me back when I was a little boy. Things I shudder even to remember.) Maria's face falls.

"Normally, at least the shit down in the coal tunnels is dead," Ben continues. "But tonight it's getting up and *walking around*. Seriously Mack, why did you even suggest this?"

I take a deep breath. (Name? Pastor Leopold Mack. Yes, ma'am. That's right. I'm here for my procedure. Uh huh. *That* procedure.)"Because it's the fastest, clearest way to Oak Park. Maybe the fastest way out of the city tonight, short of a helicopter. If we want to reach Maria's dad before Marja Mogk's people do, then it's the best way. The tunnels go straight there."

"And *are full of monsters!*" Ben counters.

Ben and I pause. We both look at Maria. We need a tiebreaker here. Probably, Maria should be the one to decide anyway, since it's her father we are trying to reach.

She looks up at her own eyebrows a moment—considering.

"If we got in, how could we be sure we'd get out again?"

I have won.

"*Maria*…you're not seriously considering—"

I cut Ben off.

"The hatches open out. They're designed so that people don't get trapped inside. If you can find a way in, then it's easy to get back out again."

"And how do we know where we're going once we get inside?" Maria says, still calculating. "Do you have a map or something?"

Ben has stopped with the verbal objections but flashes Maria an open-mouthed look to say she might as well be considering jumping off a cliff.

"Not exactly," I tell her. "I have a compass in the butt of my flashlight. As long as we keep heading northwest, we'll be making progress. If we want to leave the tunnels at any point, there are hatches every quarter mile or so. I think."

"You... *think*?" Maria says cautiously.

"Even if we just take the tunnels part of the way—just use them to get as far as Humboldt Park, say—we'll still get a big lead on Marja Mogk's people. It could make the difference between life and death for your dad."

"For my mother and sister who are *with* my dad," Maria corrects me. "That's why I'm doing this, remember?"

I nod.

Ben tries a final plea.

"Maria . . . we're no use to your family if we get trapped underground in a maze filled with zombies and monsters."

She waves him off.

"It's faster and it goes straight there?" Maria says, turning to me.

I nod, confirming it.

"Okay," she says. "Then I'm in."

★ ★ ★

"We might not even be able to gain access," I whisper to Ben as we amble north toward my uncle's old factory. "The place might be locked or guarded. Or maybe even knocked down."

"You can stop trying to sugarcoat this," Ben tells me, nearly growling. "This is going to suck and you know it."

He's right. I do.

Yet something tells me this is still the best way to reach the new mayor. Doing so successfully feels more and more important to me. Like maybe it's what God wants...like it's the reason why all of this has happened.

We pull level with the abandoned police station and its equally abandoned parking lot.

"We should stop and have a look inside," Maria states. "They might have supplies."

I rub my chin and consider it.

"She's right," Ben says. "Only Mack has a flashlight, and only Mack and I have guns. I'd like us *all* to have guns and flashlights if we're going down into the fucking coal tunnels."

"Exactly," Maria says.

"Okay then," I allow. "Maybe we have time for a quick detour."

We adjust our trajectory yet again and head across the large empty parking lot toward the dark police station. There is essentially nowhere to take cover. The lot security lights above us are sputtering but still functional. If there are any cops left inside, they will surely see us coming. Only two cars remain in a network of parking spaces that usually holds 200. As I look closer, I discern that they both have flat tires.

I contemplate calling out and announcing our presence. I know a number of south side officers, and it is likely that some of those assigned to this station will remember me. But then it occurs to me that this station might yet be occupied...but not by policemen. In light of this, I remain silent, and we slink up to the entrance as quietly as we can.

The lights are on, and the front door is unlocked. Nothing appears to move within. The only sound is the fuzzy static of an unattended radio dispatch. Ben draws his gun. We push the door open and head inside.

For some reason, I'm expecting the station's interior to be a mess. Paperwork on the floor, computers smashed, bullet holes everywhere. But that's not the case. The inside of the station is as orderly as ever. Desks are neat. Phones are still on their receivers. Computers are unsmashed and functional. It still has that police station smell, too—that strange combination of YMCA, Xerox machine, and the place where you sit and wait in the garage when they change your oil.

But no cops.

The evacuation must have been orderly. It's as if they all simply vanished. Poof! Behind the reception desk, a coffee maker is cooking a pot of Maxwell House down to a crisp.

"All right," I whisper. "Here's what we're gonna do. Ben, you're going to start looking through the desks up here. I'm going to head to the back and see if they have anyplace they keep SWAT gear. Maria, you're going to stay right here and keep an eye on the parking lot."

Maria raises an eyebrow.

"Your job is the most important," I tell her. "We don't want to get trapped inside. Anybody comes into the lot, you let us know."

Somewhat reluctantly, Maria takes a chair and points it toward the glass door to the station. She sits down and begins playing with her cell phone. Ben walks to the nearest desk, opens a drawer, and starts rifling through.

Satisfied, I head for the back of the station. I pass through a pair of swinging doors and take a linoleum staircase down one flight. I am not completely satisfied that the station is empty. I admit that part of me envisioned a cadre of cowardly CPD officers barricading themselves deep within to make a last stand. Upon further consideration, I realize the idea is ridiculous.

These men and women went home to their families. Simple as that.

The city still requires CPD officers to live within the city proper, but almost none of them are from this neighborhood. This part of the South Loop has immaculate, expensive condos (ever forcing themselves southward from the Loop proper) and moldering rat-trap buildings that share property lines with public housing. What it doesn't have is middle-class homes for city workers. The officers who work in this station are either too rich or too poor for the extremes of housing offered in the neighborhood they patrol.

I reach the lower level of the station and find a long concrete hallway. There is nobody about. Thick, functional wooden doors—like in an old high school—line the walls. Most of them are locked. The few that do open reveal administrative offices. Desks with staplers and cups of paperclips.

Just as I'm about to give up, I start to hear the low voices at the end of the hallway. I draw the Glock I took off Shawn Michael and cautiously move in to investigate.

Maria Ramirez

I'm testing my phone—trying to send text messages—when Ben comes over and stands next to me. He's pesty, like a dog that wants attention.

"Are the phones working again?"

"No," I tell him. "I was trying to text, but I don't think they're going through. Did you find anything in those desks?"

"No guns. But maybe these will be good."

He holds up several identical flashlights. They're smaller than Mack's Maglite but might do in a pinch. And this is a pinch if ever there was one.

"That's good," I say. "If it's true what you guys are saying about what's down in the tunnels, we probably need guns, too."

"It's true all right," Ben says with a shudder. "I don't even want to think about it. Things are fucked-up enough on the streets of Chicago, and Mack wants us to go to the one place that's sure to be even worse? I don't get it."

"Is it true what he said about being able to go straight to Oak Park?" I ask.

Ben looks around the room like there are ghosts hovering around to give him backup. If there are, I can't see them.

"Yeah," I say. "That's what I thought."

Giving up on my phone, I walk into the network of desks and look for a computer that isn't password protected. Frustratingly, all of the ones belonging to individual officers are. But then I try the aging Dell with the well-worn keyboard behind the reception desk . . . bingo. I open a browser window.

"Is the internet working on that computer?"

"We're about to find out," I tell him as we both crowd around the screen.

I try the websites for local newspapers first. They look broken, like someone was interrupted in the process of updating the pages. Everything is formatted in a weird, unprofessional way. We can make out a few headlines though. My favorites are "Multiple Cannibal Attacks in Loop!" "Amidst Widespread Rioting, a City on Lockdown" and "Mayor, Family Eaten Alive!!!"

"Try the national news," Ben says, reaching for the mouse.

"Back off, man!" I tell him. "I'm driving."

"Well drive then," he says petulantly.

We pull up the website of a cable news station. The headline reads, "The Dead Rise in Illinois!!! Chaos in the Windy City!!!"

"Hot damn," says Ben, clapping his hands with glee. "It's a local story! Local! And I'm at the heart of it! That Pulitzer is so fucking mine...if I can just not die."

"Hate to burst your bubble, but look at this," I say, directing Ben's attention to some of the smaller headlines further down the front page. These subheads report that people are starting to see walking corpses all over the country. In Mexico and Canada, too. The president has been called back from a summit in Japan and has scheduled a joint press conference with the CDC the moment he lands.

"Oh," says Ben, the excitement draining somewhat from his face.

"Look on the bright side," I tell him. "Even if it starts happening other places, it looks like we were *first*."

Ben tilts his head back and forth, considering this. A little bit of his smile returns.

Suddenly, the door at the back of the station bursts open, and four large men walk into the room. Luckily, one of them is Mack. The other three are thugs in orange jumpsuits. Mack is wearing a riot helmet with a clear plastic visor and pointing his handgun at the men.

"There you go," Mack says to them, gesturing to the door. "Stick to the south side, but stay away from the Harold Washington Cultural Center. That place is poison. If somebody doesn't seem right—or doesn't seem *alive*—you just run the other way. The dead are mostly frozen, but they get faster when they have a chance to thaw."

The prisoners brush past us and head out the door. They are tough men with hard faces. Men from neighborhoods where a smile indicates weakness and where eye contact with the wrong stranger can get you jumped. They don't seem particularly interested in Mack's description of the zombie outbreak into which they are about to set foot. Their expressions say *Leave me alone. I can handle this, whatever it is.*

The men exit the police station and head off in different directions.

"Really?" I say to Mack.

"They were going to starve down there," Mack says.

"The cops just left them?" Ben asks. "That's a pretty shitty thing to do."

"I don't think they planned to," Mack replies. "Think about it. The zombies start to rise up, and most of the police are called out. The emergencies all around the city get worse and worse. Eventually, you have a skeleton crew holding down the entire station. Then the lines of communication go down completely. The remaining officers start saying 'Forget it' and go home to protect their own families. I'll bet the last guy in here didn't even know he was the last."

Ben frowns. He clearly still thinks it was shitty to leave the prisoners.

"Ben found some flashlights," I say brightly. "How did you fare?"

"Badly," says Mack. "Most everything is locked up. It was lucky that the doors to the cells were automated, or I wouldn't have gotten them open either. I found this helmet though, and *this*."

From his pocket, Mack produces a heavy plastic nightstick.

"Fuck..." I exhale. "No guns at all? Not even Tasers or tear gas?"

Mack shakes his head.

"And we need to get moving," he says. "I don't want to risk Mogk's people running into us before we get into the tunnels."

"But I don't even have a gun!" I protest.

"Here," Mack says. He hands me the truncheon and places his helmet on my head.

"This feels like a bad Halloween costume," I object.

"Wait," says Ben, throwing up his hands. "Just...wait."

He walks over and gives me his handgun.

"You should have this. I hardly know how to shoot it, and you're evidently an excellent shot. I don't even know if the thing has any bullets left."

"Eight," I say, checking. "Seven in the clip and one in the chamber."

I trade with Ben—giving him the stick and riot helmet. He holds the stick between his legs and awkwardly works the helmet onto his head. Then he raises the nightstick with both hands on the hilt, like it's a sword.

"You look good," I tell him as we leave the abandoned police station. "Official."

"Thanks," he says grumpily, as though it is little consolation.

★ ★ ★

The giant warehouse where Mack's uncle used to work looms into view just north of the station. The dark streets are perfectly empty. There is a sense of impending doom as we get closer. I believe we all share it. Ben makes one last attempt to change our minds.

"I just think it sounds risky to go down into these tunnels," he says from underneath his clear plastic visor. (He says it quietly, like he wants us to think he's just talking to himself.) "I don't know if it makes sense when you look at the big picture."

I look over to Mack, wondering if we should acknowledge Ben's whining.

"*I* think..." Mack begins casually, keeping his eyes on the warehouse, "that everything after this is a risk that doesn't make sense. But going into the tunnels now is maybe the one thing that does."

We reach the edge of the abandoned warehouse property. There's a chain link fence around it that has long since been compromised with wire cutters. We pick the nearest hole and duck through.

"I don't know what happens tomorrow," Mack continues. "I don't know what happens when the sun comes up. Zombies throughout the state...maybe throughout the whole country."

"The zombies are popping up all over," I tell him. "We saw it on the internet at the police station."

"Tomorrow is a mystery," Mack continues. "But *tonight*, we have the chance to do something right. Something that restores order and decency. Something that helps people. Tomorrow, we might not have that chance."

The warehouse is enormous and old. One exterior wall features the ghost of a print advertisement for a brand of chewing tobacco that hasn't existed for sixty years. The walls are brick, but the ancient, slanted roof is made of wood—weather worn and mostly warped.

"This place looks like a haunted house," Ben says.

He's right, it totally does. Or at least the kind of place that that a bunch of art students rent out around Halloween and charge $20 a pop to scare people with fake blood and plastic monsters.

"It hasn't been operational for a while," Mack replies. "Closed down right after my uncle retired. Whoever owns it is just waiting to sell the land it sits on. It might be abandoned. I really don't know."

Ben says nothing, but I notice a little fog building on the inside of his riot helmet.

"Around back," Mack says.

We hoof it along the side of the warehouse and turn the corner. There we find loading docks for trucks and a wall of ancient, rusted garage doors. Everything is covered with graffiti, but it looks like graffiti from 1980. (Even taggers got bored with this place many years ago.) Mack stalks over to a metal door with "Authorized Personnel Only" stenciled over it.

"We could try to kick it down," Mack says. "But I wonder…"

He feels along the dirty ledge above the door.

"I don't damn believe it."

We watch as Mack's hand comes away with a key. It's filthy and sticky, covered in grease and years of dust.

"They used to leave the key here in my uncle's day. I wonder if the current owners even know it's here."

Mack brushes the gunk and grease off of the key. Then he uses it to open the door.

I look over at Ben. There is a pea-soup level of fog on his mask.

"Maybe you should wear that thing with the visor up. For now, at least."

"Yeah," he says, adjusting the helmet. "That might be a good idea."

We take out our flashlights and turn them on. Only two of the flashlights from the police station actually work. Ben and I each take one. They are good, but Mack's giant Maglite is even better.

Ben and I form up behind Mack, and we make our way into the building. Inside is a stench like burned grease or motor oil and old, undisturbed machinery.

We enter a shipping bay, which is only a small part of the larger warehouse. There are broken pallets and stacks of tires against the wall. Everything is covered with dust. Our footsteps echo. The warehouse door swings closed behind us.

The air is thick with particles. It picks up our beams and makes them stand out like lasers in a movie. Mack conducts us cautiously but steadily, like he knows where he's going. Then he stops and puts his hands to his temple like he doesn't.

"It used to be right there," Mack says, standing at the entrance to what looks like a machine shop. Unless…"

Mack strides into the dark, greasy room and takes a knee. The floor is covered with a fibrous workshop mat, something half carpet and half plastic. Mack begins to pick at the corner. It's been glued to the floor, but it starts to come up easily when Mack puts his back into it.

"Here, help me out," he says.

Ben and I set down our flashlights and help Mack pull up the flooring. It makes a ripping sound like tearing cloth that echoes off the warehouse walls. After a minute or so, Mack stops.

"Look, there."

We look.

Our ripping has revealed a metal square set into the floor. Its edges have been filled in with caulk. It looks like it hasn't been opened in years. I'm not even sure it's something that's designed to open.

I retrieve my flashlight and cast a doubtful look at Mack.

"Just need to pry it up," he says. "It'll open. Trust me."

Ben is looking down at the caulked-shut square in the floor and shaking his head.

"Wow, just wow," Ben says. "I can't believe we're about to do this."

"Stand aside," says Mack, who suddenly has a grease-covered crowbar in his hand.

We watch as Mack uses the hooked end of the crowbar to scrape away the caulk. Then he jams the crowbar into the opening and pries up the metal square. It falls to the side with a *Conk*. A dark hole in the floor beckons.

"Wow," Ben says again.

Mack shines his light down into the hole. We creep in close to take a look. There are metal handholds reaching from the tunnel opening down to the floor below. At the bottom of the shaft is a stone floor with what looks like a metal track set into it.

"Come on," says Mack, holding his flashlight in his armpit. He begins his descent into the shaft. "It's now or never."

Ben Bennington

The smell . . . my god.

We make it down into the tunnel just fine. (The handholds are precarious and slippery, but we all manage it.) The walls are fairly close (and a bright concrete-white), so there's a lot of light refraction. The floors are caked in grime, but the walls are clean. The tunnel is maybe six feet wide.

"This is one of the narrower, side shafts," Mack pronounces. "It'll widen up when we get further in."

Our voices echo, though not overmuch. The thing that gets you, though—or gets me, anyway—is the smell. Stagnant water. Filth. Grime. Nightmares.

They say that nothing can trigger memories like smells. Your mom's apple pie hot out of the oven takes you back to being six and smelling it for the first time. The stench of sweat and metal at a gym can transport you to high school football practice, juicing up for the big game against a crosstown rival. Smells transport you. Smells let you recall a feeling and a place and an attitude about the world that you thought your brain had long ago lost forever (or at least drowned to death in Vicodin and beer).

The thing about these tunnels, though, is that they bring back memories I never knew I had.

Can I "remember" the feeling of being suffocated and gasping for breath under blankets that smelled like mold? Can I—in any technical sense of the word—"recall" being trapped at the bottom of a well and screaming for help while no one comes to my rescue? Have I fallen into a machine used to grind animals into meat and waited for the device to be turned on in cold sweaty terror?

No. They are not memories. These are things from dreams. From my nightmares. Things from my lizard brain that is millions of years old. This horrible place brings these things alive, forces them to the fore of my consciousness.

And all of it—all of this "memory"—screams a differently worded version of the same message: You *should not* be down here.

★ ★ ★

Mack leads us down the tributary tunnel and into the wide central corridor where mine cars used to carry coal. There are two sets of tracks underfoot. This corridor is larger, both wider and taller. The walls are lined with pipes—some appearing to date back to the tunnel's origins, while others seem more recent. There are also markings along the walls every few feet; they're like something the city would do on your lawn when they're looking for gas lines. Little, coded doodles in spray paint. I wonder what they mean?

Mack checks the compass on the bottom of his flashlight.

"Excellent, this heads directly northwest."

Mack smiles at us as if to say we should be cheered by the news. I shudder and pull the riot helmet mask down.

We fall into a formation. Mack leads the way, Maria follows, and I take up the rear. The strange smells seem to change every fifty feet or so, but their effect on me remains consistent. Every scent in this place is otherworldly and terrifying.

I open my mouth to speak, but have second thoughts. In most situations like this, you'd talk to pass the time. Certainly, when I feel this nervous and uncomfortable, I find that talking helps me not go crazy…but one look at the back of Mack's head is enough to tell me that he's all ears. He's focused, listening intently for anything ahead of us…or behind. His chin is up as though he's sniffing the air. His gun stays in his coat…for now. I look to Maria, and see that her weapon is in her hand.

It occurs to me—absurdly, perhaps just to break the terror I feel—that if this were a video game, it would be a really, really lousy one. In video games, there tend to be finite waves of zombies and you have infinite ammunition. This is the opposite of that. The zombies may verge on the infinite, and we have something like twenty bullets between us.

A very bad video game indeed.

I risk a couple of glances backward with my flashlight.

Nothing.

It's hard to imagine that a slow-moving zombie could sneak up behind us. We're walking at a pretty good clip. Still, the idea unnerves me. Three sets of footfalls going "*clip-clop, clip-clop*" get confusing pretty quickly. Would I be able to notice if a fourth set came into the mix? If I'm being honest, probably not.

After perhaps ten minutes of silent walking, we arrive at another side-shaft. It looks almost identical to the one that led off to the warehouse. Mack does not pause to investigate or even shine his flashlight beam down its inky depths. He keeps us moving right on past it. Then, after perhaps five minutes more, we pass another side-shaft. It is boarded up. At this one, we do pause.

The shaft has been covered with a large central plank, and then several wooden ties have been added around the edges, creating a pretty tight seal. Access is prevented. Still, there are small openings and little slots in the wood where I can shine my flashlight through. I do this, but the beam reveals nothing beyond.

Mack clears his throat and taps the front of the boards with his flashlight. I follow with my eyes.

A crude skull and crossbones has been spray painted on the front of the board-up in bright orange paint. The skull has three teeth, and there is an "X" over its right eye.

"Is that a joke?" Maria whispers. It is the first time in a while that any of us has spoken.

Mack has no answer.

We continue down the tunnel, and there we find two more like it. But not exactly like it.

The next side-shaft is similarly boarded and also features an orange skull. Like the previous one, it has three teeth, but the "X" is over its *left* eye. It also has a line above it—slanting down from left to right—like an incompletely drawn hat.

A few minutes later, another boarded up shaft and another orange skull painting. This one looks much older. The paint used to render it might once have been orange, but now is a faded dark brown. The woodwork that seals the passage looks older as well. No part of it has been built with aesthetics in mind. This is purely functional. Something no one is meant to see.

Again, the skull is different. This one has three teeth, but the central tooth is colored-in. It has no "X" in its eyes.

We peer through the holes in the slapdash board-up with our flashlights. There is nothing beyond.

Then Mack says, "It's a code."

Maria and I look at one another.

"A code?" Maria whispers. "What kind of code? Why?"

I think for a moment and risk a guess.

"Like on the houses in New Orleans after Hurricane Katrina?" I ask.

"Yes," Mack answers. "The different details on the face have to mean different things about what's down the shafts."

"I wouldn't say they're 'faces' exactly," quips Maria. "Look at the mushroom-shape. Those are clearly skeleton heads. Skulls."

Mack ignores this.

"The crosses over the eyes are signals," he says. "So are the other markings. I just wish I knew what they meant. Down in New Orleans, there was a system. If you looked close, you could figure out what the search teams had found inside. D.B. stood for 'dead bodies.' G.L. was 'gas leak' and so on. You could make an educated guess. These...*skull*...pictures, though? I can't even begin to theorize."

"Shhhhh!" Maria says, putting her gun to her lips like a giant librarian's finger. "Listen to that."

"What?" I say after a moment, hearing nothing.

I look to Mack. He shrugs and shakes his head.

"Be totally quiet and listen," Maria says, scolding me.

We do.

At first nothing. Maria's final word—"listen"—echoes down the tunnels and is followed by silence. The tunnels are deep enough to block out noises from the street above. When the three of us do not move, the silence descends like thick, muffling snow.

Just as I'm about to insist to Maria that there's nothing to hear, we *do* make out a noise. The sound of something—or someone—being dragged. It is layered. There is a stutter step at regular intervals *(clip...clop, clip...clop, clip...)* and the *pshhhhhh* of something dragged along the tunnel floor behind the footfalls.

We look at one another and nod, indicating that each of us has heard it.

"Where's it coming from?" I ask. I shine my flashlight down the tunnel behind us frantically. There is nothing there.

"I don't see anything ahead," Mack announces, shining his light.

Then it occurs to me that the sound might be coming from the other side of the walled off tunnel. I put my face close to the brownish skeleton and take a listen.

"It's close," whispers Maria.

We fall silent once more. Our flashlight beams scour the tunnel as we attempt to locate the source of the approaching sound. It's still there, and it's getting louder. I start to think it's coming from somewhere above us. I wonder if the tunnels are layered. Are there tunnels on top of tunnels? Places where the coal and subway tunnels intersect?

"There!" says Mack. "Up ahead. Look."

We train our flashlights forward down the tunnel. At first, I can discern only movement. (Maybe it is simply the combined motion of our beams that I'm seeing...) Then, something comes into view with the unmistakable piston-motion of human hips and legs. But it's *just* hips and legs. We are seeing the lower half of a human being—in tattered tan pants—walking toward us down the corridor. A pair of pants and shoes walking by themselves. It takes a moment for this fact to register.

"I thought they had to have a head," I say.

I look over at Mack. He shrugs as if to say *That's what I thought too, but apparently…*

Then the thing gets closer and we hear a familiar moan.

"Look," whispers Maria. "It's *not* just a pair of legs."

She's right. As it gets nearer to us, we can see the walking thing at more of an angle. This new perspective reveals that the legs are trailing a torso, shoulders, head, and arms behind them. This is a body whose back has been broken in many places. The thing comes toward us, dragging its upper half behind it like a wounded animal dragging its viscera.

"How does it even see where it's going?" I whisper.

"I don't think it can," says Mack.

"Can it tell we're here?" asks Maria.

As if in answer, the bedraggled zombie speaks a low, brief nonsensical sentence. Really, it's more of a series of guttural burps. It is like human speech in so many ways, but, ultimately, isn't. And it's completely chilling.

"Oh fuck," I say.

"It's getting closer," Maria says. "What do we do?"

Maria and Mack draw their weapons. I hold my nightstick at the ready.

"Don't shoot it unless you have to," says Mack. "As far as I can tell, these things can hear. Using guns would be very loud, and I don't want to attract more. Maybe we can just rush past this dude. I bet it'd take him a while to turn around, broken as he is."

Maria and I look at one another and nod. The walking thing steps closer.

Twenty yards. Ten yards. Five.

At this distance, we can see that the thing is wearing khakis and dragging a body clad in REI winter wear. The broken shoulders are also dragging a backpack. The hands are gloved. The only exposed flesh is the face, which is horrible to see. It's a Caucasian man with a short beard, but large chunks of his face have been eaten away, most likely by rats. My guess is he's one of those urban explorers who investigate old buildings. His eyes— alarmingly and against all reason—are intact. They roll back and forth madly in their sockets, glistening and frozen.

He appears to have fallen a great distance. I hope for his sake that he died on impact, or at least before the rats got to him.

The dead explorer looks up from behind his own legs. He does not blink in the blinding glare of our flashlight beams. He begins to gnash his teeth mechanically.

"What do you think?" Mack asks. "Can you guys get around him?"

We have only a moment before the zombie is upon us.

"Yeah," I say. "Let's do it."

Mack goes first. Appearing—again—much younger than his years, he lithely bounds over the back-shattered undead man.

The zombie watches him. It stops for a moment, confused, as Mack flies overhead. Then its horrible eyes roll forward and sight Maria.

"Come on," Mack whispers to her urgently. "It's easy."

Maria tucks her gun into her belt, takes a couple of steps backwards, and then leaps past the reclining zombie.

Out of nowhere, the zombie's left hand—which had seemed too broken and gnarled to be of any use—shoots up and grips Maria's leg while she's midair. Maria gives a little surprised "ugh," and falls awkwardly to the ground.

The zombie suddenly folds in on her, wrapping its disgusting broken body around hers like a snake. Its separated spine contorts like a coil.

"No!" Mack shouts. I raise my nightstick and prepare to descend on the zombie. Maria writhes in its grasp.

Suddenly, the thing's head rises from the ground, extending out from the torso on a length of spine. It stares Mack right in the face and gnashes its teeth. Its lips curl into a smile.

"Holy shit," I gasp.

Then a voice says, "Get out of the way!"

I look and see Maria sitting up. One arm is still caught in the zombie's coil, but the other is training her weapon on its slowly swaying head.

"Maria, the noise!" protests Mack, even as the zombie's head dips in to bite him.

Maria pulls her trigger.

The sound is deafening. For a few moments, all I can hear is the report of the gun. It seems to last forever, captured in the echo chamber of the tunnels and repeated again and again. My hands instinctively fly to my ears but encounter the riot helmet. There is a palpable pain in my eardrums.

When I recover enough to look up, I see that Maria's bullet has destroyed the zombie's forehead. The undead explorer lies on the floor of the tunnel, unmoving.

"Oh my God that was loud," I say.

"Had to be done," Maria replies soberly, putting her gun back into her waistband.

We shine our lights down on the broken, distended zombie, making certain it no longer moves. The twisted wreckage is awful. A body so contorted should be beyond dead. The thought that this thing found a way to live again is deeply unsettling.

Satisfied that Maria's bullet has done the job, Mack shines his light back down the tunnel ahead of us. He grows still.

"Do you guys hear that?" he asks.

"No," I say. "That gun fucked up my hearing. I can't—."

Then I stop. I do hear it.

It is a long, low roar coming from somewhere ahead of us.

"What *is* that?" whispers Maria.

"I'm not certain," says Mack, "but it definitely knows we're here."

★ ★ ★

We trudge on, heading generally northwest. The pipes lining the walls increase in number, giving the passage an industrial feel. There are also lights fitted into the walls at regular intervals, but they are not functioning. Eventually, we encounter a ladder built into the side of the tunnel with a hatch above. A way out, if we want it.

"I thought you said these would be every quarter mile or something," Maria says.

"I had been misinformed, apparently," Mack manages.

"Yeah, *apparently*," Maria returns.

I gaze up at the hatch. Suddenly, I want with great intensity to stick my head back above ground and breathe air that does not smell like confinement and nightmares. The lure of it calls to me like water to a thirsty man. Just a little sip would slake me.

"Maybe we should go up and take a look," I try. "See where we are? Get our bearings?"

Mack gives me an *Are you serious?* expression.

"I *know* where we are," Mack says. "There's a long way to go still. We keep on in the tunnel."

I stare up longingly at the hatch a few moments longer.

"Damn…" I whisper softly. "Okay."

We continue down the passageway.

After ten steps, Mack raises his hand and freezes. For a moment, I'm hopeful that he's changed his mind about the hatch. Then his free hand goes to his ear. He looks back at us and raises an eyebrow. Do we hear it too?

After a moment, I do. It is the long, low roar again. Louder. Closer.

"Oh hell," Maria whispers. "That's ahead of us. That's the way we're going."

"What is it?" I ask.

Nobody responds.

Mack lowers his hand and continues forward.

Part of me wants to turn around and run back to the hatch. Fuck the Pulitzer. Fuck it all. Whatever I encounter above, it's got to be better than this. (What are we below, anyway? Chinatown?

Bridgeport? Those neighborhoods would probably be okay.) But fleeing the tunnels, I realize, would mean going it alone. Increasingly, it feels like the most valuable—and rare—things in this outbreak are people I can trust. I may not like where Mack and Maria are taking me, but think I can trust them. For the time being, at least, I decide I'll go with that.

Leopold Mack

The markings on the doorways of abandoned houses after Hurricane Katrina were utilitarian. There was no artistry to them. Their goal was to make mathematical and impersonal the most devastatingly personal information. The people in here are dead. This is how many corpses you can expect to find. (Or—in the case of the Katrina searchers who merely put a stripe down the front of a door—this house contains an *unknown* number of corpses, a more harrowing prospect entirely.)

The spray-painted designs on the boarded-off side passages are part of a code, but they are also decorated with verve and wit. As we continue to pass more of them, the skulls begin to wear hats, to smile and leer, and even to have little stick-figure bodies underneath them. Some hold things like guns, sticks, or swords. Some gesture or even dance. The skulls begin to feel more like characters from the Sunday funnies than utilitarian warnings of dangers beyond.

Then—it happens!—we find a board-up with some actual written words on it. Sort of.

"FUBAR," Ben announces, reading the orange letters on the front of the boards. They have been painted beneath a winking, leering skull who wears a crudely crafted bow-tie.

"Fucked Up Beyond All Recognition," Maria announces proudly.

"That expression has been around since before the Second World War," I inform my young friends. "Look at the age of that paint. This guy is from before you were born."

Ben looks at the board-up silently, like he's trying to guess at what it could mean.

"Are all the coal tunnels like this?" Maria asks.

It's a good question.

I can remember watching a TV series on the local PBS affiliate a couple of years ago that explored the history of Chicago's neighborhoods. In one episode, the genial bald-headed host mentioned that coal tunnels ran beneath a particular neighborhood. There were even some quick cutaway shots, purportedly showing the contemporary state of the tunnels' interior. I'm starting to think that what the PBS program showed us were either not the real coal tunnels or just a tiny showroom-area they keep clean for TV crews. What they showed us on television looked *nothing* like this.

"I don't know," I tell Maria. "But I'll tell you something. Whatever's down these blocked-up passages, people want to forget about it."

We continue northwest along the ancient tracks. Our footfalls echo off the walls. So do our voices.

"I wonder what my mother is doing right now," Maria whispers. "And my sister. God, I hope they're okay."

"I'm sure they're fine," I say to Maria.

"If they're fine, then why are we down here in these tunnels?" observes Ben.

"We're down here to make sure they *stay* fine," I shoot back.

We reach an intersection where the tunnel splits three ways. I take us up the middle path, heading north. After perhaps thirty yards, it splits three ways again.

"What do you think?" Maria asks.

"This is good," I say. "These junctions mean we're inside what used to be the busiest part of the tunnels, right near the Loop. We're making progress. We should keep going north."

We ignore the tracks veering east and west and stay on the center thoroughfare. New intersections continue to come, but we ignore them. Most of the side passages in this part are not boarded up. Now and then we explore them with our lights, but usually detect nothing. There are more stairways set into the tunnel walls with hatches above. Ben stares at them longingly.

Underneath what I estimate to be the West Loop, we sight two humanoid figures on the track ahead of us. They wear suits— one brown, one black pinstripe—and have rotted, ghastly features. They're huddled to one side of the tunnel, but not motionless. They appear to be attempting to climb over one another. We watch as one gets a few feet off the ground, slowly loses his balance, and falls to the floor with a thud. A moment later, the other uses him like a stepstool.

"They're trying to get up to that hatch," Maria says, spotting a sealed opening in the ceiling with her beam. "There must be people on the other side."

No sooner does Maria utter these words, than the zombies stop trying to climb. Both of their heads swivel around in slow unison. Brown Suit manages what looks like a smile. They begin walking toward us.

"I'll do these," I say, stepping forward. "Hold your ears."

I walk up to the zombies and draw my gun. Brown Suit's smile grows even wider as I get close, revealing horrible black-green teeth.

BLAM! BLAM!

My handgun thunders in the cavernous depths. I put a hole through each zombie's forehead. They go down, still.

"Evil bastards," Maria says, pausing to spit on the corpses as we continue past.

I smile.

To me, it feels like zombies are more a force of nature than a sentient, evil entity. Back in divinity school, I had to learn about all kinds of evil. Believe me, I'm an expert now. But which kind of evil are zombies? That question is still a head scratcher. One morning (or evening), zombies are just *there*, with the suddenness of a crashing tidal wave or a ground-rending earthquake. You wake up, and they're out on your lawn chasing down the mailman. Zombies kill and eat people, yes, but so do Bengal tigers and great white sharks. Where's the evil there?

I think, to get at real, Biblical-level, brimstone and hellfire evil, you need humans. *Living* humans. You need them for things like neglect, contempt, hatred, and avarice. Certainly, these forces are the reason why we are now 20 feet below the surface of the city, racing to prevent the new mayor from being murdered. The zombies aren't trying to kill Maria's father any more than they're trying to kill Maria herself, or Ben, or me. The *humans* are the ones with murder in their souls. The *humans* are the ones who discriminate.

Zombies are just the natural disaster. The opening in the rift for evil to come on through.

★ ★ ★

Somewhere below the northwest Loop, Ben's flashlight goes out.

"Dammit," he says, banging on the side of the light. "What the hell?"

We stop and try to fix it. We remove the batteries and reinsert them. We unscrew the back and look at the wiring inside. No luck.

"Did you *do* something to it?" Maria asks accusingly.

"No," Ben insists. "The beam got dim and went black."

"It's just out of juice," I tell them. "Don't worry. We've got two lights left. C'mon. We keep moving."

"Should I still be in back?" Ben asks, a tremor creeping into his voice. "I mean, you each have a gun and a flashlight. Now I just have this baton and no flashlight.

"Does it make sense for you to go *first* if you don't have a flashlight?" Maria asks, crossing her arms.

"I guess not," says Ben, suitably silenced.

★ ★ ★

After a half-hour of walking, we arrive in front of yet another boarded-up passageway. The skeleton face painted on the boards has two blacked-out teeth, an "X" over its right eye, and a conical hat like a wizard.

"That's a new kind of hat," Ben observes from the rear.

"Ehh, the other ones were more interesting," Maria says. "A pointy hat isn't that creative."

We stand there looking at it. There is an awkward silence as Ben and Maria wonder why I do not continue down the open tunnel ahead.

"What's up, Mack?" Maria finally says. "You see something interesting?"

"We have to go this way," I respond soberly. "Down *this* tunnel."

"Excuse me?" In the ambient glow from her flashlight, I can see her raise a skeptical eyebrow.

"Yes," I say, turning my Maglite over to show her the compass in the handle. "Take a look. For the last mile or so, this tunnel has been curving—first north, and then back east. I think we've reached the northwest corner of the Loop. Now we need a tunnel that will take us further west, out to Oak Park."

Maria says, "But how do you know it's this one? Why don't we scout ahead and see if there's an *open* tunnel heading off west?"

"It's this one," I assure her. "Look."

I point to an almost imperceptible engraving in the brick wall beside us. Covered in a hundred years of soot and grease, it reads simply: Oak Park Junction.

"Oh," Maria says, slouching her shoulders in defeat.

"How do we get inside?" Ben asks.

It is a reasonable question.

"These boards look old," I say. "Let's see what your nightstick can do."

Ben creeps to the front of the board-up. The wizard-hatted skull stares back at him, smiling. Ben selects a point off to the side where the boards look thinner, and begins to hammer.

Wham! Wham! Wham!

Right away, we see that this will work. The boards surrender easily to Ben's blows. Bits of wood caked in tunnel-dust fall to the ground. Large holes begin to appear.

"This is gonna be no problem," Ben says, pausing to kick away the debris at his feet. He has made an opening roughly the size of a computer screen. We can see into the blackness of the tunnel beyond.

Suddenly, the blackness forms into the shapes of a skeletal hand, and reaches out through the gaping hole toward him.

"Look out," I say, rushing forward. Ben is not paying attention and is fiddling with bits of wood that have gone into his shoes. He looks up but does not immediately see the arm. I grab Ben around the waist and pull him forcibly backward. At the same moment, the hand lurches forward and rakes its claws against his police helmet.

"Jesus!" Ben says, jumping backward into my arms.

"You're okay," I say, setting him down.

A pair of zombies, black as coke, are visible through the hole that Ben has created. They have eyeless faces. Their skins are withered like Egyptian mummies in a museum. Their silent mouths open and close noiselessly like Jazz Age automatons. Their decomposed nose-holes sniff the air.

"Fuck *me*," Ben says, still alarmed. "They were right on the other side of the boards! We didn't hear them or anything!"

"These look too dried out to groan," I observe.

"They just blend right into the black walls!" Ben says. "That one tried to claw my eyes out. Man . . . fuck this place!"

"Now, now," I tell him. "There are only a couple. Let me put them out of their misery, and then you keep on hacking away. You were making good progress."

"This is like a reverse zombie movie…" Maria quips from behind us. "The zombies are barricaded inside, and we're breaking through to get at *them*."

"Just shoot those fucking things," Ben says, taking off his helmet to wipe the sweat from his brow.

"All right," I say, drawing the Glock. "Here we go."

As Ben and Maria plug their ears, I expend four more valuable bullets on the shadowy mummy zombies. They're so old and brittle I expect them to just explode under the force of my bullets. They don't. My first two shots miss—one entirely. Another goes into a zombie's chest. The penetrated zombie shrugs it off, remaining upright. I squint down the barrel of the Glock and risk another step forward, standing closer to the zombies. That does the trick. Two headshots later, it is done.

"Good shooting, Mack," Maria says. She is just being kind, as she probably could have done better herself.

Maria creeps to the screen-sized opening and peeks through with her flashlight.

"Yeah, that's all of them," she announces.

"Good," I say. "Now Ben, you can finish the job."

★ ★ ★

We smash a man-sized hole through the barrier and squeeze inside. The passageway beyond is filthy and soot-smeared. It smells dank, like slime and mildew. There is a strange, persistent humidity, even in the winter air. The walls are composed of old bricks— once a healthy red, but now aged and stained to near blackness. The rail tracks below our feet lead off into the darkness beyond. The floor is dusty. There are also two sets of coal-black footprints leading up to the barrier.

"The zombies," Maria observes.

"Yes," I say. "This is as far as they got."

"Two sets of footprints…so maybe there were only two of them?" Ben tries.

"I sure hope you're right," I tell him.

The overriding sensation conjured by this side tunnel is decay. This is a place that has been forgotten so long that it has rotted away. Nobody was meant to see the inside of it—the very sights we are seeing now—ever again. It had been boarded up for the last time and was waiting patiently for the city to get up the gumption and funding to fill it in with concrete.

Funny how zombies change things.

The floor of this passageway is quiet. The dust and gunk on the floor have gained the upper hand. It is thick enough to pad our footfalls like snow. (It occurs to me that—in addition to not hearing ourselves—this also means it's now more difficult for us to hear approaching zombies.)

We advance down the pitch-dark shaft. The number of pipes lining the walls dwindles from three to two, and then to one. Hatches to the world above cease to appear with any regularity. Privately, I start to wonder if there *will* be a functional hatch once we get to Oak Park. There has to be an opening. Has to be. But might it be sealed? Blocked from above? Quite possibly. There is no way to know.

After about twenty minutes of walking, we encounter an empty suit of clothes. When my flashlight finds it, I freeze and train my gun. Maria and Ben freeze as well. I'm expecting a zombie to rise up out of it, but that doesn't happen. Maria gets brave and walks up to it. She gives the clothes a little kick. Her foot reveals only a gray pinstripe suit. It is many years old. Trousers, jacket, and vest. Three piece.

"They sure like suits down here," Maria says.

"I should have worn one like Mack did," Ben jokes. "Then I'd fit in."

They both look at me in my pinstripes and pink tie and smile.

We encounter an empty, rusted bucket. It has been rendered unusable by what looks like a blow from an axe. Maria moves it with her foot and it gives a *grrrrrr* scraping sound against the floor. We leave it where it is and continue down the dark passageway.

Then after perhaps a quarter mile's walk, we hear something. Soft, but distinct.

Grrrrrrr.

"Did you hear—?" Maria begins.

"Yes," I whisper.

Four hundred yards behind us, someone, or some*thing,* has—as they say—kicked the bucket.

"We're not alone in this shaft," Maria whispers.

"I never thought we were," I whisper back.

"Let's pick up the pace," Ben rasps from his position at our rear guard. "Zombies can't catch us if we move fast."

"We're going as fast as is prudent," I tell him.

"Then go faster than's *prudent,*" he shoots back. "Come on, chop chop."

I listen again for movement in either direction. I shine my beam back behind Ben. The bucket is out of sight, and so is whatever moved it . . . for now.

I turn back around, and we continue down the passage, perhaps walking a little faster than before.

★ ★ ★

The blackness before me becomes crushingly uniform. It is like snow blindness. I shine my light around to break up the monotony, but it is difficult to do anything with it. This much blackness—in a tunnel, under a big city, in the middle of the night—takes the upper hand. Just the thought of it is crushing. The blackness is in charge. It hangs over us like a funereal pall.

"We're over halfway there," I say, as much to cheer myself as the others.

Ben jumps a little, rattling his riot helmet. He is that much on edge.

Good, I think. It's not just me.

After what feels like a mile, the tunnel begins to widen. Not subtly. The walls are suddenly twice as far apart. This means more places you have to shine your flashlight to check for zombies. We also begin to hear noises. They are coming from a spot straight ahead.

"What is this, Mack?" Maria asks, like I'm the authority.

"The tunnel is getting bigger," I tell her. "Widening."

"I can see that," she responds. "What's that noise? Is it water? Machines?"

"It sounds like a rustling, but also like a clicking," Ben offers from the rear. "Could be we're going underneath a factory. Or, ooh, maybe a power plant!"

"I don't think so," I tell him.

"What is it then?" Ben asks aggressively. "Listen, that's like, clicks and taps and…rustling. What could that be?"

"I don't know," I answer honestly. "But I bet we find out in just a second."

We continue down the widened tunnel, looking left and right for zombies. There begins to be something more than dust and grime underfoot. There is a slickness and squishiness that wasn't there before. Oil? Grease? Maybe. The air begins to smell like the inside of a machine shop. The strange rustling grows louder. It makes me think of reeds swaying in the wind. Reeds and rain.

And here I have to watch myself. The sounds combine with the fear and the gun in my hand, and I know I am on a slippery slope that leads back to that scared nineteen-year-old kid in Vietnam. I think of the small metal cross I wear on a chain beneath my clothes and let myself notice it against my chest. I take deep breaths. I force myself to keep moving.

The tunnel gets even bigger.

"Are we going down, or is the ceiling getting taller?" Maria asks.

"Could be a little of both," I say.

The shuffling, scratching noise becomes even louder. Even more disconcertingly, the coal car tracks—which have been with us the entire way on the tunnel floor—appear to end up ahead, simply terminating into darkness. I would say we're now looking into a flat, empty wall, except that the sounds are near to cavernous. These noises aren't bouncing back off a wall, they're echoing into the darkness.

"What *is* this?" whispers Maria.

"I don't know, but tread carefully," I say.

We edge forward. Our flashlights trace the grimy floor inch by inch. Then, suddenly, we are all starkly aware of what we're seeing.

The tracks appear to end because they have fallen forward into a miniature ravine. It is perhaps 40 feet across and 7 or 8 feet deep. It is filled with metal drums and ruined coal equipment. (The tracks resume on the far side of the depression, beyond which the tunnel appears to continue.) The ravine is also filled with a terrifying collection of writhing, gibbering things that used to be human. Their jarring bones and scampering feet combine to form the strange sound we hear. Hundreds of zombies—whole and half-formed—are clamoring to get out. This pit is the lowest of the low. All the human things that Chicago throws away drifted deeper and deeper until they reached this point. The coal tunnels are the lowest point in Chicago, and this pit is the lowest point in the tunnels.

The eyeless, toothless faces below sense our proximity and scuttle toward us. They are stopped only by the steep edge of the rift. My heart jumps to my throat, my knees go weak, and, catastrophically, I lose my grip on my Maglite. It rolls forward onto the ground—rolling, rolling—and falls down over the edge of the pit.

I can only stand at the edge and look on in horror.

My errant flashlight shows me horrible things as it rolls to the bottom of the pit. If I could purge them from my mind, I would. I ask God, what can be the benefit to showing me such things? What can be the point of a floor filled with flapping, half formed human fetuses, gasping for brains like little fish gasping for water? What makes me a better Christian to know that dusty, legless mummies will drag themselves on stumps to gnash a single tooth in my direction? What is the lesson for me in a trio of freshly killed girl scouts—still in their uniforms—that look like they could be from my neighborhood: hair carefully braided, little black shiny shoes, and throats slit almost to the point of decapitation?

I start swearing. I can't tell if I'm swearing at the zombies or God or just my flashlight. I don't care anymore. (Either way, bad pastor. *Very* bad pastor.) I swear and swear and swear, all at the top of my lungs. There is no point to whispering now. The ravine of scuttling zombies is well aware of our presence.

When I calm down, I turn back to my compatriots. In the glow of our remaining flashlight, their faces reveal that we are—all of us—all at a loss.

"It makes sense," Maria says, looking down at my flashlight. "The zombies walking around in the tunnel try to cross the pit, but they fall in and can't get back out. They start to collect, and pretty soon you've got this big group. I guess a pit is a good zombie defense, if you think about it."

"It's not so good if you need to get to the other side," I observe. "Which we definitely do."

"I'll bet this was some kind of service depot," Ben says, observing the entirety of the widened corridor. "Maybe it was where they repaired the coal cars or loaded them."

"What happened to this place?" Maria wonders, still looking down into the pit as if hypnotized by the gnashing, writhing zombies. "Why is the track broken?"

"I dunno," Ben answers. "A minor earthquake? Shitty construction? Supports that collapsed due to age? Your guess is as good as mine."

I kick the grimy ground in frustration and try to think of what to do next.

"We have to get to the other side somehow. Look across—I mean straight across—from where we're standing. Maria, hit it with your light. There! See, on the other side? Those broken tracks dangle down into the pit. I bet you could climb them like a ladder."

There is a moment of silence as my friends contemplate that.

"Maybe," Ben eventually allows. "But they might be brittle and break."

"We won't know until we try, will we?" Maria says. Her tone is not optimistic. It's grim. The idea of jumping down into the pit and not finding a way out again is awful. Even if the tracks on the other side *will* work like a ladder, it's still awful. Descending into a pit filled with the undead—for any reason—seems like the most insane thing you could do. Something you would only do if you had no other choice…

"Do we have another choice?" I ask the pair.

"I don't see one," Maria responds after some thought. "Go back and try one of the other tunnels—hope it also leads to Oak Park? Go back to a hatch and do the rest of the way above ground? But then, when was the last time we saw a hatch? It's been a while."

"I don't remember," Ben adds.

"Yeah," Maria agrees. "We'd have to go a hella long way back. We'd lose hours, probably."

"That's why we have to go forward," I say.

To me, it feels do-able. The roiling mass of zombies in the pit has collected near us. That leaves the back half of the pit virtually empty.

I'll bet a reasonably strong person could take a running jump and clear most of the zombies no problem. Then it'd just be a matter of scrambling to the far side and climbing up the broken track. I think Maria and I could definitely do it, and Ben is at least a strong maybe.

Out of nowhere, Maria cries, "Oh shit!"

I ask what it is, and then I see for myself.

She is shining her flashlight back down the tunnel, back the way we came. Her beam shows us the silhouettes of several humanoids. At least three or four. Maybe more. It's hard to tell because of the way the shadows play on the walls. The figures move slowly but with great determination. They move straight for us.

"Oh no," whispers Ben.

"This looks like a lot of them," Maria whispers, drawing her gun. "Do we have enough bullets?"

"Forget bullets," I tell her. "That's the wrong direction anyway. We need to go forward. I think we can cross the pit if we take a running jump."

"What?" Maria says. Then, after a moment, adds, "Omigod… you're serious."

"Yes," I tell her. "Ben, what do *you* say? We take a running jump, leap over the bulk of the zombies, then run to the tracks and climb up to the other side."

"I…I don't know," he says rubbing his chin.

"What don't you know?" I ask, trying my most commanding voice. "If we go across the pit, we get to Oak Park before the aldermen do. We keep something bad from happening to Maria's family. We make sure evil aldermen don't steal the city. We're very close now, and you know it. But if we go backward . . . or we just stand here . . . then bad things happen. Do you understand me, Ben? *Bad* things. It's not a choice."

"But…" Ben manages, looking down into the pit of gnashing zombies. One near him is trying unsuccessfully to climb up the side. It not only fails but pulls its own index finger off in the attempt. Undeterred by the missing digit, the zombie claws up at us as if nothing had happened.

"Don't worry about the zombies," I tell him. "They can't climb ladders. And look how they're massed so close. Jump over their heads and you'll clear them. By the time they turn around, you're going to be climbing up the other side."

"I don't know," Ben says. "I just don't know."

Behind us, the other group of zombies continues to saunter toward us. It's time for action.

"Here, I'll go first," I say. "Maria, you've got our only remaining flashlight, so you're going to have to be my eyes. It'll be like I'm a performer on a stage, and you're operating the spotlight. But keep it just a little in front of me if you can, so I can see where I'm going."

"Are you sure about this?" she says.

"Yes, now get ready."

I take a few paces back from the lip of the pit so I can make a running start. Maria trains her light so I can see what I'm up against. There are four or five feet of solid zombie to clear, and then mostly nothing. (A few especially-decrepit zombies linger at the back of the pit simply because they're too broken to move properly. They should be no problem to hurdle. I hope.)

I inhale and exhale deeply. I clear my mind and sprint.

And jump.

Maria Ramirez

I hold my breath as Mack leaps over the rows of gibbering zombies and into the darkened pit. He falls faster than I expect him to, and for a moment, I lose him. It is terrifying.

I rush to the edge and point my light over the side. It's difficult to see for all the writhing, flailing zombies, but in a moment, I locate him. He has landed a few feet past the zombie horde—which is good—but it takes him a moment to stand. When he does, he teeters and rubs his side like he's hurt himself. Which is very bad.

"Mack, are you all right?" I call down.

"Yes, fine!" he shoots back, waving me off.

Remarkably, the zombies in the pit below remain focused on Ben and I, and not on Mack. Many of them appear not to have noticed his jump at all.

Mack does not immediately make for the opposite side of the pit. Instead, he cranes his neck to a spot a couple of paces off, where his lost Maglite still shines.

"Mack, don't—" I begin to call, but I'm too late. Before I can tell him it's not worth the risk, Mack turns and delivers a karate kick to the chest of a moldering zombie near him. The zombie goes down with a splat, but Mack also pauses for a moment and winces in pain. Then he lunges in and picks up the Maglite. A tiny, fetus-zombie clings to the long barrel like a koala bear clinging to a branch. Mack shakes the flashlight until the tiny creature flies off into the darkness.

The zombies nearest Mack start rotating to face him.

"Run," I shout. "They see you. Run!"

He does.

Favoring his right leg, Mack lopes across the remainder of the pit. He's got his own flashlight now, but I still try to light the way for him. He reaches the twists of broken track that hang down from the opposite side. To my great relief, he is able to pull himself up. Finding regular footholds in the wooden cross ties, he climbs the 7 or 8 feet until he is out of the ravine. He shines his light all around his new surroundings. It shows oil drums and piles of broken wood, but no zombies.

"Okay then!" Mack calls from across the gorge. "Maria, you're next. Ben, hold the light on her. I'll do the same from my end. Hurry!"

I hand my flashlight over to Ben, who accepts it nervously.

"Keep it on the edge of the pit," I tell him. "I don't want to slip at the last minute."

Copying Mack, I take a few steps back and prepare for a running start. I should feel scared, but I don't have time to. In a way, this is sort of a relief. What's happening is happening. I've got to take this jump. I've got to make this jump. There's no time to think about what happens if I fail. No time to worry about what happens once we reach the other side.

I sense something behind me...something close. Almost close enough to reach out and touch me. Something old and creaking yet imbued with unnatural life. Something that all experience and knowledge tells me should not be moving, that yet moves. My nostrils fill with the stench of the dead.

I run.

I run from whatever undead thing stands behind me. I run toward Mack and safety on the other side of the pit. I reach the edge and leap, arms and legs flying. I clear the zombies easily and hit the floor of the pit. Hard. Really hard. Like, take a moment to recover hard. (I may be a five-foot nothing, but I'm in pretty good shape. I played basketball in high school, and the drumming gives my limbs a regular workout. [Also, I don't weigh much, so I don't fall that hard. As I struggle to right myself, I think about how difficult this would be for a seventy-year-old who weighs 200 pounds.])

"Run!" Mack screams from above me. "Come on, girl, run!"

I do. My path is mostly clear. There are a couple of disabled zombies flopping around, but it's easy to avoid them. The stench, though, is almost intolerable. The floor of this place reeks of death, charnel earth, and rancid meat. It is suffocating. I feel nose-raped.

I reach the broken tracks and begin to climb. Again, I'm impressed with Mack, because the wood is full of splinters, and the metal edges are sharp as shit. By the time I get to the top, I've cut my hands up pretty good. The moment my adrenaline ebbs, I'm really going to feel it.

As I near the top, Mack grabs me by the scruff of the neck and hauls me to safety. For all of the contempt I've felt toward this man, his touch feels good. I grasp him back as he pulls me up out of the zombie pit.

"You all right?" he asks, staring down at my bleeding hands.

"Yeah, fine. The zombies coming down the corridor, they were right behind me. We need to get Ben across."

We turn and face the far side of the pit where Ben still stands.

He is holding the flashlight and looking at us from underneath his riot helmet. Some of the zombies below have started to notice that there are now more edible humans on our side of the divide. Several stumble in our direction.

"Ben!" I call. "You need to jump right now!"

Ben turns around. In the beam of his flashlight, we can see a number of zombies closing in on him. He has very little room with which to take a running jump. The expression on his face makes clear he understands this.

"Jump, young man!" Mack calls. "Do it now!"

Suddenly, Ben slips on the greasy floor and falls to the ground. His flashlight flies out of his hand and goes out completely. The space across the pit goes completely dark.

"Ben!" I call. "Bennnnnn!!!"

Mack fumbles with his Maglite.

"Come on," I tell Mack. "He can't see. Give him light."

Mack rights his fancy flashlight and trains it on the far side of the pit. It shows us only a group of six zombies, idly inspecting the edge of the pit. They look at one another and around at the walls. One of them risks a step onto the lip of the pit and promptly falls in. The remaining five hardly appear to notice their compatriot's departure.

But Ben is nowhere to be seen.

"What the fuck!" I exclaim. "Ben…Ben…where are you?"

Mack frantically explores the far side of the pit with his flashlight. The zombies are there. The pit is still there. Ben is just gone.

Did he fall in? No. The zombies in the pit would have noticed him. (There would be a feeding frenzy going on right now.) Instead, they merely jostle each other idiotically, like too many fish in a Chinatown vendor's bucket.

Did he go back down the tunnel? No. We would have heard him fleeing.

After several breathless moments of exploration, Mack's beam locates Ben's extinguished flashlight at the lip of the pit. Nothing more.

"What the hell just happened?" I whisper.

"I'm not sure," says Mack. "But I think he's gone."

Ben Bennington

"..."

Leopold Mack

After a point, there seems to be no use in looking across for him. There is no sign of human activity. No new clues. The zombies below have lost interest in that side of the pit entirely and reassembled over by where I stand next to Maria.

Ben Bennington—my Good Samaritan on this night of judgment and horror—has been taken from me as suddenly as he appeared. I have no idea what's happened. He might have ascended to the Heavens for all I know. All that's sure is that we have precious little time. We need to keep moving. We can still reach Maria's family.

I exhale deeply, signaling to Maria that we need to think about next steps. She looks at me, clearly distraught, but manages a nod.

"He liked you, you know."

"Yeah," Maria says. "I kind of picked up on that."

★ ★ ★

We discuss going back across for the remaining flashlight. Two would be better than one in this situation. However, we both ultimately agree that it's not worth the risk. As terrifying as it is to imagine being trapped in the darkness without any light, the prospect of going back across the pit is much worse. The tracks on the other side do not descend as sympathetically. It doesn't take much to imagine trying to scuttle up the side of the pit like a beetle on a slick surface—failing utterly—and being torn apart by the undead.

One light then. One light between us and the zombies. One light between us and not being able to see signs or exits from the tunnel. One light.

Ladies and gentlemen, we are working without a net.

★ ★ ★

Exhausted, shaken, and increasingly hungry, we continue down the coal tunnel passageway toward Oak Park. It narrows back to its original size, maybe 9 feet across. We are resolute and quiet. At one point, a strange thunder echoes down the tunnels behind us. Maria looks at me and raises an eyebrow. Her expression seems to ask if that could be Ben.

I shake my head solemnly.

No, Maria. Whatever that was, it's not Ben. Not anymore.

"My hands hurt," Maria whispers.

"Mine too," I tell her. "Climbing up that track was awful."

Maria nods.

"How's your leg?" she asks me.

"Fine."

This is not the entire truth. I suppose that by "fine," I mean "fine to get to Oak Park." After that, I'm not too sure.

Maria laughs to herself.

"What?" I say, confused.

"We're in a tunnel twenty feet below the street, in the middle of a zombie apocalypse—racing against people who would like to kill us—and you still don't tell the truth. We could both die at the next bend in the tunnel. Zombies could jump out and kill us. Why not be honest, Mack? Who are you possibly kidding? I saw the way you hit the floor when you made that jump."

I consider that she has a point.

"My leg hurts very badly," I tell her. "It's up high, near my hip."

"Is it, like, dislocated?"

"If it were dislocated, I wouldn't be walking," I say stoically. "But it's at least bruised…maybe a small fracture. Pain like this that doesn't go away after a while usually means something bad. I say I'm fine because I don't need you to carry me."

"I'm stronger than I look," Maria says brightly. "I could at least drag you, I bet."

"I don't doubt it," I say, smiling for the first time in a while. "You got them guns, girl."

"It's all the drumming. It's better than going to the gym. More fun, too."

The tunnel begins a gradual curve, making it difficult to see more than 30 feet ahead of us. We slow our pace and advance carefully. I keep up a back-and-forth search pattern with the flashlight's beam.

"While we're being honest…" Maria says as we ease into the turn. "There's something I wanted to ask you."

"Okay," I say cautiously.

"Are you, like…*concerned* for Richelle right now? I mean, do you even care what's happening to your daughter?"

I exhale deeply. We do not speak for a few steps. Our soft footfalls on the oily floor become the only sound. Step. Step. Step.

"I might very well ask *you* the same question," I eventually reply.

"What?" Maria shoots back. "*I* don't have a daughter!"

"You misunderstand," I insist. "Are *you* worried about Richelle?"

"No, not at all."

"Why?"

"*Because!*" Maria returns, like the answer is obvious. "She's a grown-up, capable, completely brilliant young woman. She knows how to take care of herself in any situation you can think of…and I've definitely seen her in some hairy situations."

"Mmm hmm," I agree.

"She's resourceful," Maria continues. "She's sensible. She and her boyfriend have that place together in Ravenswood, too. It's like a fucking fortress. If anybody could survive a zombie outbreak, it's Richelle."

I stay quiet for a moment so Maria will understand that she has answered her own question.

"But…" Maria stammers, unsatisfied by my silence. "Then why do you…?"

"Why do I *what*?"

"You know," Maria says, as if it's obvious.

I sigh deeply.

"Why would I wish that she would use her blessings to help her community instead of standing on a stage in a dress that shows off her breasts…"

"Just the tops of her breasts!" Maria objects.

"The *tops* of her breasts," I correct myself. "And singing songs about drugs and sex and atheism?"

"But that's *what she wants to do*! How can you have a problem with that? She's an adult. She's not twelve!"

"My daughter's gifts could be of great use on the south side of Chicago, and that is fact, not opinion."

Maria glares over at me, clearly unconvinced.

"In my neighborhood, the house is on fire," I say. "The house is on fire, and Richelle has water that could help put it out. Do you have any idea the positive impact it would have on the young women in my pews to see a girl from the neighborhood who has become successful? These young women who don't see a future for themselves—who have babies at fourteen because they don't see any reason not to—would benefit tremendously from just *seeing* a woman like Richelle in their midst. They'd see that a smart, determined young woman from South Shore can achieve anything she puts her mind to . . . and that's just if Richelle meets me halfway! That's just if she comes to church *occasionally*! What Richelle could achieve if she chose to use her talents to advocate for the community? To work alongside us for change? That thought makes me so mad...I have to force it out of my mind! Richelle could be so many things. She could help in so many ways. Our house is on fire. Our neighborhoods are on fire. Richelle knows this. She grew up there. Richelle has water—*so* much water—and she won't help me put out this fire. Instead, she uses it for...making lewd, angry songs. *That's* my problem."

Maria opens her mouth, but closes it again without speaking.

"I'm not saying there's no place for lewd, angry songs," I continue. "You'd be surprised by the things I like to listen to. But to put those songs above helping a community? Above pouring water on a burning house? That, I just don't understand."

I wonder if Maria will have more to say to me. For the moment, she doesn't. We know we disagree with one another. I know her arguments, and she knows mine. We are like long-retired senators from opposing parties, each having heard the other's speeches and invectives countless times.

And I start thinking…I could really tell Maria something now. While we're sharing, I could share something with her that I don't talk to anybody about. I could tell her the reason why I was late to Ms. Washington's house. Why I took that drive down to Merrillville. Here, in the middle of a zombie outbreak, beneath the warring city, we have the privacy of a fortress. We are beyond isolated. The zombies have made so many horrible things possible, why not let them make truth a possibility?

Why not?

We round a bend in the corridor. For the first time, we see a hatch with an opening to the world above. It does not appear soldered shut. There is a ladder. We have a way out, if we want it. It is cheering beyond description to see.

I also realize that we are near Oak Park. What happens when we arrive there and get above ground? I have no idea. But time is short.

Geronimo.

"I missed an important appointment with one of my parishioners tonight because I was at a Huey Lewis and the News concert."

I await Maria's judgment with bated breath.

"They're still touring?"

"You kidding? They did over a hundred gigs last year."

"If they can still pack 'em in, I guess it makes sense," Maria allows. "Bill Gibson, right?"

"Huh?"

"Bill Gibson is the drummer, right?" Maria clarifies.

"Yes," I answer, surprised. "That's correct."

"I mean, he's no Neil Peart or Stewart Copeland, but talk about a solid four beat," Maria continues. "You could set your watch by that guy. Never overplays. Never distracts from Huey. Lotta good drumming over the years."

"How do you know about Bill Gibson?"

"Because he's a *drummer*," Maria shoots back, as if this ought to be obvious.

Then she is silent for a moment.

"Wait a minute," she says. "How is it that you criticize your own daughter for being in a rock and roll band, and then you turn around and…"

She stops.

"Mack? *Mack*? Omigod…Mack are you *crying*?"

She leans in to leer at my tears, making certain they're not just the dance of the flashlight.

"My hip hurts," I lie. (Bad pastor.)

"No way! You're totally crying! But . . . why would Huey Lewis make you cry? I mean, yeah, I suppose it is about the whitest music ever made, and you're a black guy from the south side, but there's got to be something more than that. Right? *Right*?"

Another moment of silence.

"I can't tell *anybody* about this," I rasp, fighting back tears.

Maria seems confused.

"What is the 'this' in that sentence?" she asks. "Do you have a secret Huey Lewis room, filled with posters and album covers or something?"

Silence.

"Omigod, you *do*!"

"It's at the back of the church, just off the old rectory."

"But why…"

"*I don't know!*" I shoot back. "Maybe it's because his first few records coincide with a good time in my life when I was growing the church, growing my family, getting to know God. They were tough years but good years, and Huey was always there. I used to be a thug and a gangster. You probably didn't know that. When I came back from Vietnam, I was troubled. It took me a while to turn my life around, but I did it. When it really began to sink in—when I was sure I'd changed my ways and left the bad old Mack in the past—well, that was when Huey came around. It just happened."

"And you like his music, too," Maria says from the corner of her mouth.

"Of course, and I have no one that I can tell. Not my closest friends. Not Richelle. Certainly nobody in the congregation. That a few times a year—once a month, if I can manage it—I have to head off to wherever the nearest Huey Lewis and the News concert is. I try to stop…and I can't. I think 'This *has* to be the last time, Mack.' Then it isn't. Another month goes by, and I find myself at some riverboat casino on the Mississippi singing along to 'Hip to Be Square.'"

Maria starts to laugh. A throaty laugh, almost like a man's. It was this that I most feared. That if people knew that Pastor Leopold Mack—advocate for the people, crusader for justice in South Shore, shepherd of his flock—liked a super-white 80s rock band, his power would be taken away. Nobody would take him seriously. Nobody would turn to him when in need of assistance. His sermons would be heckled. People would laugh. And laugh. And laugh.

Then Maria says, "I'm not laughing *at* you, Mack. I'm laughing at the fact that you think anybody cares!"

"What?"

"So what if you like the whitest singer ever? How is that even anybody's business?"

"You don't understand," I tell her, shaking my head. "I have a reputation to uphold. A standard of comportment that—"

"No, *you* don't understand," Maria shoots back. "You've made something out of nothing. Why do you think those people in the pews come listen to you week after week?"

"According to you, it's because I tell them to," I counter.

"Nope," Maria says. "That was why they called you 'reverend,' which you said they don't even do."

"What, then?"

"Because they get something from it," she tells me. "Because they get *you*. They get who you are and what you're trying to do for them. They know that you give a damn about them. That you really care what happens in their lives. That that's your 'thing'—in the same way it's *not* Richelle's 'thing.' I don't think the fact you know all the cities Huey names in 'Heart of Rock & Roll' is going to change that."

I don't have an answer for her.

"We may have to respectfully disagree," I tell Maria.

"That'd be a first," she says. "The respectful part, I mean."

She has a point.

Maria Ramirez

After he talks about his Huey Lewis thing—or whatever—Mack gets kind of quiet for a while. I don't think he's mad at me, more like he just has to do some thinking. (I still don't get why it's such a big deal.)

We keep on heading northwest. This part of the tunnel is less oppressive and dirty. I don't know if 'cleaner' is the right word—the floor is still covered in disgusting greasy coal slime—but there seems to be less gunk underfoot. I point out that we haven't seen any more zombies.

"Yes," agrees Mack. "They're all back in the pit. The way the tunnel was boarded up, they had no place else to go."

No sooner are these words out of Mack's mouth than his flashlight beam lights on makeshift wooden scaffolding blocking the way ahead.

"Uh oh," I say.

"Now, now," cautions Mack. "No reason to worry…yet."

I'm reminded that we no longer have Ben's policeman's truncheon. Or Ben. Maybe we can kick it down or use the butt-end of Mack's Maglite.

We reach the bulwark. It is a thin wall of wood like we've seen before. No doubt, the opposite side will carry a skull face of some clever, coded variation.

"Why do you think these things were built?" I ask Mack as we begin looking for the weakest point. "They didn't know zombies were going to be inside them."

"I think it was the stuff that *became* zombies," Mack answers, prying loose a board with his bare hands. "The dead bodies and whatever else. We don't even know if this tunnel—the Oak Park tunnel—is typical. Maybe the others contain different things. Worse things."

"Maybe so," I answer, hoping he is wrong.

It takes only a few minutes of kicking and prying to make a hole in the wooden wall. Like last time, there are silent zombies waiting for us on the other side. But this time we're ready for them.

We work in tandem. I hold the flashlight and Mack takes them out with his Glock. Two are old—practically mummified—and Mack targets them easily. One shot to the forehead each. They puff out dust like when you smack your grandmother's old couch. Down they go, collapsing to the tunnel floor.

Behind the two mummies is a fresher, newer zombie—so fresh that at first we mistake him for a human. It's a city worker. African American, maybe late 40s. He wears a bright orange hard hat and a reflective yellow Streets and Sanitation vest over his work overalls. His lower jaw hangs open expectantly like someone in the thrall of a good anecdote—the punch line always an instant away.

"Look out, m'man!" Mack says instinctively when the zombie lopes into view.

"Zombie!" I advise Mack. "Look at the eyes."

Or rather, the lack of them. The city worker's organs of sight have been eaten out of his head, probably by rats.

"Dang," says Mack. "This guy couldn't be more than a week old."

"Here, let me get his hat off."

I carefully reach in with the Maglite and knock the zombie's hardhat away. The creature roars and tries to seize me, but I'm too quick.

BLAM!

Mack finishes it off. The former city worker falls to the tunnel floor and takes his place next to the crusty mummies.

We step over the motionless corpses of corpses and continue our lonely parade down the tunnel.

★ ★ ★

"What time is it?" I ask, handing him back the flashlight. "I've lost all sense of time."

"Don't you wear a watch, young lady?"

"No, I use my cell phone like a *normal person*. My guess is five in the morning. I'm hungry and thirsty and I feel like I could sleep for a week."

"I understand those feelings," Mack says, bending the light to check his wristwatch. "Wow. It's closer to seven."

"It'll be light out soon. I mean…up there."

No sooner are the words out of my mouth than the strong brilliant beam of Mack's Maglite flickers and grows dim.

"Oh shit," I whisper, as if it will hear us. (I shouldn't have mentioned the word light. I have somehow upset the heavy metal cylinder that is the difference between life and death for us right now. It heard me. It knows.)

"Ehh, I'm not surprised," Mack says unperturbedly, as if the dire implications of this development are not clear to him. "I can't remember when I last replaced the batteries."

I look at Mack, now less distinct in the limited glow.

"Should we, like, turn it off for a while? Maybe just shine it every few feet. It'll be like coasting in your car when it's almost out of gas. Sort of."

"I don't—"

And that's all Mack has time to say before the flashlight fails completely and we are plunged into darkness.

"Omigod."

"Come to me, child. Follow my voice. I'm right here."

I walk in the darkest blackness I have ever seen. It's coal black. Blue-black. Make you think your eyes are broken black.

"Omigod," I say again. I reach out and find Mack's slick leather coat in the darkness. Then his arm. Then his hand. It is warm, and I grip it hard.

"Here," he says. "I've got you."

The utter, smothering nature of this darkness is more than I can describe. It's not like being in a darkened room. It's like your optic nerves got pulled out of your head. That part of you is gone. You don't just "not see." You forget what seeing was ever like.

This is it.

Game over.

Unless...

"Can you do anything with the light, Mack? Can you fix it?"

"It's the batteries. I think if we wait a few minutes, they will charge back up a bit. Then I think we should do your plan of flicking it on and off. I think we'll *have* to do that."

"Jesus, this is horrible."

"It's okay," says Mack. Somehow, he is not terrified.

I huddle close. I can smell Mack's musk, aftershave, and sweat. I can smell the horrible oil stench of the tunnel. I can hear...

Wait.

"Mack, do you hear that?"

We both listen.

"Yes," he says.

"It's like a scraping…a metal scraping."

Suddenly, the tunnel in front of us grows perceptibly brighter. There is a thin blue light against the darkness. We can begin to see the outlines of the track in the floor. I can see Mack's face and just how scared he looks (despite his air of confidence). I'm sure I look the same.

"What *is* that?" I whisper.

Mack's eyes go back and forth as he searches for an explanation. Then it hits him.

"That's our only chance! That's what it is!"

He takes off down the tunnel as fast as his bad hip will carry him, nearly casting me to the floor in the process.

"What?" I say, stumbling forward.

"Someone has opened up a shaft! A shaft to the surface! A way out! Come on!"

"What if it's someone who isn't friendly?" I object, running after him.

"We're takin' that chance!" Mack replies.

I follow him around the gentle curve of the tunnel. The blue-white glow becomes more and more pronounced. I can see the walls of the tunnel and Mack's flopping jacket as he races forward.

"Hello!!!!" Mack calls as he runs. "Hellooooo!!! Is anyone there!!! We're down here!!! Don't close it up!!!"

We round a long corner and finally see the source. A two-foot beam of light penetrates the darkness. It's so bright that it forces me to squint. Mack shields his eyes with his forearm but doesn't stop running.

A manhole-like covering at the top of the tunnel has been pried open. There are stone footholds and a metal handrail set into the wall below it. I force myself to head directly for this makeshift ladder, so that even if the light from above is extinguished I won't run past.

Mack speeds ahead and stops only when he stands underneath the opening, directly in the beam. I catch up and hunker at the edge of the light. After so many hours beneath the city, we've become like moles. We shield our eyes and struggle to glimpse the topside world.

"Hello there!" Mack calls up to the opening.

Both of us squint and try to see. An enormous figure looms into of the circle of light above us, blocking nearly half the beam. It's a man—a giant man—thick-necked like a football player and wearing a turtleneck sweater to increase his general girth.

A voice, eerily similar to Mack's, booms down.

"Hello down there!" it says. "I heard y'all could use you some light."

Mack claps his hands and dances around, once, in a circle—rotating in the beam like a brilliant jewel in a motorized display case.

"*The entrance of thy words giveth light!*" Mack cries, a smile curling to his lips.

"Mmm hmm," returns the voice, with playful skepticism. "In this case though, I believe my light giveth light. The light from the sun, that is. What you doing down in that sloppy old tunnel, Pastor Mack? Oh, hang on, your man here tried to tell me..."

"My man?" Mack asks.

Another head appears in the opening above. It has a familiar shape. And thick black glasses.

"Ben?" I call out. "Ben, is that you?"

"Yeah," Ben's voice descends. "Come up here! You're almost to Oak Park!"

"My Good Samaritan!!!" Mack says, and erupts into laughter.

I look on, scarce believing my eyes. Mack continues to rotate. He is dancing. He holds out his arms.

"My Good Samaritan!" Mack cries out again. "Hallelujah!"

And he stays there for a while like that, just rotating.

★ ★ ★

Back on the surface world, we learn that we are at the edge of a mostly African-American west side neighborhood called Austin. It abuts Oak Park. We are practically there. In our time in the tunnels, we've traveled something like eight miles.

The large, turtlenecked man is an old friend of Mack's. (Mack introduces us when he gets through hugging him, which is after a damn while.)

"This is Moses Rivers," Mack explains enthusiastically, "Pastor of The Church of Christ in God."

"We go by 'cockage,'" he says in a baritone equal to Mack's. After an awkward moment, I realize he is parsing "COCIG."

I take a look around. The streets in this neighborhood were pretty bleak *before* a zombie outbreak. Now they are doubly so. There's a mix of single family homes and apartment buildings, but nearly half of them are board-ups. The ones that were not closed by the city for tax delinquency or abandoned have been barricaded against the walking dead. Empty lots full of trash and detritus separate the homes like pits of decay separating teeth in a smile. (It is in one of these undeveloped lots that Pastor Rivers has accessed the tunnels to free us, removing the bolts on a square plate set into the ground.) At the end of the block is a no-name cell phone store and a fish-fry shack, both burned and looted. On the sidewalk across the street from us is an old brown couch with two elderly men relaxing on it. It takes me a few moments to realize that both of them are dead.

Ben Bennington, still apparently hale and whole, is standing next to Pastor Rivers. Mack hugs him next, just for good measure.

"Wow . . . good to see you, too," Ben says.

"What happened, Ben?" I ask urgently. "We were sure those zombies got you."

Ben looks at Pastor Rivers and says, "You want to tell them?"

Rivers shrugs.

"Since these things first started coming up, we've been trying to stamp 'em out and clear the neighborhood," Rivers begins. "Try to ensure everybody in the congregation was safe."

"Just like what we did at Mack's church!" Ben says brightly.

"I don't envy Pastor Mack," Rivers says. "You're right between the lake and Crenshaw Cemetery. Plus, your congregation is bigger than mine. We get a lot of bodies out here on the west side, but the police usually find 'em a few hours after they drop. Down in South Shore, you boys got a whole other story. Put a body in that lake, ain't no tellin' how long it stays down. Anyway, we been at this since last night. And those *things* kept coming up long after I was sure there couldn't be no more. I got to thinking they could be coming from the old tunnels, 'cause I was seeing ones that were old. *Real* old. Men that had died back in my grandfather's days, rotted down to almost nothing but bones and a suit."

"We saw a lot of that in the tunnels," I say. "You were right."

"There are three entrances I know of here in Austin," mentions Pastor Rivers. "First one I tried, there weren't nothin' below. Empty and spider webs. The second opening—it's inside an old sausage plant off Central Avenue—I look inside and what do I see but this young man about to get hisself eaten by a bunch of the damn things. I reach down and grab him, hoist him back up to the factory floor, and close that door. All in about two seconds."

"But we didn't see that!" I object. "How did you…?"

"There was a hatch right above the lip of that pit," Ben says. "We were so distracted looking down at the zombies that we didn't even notice it. When Pastor Rivers grabbed me, I had no idea what was happening. The interior of the sausage plant was dark too."

"Mmm hmm," agrees Rivers. "You take it from here, young man."

Ben looks sheepish for a moment.

"Come now," Rivers cajoles. "The dead are walkin', son. Ain't no time to worry what people think."

Mack and I exchange the briefest of glances at this comment. I say nothing though. His secret is safe with me.

"I passed out," Ben says quietly. "I didn't know what was happening. I saw the zombies coming, and I was worried about making that jump into the pit. Then there were these hands pulling me around the waist—pulling me up out of nowhere—and I got lightheaded and that was it."

"I thought he might be dead or about to come back as one of those *things*," Rivers tells us. "He was out a good twenty minutes. When he woke up normal and explained what you all were doing, we went back and opened the hatch. We looked and looked, but you were already gone. Our only chance was to try to catch you further down the line, at *this* hatch. But we scurried and done it."

"In the nick of time, too," says Mack. "We lost our light."

"Damn," replies Rivers. "Down there with those things...*in the dark*. Ouch."

"Yeah, it was pretty 'ouch' there for a while," I say.

"Did Ben tell you what we're trying to do?" Mack asks. "What we're up against?"

Rivers nods. "He did, and I ain't surprised. Disappointed maybe, but not surprised. You always could smell the stank coming off Marja Mogk from about a mile away. She's got some allies out here on the west side, too. But I don't know if she's been able to get to them yet."

"Are the phones and everything still down?" I ask, remembering my cell in my pocket.

"Oh yeah," says Pastor Rivers. "Internets too."

"Then we've still got a chance to get to my father...before she does," I say.

"I can drive you the rest of the way," says Rivers. "South part of Austin is jammed up good. People got stuck trying to get on the expressway and abandoned they cars around midnight. Where we are though—a bit north of the highway—we got a straight shot into Oak Park."

"Sounds good to me," I tell him. "After all that walking, I will damn-straight accept a ride."

★ ★ ★

Rivers's car is not as nice as Mack's but still has the preacher look to it. (Mack's house of worship might not be a clean new mega-church with ten thousand parishioners, but it could still look plenty enviable to a west side startup congregation operating out of a storefront that gets fifty attendees on a good Sunday.) We pile in. I take a spot in the back seat next to Ben. As we wait for the heater to kick in, I realize just how tired and hungry I am. Ben seems to sense this.

"Here you go," Ben says, producing a half-eaten stick of beef jerky from under his coat. "Rivers gave it to me."

"Ugh," I say. "*That* stuff."

"Do you want it?"

"Of course I do," I tell him. I grab the preserved sausage stick and take a bite. Meaty saltiness washes over me. Balm of Gilead. Ambrosia. I have never tasted anything so fine. My stomach rumbles as I begin to fill it with processed meat.

I give Rivers my cousin's address and he pulls the car away from the curb.

The neighborhoods through which we pass show signs of chaos and carnage but are quiet for the moment. In the cool light of dawn, they reveal themselves as utterly still. Abandoned cars are everywhere. Many streets are blocked—some with personal cars but some with police cruisers and fire trucks, as if as part of some coordinated municipal effort. A garbage truck has been used to completely cut off traffic to a side street. A fire truck's ladder has been extended horizontally to prevent automobile traffic from taking an exit. Was this some mad, last-ditch attempt to funnel people away from the highway? It seems impossible to tell. Rivers appears to know the neighborhood, however, and easily maneuvers us around the blockage, driving across yards and up on sidewalks when he has to.

Corpses litter the landscape, especially in the gutters. From a distance, they look like piles of clothes. Some are dead zombies, shot through their stinking heads. Others are human, either too destroyed and dashed to reanimate…or too *recent* for reanimation to have yet occurred.

We mostly ride in silence. Going from the stark alien darkness of the tunnels to the familiar inside of an automobile is jarring. I think we are all letting it sink in. I can't speak for the others, but I feel like I could sleep for about a year.

"You inhaled that sausage," Ben observes.

"Got any more?"

"Nope, that was the last one."

I frown, wanting about ten more of them. Then something occurs to me.

"Is there anything on the radio?"

"Ehh, wasn't much before," Rivers replies with some amusement. "Let's see if they got their act together."

Rivers turns on the radio and begins scanning through channels. Most of them—the stations I recognize—seem to be gone. The ones that do come in are all playing the same recorded message. It starts with the distorted whine of the Emergency Broadcast Service. Then a computerized-sounding voice comes on. It advises residents to stay inside their homes, obey any orders from police or military, and, oddly, to "give no comfort or aid to aggressive foreign elements."

"What the hell does that mean?" I ask after the message has repeated a couple of times.

"I don't think they had a pre-recorded emergency message for 'Zombie Outbreak' waiting in the can," says Mack. "They probably went with whatever seemed closest."

"Yessir," agrees Pastor Rivers with a laugh. "That one sounds like 'Russkie Invasion' to me. Somebody must'a had to dig through the archives for that."

"I bet you're right," says Mack.

"The radio mentions army and police," I say. "Have you *seen* any army or police?"

"Not on duty and not alive," Rivers replies, shaking his head.

We enter the strip where Austin ends and Oak Park begins. Normally, I would observe that the homes get a little nicer as we continue west, but what's "nicer" when it would be "nice" not to get eaten by zombies or killed by looters? Is a Frank Lloyd Wright prairie-style house an advantage if your long, low front window and the grand piano behind it are no longer protected by a security system?

Despite some architectural setbacks, I see evidence that the upper middle class have done their best to hunker down against the walking dead. Ignoring carefully maintained yards, SUVs have been driven across flowerbeds and parked in front of vulnerable glass doors. Windows have been boarded up with broken furniture and nailed shut. In one case, a Harvard University flag has been used to tie down the opening to a cellar door.

A few houses have been left utterly undefended by residents who I assume simply headed for the hills. These are almost uniformly ransacked—windows smashed, doors torn from hinges, possessions scattered everywhere (sometimes out across the front lawns). There are also signs of zombie attacks. Alarming red swaths of blood smeared across white picket fences and garage doors. Bright red handprints—some, heartbreakingly, child-sized—mottle the sides of houses like art projects. (These are not the aftermath of looters and gun-packing criminals. No thief bothers to draw that much blood. These victims were sanguinated by hordes of dragging, scratching, biting zombies.)

It doesn't take much for me to imagine the confused residents of this neighborhood in the first moments of the attack. I see them running across lawns in mounting terror, searching in vain for loved ones, and finding themselves cornered in back yards by stumbling undead.

It happened here too. And if my family—my father, mother, and sister—made it out here, then what did they find? Was my cousin Franco one of the ones to turn his house into a fort, or was he one of the ones who fled? I look at the alternately fortified and destroyed homes and wonder which kind we're going to find.

"It's down here," I call up to the front. "Take a left after the playground...if you can."

The neighborhood is so utterly changed by the outbreak that it's hard for me to recognize where we are. I'm mostly going by street names.

"Quick question, everybody," I say to the whole car. "What happens when we get there?"

"I talked to Pastor Rivers already," Ben says. "We discussed escape plans for the mayor."

"You knew you could trust him?" I shoot back, forgetting for a moment that Rivers is inside the car with us.

"He saved me from zombies, didn't he? Plus, I didn't have much of a choice. I had to tell him my story. It was him or nothing."

"The young lady has a reasonable concern," Rivers allows from the front seat. "There *are* a lot of corrupt people who'd love to help Mogk take over the city. A lot of 'em would do it for next to nothing. For a scrap. For a sandwich. There's people in this town *dyin'* to sell out somebody, just so they can get a little bit ahead. When you ran into me, you got lucky. I'm incorruptible."

"So what did you decide?" I ask.

"What you need—what your father and all your family members need—is somewhere to hide," Rivers says. "Somewhere with no connection to the rest of your lives. Your priority is to put the mayor someplace where Marja Mogk's people will never think to look."

"Like?" I ask.

"Like how 'bout the basement of a church in Austin?" Rivers suggests.

I nod. That sounds okay.

"Gonna be a tight squeeze to fit everybody in this car," I point out. I hope the Pastor will not think I am criticizing his smaller size preacher car. I am only stating a fact.

"If sitting in laps is our biggest problem, we are gonna be a blessed group of people," says Mack.

Moments later, Franco's house comes into view. I take a deep breath. Whatever's going to happen, it happens now.

Ben Bennington

The Oak Park home containing the new mayor of Chicago is at the end of a block filled with burned-out cars and bodies littering the gutters. It looks like TV footage from a third world country, not a city in the United States. The house is, compared to its neighbors, relatively modest—a white, two-story affair; probably no more than two bedrooms. It has not been abandoned to zombies and criminals, which we are very relieved to see. Indeed, in stark contrast to some of its smashed and looted neighbors, it has been protected in a variety of ways. Furniture and boxes have been heaped against windows. Two cars have been parked in front of the garage door, blocking access. Another car has been parked against a side door, with its front bumper physically pinning the door shut. Every shutter has been closed, and every shade has been lowered. Somebody has definitely battened down the hatches.

It's eight in the morning now, but the house is still dark. At Mack's insistence, Rivers pulls his car to the side of the road some distance away. We step outside into the bracing cold street. I can't tell if the temperature has fallen or if I'm just weak from exhaustion. Probably both.

"Careful now," Mack says, drawing his Glock.

"Put that away!" Maria objects. "You want to scare them?"

"No, but I might want to scare some other people."

Maria seems to consider this and draws her own gun.

We stay in a tight bunch, cutting through front yards and staying close to trees and fences, as if taking cover from snipers above. Maria takes the lead. At one point, I stop to rest against a five-foot iron fence with pointed, spear-like tips. After a moment, I notice that a human eyeball has been impaled on the tip nearest me. (Is it my imagination, or is it looking at me?)

In a few moments, we are in front of the right house.

"Franco!" Maria calls loudly. "Franco, it's me!"

We head up the driveway.

"Rifle on us," Mack says from the corner of his mouth. "Upstairs window. You recognize him?"

Maria takes a glance at the bedroom window from which a gun barrel is emerging.

"No," Maria says. "I don't."

Maria stops advancing. So do the rest of us. There's this awful moment where we all start to wonder if we've got the wrong place, or if Marja Mogk's people have beat us here and we're walking into an ambush. Then the front door opens and a man about my age in a Blackhawks jersey steps onto the porch. He holds a handgun but keeps it pointed at the ground.

"Maria?" the man asks.

"Franco!" Maria returns with relief.

"Maria, who are these people? What's going on?"

"These are my friends."

"I need to talk to you," Franco says, cautiously. "And they need to stay outside…for now."

"Franco, what the fuck?" Maria returns, scowling and frustrated.

Mack leans in to Maria and whispers, "Maybe you should tell him *who* and *what* is on the way to his house."

Maria nods.

"Franco, we're here because we're trying to protect my dad. He's the fucking mayor now. Did he tell you that? Did he also tell you that most of the city council is trying to kill him? Because they are. And they're coming *here*."

Franco's face falls.

"These people have helped me get here," she continues, indicating our motley crew with a flick of her gun. "I would be dead if it weren't for them. You can trust them, okay? Now let us inside!"

Franco sets his handgun on the porch railing and runs his fingers through his hair. He looks—probably as we all do—like he hasn't slept in twenty-four hours. He glances around his neighborhood at the shuttered and looted homes.

"Yeah, okay," Franco allows quietly. "Come on inside."

We file up to the porch, Maria first. Above us, the rifle barrel slowly retracts.

The inside is a mess, like the house of somebody in the middle of moving. Furniture and clothes are piled everywhere. There are two armed men about Franco's age, drinking coffee in the kitchen just off the entryway. Another man with a rifle descends from the second floor staircase and joins them, making three in all. They regard us and look to Franco for a cue.

"Franco, where is he?" Maria asks.

"In the back bedroom," Franco returns.

"And my mother and my sister?"

"Down in the basement rec room, sleeping."

"I want to see them, Franco...*now*."

Franco nods solemnly and conducts Maria away to the back of the house. A few moments later, he returns alone.

"You got any more of that coffee?" Mack asks the men in the kitchen.

"I'd take some too," says Rivers. "And I 'spect so would my man here."

I nod. I would.

We are poured coffee and sit at the kitchen table with Franco and his friends.

"Tell us everything," Franco says.

Restored by Folgers, the three of us oblige.

★ ★ ★

After giving Franco the basics, we all agree that—if Mogk's troops *are* coming—the next priority is getting everyone to a new location, including the mayor. Using Rivers's car sounds like a good plan.

Moments later, Maria returns from the basement. She has obviously been crying, but her expression is now placid. Serene. Maybe it was good-crying.

She wipes away a tear.

"Okay," she says. "Now I need to talk to him."

"Respectfully," Mack interjects, "I think *all of us* need to talk to him."

We file to the back bedroom. The cream-colored carpeting in the hallways has been trampled to an ugly Chicago-grey by snowy boots. Passing through the home, I see that every piece of furniture in each room has been piled against the windows.

Franco raps on the door with a thick set of knuckles.

"Frankie!" he calls. "Uncle!"

For a moment, there is no response.

"Mister Mayor!" Mack tries in his deepest voice.

That does the trick.

The bedroom door opens abruptly, and Maria's father stands before us. The new king of Chicago is hardly regal. He wears a tattered bathrobe that hangs open most of the way. Underneath he is naked, except for a pair of cheap white boxer shorts. His belly protrudes like a giant tractor tire. He looks exhausted and smells of sweat and fear.

Maria pushes her cousin aside and strides into the room. She stands in front of the mayor and looks up into his eyes . . . and then slaps him across the face.

"What did you do, *Papi*?" she says coldly. "What in the name of God did you do?"

The mayor's face falls. He looks away.

"Could we please..." the mayor begins, faltering. "Can we talk about this in private, Maria?"

"Okay," Maria says, then adds, "But wait. Ben, Mack...you two stay. This concerns you."

"How does this concern *them*?" the mayor objects, looking back and forth.

"Because they were almost killed by the shit you pulled!" Maria shoots back. "By the shit that you better start explaining *right fucking now*."

The mayor ties his robe and sits Indian-style on the edge of the bed. Mack shuts the door. He stands in front of it with his arms crossed, staring down the mayor. His body language seems to say that *none* of us will be leaving this room until Maria gets some answers.

"What the fuck was going on at Crenshaw Cemetery?" Maria says like a prosecuting attorney. "Give us the truth and we might just save your life."

For a moment, the mayor looks at Maria with an angry, arrogant expression. His face seems to ask who she is to address him in this way. Then, slowly, he appears to remember that he is an exhausted man in a filthy bathrobe who is unarmed and afraid for his life. And that his own daughter now holds the upper hand.

"First of all, it was never me," the mayor begins, looking down at the bed. "It was Alderman Mogk and Alderman Szuter. Their system had been in place since before I was elected. That fucking system...I just *inherited* it. One day—not a week after I started my first term as alderman—we were meeting in Marja's office after the dedication of a new community center. I thought it was just a friendly, get-acquainted sort of meeting, you know? But that was when she told me how they did it."

"Did *what*?" Maria returns icily.

"There's a lot of change happening in our three wards...a lot of *movement*, let's say," the mayor begins cautiously.

"No, let's *not* say," Maria spits back. "There's no time for euphemisms, Dad. The zombies are at the gates. Just tell us what the fuck you did!"

"*I'm trying to!*" the mayor roars back, frustrated.

"All right then..." Maria says. "So tell us in plain words."

"There is a lot of moving around between constituencies in the neighborhoods where our three aldermanic wards meet," the mayor says slowly, as if he is talking to a child.

"By 'constituencies,' you mean 'races,'" Mack states from across the room. "Black and white and brown people moving around."

"Yes," says the mayor. "Szuter's ward is white people, pushing down from the Loop. Mogk's ward is where the black south side begins, and my ward is the little Hispanic pocket that sort of separates them. But it's not that easy."

"How so?" Maria presses. "And what the fuck does it have to do with bodies where they shouldn't be in Crenshaw Cemetery?"

The mayor takes a deep breath.

"As Marja explained to me, the people in our wards move around *more* than people in other wards in this city. It's a volatile area, demographically speaking. The tip of the spear for gentrification. A new strip of condos can make a block that was affordable for renters six months ago suddenly too expensive, forcing them to move. They move somewhere close, and then the neighboring ward changes. Pretty soon, everyone is all mixed up. The city redraws the ward maps every ten years, but our ward-changes happen faster than that...much faster. If you're not careful, the people in the alderman's ward might not look like the alderman come election time. And these new voters might not know all the good things that that alderman had done for the community ... *Unless you do something about it.* That was where Burge Wheeler came in."

The mayor pauses for a moment. The name of Chicago's most infamous cop hangs heavy in the air.

"Wheeler helped make sure that things didn't change too quickly in our wards. He was their hired man. That was where I said 'no' to Marja and Igor, by the way. That was where I said I wanted no part of it."

"Burge Wheeler worked for Marja Mogk and Igor Szuter?" Mack asks.

"And my predecessor," says the mayor. "But *never for me*. I refused to be involved with that…ugliness."

"What changed your mind?" Maria asks with a smirk.

And, for the first time, an expression crosses the mayor's face that makes me think he is not an entirely evil man. A scumbag? Sure. A corrupt politician who only wanted to use the system to make himself rich? Oh absolutely. But a killer? Well… maybe not.

"It was murder!" the mayor says, as if this fact should be obvious. "Under the direction of Mogk and Szuter—and, formerly, *my* predecessor—Burge Wheeler would carry out murders and disappearances in our wards. Gangbangers start to hang out in a neighborhood that needs to stay nice? They end up in Crenshaw. People from the wrong race move onto the wrong street that's not ready to gentrify yet? Some of them—not all of them, but some of them—go to Crenshaw. Enough to send a message. Burge Wheeler was killing people for them. *Killing* people. He had been for years. And the cemetery manager was always happy to take a bribe to make the bodies go away."

"And bury them underneath the landscaping," Mack adds, shaking his head in disapproval.

"But Burge Wheeler can't have come cheap," I interject. "I mean, corrupt cops are corrupt for money, not just because they like corruption. These aldermen must have had to pay some hefty bribes. Was it worth all that, just for an alderman's salary?"

Chicago aldermen are probably the highest-paid city council in the nation, if not the world. Six figures and a pension for life. But still, I reason, paying for murders has to add up fast.

I look over at Mack for backup. He nods to say my point is indeed legitimate.

"You have to understand, it was about much more than getting reelected," says the mayor. "That's small-time thinking. What aldermen make? That's peanuts. Mogk and Szuter were onto something greater. Something grander! They had realized that with just a few strokes of...*selective* law enforcement, you could do more than just keep white neighborhoods white, black neighborhoods black, and Latin neighborhoods Latin. You could control gentrification itself!"

The mayor pauses dramatically, as if we need time to let this idea sink in. When we appear less than completely bowled over, he continues.

"The thing about real estate...it's essentially gambling, right? You're betting on the market. Betting that neighborhoods will change. You buy up a nasty old block in a crime-ridden area and hope that it changes from bad to good quickly so you can build some overpriced condos that rich people will pay out the ass for. Sometimes it works, and you get a windfall. Sometimes it doesn't, and you're stuck with a worthless, nasty block that nobody wants to live on. But what if somebody could *guarantee* that a neighborhood could change for the better—and change quickly—for a fee?"

"Or guarantee that it wouldn't change, *unless* there was a fee," Mack adds, seeing the implications.

"Exactly," says the mayor. "Burge Wheeler did more than maintain the demographics for election day. When a block needed to improve and crime needed to go away, he could make that happen—step up enforcement, make drug dealers and thugs 'disappear' or torture them into a confession. But he could also send stuff the other way. When Marja told him a block needed *more* crime—because a developer hadn't paid their 'gentrification fee'—Burge Wheeler could provide that too."

"He and his men just didn't enforce the laws?" I ask. "Like on that 'Amsterdam' episode of *The Wire*?"

"That was part of it, but not *all* of it. You want me to say it again? I'll say it again. He did murders! He created the crime. New people move to a neighborhood that Mogk and Szuter don't want to change? Maybe they get shot in a drive-by. Maybe they just go for a walk one night and never come back. Either way, they can't pay the mortgage anymore. The neighborhood goes back to the way it was."

There is an uncomfortable moment of silence, that kind you get when the worst is confirmed. Mack and I look at one another, then down at the floor. Maria just shakes her head.

For whatever reason, I'm still thinking like a reporter.

"Why didn't Burge Wheeler flip on you when the feds came for him?" I ask the mayor.

"Flip on Marja Mogk and Igor Szuter, you mean," says the mayor. "Yes, I think he might have done that...if he'd thought he'd get a real sentence. If they'd had *any* evidence about the murders. But they didn't. They had nothing, remember? What did they get Burge Wheeler for? Failing to follow interrogation procedures, some bullshit like that. Burge Wheeler isn't going to die in jail, and he knows it. I'll bet there's a bathtub full of unmarked bills waiting for him when he gets out, too. And he takes it down to Florida, and we never hear from him again."

"I hate to say it, but that actually sounds believable," I tell him.

"But I told them to leave me out of it!" insists the mayor. "I want to make that clear. You have to believe me! I told Marja and Igor that I wanted *no* part of it. They could do their thing—run their little gentrification-for-hire business—but I didn't want in. I would not be involved."

"You didn't turn them in, either!" Maria shoots back. "You didn't tell them to stop! You actually sound proud of yourself, but you didn't do anything."

"You'd be surprised by what I've turned down in back rooms and basements around this city. Besides...they would have killed me."

"That can still happen," I advise the mayor.

"Yes," the mayor agrees soberly. "Marja Mogk has two reasons to want me dead. I know about the killings...and I'm the only thing standing between her and the mayor's office."

"We went to Crenshaw last night," Mack says. "Marja's troops were putting down the zombies. All the people Burge Wheeler had buried over the years were coming back up."

"I'm sure they were," says the mayor, nodding. "Like a lot of murderers in Chicago, she's very busy right now tying up loose ends."

The mayor's face falls.

"She doesn't know about *this* place!" he says. The thought has only now struck him.

"She *does*," Maria confirms. "Her people are on the way."

The mayor's jaw drops a little. His shoulders go slack, and his belly pooches out even more.

Maria gives her father a quick version of our story. During the more fantastic moments, the mayor looks around the room doubtfully. Mack and I nod sternly, insisting that no part of our Odyssey is being exaggerated by his daughter.

"You did all that just to get to me?" he says after she finishes.

"Were you even listening?" Maria says. "*I* came here because my mother and sister are with you, which means they're in danger. Ben and Mack might be curious about what happens to you, but I'm not."

Maria gestures across the room at us.

"You've got a lot of nerve thinking I did this for *you*. I fucking hate you. You were a virus I had to keep from infecting our family. You were a giant horrible octopus who wanted to pull us down into the depths. I had to spend months and years untangling us from your suckers and tentacles. The balance of my life has been spent thinking of ways I could keep you from hurting the people I actually love. Do you understand that, Dad? Do you?"

Maria crosses her arms and glares.

And for a moment there is no mayor, at least not in here in the room with us. There is no title and no weight of office. There is just a sad, paunchy man in his underwear and a robe. There is only a father who has neglected the things that actually matter, and is beginning to realize it.

The mayor stares up at his daughter—he's taller than her by a foot or so, but she towers over him as he sits on the bed—and waits for this to be over. He has the expression of a powerless man taking a beating. He waits for her to be done. It is what it is.

"Now…" continues Maria. "I'm going to take my mother and my sister, and the three of us are getting out of here. I suppose you should leave too…unless you want to die. Which would probably be what you deserve."

For whatever reason, I again remember that I'm a reporter and that this pitiful man in front of me may one day be the mayor of a major American city in a proper sense. If Chicago is ever going to be saved—from the zombies—from the violence—from itself—*he* will probably be necessary. I don't know if laws still exist, but if we want them to, then it has to start with the person who is *legally* in charge.

"Mister Mayor," I say loudly, formally, almost as if I'm hoping to be called on at a press conference. "We need to get you to safety, sir. We need to keep you protected and find a way to connect you with your constituents when the phone and internet come back on. People are going to be scared, and they're going to need to hear from you. We have to make sure that happens."

Fuck the Pulitzer, I'm gonna *make* the news.

Leopold Mack

Clearly, there is a profound hurt within Maria. I may have been too preoccupied to notice it before. But, my God, what this young lady has been through....

And the way her words take down her father—reduce the mayor to a big fat nothing—well, I've never seen anything quite like it.

It's hard to think about what comes next for the mayor. He didn't expect to start his administration hiding in the basement of a church in Austin, but that's the plan. Right now I don't have a better idea. Maybe there have been more inauspicious starts and we just don't know about them. (I can actually think of a few mayors who would have *benefitted* from a forced immersion into their more underserved communities. As I look into the mayor's wan, sad eyes, I consider that this may be just what a man needs to start over. Change and correct himself. Mend his ways. If anything is a ground-clearing, life-altering experience, it's a zombie outbreak. I hope that the mayor is seeing the error of his past actions, and that—if God has so ordained it—he will one day find the strength to rebuild this city.)

As the mayor is pulling on a pair of blue jeans and looking for a shirt, shouts of alarm erupt from the front of the house. There is the sound of scuttling feet across the kitchen floor, which is followed by more raised voices. Then a moment of silence. Then, abruptly, the loud *Ka-chang! Ka-chang!* of powerful guns being discharged. The mayor ducks his head but finishes putting on his pants.

Maria and I look at one another and draw our guns.

"I don't know who—" the mayor begins to say, but he's cut off by an explosion so great I wonder if the front of the house is still there. The foundations seem to shake. The roof creaks above us. It feels like the house just jumped a foot and then resettled.

Maria's cousin comes barreling through the bedroom door, gun in hand. The left side of his face is full of tiny cuts. He is covered in the fine white dust of exploded drywall. The air behind him is swimming with thick gray particles.

"A bunch of guys with guns," he says, spitting the dust from his lips. "Oh, Jesus. They just threw a fucking grenade at the front of the house."

"Is it the alderman's goon squad?" Ben asks me. "Could they be here already?"

"It has to be," I say. "Looters wouldn't attack a fortified home."

"We should have been quicker!" Ben says. "Dammit!"

"Mom and Yuliana are still in the basement!" Maria shouts in alarm.

No sooner are the words out of her mouth than a woman of about fifty and a scared-looking teenager come barreling through the doorway.

"Get in here!" Maria shouts.

The two women run inside the room. For a moment they regard the half-dressed mayor—he smiles at them awkwardly—and then fall on Maria, embracing. They cling to her. Maria seems pleased by this. She stares over at her father and smiles contemptuously.

"My friends!" Franco cries. "They all got exploded out there. Jesus…"

"Where is Pastor Rivers?" I ask seriously.

Franco just shakes his head.

"They came up out of nowhere. They looked like they wanted to start some trouble. They pulled out guns, and so we started shooting at them—just warning shots, you know? And then one of them threw a grenade."

"I heard Shawn Michael Recinto say they wanted to make it look like a random killing—not even leave shell casings," Maria says from the corner of her mouth. "I guess *that* plan's out the window."

"We shouldn't be huddled in this room," I announce. "We need to spread out and defend ourselves. They're out there wondering if that grenade got us all. Pretty soon, they'll get brave and come find out."

I can hardly believe what's happening. Marja Mogk's troops have caught up to us. I'd thought we had hours on them. Instead, they have almost kept pace. They've found their way through the rubble and barricaded neighborhoods of Chicago, and now they are here to kill the mayor.

But I haven't come this far to give the mayor up without a fight, even if he *is* a corrupt sad sack who takes his damn time putting on his pants. He's bad, no doubt there…but there are worse elements. Worse elements who will take over this city…unless we do something.

Like fight back.

I open the bedroom door. The dust is settling, and the corridor beyond is clear. I gaze up to the front of the house. It hasn't exactly "exploded," but the damage is severe. The windows have been blasted out of the front kitchen area, and there are softball-sized holes in the wall. My gun at the ready, I creep down the hallway. Through the broken windows, I see a couple of furtive young men outside taking cover behind trees and cars. At least I think they are young and men. Their sexes, ages, and other defining features are almost completely obscured by winterwear.

Around the kitchen, I encounter the remains of Franco's friends. Moments before, we had been drinking coffee and telling our story to these men. Now they are lying in pieces. Near the oven, a bloody torso presents itself like a roast waiting to be cooked. I step over it as respectfully as I can.

I move to the front staircase where I encounter the body of Pastor Rivers. His giant, genial bulk has been blasted against a side pantry. Now he lies like a beached walrus, large and unmoving on the floor, with part of his spine protruding through the back of his turtleneck. The position of his body makes it clear that there is no way he can still be alive.

I lean forward and hazard glances through the broken front windows. Our attackers have assumed defensive positions.

The men—and they *are* men, I now realize—are beginning to spread out. I can see two huddled behind a yellow car directly across the street. They keep looking around to the side of the house though. We are being flanked.

"Maria, Ben," I call back down the hallway. "South side of the house. Get on it, now!"

My compatriots leave the back bedroom, keeping low. Remembering that Ben is unarmed, I indicate a weapon next to one of Franco's exploded friends. Ignoring the gore that encases it, Ben bravely picks up a bloodslick automatic.

Ben and Maria skulk to a side window near the den. Maria carefully peeks through the blinds. A moment later, she gingerly takes aim.

Ka-pow! Ka-pow! Maria fires twice.

"Winged him!" she calls.

Moments later I see one of the thugs hobbling back to the front of the yard. He has been shot through the calf and blood is turning one of his white tennis shoes bright red. More of these men could be creeping in from any direction. We need to get a better view.

"Ben," I call. "Take your gun and go upstairs. See what you can see from the windows up there."

Ben looks warily at the blasted front wall—from where, it feels, we are most vulnerable to another attack—and runs past me up the stairs.

Back on the lawn, I watch the wounded man limp until he is behind the dingy yellow car with the others. A shape moves out from behind it to receive him. It is a large man with his nose padded in gauze and crudely bandaged with medical tape. Shawn Michael Recinto.

He made it after all.

Shawn Michael frowns at his colleague, showing no concern for the wounded man, only annoyance that he has failed at his infiltration. (What had the man hoped to do? Lob in another grenade? Set the side of the house on fire? I suppose both of those might have worked.)

At least we know that this group has a leader. And if the group can be reasoned with—which I'm not sure it can—then he will be the conduit.

I creep to the edge of the shrapnel-riddled front wall. Trying to keep out of the gangsters' line of sight, I crouch down beneath a glassless window.

"Shawn Michael!" I call loudly. "We've got to talk about this, young man."

For a moment there is silence. Then I hear the sound of a gun being cocked.

"I don't know what you think you're up to…" I call to him. "But one…you can't do it. We won't let you. And two…you don't need to do it."

At this, I risk a peek around the blasted window frame. There is no visible reaction from the men. Shawn Michael does not show himself. I dip back into cover.

"Fact is, a lot of people already know," I continue, trying to project so he can hear me. (I have been spoiled, lately, by the microphone system in my pulpit.) "We've spread the word around, son. Told half the city! When this all settles down, everybody's gonna know what Marja Mogk did. Everybody'll know she's a murderer, and murderers can't be mayor, even in Chicago. Unless—that is—you don't do this. If you walk away now, people will say they must have heard wrong. That Pastor Mack is a liar. If Marja were here, she'd tell you to walk away. You know I'm right, son."

There is a powerful silence. I look over at the remains of Franco's exploded friends, then over at Pastor Rivers, and utter a silent prayer. Please let me reach him. Please, God. No more killing.

Silence.

I wonder if Shawn Michael is formulating a response. Maybe he has elected not to speak with us at all. Maybe he can't even hear me.

I hazard another glance out front. Our attackers remain hidden. I detect movement, however, in the far yard across the street behind Shawn Michael. I rub my eyes and squint. It's…a ragged pair of zombies. The corpses of homeless addicts, it looks like. They parade confidently, like high noon in a Western, hands on their hips. Shawn Michael and his men are bound to notice them soon and to make short work of them. A distraction, but not a threat.

Shawn Michael's voice comes back across the lawn.

"I know you," he says. "You broke my nose."

"And I know *you*," I return quickly. "I've seen you with Marja. You're always by her side. Big man on the scene. I'm me; you're you. Who we are is no secret. Neither is what we do. If your men back away now, maybe this was all just a misunderstanding. If you don't, people are gonna know."

I pray that my words will reach Shawn Michael.

Come on, dammit. See reason.

"Nothing to do about it," Shawn Michael says. "We both know I got my orders."

I sigh in defeat.

Shawn Michael is right. He has his orders.

That's the problem with Chicago-style politics. It doesn't encourage thinking. You can be somebody who's not paid to think and still rise very high in the ranks. Actually, the less you think, maybe the faster you can count on rising. Shawn Michael is not his own person, really. He's just Marja Mogk's arm. A big, muscled arm that threatens to knock people down whenever they disagree with her.

By telling me he has his orders, he is reminding me that he is an arm. Not a brain. Not a heart. Not any other thinking or feeling apparatus. An arm. There will be no getting through to him.

The young men in South Shore who I counsel about the dangers of gang life are this way. (Hell, I was this way forty-some years ago, when I had a habit to support.) Shawn Michael has turned off the aspect of his brain that registers that other humans also have feelings. You got to turn off that part of your brain to do a crime. To hurt somebody. Otherwise, you won't do it. But some people—once they turn it off—can never turn it back on again. Their switch is broken. Stuck on "off" forever.

I have no chance of convincing Shawn Michael not to kill us. I never did.

There is a clamor behind me at the stop of the stairs.

"Mack," Ben calls down. "I can see all of them from up here. There are three out front behind a yellow car. And there's also one to the north with a rifle, hiding on the neighbor's back deck. Four total."

"That's counting Shawn Michael?"

"Yeah," Ben confirms. "Four total."

At the back of the house, Maria's cousin Franco creeps forward out of the bedroom. He has wiped the blood away from his face, but his cheek looks pretty torn up. He holds a handgun low and at the ready. He gives me a nod, signaling that he is prepared to fight with us.

Looks like it's four against four, and one on each side is already wounded. A fair fight.

Back outside, Shawn Michael is risking a glance out from the side of the car. Can he also tell that it's four against four? (I once read that in medieval battles, the attackers who come to sack a castle should always outnumber the defenders two to one. Maybe Shawn Michael has some sense of this notion and understands he lacks the power to overwhelm us.) I can still see the soullessness in his eyes: a stare more lifeless and hollow than that of the two zombies who approach behind him.

I have an idea.

"Come here," I whisper to Maria and Franco. "Ben, you too."

I motion for Ben to come down to the foot of the staircase. He quickly descends.

"Here's what we do. There are two zombies in that far yard, and they've noticed Shawn Michael. Pretty soon, Shawn Michael and his people will have to deal with them. It won't be much, but they'll have to turn around to kill the zombies. Shoot until they hit the brain. The moment his group does that, I want Ben to start shooting from upstairs. Worst case, they'll get pinned for a while. Best case, you pick a couple off."

"Aim for Shawn Michael," Maria says stoically.

"Once we hear you shooting, the rest of us will go after the lone wolf to the north on the neighbor's deck," I say.

"What, charge him?" Franco asks.

I had actually been anticipating doing that very thing—making a break across the lawn and presenting him with too many targets to shoot. The tone in Franco's voice tells me he believes this would be a bad idea. I realize I may not be thinking clearly. Exhaustion has taken its toll. I try to shake it off.

"I want to use our three-to-one advantage while we have it," I say, staying general about the specifics of my plan.

"Can we go out the back and try to flank him?" Maria offers.

"No," Franco answers seriously. "He can see the back door from that deck. I think that's why he's there—to shoot us in case we try to sneak out the rear."

I look down the hallway into the bedroom, wishing for more help. I see the mayor sitting on the corner of the bed, his head in his hands. He sways back and forth like a top spinning on a table, ready to topple at any moment. Maria's mother and sister look on. Maria's mother tentatively puts a consoling hand on the mayor's shoulder. Somehow, she can bring herself to comfort a man who—from what I can gather—has betrayed her many, many times.

The sight fills me with a red-hot rage. This is the man who agreed to lead our city, and he has dissolved into a whimpering, simpering nothing. What's wrong with us as citizens? How were we ever "okay" with this arrangement? I can't get mad at the mayor for being a coward. Some people are just born cowards.

But I'm furious with the people of this city for putting a bunch of cowards in charge. For thinking that was fine.

I look at this blubbering mayor and decide he is an example from God. He is here at this moment to show me what *not* to do. (In Chicago, if you want to do the morally correct thing, think to yourself "What would the mayor do?" Then do the opposite.)

"I'll charge the guy on the deck," I tell the assemblage at the foot of the stairs.

"What?" Maria protests. "You can't. Your hip is hurt."

"Yeah, and it's too dangerous," Franco adds.

"I've got more combat training than anyone here," I tell them. "I know how to move under cover and how to shoot to kill. When the group out front is pinned by Ben and the zombies, I want you two to start shooting out the northside widow at the guy on the deck. Keep him in cover. Then, I'll go out the front door, around the side of the house, and take out his position. We get him, and suddenly it's four-against-three, and we have the advantage. No objections. Just do what I say. This is the plan. Trust me."

Maria Ramirez

I take position next to Franco under a first-floor window on the north side of the house. Ben goes back upstairs. Mack crawls next to the front door where he prepares to make a break for it.

"How you doing?" I ask Franco as we huddle underneath the windowsill.

"Ehh, you know…" he says.

"We're gonna have some fucking good stories at the next family reunion."

Franco smiles weakly.

It's in my nature to be flip, but I'm not really feeling it. Mostly, I'm worried about providing cover for Mack. I can't even see the shooter on the deck. We're just taking Ben's word that he's there. I hazard a couple of glances outside and contemplate the best way to lay down fire.

Sooner than seems possible, Ben's gun thunders down from the second floor of the house. *Ka-pow! Ka-pow! Ka-pow!*

Mack draws his Glock. He gives Franco and me a nod and then slips out the front door.

My cousin and I rise from our crouches and look out the north-facing window. At first we see nothing. No target. Then he shoots, and we glimpse the unmissable muzzle flash by the side of the deck. It's not clear if he has a target or is just shooting to shoot, but we duck instinctively. He's probably spraying and praying. We start to return fire, really opening up on him. Splinters fly as our guns begin to eat up the deck and the wooden railing around it.

Upstairs, Ben continues to shoot intermittently. I can hear what might be the gangsters out front firing too, but there are now enough people shooting that it's difficult to tell. (It's all very wordless and weird. Close your eyes, and we could be a bunch of people at a shooting range.)

I squeeze off a few more shots before Mack comes into view. He has edged around the side of the house and is moving fast and low as he closes in on the shooter.

I start to feel sick as adrenaline surges through my body once more. Usually adrenaline takes away the pain, but I've been asking a lot from myself over the last ten hours. This puts me near overload. A feeling of *wrongness* courses through my veins. It's like drinking an espresso when you've already had two pots of coffee or doing whiskey shots on top of a raging hangover. More adren-aline is the *last* thing my body wants. My gun bucks in my hand. Each time it does, I feel a little more sick and stretched thin.

Mack takes cover next to a hedge just inside Franco's property line. The twists of branches and bramble will not stop a rifle bullet, but he is concealed. Next, he begins to crawl *away* from the shooter on his elbows. At first I think he's just orienting himself; it would make more sense to crawl west and get closer. I realize Mack must be aware of this. He's making the counterin-tuitive move. He's going to go down the hedge a ways *then* pop up. He'll have to pick off the shooter at an angle, but his target will never see it coming.

Suddenly, there is a furtive movement atop the deck. I see the barrel and stock of a rifle bobbing as the shooter changes position.

Uh oh.

Then, before I can act—or think—a white flash comes from the muzzle. Mack crumples to the ground.

Franco and I open up on the shooter, who knows he's been spotted. He stands up and tries to run—the worst thing he could possibly do. One of us hits him square in the back. He slumps over, dead.

"Mack!" I cry.

He isn't dead, but he isn't moving much either. He balls up and turns on his side, like a sleeping dog. My God, I hope he's only been winged. (Though in a world where the hospitals probably aren't operating anymore, the implications of a flesh wound are increasingly dire.)

Then disaster strikes.

I'm preparing to leap out of the window and onto the lawn, when a giant shape looms behind Franco. In my peripheral vision, it only registers as movement. Very large movement. I pivot to take a proper look, and something hits the side of my head and sends me reeling to the floor. Then Franco starts screaming.

I look up and see that the massive corpse of Pastor Rivers has risen. The grenade explosion has filled its front with wooden splinters, but its brain remains intact. The face looks like someone going for the Guinness record for piercings, but this is no body modification. This is a zombie who has been transformed into a spiny porcupine.

Before I can react, the Rivers-thing grips Franco from behind. The pastor's massive muscles flex and lift my screaming cousin skyward. The splinter-covered mouth opens to take a bite.

Franco struggles and bucks, but the Pastor only grips him tighter. Hideously, I realize that Franco's screams are not from terror. The splinters from the pastor's chest—and arms and hands—are entering Franco's body. Rivers has become a walking iron maiden.

I fumble with my gun, losing crucial seconds. I try to aim from my supine position, but Franco is flailing in the way. The Rivers-thing begins biting into the top of his skull. Franco understands what is happening, and a horrible knowing comes over his face. I manage to get to my feet. Franco continues to struggle. I step in close and put my gun against the Rivers-thing's head.

BLAM!

The giant zombie's eyes cross, and it falls to the floor in a heap. Franco screams as the splinters retract from his body. Other splinters—I quickly see—are left behind. Like the zombie, he also falls to the ground. His wounds do not look fatal, but he's bleeding a lot and full of wood. I don't see any way he can continue to fight. His screams ebb to a moan, then to near silence.

"...fuck..." he manages.

"Don't try to move," I tell him. "I have to get Mack. I'll be right back."

Franco nods to say he understands. As I bend to pick up his gun, he slowly pulls the first of about fifty splinters from his body.

I stalk to the back of the house where the rest of my family is huddled.

"Papi," I say. "I need your help."

Ben Bennington

Sooner than I like, I run out of bullets. I have not been able to hit any of my targets. Our attackers remain huddled behind the car, very much alive. They have expended a few bullets shooting the zombies that ambled up behind them, but they haven't returned fire at me. (Which they haven't really needed to…because I suck at shooting.)

I have no idea if Mack has taken out the shooter to the north of the house. Until I hear otherwise, I want to keep Shawn Michael and his goons pinned. But I can't do that with zero bullets.

I run to the top of the staircase, hoping to pick up another discarded firearm from somewhere. Down below, I see a determined-looking Maria huddled with her father near the front door.

"Ben, c'mere," she urges.

I clomp down the stairs as quickly as I can. The front door is open, and I can see the yellow car beyond. I worry about being shot through the door.

"I ran out of bullets," I tell her. "I didn't hit any of them."

Wordlessly, Maria hands me a heavy black Glock.

"That has a full magazine," Maria says. "Fifteen rounds. I need you to use it to lay down fire on Shawn Michael again. Mack got shot, but we got the shooter. Mack's still alive. My dad and I are gonna drag him to safety."

Next to Maria, the mayor looks like he's hearing this plan for the first time. He looks up at me like I can provide confirmation.

"Whatever you say," I tell Maria. I take the gun and head back up the stairs to my firing-perch.

"Just start shooting," Maria calls after me. "We'll take it from there."

The mayor looks over at her as if to say *We will?*

I get back upstairs and draw a bead on the yellow car.

More and more, I'm starting to wonder if the best plan might not be trying to wait them out. The men out front have no shelter (outside of busted cars) and no food or water (that I can see). It will get seriously cold when the sun gets low. They will have to find sustenance and shelter. Maybe all we have to do is outlast them for the rest of the day, then they'll go look for food and warmth and we can escape.

Whatever the case, that comes later. Now we've got to get Mack off the lawn. Now it's shooting time.

I see Shawn Michael talking to his boys down below. One of them leans around the side of the car like he might want to charge us. He braces himself against the car like a runner in the starting blocks.

No you fucking don't.

I point the Glock and squeeze off a round. The man flinches and jumps back behind the car. Below me, I hear the sound of Maria and the mayor heading out the front door.

How many of these did Maria say I had? Fifteen? Got to make them last. I point the gun at the car and pull the trigger again. This time, I actually hit something; my bullet makes a round silver hole in the hood. Fuck yeah.

I wait. Nothing happens. Shawn Michael and his cohorts don't shoot back. They don't even move. Even so, I send another bullet in their direction every few seconds. I try to keep track of how many I have left.

When I am down to five, I hear the sound of movement again on the doorstep below me. There is the shuffling of feet, but also a baritone moan that can only be from Mack. He is with them and—for the moment at least—apparently still alive.

I decide to squeeze off another shot before heading downstairs. I take a deep breath like I've seen snipers do in movies. *Hold it Ben, hold it.* I try to get Shawn Michael in my sights. (I'm a terrible shot and I know it, but maybe this time . . . just *maybe*. . .) My body tenses as I prepare to pull the trigger.

Then I hear one of the men behind the car scream "Aww, hell yeah!" *really* loud.

Another adds "That's I'm talkin' 'bout. Ow! My mother*fuckers*!"

It is unnerving. I hesitate. I don't pull the trigger. Something in the vibration of the air has changed, and I can feel it. I lower the Glock. I then look out past the yellow car and see what it is.

Coming up the block is a group of men and women in heavy winter coats. Fifty people at least. They are armed to the teeth— in some cases literally—but they don't behave aggressively toward Shawn Michael's group. Rifles are slung over shoulders. Handguns are displayed openly in waistbands. One gentleman holds a glistening knife in his mouth, despite the cold.

Most unnerving of all, they don't look like gangsters—they look like the local politicians and community leaders I see in meetings across the city every day. Which—terrifyingly—is what they are.

This part of the mob could be a priest and some parishioners from the Polish Catholic League, heading to a city forum to express displeasure with a new pornographic billboard. Next to them might be a collection of youth mentors from the Roberto Clemente outreach gang violence program in Humboldt Park. And next to these could be a smiling, convivial detachment from the Ping Tom Improvement Association in Chinatown.

My heart jumps to my throat. Can these people be with Marja Mogk? *All* of them? Has the corruption spread that far?

Erasing all doubt, Shawn Michael Recinto gives the group a hearty wave from behind the car. He then indicates my position with his index finger. A moment later, someone from the advancing horde takes a potshot at me. A bullet *SPATS* into the side of the wall, only a few feet from my face.

This is the worst part of a zombie outbreak. People you know—people who were your friends and associates just the day before—are now roaming the streets and trying to kill you. But they're not the zombies. They're the horrible people who want to run the city.

I retreat back inside the bedroom and head frantically for the stairs.

"Holy shit!" I shout to whoever is left alive below. "There's fifty more coming down the street! Fifty more!"

I race to the bottom of the staircase and shut the front door of the house. Everyone's at the back. Maria, Mack, the mayor, and even Franco—who is apparently filled with wooden splinters—have retreated to the back bedroom with Maria's mother and sister. They all look up as I race down the hallway toward them. I skitter like a cat on the linoleum and blood, then come flailing into the bedroom like a wild man. I slam the door behind me.

"Fifty more?" says Maria. "What're you—"

"Shawn Michael's group wasn't sent here to kill us," I cry breathing hard. "They were the scouting party. They were sent ahead to trap the mayor until the *real* killers could get mustered. And I think they just did."

"My God," says the mayor. "They must really want me dead."

"Each one of those people has been promised a reward if they help Marja kill you," I say dourly. "Each one of them has decided to sell a little bit of his or her soul to get ahead. That's the Chicago way."

"I think the mayor knows that already," Mack says from his position on the floor.

For a moment, it's hard to tell who is speaking. All strength and sonorousness has disappeared from his voice. It's like hearing a mighty brasswind reduced to a buzzing mouthpiece.

I look him over and see that the bullet has travelled through Mack's left shoulder. There is a sizable wound. With his right hand, Mack reaches across his chest and tries to hold it closed. There is, however, an exit wound in his back which he cannot reach. Blood is escaping from it and pooling underneath him. It turns the tan carpet red. Without the intercession of a doctor, Mack does not have long to live.

"I have to give myself up," the mayor says. "There's no point to more fighting."

"That won't save any of us," I explain. "They need us dead. There can't be witnesses."

"Well then," says the mayor, "what is there left to do but die?"

I lean against the wall, trying to think of an answer.

Leopold Mack

I've sat with the dying many, many times.

Most of these visits have been with the elderly who were preparing to pass away from natural causes. Yet, I've seen more than my fair share—anyone's fair share—of young people dying from gun violence. I've held their hands and listened to their breath wheeze out of them through bullet holes and punctured lungs.

And here I am, a grizzled old geezer who's been shot like a youngster. What a thing! Pastor Mack, what *were* you trying to prove?

★ ★ ★

The good book contains no shortage of passages about death. My favorite has always been in the Book of Ecclesiastes, where it says: "A good name is better than a precious perfume, and the day of one's death is better than the day of one's birth."

However, I find that lying here with a hole in my shoulder has somewhat altered my perspective. Sorry, Mr. Ecclesiastes, but birthdays are pretty fun…and I've smelled some damn fine perfume in my time.

In those final moments—when all I can feel is the blood leaving my body and the cold shudders of death coming on—I try to think about what is going to be left after I've departed. I wonder what my life has meant. I know I'm an old guy, but it felt reasonable to think that I had another fifteen years or so.

Suddenly, though, I don't. Suddenly, whatever I've done…well, that's *all* that I was gonna do.

All my life has been about helping South Shore. Helping the neighborhood improve. Making life a little better for black folk on the south side. But now the dead come back to life and people are running amok like anarchists and … and …

And I don't know.

Does it wipe away everything I did down in my neighborhood? All that work? Have I spent my life trying to repair a sand castle that just got washed away by a tidal wave?

No.

I can't think about it. It hurts too much. My shoulder, yes, but that idea too.

I don't know. I will never know. Only God does. Only He ever really gets to see the big picture.

★ ★ ★

I commend my soul to God and close my eyes. I thank him for giving me so many years on this earth and for the chance at redemption. I pray that he will watch over and protect my daughter, though I already know she'll take care of herself. And I pray that he will watch over my flock in South Shore and guide them through this time of trial. Then I stop praying and prepare to die.

The room has grown cold. It begins to spin slowly, like when I used to pass out drunk. It's hard to feel my fingers.

When I finally hear the cavitations outside—those flapping sounds coming from up above—I'm not ashamed to admit I wonder if they might be angels.

Maria Ramirez

So we're sitting there, trying to figure out if something can be done. Mack is nearly dead. The blood beneath him is spreading so much that it looks like he's lying on a red beach towel. His leather jacket is drenched.

There is a weird sound outside the house. It's not the mob, more like something mechanical on the edge of hearing. A distant engine or motor, muffled by the walls that enclose us. A repeating noise. What exactly can it be?

Immediately following the mechanical noise *is* a sound from the crowd of killers. It starts as a few shouts but in seconds turns into a full-on uproar. People outside start screaming. Cries of alarm and cries of fear. Several guns are discharged.

"The fuck?" says Ben, wrinkling his eyebrows.

I give him a look that says, "If we're dead anyway, then let's go take a look."

Ben smiles at the idea. I open the door to the bedroom and we walk out together.

We pass through the bloody hallway and peer out of a blasted window in the kitchen. Beyond is a great commotion. The street outside is in chaos. People are running every direction. A group that couldn't be more different—men and women from all over the city are trying to find cover. (From what, I wonder.) They're armed, but many are now dropping their weapons and sprinting away. The mechanical sound gets louder. Soon it feels omnipresent. Thunder from the heavens. Vibrations from under the earth.

A couple from the fleeing mob head straight toward the house. Ben and I raise our weapons and point them menacingly. The mob members' eyes go wide. They turn around and try somewhere else.

The mechanical noise gets louder…and *recognizable*. I slowly realize what is happening, and I start to smile.

"Is that…?" Ben asks, tilting his head.

"A helicopter," I say, nodding slowly. "And look, down the street!"

Ben swivels his head.

At the far end of the street, three armored personnel carriers are slowly making their way toward us. They sometimes struggle to negotiate the abandoned cars and debris that litter the way, but they make consistent progress. A few mob members who had fled in the direction of these vehicles quickly change their courses.

"Who can it be?" Ben asks.

"There are a few options," I tell him. "I sent text messages to, like, everybody."

"What?" Ben says.

"You know," I tell him. "The Army. The Coast Guard. The National Guard. I texted them all."

"When did you…?" Ben begins.

"I found a list of emergency contacts when we were in the police station. I sent texts saying what was happening and where they could find the mayor of Chicago. Remember, you came up and bothered me when I was doing it? Anyhow, I didn't think the messages went through—my phone's been acting weird like everybody else's—but damn, I guess they did."

"The military got your *text messages*?!" Ben says like he still can't believe it.

"I don't have a better explanation," I tell him. "Do you? Maybe the military just came here randomly . . . roll with it, okay? You worry too much."

Ben cracks a smile and relaxes a little. We continue to watch the chaos outside through the front window.

The armored troop transports pull up directly in front of the house. One of them lowers a hatch like a giant mouth opening at the back of the vehicle. Armed soldiers begin to stream out.

"It's National Guard," Ben says quietly. "You can tell by the uniforms."

"We should probably put down our guns," I say.

"Yeah," Ben answers. "Good thinking."

We throw our weapons to the floor. Ben also kicks his away for some reason, like we're on a cop show. I carefully open the shrapnel-riddled front door of Franco's house.

The soldiers are on the front lawn now. They see us, and one of them raises a weapon. It is a young woman about my own age. She's pretty...or would be in other circumstances. Her face carries a strange combination of fear and determination. Her eyes meet mine.

"He's in here!" I call brightly. "He's still alive!"

That's all I need to say.

★ ★ ★

Minutes later, we are riding in the back of armored personnel carriers, heading north out of the city. They put my dad in the first carrier by himself. My mother and sister go in the second, and Ben and I end up in the third. Everyone is present and accounted for, except for Mack and Franco, who have been placed aboard a helicopter and airlifted to a military hospital.

It's cramped inside the carrier. I am squished against the pretty young soldier. She has more stripes on her shoulder than the others. I ask her name, and she says Emily Jean.

"We're lucky you showed up when you did, Emily Jean," I tell her.

Emily Jean looks around the crammed carrier.

"I think every part of this was lucky," she says. "We almost didn't come. Plenty of people thought your text messages were fake, or even a trap. A lot of people thought we should just ignore them."

"Then the fact that you *did* come...probably means you didn't have a better lead on the mayor."

"That's accurate," Emily Jean says stoically.

"How did you get Maria's texts?" Ben asks from across the bumpy, loud carrier. "Isn't everything still down?"

"*Civilian* communications are, yes. *Our* stuff is up and running. It may have looked like you didn't get through, but you did."

"Fucking *apparently*," Ben says, gazing around at all the soldiers.

"What's going to happen to Marja Mogk and all those people who wanted to kill my dad?" I ask.

The soldier shakes her head.

"Our priorities are to secure the chain of command. That includes the mayor of Chicago. That's why we're here. As far as what law enforcement is going to do—or what form it's going to take—that's not my place to guess."

"But the mayor of Chicago—Maria's *dad*—will be supported by the full faith of the United States military, right?" Ben asks. He sounds formal, like a lawyer. I wonder if he is still planning on writing an article about this.

"That...yes, that's my understanding," Emily Jean manages.

"You see?" Ben says.

"See what?" I tell him. "I don't want Marja or Igor or Shawn Michael to get away with this."

"They can't," Ben says. "At least they can't be mayor. The military has the person they think is the legitimate leader of Chicago. So it's done. Over. No amount of secret meetings between aldermen is going to change that. There're no favors left for Marja and Igor to buy."

"Hmmm," I say, feeling unsure. "So my dad is, like, *definitely* mayor?"

Ben nods and smiles, more to himself than to me. That's how I know it's for real.

"Well...good, I guess," I say, relaxing. "I wish there was some way the military could have done this years ago. Just come into the city and cleaned house."

"Speaking as a person who grew up inside of Cook County, I don't disagree with you," allows Emily Jean.

Across the carrier, Ben chuckles. So do a few of the other soldiers.

"Do you know what happens next?" I ask Emily Jean.

She smiles wryly. "I can tell you what happens next, but not *next* next, if you follow me. Your dad is probably getting the same debriefing right now. Headquarters, for the moment, is up north on the base in Lake County. That's where the orders from Washington come from. This zombie stuff started in Illinois last night, but now it's spread around the world, to just about every country, every city."

"Jesus," I say, trying to imagine the entire Earth crawling with these things.

"Apart from making sure this outbreak doesn't somehow start a nuclear war, I think what the government cares about is keeping a coherent chain of command," Emily Jean continues. "That's all anybody is using to define failure or success at this point. 'Did we maintain the chain of command?' That's why we were willing to risk a goose chase to Oak Park if it meant we might find Chicago's mayor."

"Wow," I tell her. "I'm glad you did. We would have been killed by that mob in, like, seconds. Our friend Mack would have died for sure."

"Yeah..." Emily Jean says absently. "But in terms of where we go from here—to answer your question in the bigger sense—your guess is as good as mine."

Emily Jean looks away from me and back to her squad. She takes a deep breath. I realize that while this is the end of our story, it is probably just the beginning of theirs. Some have sad, wan faces, like this is the last place they want to be. Others look plain exhausted. Others still look alert and excited, like they have been waiting for a zombie outbreak their entire lives.

The armored personnel carrier continues north toward Lake County. I lean back against the jostling metal side. Almost before I realize what is happening, I have drifted off to sleep.

Epilogue

If charnel-houses and our graves must send
Those that we bury back, our monuments
Shall be the maws of kites.

—Macbeth (III, iv)

Ben Bennington

Nelson Algren once said that loving Chicago is like loving a woman with a broken nose. But he said that back in the 20th century…back before the outbreak. These days, loving Chicago is more like loving a woman whose nose has been bitten off by a zombie.

There's a gaping hole that's impossible to miss right in the middle of her face; a couple of tunnels where you can see up into her sinuses (eww!); and a terrifying, cadaverous aspect to her profile now. It just doesn't look right, no matter what angle you see her from. But maybe she covers the nose-hole with a designer scarf. Maybe she wears a fancy, bejeweled Tycho Brahe fake nose. Maybe she just lets it all hang out and doesn't give a shit.

And you look at her, and, I mean, the noselessness is glaring. *Glaring.* You can't miss it. The fact that it's not the first thing both of you talk about when you first get introduced is utterly absurd.

But still…

Despite it all, she looks *damn good.* You look her over—head to toe and lack of nose—and you're still onboard. You love her just the same.

Maybe, in some weird way, you love her even more.

★ ★ ★

I don't know how this next part happens. I mean, from what I've heard, if civilization is going to come back, it's going to start in cities and spread outward. People are saying we've reverted back to Medieval times. What they mean is that in cities there's still law and order. Courts. Police. An army. A government. Out in the countryside though—where the army can't reach—it's just lawless. Every man for himself. It's also where all the libertarian survivalists fled, and they didn't like government to *begin* with.

There's going to be a lot of resistance to bringing the countryside back under federal or state control. The "countryside"— by which I mean any Illinois county with a population of less than 100,000—is going to have to be resettled inch by inch. People will have to become pioneers all over again. Instead of taking over the country from American Indians, they're going to have to reclaim it from people who want to shoot their own food and not pay taxes. So be it. Civilization has faced worse. It has won before, and it will win again...eventually. (But for the time being, I'm staying in Chicago.)

I'm pleased that Washington, D.C. understands this as well. You must, after all, if you rolled in to save the mayor like that. By not just letting bandits and criminals take over the city, you insisted that laws matter even if zombies have broken out. Maybe *especially* when zombies have broken out.

Anyway, nobody will tell you this, but you did something good. We appreciate it. Whether or not people know it, you just saved Chicago from itself.

Mogk and Szuter? Are you kidding? What you're doing warms my heart. Seriously.

Providing this deposition has been a real pleasure. I hope you understand that. And like I told the prosecutors before, I'll testify in court if you need me to. I love the fact that there are still zombies in the streets some places, and we're going to have a trial. That's how we bring civilization back! As long as we still have court systems, Mogk and Szuter should get a trial. That will be justice. They "disappeared" so many people. We should show them that we don't do that. That's not how you play the game. We should lead by example.

★ ★ ★

I don't even know if I can write about all this, you know? At least, not in an article. I mean, newspaper reporters aren't supposed to make the news. They aren't supposed to put themselves *in* their stories. But I was personally present for so much of what happened that it'd be strange if I did an article about how the mayor escaped being murdered and got to safety, and I omitted myself. Not that the papers will be publishing for a while. Maybe a book deal won't be out of the question though, when the publishers in New York come back.

So, has this helped? I *hope* it has.

Mack and Maria's stories should line up with mine and fill in any holes. I still have Jessy Knowlton's notes if you need them.

You just get Mogk and Szuter and their cronies like Shawn Michael—and hell, make sure Burge Wheeler gets some extra years tacked on—and you'll have done something good. That's what I'm convinced of.

Even in a zombie apocalypse, you can find a way to do the right thing.

★ ★ ★

Did this fix Illinois? What a question! Yes. No. I don't know. It's a pretty corrupt state.

I feel like what this did was hit the reset button. Now we get to start over. Now people have seen why it's not cool to have incompetent, corrupt politicians who can't handle a crisis and only promote their friends. Now we will want people in charge who actually know what they're doing.

At least I hope we will.

No promises.

I mean, after all, this is Illinois.

Leopold Mack

This has not been easy. Dictating my story from a cot in your infirmary has certainly been a challenge, but so are most things worth doing. I've managed it, haven't I?

I apologize if my testimony has, at times, strayed to the informal. I communicate much more clearly when I can write something down. I've said things to you I wouldn't normally say. What do they call it? "Free-associating?" Yes. For some of this, I've merely been free-associating.

Your doctor says I'm lucky to be alive. Said he's never seen somebody lose so much blood and not die, and that counts what he saw in Iraq.

And I think he's right. I think I am very lucky.

But not just because I didn't pass away.

★ ★ ★

So that should just about cover what I wanted to tell you. I don't know if I think it will do much good—your prosecution of the aldermen—but maybe it can serve as an example. Show people that Chicago might have been one way before zombies, but now it has changed. The old ways are gone. Now there are new and better ways. New and better people.

I didn't think much of our mayor when I first met him, but I remember him dragging me to safety after I got shot. There was a moment at the end when he got his courage up to charge out of that house and help. Maybe he can keep that momentum going, if you know what I mean. I hope to God he does right for this city. I hope there is some more good in him. Maybe it's hidden deep inside. Maybe it just needs to be nurtured, and it will grow.

As for me, I need to get well enough to get back home. Back to The Church of Heaven's God in Christ Lord Jesus. That's my only concern. The people in South Shore need me. But I think, even more than that, I need them.

★ ★ ★

Right before the military showed up—when I was dying in that bedroom watching the mayor watch me—I didn't know if my life had been well spent. (Honestly, I thought maybe it had been wasted trying to improve neighborhoods that can never improve.)

Then I got here, and I started to hear the stories. You know the ones, I'm sure. That the south side of Chicago did the best during the outbreak. That it had things like block clubs and community groups and church groups and neighbors who actually *knew* one another. That it had been depending on itself for so long, that doing so in a zombie outbreak came naturally.

What we were able to accomplish at my church was *the rule*, not the exception. When the rest of the city relied on electronics that didn't work and policemen who weren't there, we relied on each other. We looked out for one another. And it worked.

That's something good. Something damn good. And I think if I helped to make *that* happen, then maybe I haven't wasted my life after all.

Now, when communities around the country—or, my Lord, around the *world*—are trying to figure out what they need to survive—are looking for a model to follow—they look to the south side of Chicago. They ask, "What is South Shore doing right?" and "How can we be like them?"

It all feels like a dream, doesn't it? But it's real.

I swear to God, it's all real.

Maria Ramirez

All anyone talks about now is what'll be the next thing to return. Like, when will the newspapers start printing again? When will they have TV shows that aren't just news broadcasts? When will they clear the last of the zombies from the subway tunnels and get the El up and running?

But nobody is talking about punk rock.

What the fuck, right?

We need to get this town's punk scene back on track, ASAP. That's *my* project. You guys and my dad sound like you have all the boring logistical bullshit covered. Now we gotta get about to rocking.

That's why I'm organizing an outdoor punk show in Millennium Park as my first order of business. Are there still zombies in Millennium Park, hiding in the landscaping and submerged in the fountains? Probably. Will that make going to a punk show there even more dangerous and exciting? I damn sure hope so.

Seriously, just think . . . the first punk rock show in New Chicago. A mosh pit that might have a zombie or two mixed in. A bunch of survivors who have all this pent-up zombie killing energy and need to cut loose. Talk about excitement. And Strawberry Brite Vagina Dentata to headline, with all members present and accounted for? Hell to the fucking yeah! That's the best part of all.

★ ★ ★

I mean, I don't know what else I can tell you at this point, really.

You know pretty much everything. At least, everything I was there for.

I don't know what Ben and Mack said, but I'm not particularly worried about Marja Mogk. You guys are going to take care of her. That will be that, and then we can forget about her forever.

At the end of the day, if you look at what she did—what she *actually* did—it was boring. Uninspired. It takes *nothing* to decide to murder your way up the food chain, you know? To kill people and take power when the lights go out? Any idiot could do that.

Do I want her to go to jail? Sure. She deserves to. So do Igor Szuter and Shawn Michael and everybody else who was involved. But I don't, you know, want to think about Marja ever again. She's just a murderer, and there's nothing to that.

All the worst things are boring. Murder is the worst of the worst things, so it is also the most boring.

★ ★ ★

Oh, okay…and speaking of things coming back … did I mention that beer is back? Finally!

It's back in a few places, at least. Ben says he knows a guy with a hookup. He asked if he could take me sometime. (I'm still going, but that part was creeper-y. Not the asking, but the *way* he did it. "Take me." Like, "May I take you, Madame?" What's up with that? Whatever.)

Ben is nice. A little serious, but nice.

He's no Stewart Copeland, but we'll see what happens.

Author's Note

I have tried to portray the geography of Illinois with something approaching accuracy. However, amateur spelunkers should note that Chicago's coal tunnels terminate just west of the Loop and do not—to my certain knowledge—extend as far as Oak Park.